THE UGANDA PROTOCOL

JEFFREY JAMES HIGGINS

SEVERN RIVER PUBLISHING

Severn River Publishing
www.SevernRiverBooks.com

ISBN: 978-1-64875-713-6 (Paperback)

ALSO BY JEFFREY JAMES HIGGINS

The Nathan Burke Thrillers

The Havana Syndrome

The Khorasan Retribution

The China Gambit

The Uganda Protocol

To find out more, visit

severnriverbooks.com

For Cynthia Farahat Higgins, my number one fan.

1

"Mayday, Mayday, Mayday, Magnus Air 1522 heavy," the radio squawked inside John F. Kennedy International Airport's control tower.

Traffic controller Arthur Meyer bolted upright in his chair inside Terminal Radar Approach Control and almost spit out his mouthful of cold coffee. Nothing got his heart beating faster than a Mayday call in the last hour of a double shift.

"Magnus 1522, Kennedy Tower. Go ahead with your emergency."

"Mayday, Mayday, Mayday, Magnus 1522 heavy, declaring an emergency."

"Magnus 1522, Kennedy Tower. State the nature of your emergency."

"Leak . . . cabin . . ."

"Magnus 1522, Kennedy Tower, say again. You're coming in broken."

"Kennedy Tower, American 622," another pilot transmitted.

"Break, break. All aircraft, Kennedy Tower, radio discipline. Magnus 1522, repeat your emergency."

Static.

"Magnus 1522, Kennedy Tower."

"Kennedy Tower, Magnus 1522. Requesting emergency landing clearance. Odor in the cabin. Pilot incapacitated. We need to land now."

"Magnus 1522, Kennedy Tower. Copy. You're cleared to land on runway 13-Left. Descend to two thousand, heading 120 for final approach."

"1522 . . . dizzy . . ."

"Report injuries, remaining fuel, and souls on board."

Static.

Arthur's supervisor leaned over his shoulder and depressed the manual transmit button. "Magnus 1522, Kennedy Tower. What's the condition of your aircraft?"

"Kennedy Tower, Magnus 1522, all systems green, but my pilot is incapacitated. There's some kind of leak in the cabin."

"I've got you twenty-two miles out on final," Arthur transmitted. "Fly heading 120, cleared to land on runway 13-Left."

Arthur's supervisor yelled across the room. "Divert all flights from 13-Left. Emergency traffic coming in. Put conflicts into holding patterns. Give this guy a clear lane."

"Kennedy, Magnus 1522, I need to put her down."

His supervisor pointed at his deputy. "Scramble emergency services. That's a 777 jumbo out of there from—" He looked at Arthur and snapped his fingers.

"Magnus 1522 direct from Munich," Arthur said.

"I want fire, ambulance, and LEO response." He scratched his head and looked back at his deputy. "And get hazmat out there. I don't know what's leaking in that fucking cabin, but once they evacuate the aircraft, nobody leaves the tarmac until we figure it out."

2

———————

"They're all dead," FBI Special Agent Nathan Burke said as he stared out the thick glass of the terminal window at JFK.

Special Agent Bridget Quinn turned to him with wide eyes. "Who?"

"Everyone on that plane, except whoever landed it."

"Why would you say that?"

"No radio communications since they landed. No cell phone calls from our guys or anyone else. No raised window shades."

"Could be a hijacking," she said, "and someone's preventing the crew and passengers from making contact."

"Maybe."

They'd been waiting for the flight from Harare, Zimbabwe, via Munich, so their agents could deliver the most-wanted man in America—Imam Omar Yemeni. Two years before, Yemeni had facilitated the Phantoms' operations across the United States—the deadliest terrorist attacks since al-Qaeda brought down the Twin Towers.

Ideology and theology motivated Yemeni but shielded his mind from logic and reason. He sought only one thing—enforcing the will of Allah—and terror was his only option. But Yemeni couldn't spread fear from a prison cell. The FBI had snatched him in Zimbabwe on his way to Uganda, and then extradited him to face prosecution. Yemeni would never hurt anyone again. Not if they could help it.

"What's freaking happening?" Bridget asked.

"They've been down for five minutes," Nathan said. "Whatever's wrong, it's bad."

Bridget dialed her cell, then hung up and dialed again. "Rick and Alfonso's phones are still off."

Red lights flashed below as emergency vehicles raced across the tarmac, and airport personnel scurried around. The Boeing 777-300ER had landed, but instead of taxiing to the gate, it'd continued down the runway. Emergency vehicles raced down the access road after it.

Nathan checked his phone for a text message from Meili Chan, his former supervisor and current girlfriend. No messages or missed calls. After their incident on the Macao–Hong Kong Bridge, the Office of Professional Responsibility had reviewed their conduct, and Nathan and Meili's romantic involvement had surfaced. Nathan had been forced to transfer out of her group, so he'd returned to the AF-Pak terrorism group. That meant they didn't see each other much, and Meili seemed okay with that. Their relationship was in trouble.

Footsteps pounded the floor, and Nathan turned.

Supervisory Special Agent José García, the FBI's point man at JFK, hurried across the terminal to them, in a half run, half walk that made him look like he balanced on the deck of a ship. He lumbered to a stop, breathless.

"Okay, here's the deal," José said. "The pilot, er, the first officer called in the Mayday when they were on final. He said he had vapor in the cabin and an incapacitated captain."

"Why didn't they taxi to the gate?" Bridget asked.

"They don't know what type of gas leaked," José said.

"What about the passengers?" Nathan asked.

José shook his head and stretched his back. Judging from the gut hanging over his belt, he hadn't moved that fast in years. "The first officer hasn't responded . . . or at least he hadn't when I left the control room. Until they determine what the gas is, they're gonna quarantine everybody."

"Let's head to the runway," Nathan said.

José led them to a door for authorized personnel and used one of the dozen IDs hanging from his lanyard to open it. They followed him downstairs onto the tarmac.

Two golf carts screeched to a stop beside them. A giant wearing a suit and tie sat behind the wheel of the first cart. The second vehicle contained two TSA agents and two NYPD officers. The giant waved them over.

"That's Ron Black, JFK's chief security officer," José said.

"José, jump in," Black yelled.

Bridget, José, and Nathan climbed into the cart, and it lurched forward. Black drove at full speed, manipulating the wheel with two fingers, as if out for a Sunday drive. He leaned over his shoulder. "Who are you?"

"FBI Agents Burke and Quinn," Bridget said.

"Any injuries on board?" Nathan asked.

"We'll see," Black said. "No word from the first officer for eight minutes."

Tires hummed over the tarmac, and the vibration rattled Nathan's teeth. The cart swayed as Black navigated to the runway threshold, where the plane idled. It towered above them like a prehistoric beast.

Black communicated with Ground Control as he drove, then they jerked to a stop and disembarked beside the plane's extended raked wingtips. Its engines ticked. Most window shades were drawn, normal for the transatlantic flight.

"She's a 777-300ER with General Electric GE90-115B engines, extra fuel tanks, and a 212-foot wingspan," Black said.

"I've got to get inside," Nathan said. "The world's most-wanted terrorist is on board, and it took us two years to nab him. I'm not letting something happen this close to the end. That asshole's gotta face justice."

"I know who's in there," Black said, "but that flight's half full, and I've got 192 other passengers to worry about."

"Then roll a stairwell over and let me inside," Nathan said.

Black's face reddened, and he stabbed his finger at the plane. "That's a wide-body, a 242-foot-long metal tube filled with an unknown gas. The flight crew should have activated the emergency exits and evacuated already. That's standard SOP. When we crack that hatch, God knows what we'll unleash."

Shit. He was right. That aircraft could be a biohazard. Why hadn't they evacuated or at least opened the hatches?

"What about the passengers?" Bridget asked. "If that gas is toxic, they need medical attention."

"This requires a hazmat response," Black said. "I won't expose my team. No one else is getting injured because we're rushing into a situation we know nothing about."

"Did the first officer mention the passengers?" José asked.

Black shook his head. "We're trying to raise him. He landed and shut down his engines, then radio silence."

Alfonso and Rick, two FBI agents from Nathan's team, had escorted their prisoner from Zimbabwe, through the layover in Munich, and on the final leg. A thought shook him. Both agents had cell phones, so why hadn't they called?

Nathan's stomach hardened. "Then what do we—"

Tires barked as a white van veered off the access road and raced toward them. It parked thirty feet away, and men dressed in white hazmat suits jumped out. They unloaded black plastic cargo boxes and duffel bags, and piled gear on the tarmac.

"Nathan's right," Bridget said. "We don't have time. We need to go in now."

"Absolutely not," Black said. "We follow NFPA 472 standards to the letter in hazardous materials incident response."

"But people could be dying," Bridget said.

"And we'll add to the casualty count if we rush in unprepared. There's nothing we can do. That plane could be filled with deadly—"

Something clicked inside the plane. They all looked up as the passenger hatch whooshed open.

3

———————

Nathan's hand moved to the Glock on his hip as the plane's hatch slid back. The armed slide activated and inflated.

A man wearing a white shirt, black tie, and black trousers stepped into the opening with an oxygen mask over his mouth and nose and an aluminum cylinder strapped to his back. The first officer. Shadows bathed the interior behind him, and the sharp angle from the ground only revealed the ceiling panels.

"Everyone back," Black said.

The group needed little encouragement, and first responders shuffled away from the plane as more emergency vehicles converged on the scene.

"Stay there," Black shouted to the first officer. "We'll get the airstairs to you once our team's ready."

The first officer glanced back inside and then down at them. He held the hatch for support. He looked ill. Where were the other crew members?

"Why's this taking so long?" Bridget asked.

Nathan shifted, venting frustration. People could be dying. He had become an agent to save lives, and his inability to help rattled his core.

"I'm making entry with them," Nathan said.

"Whoa, hold on there," José said. "This is JFK's show. You're here out of professional courtesy."

"Our prisoner's inside," Nathan said. "And our agents."

"You're not trained to respond to chemical biological attacks."

"Actually, we are," Nathan said. "Bridget and I are both certified."

Beside him, Bridget stiffened, and her forehead wrinkled. She wore her near-death experience in Philadelphia like a scar.

"Doesn't matter," José said. "This scene is—"

Nathan approached Black, who issued orders like a field commander in combat.

"I need to get inside," Nathan said. "I'm trained in hazmat, and our most-wanted fugitive is in there."

"Not a chance," Black said. "My tactical response team works as a unit. Your prisoner isn't even armed."

"That's not an assumption I'd make."

"We can handle armed suspects without the FBI."

"They don't know him, and you've got hundreds of people inside."

Black exhaled. "Current certification?"

"Yep."

"The team's about to enter. Follow them, but stay back until they clear the compartment."

"Roger."

"Anything happens to you, it's not my responsibility."

"Understood." Nathan's pulse increased.

"Get dressed. You've got four minutes."

4

Nightingales fluttered in Leila Kabiri's stomach as she prepared for her first day as a federal interpreter. She inspected her makeup in the hallway mirror and then scanned her chestnut hair for signs of gray, something she'd done every morning since finding her first white hair a week ago. Thirty-two was too young for her hair to turn. Her mother was sixty-six, and she retained most of her black hair. Maybe stress had caused it. She'd experienced a lifetime of anxiety over the last year.

She swallowed hard.

The last-minute call from the court in the Southern District of New York asking her to substitute for a missing interpreter had filled her with terror. But this was the job she sought—the only position that utilized her language skills and would pay enough to support her son and mother. If she couldn't succeed as a Persian and Arabic translator, then all her efforts would be wasted. She didn't have many translation opportunities, and this was a tryout, so she needed to deliver a strong performance.

Her family's livelihood depended on it.

Her ten-year-old son, Darius, slouched at the kitchen table and tapped his spoon against his cereal bowl. He'd do that ten times exactly, because his obsessive behavior always came in groups of ten or in even divisions.

That's what neurodivergent kids did. Repetition and routine brought them comfort, according to his school psychologist.

The clinking continued and exacerbated her tension.

"Ri, please stop," she said.

He looked up with brown eyes full of hurt and shock. He grabbed his knees and rocked.

Oh, shit.

A wave of guilt washed over her. He coped in the only way he knew how. They'd escaped her abusive husband, Ri's father, and fled Iran just six months before. Ri's behavior was his mechanism for bringing order to a chaotic world.

"I'm sorry," she said.

He stared into his cereal bowl with intensity, as if he were studying his physics textbook, something she'd caught him doing a few days before. The kid was neurodivergent and brilliant. She must have good genes, because Ri hadn't inherited them from his father.

Ri looked up and smiled. Relief washed over her.

The clinking continued.

A line of makeup ran down the corner of her eye. She rubbed it, but it didn't come off. She licked the tip of her finger and poked at the streak again. Still there. It wasn't makeup. A wrinkle. Crow's feet. When had that happened? Maybe she was dehydrated.

Her mother, Shirin, came out of their shared bedroom wearing fluffy blue slippers and a ratty bathrobe. Leila would buy her a new one for her birthday. Everything needed to be replaced, even their one-bedroom apartment in upper Manhattan. Washington Heights was like the Upper West Side after an apocalypse. Dominican Republic flags papered the low-income neighborhood and made the bordering neighborhood of Harlem look safe. Several of her neighbors trafficked drugs, though she had no idea what kind. She would've moved them to New Jersey, but she needed to stay close to the courts in Manhattan. If she did well on this job, she'd make money. Her stomach hardened more, and heartburn sizzled inside her throat.

"I don't know why you brought us to this dump," Shirin said. "Our people move to Queens."

"These are your people," Leila said. "We're Americans now."

"I am a resident, not a citizen, and Darius needs his culture."

Leila's stomach tightened, spreading tension through her. Why didn't she understand Ri needed to assimilate? They all did. They'd fled Iran, and they weren't going back. Not ever. They had the same argument over and over.

"I can't do this," Leila said. "I'll be late."

"They shouldn't call you without notice."

Leila sighed. "I'm an alternate. Something happened with Mr. Tarek Fadel, the defense attorney's interpreter. He handles most Arabic translation in the Southern District, but he couldn't make it today."

"You didn't need a job back home."

"We *are* home, and this is an opportunity."

"You have a husband."

Anger flared inside Leila, warming her face. "You know what he did to me."

Shirin's face stretched, and she turned away. "A woman shouldn't be alone."

"I have you and Ri."

"Living in a place half the size of our home in Tehran."

Leila couldn't get drawn into another argument. She'd been caught in that trap too many times. Her decision to leave her husband and bring them to America always simmered inside her mother.

"I'm leaving," Leila said. "If I'm late, they won't call me again. They look for reliability."

"Tell that to Mr. Fadel."

Leila checked the time on her phone. *Dammit.* No time to walk to the subway and wait for a train, and paying for a taxi cost money—something she didn't have—but this was an investment. She couldn't be late. This was her chance.

Leila kissed Darius on his head. He'd stopped tapping and accepted her kiss without protest. Showing physical affection didn't come naturally to him, and he often mimicked what he'd seen others do, but he let her hug him, and that was all that mattered. Everything she did, she did for him. Leila grabbed her purse off the counter and headed out the door.

Showtime.

5

____

The first officer had pulled the girt handle and detached the slide to allow the airstairs to reach the hatch, and Nathan had followed the hazmat team up as they made entry. Nathan tried not to hyperventilate as he stood atop the mobile airstairs and gawked at the horror scene inside the Boeing 777-300's passenger cabin. His breath clouded the hazmat suit's face shield. Eight passengers in first class stared back with unseeing eyes—all dead.

The hazmat tactical response team snaked down the main cabin's aisles, aiming their H&K MP5A3 submachine guns at row after row after row of dead passengers.

The sight of corpses wasn't novel, but fully dressed people without visible injury seemed surreal, like a plane full of mannequins. Whatever toxin had killed them must still infect the air, and Nathan's survival instinct urged him to run. A film of sweat cooled his skin.

He leaned inside and stretched to see over the team. Alphonso and Rick would be in the last row, too far away to identify.

Nathan couldn't wait. He must discover the fate of his colleagues and the target of his two-year manhunt. Dread filled him. He could've been on that plane escorting Yemeni as easily as Alfonso or Rick. Agents didn't survive into old age just because they were talented. Chance played a role.

Nathan looked back down where José and Black watched from the tarmac. Black had ordered Nathan to wait until the tactical team cleared the aircraft.

Screw it.

Nathan entered the cabin. His fully encapsulated and pressurized Level A hazmat suit would protect him from chemicals and biological agents. In theory. But his confidence in technology faded as two hundred corpses stared at him. His padded boots squished on the aisle's carpet. He headed aft, and his suit swished as it brushed against armrests. He tucked in his arms to avoid touching passengers.

An ancient fear chilled him.

Nathan paused and inhaled a deep breath. Irrational terror couldn't interfere with his mission. The surrounding corpses proved evil existed, and the world needed paladins to fight it.

Nathan hunted predators.

He forced himself to examine passengers' faces. The two-class configuration comprised 42 seats in first class and 385 in coach. Nathan inched forward, ensuring Yemeni wasn't among the dead, but he didn't linger. Fixating on anyone would make him think of their families waiting at home, and the lives they'd never experience. Empathy was poison to those who dealt in death.

He entered the galley, where two chubby flight attendants in blue uniforms lay face down on the floor.

Nathan entered the first of three economy sections, each with thirteen ten-seat rows. This was harder. Men, women, and children occupied the seats. Beautiful people—all dead.

The tactical team reached the last section, and the officers disappeared into the aft galley. First responders in hazmat suits trailed them, moving row to row, checking for survivors.

Nathan lumbered forward, scanning like an automaton. He buried his emotions to protect his soul. This carnage could devour his humanity—if he let it. He stopped halfway through the cabin.

Rick slumped in the last row with his head hanging forward. Nathan moved closer. Alfonso lay on the deck beside the open lavatory door with his dead eyes staring up at nothing. Losing Nathan's fellow agents lanced his chest. If he hadn't flown back to prepare for the arraignment, he'd be dead too. Life was precious. And fragile. It could end in a second. Nathan swallowed hard. The seats beside Rick were empty.

Imam Omar Yemeni was gone.

"Fuck." Nathan keyed the built-in microphone in his suit. "Yemeni escaped."

"RT-1 to unit transmitting," Black said. "Say again."

"Our prisoner isn't here. José, are you on?"

"FBI-1's got you on speaker. What's the sitrep?"

"Yemeni's seat's unoccupied, and I didn't see him among the passengers."

"Alfonso and Rick?" Bridget transmitted. Her voice sounded frail.

"They're gone."

"Gone?"

"Dead."

Nathan forced himself forward, scanning corpses with more urgency. No sign of life. A few overhead bins were open.

A first responder in full gear emerged from the stern and headed toward him. Nathan squeezed against a row to allow him to pass, and their protective outerwear grazed. Nathan leaned over a heavyset man. Spittle had dried on the man's lips. Nathan breathed shallowly. Whatever had killed him must still be present.

Nathan continued toward his dead colleagues, then glanced back at the EMTs assessing passengers. Yemeni hid somewhere inside the plane, and there couldn't be many places to conceal himself. Evading Alfonso and Rick seemed unlikely, but not as impossible as escaping whatever deadly toxin had poisoned the air and stolen the lives of everyone else.

Nathan reached the last row as two members of the tactical team emerged from the galley in the aircraft's tail. An empty luggage compartment lay open beside the dead agents.

Nathan pointed at the empty seat. "We've got to search every nook and cranny on this plane. Yemeni's here somewhere, and we need to assume he's armed."

6

Nathan fixated on Rick's and Alfonso's cadavers. Their eyes had taken on the thick, glassy texture that only happened in death. He shook it off.

Powers, the hazmat team leader, stopped beside him and keyed his microphone. "Lead to RT-1."

"Go," Black responded.

"FBI's package is loose. We're searching the crew rest area."

"Copy."

Powers mounted his MP5 on his shoulder and turned toward the aft galley.

Nathan followed. "Where are the crew quarters?"

"Fuselage crown above us."

Powers and two operators aimed at a white door with a keypad beside it. Powers motioned to an operator, who advanced with a metal cylinder in his hand. He bypassed the keypad and pressed the device against the lock. He banged it with his fist, then twisted it. He yanked the tool back, and the lock came off with it.

The door popped open.

Powers nodded, and the second operator opened the door, revealing a circular staircase that curved up into the ceiling.

"Go," Powers said.

The operator poked his head into the opening and aimed his MP5 upward. He ascended one step at a time, leaning against the bulkhead for support. He climbed into the fuselage crown and looked over the top step.

"Clear."

He disappeared into the crew quarters with the second operator and Powers on his heels. Nathan followed them into a sleeper carriage that ran the length of the aft economy section. Sleeping berths lined a narrow hallway beneath a low, rounded ceiling. Nathan peeked through the first berth's open curtain at a mattress with bedding, and individual lighting and environmental controls.

The operators shuffled forward in a diamond formation, with one gun pointed forward and the others to the sides. Powers stopped at the next bunk, and the operators behind him moved up. They flung open the curtains and aimed into both compartments.

"Clear."

"Clear."

Powers continued, and they repeated the process. They reached the end, then Powers pivoted and led them back to Nathan. He stopped at a bunk near the staircase.

"Check the escape hatch," Powers said. He pointed to one bunk with an emergency exit sign attached to its frame.

The operator closest to Nathan dragged the mattress onto the deck, revealing a handle recessed in the molded fiberglass. A red arrow indicated the direction to turn it. He opened the hatch and looked over his MP5 into a passageway.

"The compartment's open," he said.

"Where does that lead?" Nathan asked.

"Back into economy," Powers said. "It's a secondary escape route, and the luggage compartment below is open."

"If someone used it, wouldn't the mattress have been askew?" Nathan asked.

"The stairwell hatch functioned, so there's no reason to use the escape hatch."

"Then why's the luggage compartment open down?"

Powers shook his head. "I don't know. Everyone back downstairs."

They returned to the main deck, and Nathan examined the elongated compartment. It looked like every other luggage cabinet, only it didn't have an exterior handle. Nathan hadn't noticed that when he'd passed it. He peered into the space at the berth above. Empty.

"Is there access to luggage storage belowdecks?" Nathan asked.

"Negative," Power said. "Not on this model aircraft. Those things aren't climate controlled, and they're too dangerous to access during flight."

"Then where the hell is he?"

"Open the overheads," Powers ordered.

Powers watched his men squeeze around EMTs, who continued to check casualties for signs of life. Operators aimed at the overhead compartments while others popped open the latches. Baggage tumbled into the aisles. Could Yemeni have climbed inside? He appeared wiry for sixty-four, but climbing into a compartment would take agility and strength.

Something banged, and Nathan spun around.

Baggage had toppled out of a compartment near first class. No sign of Yemeni.

Nathan's mind whirled. Alfonso and Rick wouldn't have allowed Yemeni to wander around unescorted. The lavatory door was open. What if Yemeni had used it and Alfonso had stood guard? That could explain why Alfonso wasn't seated, and Rick remained seat-belted in.

Nathan peered into the lavatory. The fiberglass closet smelled like a city bus. The toilet lid was up, and droplets of water covered the sink. Could Yemeni have folded himself inside the cabinet?

"We've got uncleared spaces in the lavatories," Nathan said.

Powers raised his MP5 and pushed past Nathan. Maneuvering tight spaces in a hazmat suit wasn't easy. Powers knelt and snapped open the cabinet.

He faced Nathan. "Nada."

"Where is he?"

"He won't escape. We've got the plane locked down, and we'll search every inch of this aircraft."

Powers grabbed the cabinet and hoisted himself up. He stumbled and banged against the toilet. Something clinked against the deck.

"Careful," Nathan said. "Let's not destroy the crime scene. I want to check the cockpit to figure out how the first officer survived."

"Wait," Powers said. "What's that?" He pointed at a tiny metal canister beside the toilet.

"Let me in there," Nathan said.

Nathan slipped into the lavatory and removed his phone from a Velcro pocket on his suit. He snapped photographs of the canister. He stowed his phone and picked it up. The six-inch aluminum tube had a red button and a plastic mouthpiece attached, like a futuristic asthma inhaler.

A miniature oxygen bottle.

"That's the key to what happened," Nathan said.

"A portable breather?"

"Yemeni used the lavatory and recovered a respirator someone left for him. Yemeni knew what would happen. He donned the respirator at the designated time and protected himself from whatever deadly shit's in the air. When everybody was dead, he came out."

"That doesn't explain how he could escape a sealed aircraft and slip past us," Powers said.

He was right. Even if Yemeni had survived the toxin, how had he evaded them? Whatever had happened, Yemeni was free—and in America.

Nathan perched on the ambulance's tailgate and watched as medical personnel in hazmat gear climbed down the airstairs. José and Bridget watched too. Everyone on board was dead—except the first officer—but EMTs had to confirm they were deceased. Stranger things had happened.

A combination of Nathan's pressurized suit and primal fear had soaked his clothes with perspiration. Proximity to death did that, especially when the unseen contagion remained unidentified. Something deadly hid inside that plane.

But not Yemeni.

Nathan had insisted they photograph every victim so he could confirm Yemeni hadn't switched places with a passenger, but they wouldn't find him. Yemeni had accomplished the impossible and escaped.

Nathan checked his phone. Still nothing from Meili.

Bridget ended her call. "Rahimya's en route with the ASAC."

He sighed. "Wonderful." Having their group supervisor, Rahimya Nawaz, on scene to manage evidence collection and run interference with other agencies would help, but Debbie Giacomo, their new assistant special agent in charge, would only gum up the works. Giacomo was a classic desk jockey who cared more about career advancement than locking up bad guys.

"You tell Meili what's happening?" Bridget asked.

Hearing Meili's name triggered a surge of longing inside him. The surrounding death had made him fragile. "We haven't talked in a few days."

"Trouble?"

"I can't think about that right now."

Bridget looked up at the airplane. "How many people?"

"They've identified 195 passengers," José said. "Well, 194 without your prisoner."

Nathan winced.

"Plus eight flight crew. In a way, we're lucky."

The callous statement jolted Nathan out of his depression. "Lucky?"

"You know what I mean," José said. "This model can carry up to 396 passengers and a crew compliment of fifteen. Flying Yemeni back on a slow day meant we had half the normal passengers and crew."

"We avoid crowded flights," Nathan said.

"What killed them?" Bridget asked.

"My money's on a biological agent," José said.

Emergency personnel had enclosed the airstairs in a pressurized compartment to prevent anything leaking out. Emergency personnel exited the plane and traveled through the encapsulated tunnel into a decontamination tent. It had taken Nathan half an hour to strip out of his gear, scrub down, and receive medical clearance.

"How did our fugitive survive that and escape?" Nathan asked.

"Could he have jumped off as it taxied?" Bridget asked.

"Not a chance," José said. "Black rolled emergency services when they declared an emergency, and they pre-positioned before the flight touched down. The police had a perimeter the second it stopped."

"We saw emergency vehicles heading to it after it landed," Bridget said.

"That was hazmat, but police and fire were present when the plane touched down, and the hatches were closed when we arrived."

"Maybe he jumped, and someone closed the hatch after him," she said.

"Everyone is dead."

"Not the first officer," Nathan said.

"Dozens of emergency personnel observed the plane roll down the taxiway. Nothing got on or off. The black box will confirm it."

"Then how'd he do it?" Bridget asked.

Nathan rubbed his neck. "He's got to be on board. Nothing else makes sense."

"We need to lock down the airport," Bridget said.

José snorted. "Shut down JFK? Never gonna happen. I transmitted Yemeni's description to NYPD, airport security, and every agency on our channel, but don't hold your breath."

"Is it possible he didn't board the plane?" Bridget asked.

Nathan shook his head. "Rick texted me when they were wheels up from Entebbe."

"But they refueled."

"Rick emailed me from Frankfurt," Nathan said. "Nobody got on or off, and the passengers died during the transatlantic flight."

"We'll know more after the autopsies," José said, "but the first officer didn't declare an emergency until final approach. If passengers died long before that, then he's involved."

"Commercial aircraft that size don't use autopilot to land," Nathan said. "Yemeni needed a pilot."

Nathan surveyed the tarmac. Emergency lights from forty vehicles danced across the plane's fuselage. If Yemeni had dropped out as they taxied, dozens of people would've seen him. Not feasible.

Nathan stood.

"What?" Bridget asked.

"The portable oxygen tank proves one thing."

"What's that?"

"Yemeni was on that flight."

8

The US Attorney's Office overlooked Saint Andrew's Plaza, a block from the Daniel Patrick Moynihan United States Courthouse behind Saint Andrew Roman Catholic Church and the Metropolitan Correctional Center. MCC had been used to temporarily house federal inmates, but it had closed due to its decrepit condition. As a result, federal detainees attending court were held in the Metropolitan Detention Center in Brooklyn, forcing agents to commute across the Brooklyn Bridge to pick up defendants for meetings—a drive that could take an hour, depending on traffic.

Bridget and Nathan drove from the airport to MDC to pick up a cooperator.

"Did Meili get in trouble over Macao?"

His chest tightened. "Dating me got her in more hot water. I transferred so she didn't need to take a demotion."

"That what's wrong between you?"

"It's more than that. She's focused on her career, and she's not ready for a family."

"You talking about Amelia or a baby?"

"She loves Amelia, but dating me means she gets a whole family at once, and yeah, I'd like another kid."

Bridget's eyes widened. "Give her time—"

"That's what Meili said, but this has more to do with how she feels about me."

"Sorry."

"Thanks." He clenched his jaw and stared out the window.

"Who's watching Amelia?" Bridget asked.

Guilt from shuffling his daughter between his ex-wife and a series of babysitters tightened Nathan's traps. How many nights had he left her alone so he could meet a panicked confidential human source? Those were the perils of working counterterrorism cases and hunting America's enemies—but that did nothing for an eleven-year-old girl growing up with an absentee father.

"Reagan picked her up."

"Is her new job keeping her busy?"

President Archie James had appointed Reagan as the inspector general, a position he'd said she'd earned because of the corruption analysis she'd done at State and the integrity she'd shown by criticizing her own party and exposing foreign influence in the election.

Nathan couldn't keep the pain off his face. "She's working ninety-hour weeks, and she wasn't thrilled about me leaving the country. Neither was Amelia."

Bridget softened. "She's a good kid. She knows you're doing important work."

"Yeah, right."

"How'd she react to the incident?"

"I didn't give her any details, but she saw it on the internet. I caught her crying in her room."

"It was horrific," Bridget said. "A lot of us cried."

"It's not just the loss of life. She's worried about losing me. I've had too many close calls."

"You and me both."

Bridget stayed behind a slow-moving Subaru in the left lane.

"Go around him," Nathan said. Drivers who blocked the passing lane topped his pet peeves.

"Traffic's everywhere," Bridget said. "Relax."

Acid reflux burned Nathan's throat, and being told to relax didn't help. He released a silent belch and dialed Assistant US Attorney Sam White.

"You can turn around," Sam said. "I caught the marshals before they put Sameer back on the bus to upstate."

"Head back to Southern," Nathan told Bridget.

"What's your ETA?" Sam asked.

"Fighting traffic in Brooklyn," Nathan said. "Maybe thirty minutes. Any chance someone else can walk him to your office?"

"No luck," Sam said. "You'll have to escort him. I reserved a room, but I doubt this proffer will bear fruit."

"Sameer lied. We've gotta hold him to account for that and find out where Yemeni went."

"Sameer's information led you to Yemeni," Sam said. "You couldn't have arrested him without it."

"I'm worried about a darker explanation."

"Meaning?"

"Yemeni knew we were close after we almost snatched him in Cairo. He's smart. What if he had Sameer give us his location?"

"You're suggesting Yemeni wanted us to catch him and fly him to New York so he could escape?"

"Maybe I'm turning into a conspiracy nut. Either way, we need to learn how Yemeni got off that plane."

"And Sameer has the answer?"

"He's our only link to Yemeni."

Sam sighed through the receiver. "I'm skeptical, but we'll see when you get here. Oh, and Nathan?"

"Yeah?"

"Don't talk to Sameer before you get him in the room."

"He signed the proffer agreement," Nathan said. "He's our CI now."

"I called Carter to let her know what happened, and she insisted she be present when we talk to him."

"Why would you call his defense attorney? That'll complicate things."

"If Sameer's involved, I'll threaten to tear up his agreement, and his attorney can advocate for him to be honest."

"And if he lawyers up?"

"Then we'll have our answer."

They hung up, and Nathan's phone rang. He answered. "Burke."

"It's José."

"We're heading to an interview."

"This'll be quick," José said. "We found another oxygen canister in the cockpit."

Nathan cocked his head. "Where, exactly?"

"Hold on." Muffled voices in the background.

"What's up?" Bridget asked.

"They found another respirator," Nathan said. "That's our confirmation of how Yemeni and the first officer survived."

"I need more," she said.

Nathan closed his eyes, picturing the inside of the commercial passenger cabin. "Yemeni asks to use the restroom, and Alfonso escorts him to the lavatory. Yemeni enters, recovers the respirator, and uses it until everyone's incapacitated."

"Hold on," Bridget said. "He didn't have a watch, so how'd he know when the gas would be released?"

"Maybe he saw an entertainment screen. Or the first officer signaled him."

"Tracking," Bridget said.

"Yemeni exits and confirms everyone's either dead or dying. He climbs into the crew quarters, where the first officer or someone else has stashed a bigger oxygen tank and maybe protective gear. He dons it and hides inside the emergency hatch, then waits for us to enter."

"How'd he get past us?"

"He waits for the tac team to pass and finds a way to slip out."

"Even if that's possible, how did he disappear?"

"Don't know. If he—"

"You still there?" José asked.

"Go ahead."

"Powers found the respirator crammed into a space beside the pilot's seat."

"That's it. The first officer's in on it. Where is he?"

"Being medically evaluated."

"Cuff him," Nathan said.
"Stand by . . . shit."
"What?" Nathan asked.
"He was here a minute ago."
"The first officer?"
"He's gone."

9

Leila entered the Interpreters Court Unit in room 270 of the Daniel Patrick Moynihan United States Courthouse. She'd arrived on time, but it had taken forever to pass through the metal detectors. She lined up at the assignments desk behind a woman filling out paperwork. An older man with a thick white mustache, a paunch, and worn leather shoes came in behind her. Leila glanced at the clock on the wall. She'd better get to her assignment soon or she'd be late.

"Are you new?" the man behind her asked.

She turned, and he smiled with kind eyes. Men noticed her, but this felt more fatherly than the usual lusty leers that tracked her on the street.

"I finished training, and this will be my first assignment."

"Khalil Mansour." He offered his hand.

She shook it. "Leila Kabiri. You're an interpreter?"

"Fifteen years. Welcome to our team."

"Is there anything I should know about—"

"Next," the man behind the desk said.

Leila hurried over and showed her credentials.

"You're on thirty-seven," he said. He glanced at the clock and frowned. "You're supposed to start in ten minutes."

"I know. I'm late." Leila collected her papers, but something didn't seem right. "The courthouse has thirty-seven floors?"

"You're at the USAO."

Doom spread through Leila's chest. "Where's that?"

"I'll help her," Khalil said.

Relief washed over the scheduler's face, and he smiled at Khalil.

"Come on," Khalil said. "I've got time."

"That's so kind."

"Plant goodness, and you'll reap goodness," he said. "An old Lebanese proverb. I hope my girls are treated with kindness in the world."

Khalil led her through the courthouse, across Pearl Street, and down Cardinal Place, past MCC. He pointed up at the US Attorney's Office atop the flight of cement stairs. "Good luck."

"Thank you," she said with as much enthusiasm as she could muster. She only had two minutes left.

Her heels clicked on the brick as she darted across the plaza beside Saint Andrew Roman Catholic Church. She climbed two flights to the walkway, then raced into the building. The bleak lobby smelled like the regime's buildings in Tehran. Did all governments use the same uninspired decorators?

"Leila Kabiri," she told the security officer behind the desk. "I'm here for a meeting with defense counsel and the prosecutor on thirty-seven."

"Sign in to the book, and I need your ID," the man said. He appeared to be in his sixties, with white hair and stooped shoulders. Probably a retired cop. He seemed bored.

She signed in, then plopped into a worn plastic chair to wait and checked her phone. Courts were sticklers about such things, but the US Attorney's Office allowed them. No calls from Shirin. At least Ri was okay.

The door beside security opened, and a young, pretty woman with blond hair and a lanyard full of IDs and magnetic keys leaned out. "Miss Kabiri?"

"Here." Her butterflies returned.

Get it together.

The girl led her through security, then up in an elevator that creaked and groaned, like those in Tehran. They exited into a hallway with thick glass windows on either end. The woman keyed them into a lobby with soiled carpeting. She opened the first door off the hallway and showed her into a tiny room with a wooden desk and plastic chairs.

An elegant black woman with coiffed hair and a powder-blue pantsuit that must've cost thousands spoke on her cell phone. A stack of folders cluttered the desk in front of her. She looked annoyed, as if representing her client was an inconvenience. Or had Leila read too much into her expression?

"That's not what the judge ordered," the woman said into her phone. "We requested full discovery, and that includes agents' notes . . . I don't care. He was involved with this case."

Leila stood awkwardly, trying not to eavesdrop. The defendant must be en route.

The woman's face reddened. "That's unacceptable. If we don't get it by tomorrow night, we're filing a new motion with the judge, and we'll let her decide." She listened for a few seconds, then slammed the phone on the desk. She glowered at Leila.

"I'm Leila Kabiri from interpreter services." She placed her session form on the table.

"Tanisha Carter." She scribbled her signature on the form.

Leila retrieved it. Carter's handwriting was illegible, but her name was typed at the top. Nothing went like in training, which had lacked the human element.

Leila should keep her mouth shut and learn. She was there to serve, after all. Technically, she represented the court and was tasked to provide an objective interpretation that favored neither the prosecution nor the defense. She didn't represent any of these people, just the concept of impartiality. Leila sat straighter in her chair.

"When will your client—"

The door opened, and two young men with silver marshal's badges led the defendant inside. They brought him around the table and sat him between Leila and Carter.

Leila's pulse sped up. What had he done? Had he hurt people or killed someone? Was he dangerous? She licked her dry lips. If he cooperated with the prosecutor, she'd know everything soon enough. Even if he'd committed horrific crimes, he deserved representation, and her role was to facilitate communication. Justice would be done, but not if she performed poorly. His fate wasn't the only one that hung in the balance. Her career and financial stability did too.

The marshal left the defendant's handcuffs and leg irons on. "The agents just brought him over. They're talking to the AUSA."

"We'll be fine," Carter said. "Please give us a moment alone to confer."

The marshal glared at the defendant like an errant child. "We'll be outside if you need anything."

Carter didn't respond as she filed through her papers. The marshals exited and closed the door. Carter dropped her papers, apparently no longer interested in them, and swiveled toward the defendant.

"Mr. Khan, Ms. Kabiri will interpret for you."

"I speak the English," he said.

"Use the translator," Carter said with an edge to her voice.

Leila introduced herself and repeated what Carter had said into Arabic.

"I want you to be clear what the AUSA is asking," Carter continued. "Pause before you respond to allow me the opportunity to interject if I don't like the question. Understand?"

"What do they want?"

"Your information allowed them to arrest Imam Omar Yemeni and bring him back for prosecution, but he's escaped."

"I won't testify."

"We've been clear about that."

"Then why am I here?"

Muffled voices came from the hallway.

"We're about to find out."

The interview room door opened, and Leila tensed beside the defendant as a man in a dark suit stepped inside. Heavy dark bags hung under his eyes.

"Ms. Carter," he said.

"Mr. White," she said.

They spoke formally, but White's eyes gleamed, and the chemistry between them was palpable. Did the prosecutor and defense attorney have a romantic history?

Another man entered behind him. He wore khaki pants and a blue Oxford shirt with a black sport jacket.

A red-haired woman watched from the doorway. Her gold badge hung from a leather holder on her belt. "I'm gonna grab a coffee, then I'll be outside in case you need me."

"Thanks, Bridget," the first agent said.

The prosecutor looked at Leila. "I'm Assistant US Attorney Samuel White, and this is FBI Agent Nathan Burke." White turned to Sameer. "We need to reevaluate your cooperation."

Everyone was silent. White and Burke looked at Leila.

She'd forgotten to interpret. She faced Khan and interpreted White's statement into Arabic. She looked at the prosecutor. "I can perform simultaneous."

He nodded and returned his attention to Khan. "I know you've reviewed your previous proffer agreement with your attorney, but I want to make sure you understand your obligations as a signed cooperator. Your value as a witness, whether testifying in court or providing actionable information, depends on truthfulness."

Leila interpreted everything, leaning close to the defendant. Her intense concentration masked her fear. Simultaneous interpretation wasn't easy, but she'd become proficient—a language machine.

"We made no promises, and if you withheld anything, you jeopardize your agreement. Now, nothing you say here will be used against you, unless you later contradict your statements under oath. We won't tolerate lying, including lies by omission. If you fabricate anything, this meeting is over. Understand?"

Something vibrated, a low hum that clattered against something. It rumbled again. A vibrating cell phone. Was that . . . *oh no.* It was hers. Mortification constricted her chest. Her phone vibrated again.

Agent Burke looked at the floor where her purse rested against a table leg. White stammered, losing his train of thought. He tugged down his tie and unbuttoned the top button on his shirt. "Will you answer that?"

Carter glared at her.

"I'm so sorry," Leila said. How had she forgotten to turn it off? She dug her phone out as it continued to vibrate. An incoming call from Shirin. She froze, her embarrassment overcome by concern. Mother was under strict orders not to call while she was at work. Was this an emergency, or did Mother want her to lose the job and return them to Tehran? Shirin wasn't that spiteful or devious. Was she? The call ended.

"May we continue?" White asked.

"My apologies."

The phone vibrated again. She had to answer.

Carter snorted. White leaned back and tapped the table with his pen. Only Burke offered an empathetic smile. Did he have a child too? A parent would understand.

She leaned away from the defendant and answered.

"Leila?"

Who else? "Yes, Mother," Leila said in Persian. "I'm in a meeting."

"It's Darius."

Leila's heart leaped into her throat. She couldn't breathe.

"What is it?" she asked, switching to English without thinking.

"He's upset you're gone. He keeps asking for you, and he won't calm down."

"Is he hurt?"

"He doesn't understand where you went."

Relief and anger battled for control. "I'll be home when I finish. I'm shutting off my phone."

Leila hung up and powered off her phone. She looked up.

"We care for them so much," Sameer said in Arabic. "And then one day —they are gone forever."

Her skin chilled.

"Is that thing off?" Carter asked. Her eyes burned holes into Leila.

"I'm sorry, it won't disturb us again."

"I should hope not."

11

Sameer Khan perched on a dirty plastic chair in a windowless proffer room that barely fit all five of them. Sameer's body hummed with energy. Was he nervous about the last-minute call for a meeting, or had he received advance knowledge about Yemeni's escape. Sameer's defense attorney, Tanisha Carter, held her pen over her notepad, ready to take notes or stop her client from talking.

Nathan's eyes kept darting to Leila Kabiri, the stunning interpreter. Intelligence radiated behind her eyes, but she looked nervous.

"Yemeni escaped," Sam said.

Sameer nodded.

"You don't seem surprised," Sam said.

"As Allah wills it," Leila translated.

Anger and frustration boiled inside Nathan, and he wanted to get up and pace, but the confines of the room wouldn't allow it.

"Do you have knowledge about this?" Sam asked.

"No."

Nathan's stomach twisted, and he shifted in his seat. He ran his sources, but Sam had taken the lead in the proffers after Sameer's arrest that had led to his cooperation, and Sam had fallen back into that lead role. They were in Sam's office.

"You're inside information led us to Zimbabwe, but your agreement didn't end there."

Leila translated and Sameer nodded.

"The proffer agreement requires total honesty," Sam said. "The quality of your cooperation determines what sentence we ask a judge to consider. If you're holding back or lying, I'm ready to move forward with our prosecution."

"Easy, counselor." Carter held up her palms in surrender. "My client cooperated, and without him, you wouldn't have arrested Mr. Yemeni."

"Withholding information is lying," Sam said. "He—"

"Not exactly," Carter said.

"They're lies by omission, assuming he knew Yemeni's intentions."

"He's answered your questions to the best of his ability," Carter said. "If you're not asking the right questions, that's not my client's fault."

"Then let's bridge that gap," White said. He looked at Sameer. "Did you know about Yemeni's plan to escape?"

Sameer's eyes drifted down, and he lowered his voice, forcing Leila to lean close.

"I did not know this thing," Leila interpreted.

White cleared his throat. "If you're less than truthful, you're endangering your cooperation agreement and your chance of receiving a sentencing reduction letter recommendation."

"This is the time to tell them," Carter said.

Anger built inside Nathan, and his skin stretched like a balloon, ready to pop. He turned to Sam. "Let me take a crack at this."

Sam gestured for him to go ahead.

Nathan glared at Sameer. "Cut the shit. Yemeni didn't escape by himself."

"You asked me to find Yemeni, and my cousins did that. I gave you what you wanted."

"You're lying," Nathan said. "This was coordinated. They pre-positioned respirators, which means Yemeni's people had airside access. We caught the first officer trying to slip out of the airport and arrested him. It's only a matter of time until he cooperates."

Sameer spoke but didn't meet Nathan's eyes—body language that screamed deception. "My cousins found Yemeni's hiding place, and I told you. That's it."

"Another lie," Nathan said. "We raided Yemeni's apartment less than thirty-six hours after you passed the information—not enough time for Yemeni to orchestrate his aircraft escape. He knew we were coming to arrest him."

Sameer's eyes shifted to his attorney.

"You set us up," Nathan said.

"Let's pause here," Carter said. "I'd like to speak with my client."

Nathan's argument had hit home. Carter understood the logic in the timeline. She knew Yemeni had an escape plan prepared, which meant Sameer had likely lied.

"We'll step outside," White said. "Knock when you're ready."

Nathan followed them out. Bridget dialed her cell as she sauntered away, and White checked email on his phone. Having the defense present for a meeting with a signed cooperator was unusual, but Carter would help them convince Sameer to be truthful. He had already admitted his involvement with the Phantoms to avoid a life sentence, but he needed that sentencing reduction letter.

The door opened and Carter leaned out. "We're ready."

Nathan waved to Bridget, and they followed Carter inside. Sameer looked sheepish as they took their seats.

"Okay," Carter said. "My client misunderstood your questions. He wants to provide more information, but only if the cooperation agreement remains intact and you transfer him to a new facility for his safety."

Sam leaned back. "Withholding information gives us grounds to revoke our agreement, but, if Sameer wants to tell us everything, I'm inclined to continue working together."

Carter looked at Sameer. "Repeat what you told me."

Sameer faced Leila and rattled off a guttural string of Arabic. His head hung lower as he spoke.

When he finished, Leila looked at Sam. "My cousin who told me where Yemeni hid in Mozambique works for Yemeni. Maybe my cousin knew about the escape and Yemeni told him what to say."

"Okay," Sam said.

Sameer was full of shit. He passed Yemeni's message knowing he wanted to escape, but confronting him more would either end his cooperation or go nowhere, and Nathan needed him to hunt Yemeni.

"Where is your cousin now?" Nathan asked.

"I dunno."

"Here's what's going to happen," Nathan said. "You'll contact your cousin and have him locate Yemeni's people. We'll protect you."

"I don't know where he is."

"Pick a team," Nathan said. "Ours or theirs. Everyone who opposes us will either be incarcerated or dead by the end of this investigation. You've got to choose right now."

"There's no need to threaten my client," Carter said, though her tone lacked conviction. Nobody in New York had sympathy for these terrorists— not after what they'd done.

"I'm not threatening," Nathan said. "I'm telling him that terror group will be neutralized. Join us, and he may breathe fresh air again, but help Yemeni, and he'll never get out of jail. That's a promise."

Sameer sighed.

"I need to confer with my client again—"

Sameer muttered something, and Leila glanced at Nathan. "His cousin is headed to Uganda."

12

———

Leila took the elevator down in the US Attorney's Office and exited into the front lobby. Her body vibrated as she replayed moments from the meeting with Sameer Khan and the AUSA. Sameer had denied knowing anything when the AUSA questioned him, but then that FBI agent had been aggressive and Sameer had given them a good lead. If Sameer had told the truth.

Did meetings always go like that? Tension had electrified the room, and the stakes couldn't have been higher. They chased a mass-murdering terrorist, and the prosecution team could—

"How'd it go?" a man asked.

Leila spun around and faced Federico Massimi, the coordinator for the Interpreters Court Unit—her immediate supervisor. Was this a chance meeting, or had he come to check on her?

"Good morning, Mr. Massimi. It went well . . . I think. No complaints from Ms. Carter or her client."

"And Sam White?"

"The prosecutor thanked me. He seemed satisfied that I'd answered all his questions."

"You answered?"

"The defendant, Mr. Khan, I mean—"

Massimi laughed. "I know what you meant. I'm busting your chops."

She relaxed. "Whew. I followed the rules. It was good . . . smooth." She'd gained confidence, but had she overstated her performance?

"What did Mr. Khan say?"

Leila jolted. The conversations she translated between a client and an attorney were confidential, especially those where the government explored collaboration. But Massimi was her boss. Did he want details, or was he testing her?

"I, uh, I translated his attorney's questions for him, and whatever the prosecutor wanted to say."

His eyes narrowed. "Was an agent present?"

"The prosecutor and an agent."

"Who was it?"

Why all these questions? Did he want to see if she remembered the participants? She'd recorded everyone's names in her notes and documented everything in case the meeting was challenged in court. Their conversation hadn't been recorded, but the agent and attorneys had taken notes. Massimi could find that information without asking her, and the names weren't confidential. Her mind reeled as she tried to remember her training. They hadn't covered a scenario like this.

"Agent Burke, with an FBI counterterrorism unit," she said.

Massimi flashed a warm smile. "Did he treat you well?"

Leila relaxed. He'd come for an after-action report on her first assignment. Standard stuff. And his concern over her treatment meant she wasn't alone. She'd joined an informal trial team of interpreters, lawyers, and judges to run the most transparent judicial system in the world. Nothing like this existed in Iran.

"Everyone treated me professionally."

No sense in complaining about Carter's attitude. Besides, the defense attorney probably hadn't meant it personally. She was overworked, like everyone else in the court system, and the stakes were so high for her client. It couldn't be easy being a woman, battling male agents and prosecutors. Did female prosecutors face the same obstacles? Women in America complained about chauvinism, but Leila came from an actual patriarchy that treated women like cattle. Feminists should spend a week in Tehran before criticizing the United States. They seemed oblivious to the plight of women in other societies. They must be ignorant, or they wouldn't support groups that advocated for Sharia law.

"That's good," Massimi said. "Very good." He licked his lips. "Did they sign on the dotted line?"

"Yes."

His eyes widened. "Really?"

"That's what I'm supposed to do," she said. "The defense attorney signed my form and then the prosecutor."

The smile slid off his face. "Not your form. The proffer agreement. I'm asking if the meeting was successful."

"I, uh, I'm not supposed to talk about what happened. That's what they told us in training."

"Good, very good. That's correct. You shouldn't discuss your assignments with outsiders, but I'm your supervisor, and I need to know."

"Still—"

"This was your first assignment, and I'm trying to evaluate your performance, and you're giving me flak. Are you a team player?"

Leila's heart pounded, and cool sweat beaded on her forehead. She was blowing it. Her very first meeting, and she argued with her superior. If she angered him, she'd never work in the SDNY again. And what he said made sense. As her boss, he could've attended the session.

"They didn't sign anything," she said, "but I think they'll meet again."

He smiled. "Thank you. Was that so hard? All I wanna do is determine your services result in productive meetings."

"It was excellent. I feel good about it."

"Well done. Keep me informed." He pivoted and made for the security desk.

What the hell did he mean by keep him informed? "Mr. Massimi?"

He stopped and turned. "Yes?"

"What's the situation with Mr. Fadel? Will he be back tomorrow?" She ignored the glimmer of hope that she'd have another paid assignment.

He frowned. "You didn't hear?"

"Hear what?"

"They found Fadel in his apartment this morning—dead."

The shock jolted her. "I didn't know. I'm so sorry."

His eyes drifted down as he thought about something.

"May I ask what happened?" she asked.

"An apparent overdose, but that stays between us. You'll cover Mr. Fadel's cases until we decide how to replace him. Can you handle that?"

"Yes."

Excitement flashed inside her, then disappeared. She couldn't summon the happiness and relief she'd expected to feel. She only met Fadel once, but now he was gone forever. Dread filled her as she watched Massimi pass through security. She hurried to the subway to get home to Ri.

13

Nathan sat at an open desk in the FBI's Joint Terrorism Task Force office at 26 Federal Plaza in New York. His dry eyes ached, and his eyelids were puffy and sore. He blinked and diverted his gaze from his glowing computer screen. Reviewing hours of airport surveillance videos exhausted him, and sitting still stiffened his joints and fueled his frustration.

"What you hoping to find?" Bridget asked as she walked toward him.

"I'll know it when I see it."

"We've scoured video from fifty cameras, and he's not in them. He disappeared."

"He's not a ghost," Nathan said. "He vanished somewhere between wheels up in Frankfurt and touchdown at JFK. He couldn't have—"

A thought jogged his mind, and he lightened before the realization crystallized.

Bridget cocked her head and looked quizzically at him. "What is it?"

"He didn't parachute out. It's almost impossible, and we'd have seen damage from an open hatch. The black box data didn't show anomalies, and they flew too fast."

"Then what are you—"

"Yemeni exited the aircraft after they landed. It's possible he jumped off before the aircraft stopped, and the first officer resealed the aircraft, but the odds of that are close to zero. Exterior cameras didn't capture anyone walking on the tarmac."

"The plane stopped next to a dozen emergency vehicles," Bridget said. "If he'd jumped out, dozens of cops, EMTs, and firefighters would've seen him."

"Exactly."

"I'm not following," Bridget said.

"They searched every inch of that aircraft, and he wasn't on board."

"So . . ."

"Yemeni got off after the plane landed."

"Nobody deplaned before we arrived except—" Bridget's eyes widened.

"You got it?"

"He impersonated the first officer?"

"You're almost there. The only people in and out were first responders."

"Yemeni wore a hazmat suit."

"That's the only answer," he said.

"But how—"

"He planned his escape in advance. What if he passed us his location so we'd capture him?"

"Why would he do that?"

Nathan shook his head. "Maybe he felt the noose closing around him, or . . . shit."

"Why is it I'm never happy with your revelations?" Bridget said.

"What if he wanted us to bring him here?"

"That's sinister."

"Maybe I'm wrong about that, but he must've escaped wearing a hazmat suit."

Investigations involved layers of unknowns and questions upon questions. Deciphering suspects' behavior and predicting their next moves was both the challenge and frustration of being a special agent.

"It's possible he had an emergency escape plan prepared, and he activated it when we grabbed him."

The image of the EMT who'd brushed past Nathan in the cabin came to him. He closed his eyes and concentrated on the man's face behind his foggy face shield. Nathan had seen a flash of dark hair, and—dammit—a fleck of gray. How many tactical EMTs had gray hair?

"I need to see airport personnel photographs, and I need them now."

14

Nathan sat alone in the dark JTTF office surrounded by empty Styrofoam cups. He leaned closer to the computer monitor, and his pulse increased. He scrolled back thirty seconds on the surveillance video and counted the first responders disembarking from the plane. He tapped them on the screen to be sure he didn't miscount. This would explain everything. It would—

His cell phone rang. He read the screen. Amelia.

"Hi, sweetheart," he answered. "Why are you up this late?"

"Why are you still at the office?"

"I'm working the case. They need all hands on—"

"Nobody's here," Amelia said, her voice tiny and afraid.

"I know, baby, but your mom is in DC and her husband . . ." Using that word about Reagan still felt weird, even after all this time. "Vince is in Santo Domingo, and I couldn't find a babysitter on short notice."

"I'm not a baby." Her voice sounded stronger, indignant.

Nathan paused. Amelia fluctuated from being a child in need of care one moment to a teenager seeking independence the next. She was so smart and capable, he often forgot she was only an eleven-year-old fifth grader.

"I know you're not a baby. You're growing up fast, and I thought you could handle being home alone for a few hours."

"Da-ad," she said, elongating the word. "I woke up, and I didn't know where you were. Bruno's snoring at the foot of my bed. He does that when you're not home."

Good boy. "I'll be back in DC as soon as I'm finished."

"What about Meili?"

The question plunged into Nathan's heart like a dagger. "She's, uh, she needs space, so I'm giving it to her."

"Space away from me?"

His heart collapsed inward like a dying star. "No, baby, not at all. You know she loves you."

"Then what does she need to escape?"

He sighed. "Me."

Amelia was silent.

This was the danger with introducing a girlfriend into his life. He and Meili loved each other, but she claimed things had become too serious. Had he pushed her into something she didn't want? He'd offered her an insta-family, and she'd balked. But what choice did he have? He had an ex-wife and a daughter. That was his life.

"What happened to all those people in New York?" Amelia asked.

Nathan was relieved to change the subject, but how should he answer that? She must've seen details on the news. Every outlet was reporting it. She'd known there'd been a huge loss of life, but he'd kept the graphic details away from her. She was far too young to understand the fleeting nature of life and how quickly everything could be snatched away forever. Those lessons would come with time.

"It's a bad one, honey. I'm needed here, but I'll be home soon."

"'Night, Dad."

"Good night, baby."

She hung up. Nathan held the phone to his ear for a moment, as guilt gnawed away his confidence. That happened whenever he chose work over family. His country needed him, but so did his daughter—even more after a horrific terrorist attack. Her late call proved she wasn't sleeping well. Nathan's vigilance made him a better agent . . . but a terrible father.

Nathan checked his recent calls. Nothing from Meili. He opened his email app. Nothing there either. He'd sent her a text earlier in the day, and she hadn't replied. She must have seen his missed call from last night. He thought about her when they weren't together. Apparently, she didn't.

He rewound the video. Rahimya Nawaz, Nathan's supervisory special agent, entered the room and stood beside him. She'd driven up from Washington after they'd confirmed Yemeni's escape. He ignored her and continued counting until he was satisfied. His hunch had been right.

"Anything?" Rahimya asked.

Nathan stabbed his finger at the computer screen. "There it is. Thirty-two."

Rahimya slid closer and nodded. "You're right. Thirty-one emergency personnel entered that plane on the tarmac, but thirty-two exited."

"We let that fucking guy walk right past us."

"You couldn't have known that—"

"There's no excuse," Nathan said. "And when this gets out, we're gonna look like fools. And we should. We let the most dangerous man on earth play dress-up and slip through our fingers. We should surrender our badges."

"Mistakes happen," Rahimya said. "You had to cope with a crime scene with 198 fatalities and toxic gas."

"Excuses are for losers."

"Beating yourself up won't help."

"I lost him."

"What's your solution? Resign and admit defeat?"

He rubbed his neck. "My only redemption will be to catch him and bring him to justice. And I gotta do it fast."

"Before the media rakes us over the coals?"

"Before he kills again."

His failure weighed him down like gravity. He wanted to shut his eyes and sleep for a week, but his only path out of his depression was to fix things. He needed to get proactive.

"I've got Bridget pulling more tape of the runway," Nathan said. "Yemeni must have passed through decon, but if he hung around, somebody would've noticed him."

"They had dozens of cameras out there. One of them must've caught something."

As if on cue, Bridget raced into the room, holding a photograph that flapped in the air. She arrived breathless and brimming with excitement.

"Got him," she said. She displayed the grainy photo. "The one walking past the fire engine. If you back up the video, you'll see him exit decon. He puts on a hat and keeps his head down as he walks away."

"Where'd he go?" Nathan asked.

"I had to follow him across six different cameras," Bridget said. "He walks past all the vehicles and gets halfway to the terminal before an ambulance picks him up."

Nathan deflated. "The ambulance driver knew him."

"Yeah, but that's where it gets interesting," Bridget said. "The ambulance doesn't belong to a local hospital. I thought it was a contracted transport service, because they called out everybody for the mass casualty, but I couldn't find a record of it."

"License plate?"

Bridget pulled a video still out of her pocket. The plate was fuzzy, but readable. She smiled.

"What?" he asked.

"The plate's stolen."

Nathan's pulse quickened. "Where did the ambulance go?"

"I followed it from camera to camera. There were a few blind spots, but it jumped on the access road and exited the airport."

"We can check the tunnel and traffic cameras."

"Already did."

15

Darius walked beside his grandmother down 181st Street through a mob more hurried than any he'd seen in Tehran. Why did everyone in New York rush everywhere, instead of sitting and having tea like back home? He hadn't lived in America for long, but already, his memory of Iran faded.

He missed the green spaces around their Tehran home and those afternoons he'd spend alone in the garden, away from everyone's judgment—his favorite times. The best part had been climbing the majestic Zagros field elm that towered over their garden. When his mother wasn't looking, he'd shimmy high up the rough bark and climb out on a long branch. He could see half the city from there. It had become his refuge.

But New York City offered none of that.

Darius glanced up at Bibi, moving only his eyes. Whenever she caught him staring, she'd unleash some kind of criticism, or worse, a list of chores. She was a human task machine that never tired of issuing unending assignments. He'd learned long ago to avoid poking the tiger.

A gorgeous woman with a bronze tan and long blond hair tied back in a ponytail jogged toward them wearing black tights and a halter top. Women in New York brazenly flaunted their bodies. He loved it. He leered, which was rude, but he couldn't restrain himself. Women didn't dress that way in Iran. But they should.

America amazed him.

The woman sidestepped along the curb to avoid a fat man eating an ice cream cone and raced past them. Darius turned and watched her go. He felt a familiar stirring. These new sensations consumed his every waking moment. He couldn't tear his eyes off her. He fixated on things that attracted his interest, and his intense focus revealed things like math and science—but not people.

How could anyone look at someone and know what they were thinking? People's inner worlds remained a mystery. Even when people expressed their emotions, they made little sense. He understood their words, but not their experience. None of Americans' behavior made sense. At least the women weren't shy.

Bibi took his hand and scowled at him.

He yanked out of her grasp. Why did she do that in public? He wasn't a child.

"Don't look," she said.

"Don't look, don't look, don't look." Repetition comforted him.

"That's what I said." She sounded annoyed.

"Look at what?"

She narrowed her eyes. "Women here are shameless."

His cheeks flushed with warmth. "Shameless."

"Yes."

"They seem happy."

"Life isn't about happiness," Bibi said. "It's about serving Allah, and your family."

Another woman strode toward them, thin and beautiful like a model. She wore high heels yet moved fast. How did women do that?

Bibi's glare prickled his skin, but he couldn't look away.

"I like her face," Darius said.

"Don't say things like that about pretty women. I've told you a million times."

"Pretty women, pretty women, pretty women," Darius said. He verbalized whatever he thought, but Bibi rarely approved, unless he complimented her cooking. Maman told him to keep things to himself too, but he couldn't. Why hide his thoughts?

Bibi grabbed his hand and pulled him close to her. The woman stared at him, and he flushed again, this time with embarrassment. Bibi treated him like a child, but he was almost a man. *If you could only stop blurting.*

"We need groceries," she said.

Panic swirled in Darius's chest. "What time is it?"

"I want dinner on the table when your mother returns."

"We need to eat at six o'clock. Six exactly."

"Then we better hurry."

They must follow their routine. How did anyone live without knowing what came next? Order calmed him. Everything had a schedule, and dinner should be ready at six o'clock. If that didn't happen, the world would collapse.

Darius picked up the pace.

16

———

Nathan slouched in the passenger seat of a lawn-care pickup truck with maintenance equipment piled high in its bed. Bridget had her hair pulled up under a baseball cap, and they both wore coveralls. They'd parked Bridget's Chevrolet Malibu, a car that had over 100,000 miles and three fender benders on it, at the Kings Point Police Department, which covered the Great Neck Peninsula on Long Island. She responded to texts while he stared in the side-view mirror at the driveway two hundred feet behind them.

That house was their only lead on Yemeni.

The video images of Yemeni exiting the aircraft and fleeing the airport were poor, but once they identified the ambulance with the stolen license plate that had picked him up on the tarmac, they backtracked and found a picture of the driver taken from the parking garage security camera. Nathan held the fuzzy photo on his lap and compared it to passing faces, but the neighborhood saw little afternoon traffic.

"What's this freaking asshole doing out here?" Bridget mumbled.

"There's a large Persian population in Great Neck. He may have allies here."

"I'd be as far from New York as possible. He must know the manhunt's centered here."

The FBI's New York Division and two groups from DC had been dedicated to the manhunt. They needed manpower to track the ambulance through a gauntlet of public and private security cameras. Rahimya approved dozens of administrative subpoenas so agents on the ground could request footage from convenience stores and banks. FBI agents descended on Queens like an invading army. They viewed footage to confirm direction of travel of the ambulance. They followed the ambulance like time travelers, several hours behind, but watching black-and-white images of the vehicle heading onto the Beltway, then north on the Cross Island Parkway.

Had the ambulance taken secondary roads, or had Yemeni stopped and switched vehicles on a residential street, they would've been screwed, but he stuck to the fastest route, and they caught glimpses of him as he traveled north. They checked footage from traffic cameras and businesses at every exit until they spotted it heading east on Northern Boulevard.

The ambulance had parked outside a bodega with a working security camera. Both men had exited and entered a 2020 Nissan Datsun. The store's camera had picked up both the car and the license plate. Sometimes, luck played a role. He'd experienced plenty of misfortune over the years too, and he deserved a break.

The Datsun disappeared for a time, then they caught sight of it on Bayview Drive, where it continued north through Great Neck Estates and Saddle Rock and into Kings Point.

Then they'd lost it.

But the Nissan was registered to the address on West Shore Road, a few blocks from Little Neck Bay—the residence that Nathan now surveilled.

In the city's shadow, Kings Point was wooded and suburban, speckled with palatial homes. Ten FBI agents spread out in a surveillance pattern in the neighborhood, ready to take away the car if it emerged. Drone surveillance confirmed the Datsun had parked at the house, though it wasn't visible from the road. Detectives from Kings Point and Nasau County were also present. Normally, the FBI would do this without local law enforcement, but speed was important to catch a fugitive, and they needed to execute search warrants on the car, residence, and anything else they could link to Yemeni.

Nathan's body ached with the stiffness that came from sitting for long hours, an ailment that worsened with age. Ten years ago, he could camp in a vehicle for twenty-four hours, pee into an empty water bottle, and stay attentive. But not now. His back hurt, his calves tightened into knots, and the scar covering the bullet wound in his shoulder itched incessantly. He usually ignored pain, but during intense periods of boredom, he couldn't silence his body's complaints. The older he got, the more he questioned the use of his time watching and waiting for bad guys to act. Time was the one resource he couldn't replenish. Keeping focus grew harder with each passing minute.

"All units, Tac-One, we got movement," the FBI team leader broadcast.

Nathan looked at his radio propped up in the center console's cupholder. He'd asked Bridget to turn off her radio to save its battery, but in truth, he'd become a control freak. Life did that. The more mistakes he saw others make, the less he counted on them, especially when the stakes rose.

"Tac-One, the drone has the Datsun moving. Unclear who the occupants are."

"Copy," another unit responded.

Nathan scrunched down and concentrated on his rearview mirror. His pulse increased.

The Datsun, a rust-colored jalopy on its last legs, jetted down the driveway trailed by a cloud of dust. A thirty-year-old man with black hair sat behind the wheel. Nathan glanced at the photo on his lap. It could be the ambulance driver.

"Target vehicle turning south onto West Shore Road," Bridget broadcast. She rattled off the license plate as the car disappeared into the distance.

Nathan snatched his phone and dialed Rahimya. "Pick me up."

"En route," Rahimya said.

Nathan wanted to stay at a residence they prepared to search, but that driver could be headed to meet Yemeni, and a case agent needed to monitor the moving surveillance.

"Stay here," Nathan told Bridget.

"Gee, thanks," she said. "You get to have all the fun."

"Yemeni could be inside this house. If our subject returns, have SWAT grab him outside and then execute the warrant."

Her face brightened. "Will do."

Rahimya parked behind them.

Nathan jumped out and slipped into her passenger seat. "Let's get in the game."

17

Ten FBI vehicles executed an investigative dance through congested streets from Kings Point to Jackson Heights, Queens. The lead agent stayed several cars behind the Datsun, while the others paralleled and covered upcoming intersections. Moving surveillances require a delicate balance between staying within range to avoid losing the subject and not getting too close and burning it. Half technique and half art, the agents maneuvered, driven by experience and instinct. Nathan could have requested the FBI surveillance group, but those teams had ruined his investigations before, and catching Yemeni was too important.

"Get a good look at the driver?" Rahimya asked.

"Sort of."

She shot him side-eye. "Not the answer I need. Can you ID him as the ambulance driver?"

That was the question. "He's the right age and size with similar features, but the video was dark and grainy."

"Could you testify in court that Ali Mohammed helped Yemeni escape?"

Nathan's stomach knotted. "We only need probable cause, and the judge will sign based on our tracking that Datson to the ambulance that came from JFK. This guy's description is close enough to hold him."

"Detain or arrest?"

"Let's see if he leads us to our fugitive."

Rahimya rolled her tongue and made that clicking sound she did when deep in thought. "If we're forced to take him," Rahimya said, "can you swear in an affidavit that he's the guy in the ambulance or not?"

Nathan fidgeted. He'd say whatever was necessary to flip a suspect, but he'd never lie on an affidavit or in court. When he swore to tell the truth, he meant it.

"He looks like Yemeni's co-conspirator, and we have reasonable suspicion to stop him and investigate, but I wouldn't be comfortable arresting him."

Rahimya's face fell. "I respect your honesty, but you're driving me crazy."

"I need to see him up close."

"Oh-Seven," an agent transmitted. "Target's slowing down on Northern Boulevard. He's looking to park."

"Oh-Eight's got the eye," Agent Russell said.

"Oh-Seven, breaking off."

Frequent passing of the eye prevented the subject from seeing the same car for too long, but the constant shuffling made surveillance difficult. A subject trained in countersurveillance would memorize cars and faces and look for unusual behavioral patterns, but a ten-agent team would be hard to detect.

"Oh-Eight, he's parking on Northern, a few yards from 71st."

"That's a block away," Nathan said to Rahimya. "Pull over and let me out. I gotta get a closer look at this guy."

The British teams Nathan had worked with overseas often rode two officers to a car, allowing one to jump out on foot when necessary, but that happened more often in small European towns with narrow roads, where people walked everywhere. In America, citizens seem tied to their cars.

Rahimya accelerated up the block and stopped before the intersection with Northern Boulevard. Nathan shrugged off his coveralls, slipped his radio into his pocket, and reduced the volume. He rushed down the block and slowed as he rounded the corner.

Ali Mohammed exited the Datsun. Mohammed was the name they tied to the house and car, though it was possible he wasn't the ambulance driver. They used his black mustache to identify him over the radio.

Nathan reached into his jacket and keyed his radio. "Oh-Two, Mustache is out. I have the eye."

Nathan's heart beat faster with the responsibility of watching their target. Stationary surveillance was hard enough, but a mobile target upped the difficulty. If Nathan lost him, they could miss their chance to catch Yemeni, and when investigating terrorism, they measured failure in lost lives.

Ali walked along Northern Boulevard, and Nathan paralleled him.

"Oh-Two. Mustache is traveling east. Doesn't appear to be looking around. He's moving at a good clip, like he knows where he's going."

Nathan stayed twenty feet back and matched Ali's pace. Nathan glued his eyes to Ali's back as he weaved through the crowd.

Ali slowed at a tiny shop called Luxury Carpets.

"Oh-Two, subject stopped at—" Nathan's radio squelched, and he released the button.

"—inside a business," Oh-Eight transmitted.

Nathan hadn't passed off the eye, so why had Oh-Eight stepped on his transmission? Had the surveillance team heard either of them?

Nathan stopped out of view of anyone inside the store.

"Oh-Two. Mustache entered the Luxury Carpets business on Northern Boulevard, about mid-block between 71st and 72nd Streets."

Assuming Ali had aided Yemeni's escape, he wasn't there to redecorate his living room. Either the business was involved, or Ali was meeting someone. Could Yemeni be inside?

"Oh-Eight, I'm on the sidewalk outside, and I've got eyes."

Nathan sighed.

Russell had only been on the job for a year, and he'd been assigned to a money laundering case, so he lacked surveillance experience. He exhibited a dangerous combination of enthusiasm and inexperience.

Nathan keyed his radio to call him off, then thought better of it. Russell was closer to the store, which would give him a better vantage point, if he kept his distance from—

Russell peered around the window frame. What was he doing?

Nathan transmitted. "Oh-Two, Oh-Eight. Stay away from the windows." Tension tightened Nathan's chest. Calling out poor surveillance technique must've embarrassed Russell, but this was too important to worry about his feelings.

The key to staying undetected was blending in and not doing anything out of the ordinary—like peeking into a window. If anyone looked out, they'd spot Russell, and if Ali had countersurveillance, they were already screwed. But maybe Ali wasn't that paranoid. Maybe—

Russell jerked back, startled.

The shop's side door opened, and Ali stepped out. He glanced back at Northern Boulevard, then he turned and bolted down the alley.

18

Leila waited for her next meeting in the cafeteria on the eighth floor of the federal courthouse and nibbled on a tuna sandwich. It wasn't awful, but American cuisine had less spice than Iranian dishes, and food in government buildings always tasted bland. A dozen people dined around her, most alone and reading paperwork. Nerves buzzed in her belly. She'd covered several meetings, but today would be her first court appearance interpreting before a crowd.

She exhaled. Federal cases involved high stakes where freedom hung in the balance, and any mistake could affect the outcome. Interpreters played a support role in the judicial system, yet nuances in their craft could have life-altering consequences. Many wouldn't notice her, but everything depended on her narrative.

"Excuse me, is this seat taken?"

She looked up at a handsome man smiling at her. He had a mocha complexion, rich, brown eyes, and lustrous black hair combed back in a wave. His silk suit screamed Giorgio Armani.

"Yes, I mean, no. It's available." He'd startled and flustered her.

The man pulled back a chair and set his leather briefcase beside it. He locked her with his eyes. She warmed and shifted on her seat.

"Lucas Robert," he said, using the French pronunciation.

"Leila Kabiri."

He extended his hand, and she took it. He had a firm grip. When was the last time she held hands with a man? She folded her hands in her lap and suppressed her attraction.

"Are you an attorney?" he asked.

"I'm employed by the court, sort of. I'm an interpreter, but I'm not full-time yet." Why couldn't she form sentences?

"That makes sense. A beautiful woman such as yourself would have marketable skills. I didn't think you were another cog in the administrative machine."

He leaned toward her, and she mirrored his movement as if drawn by the sun's gravity. "What do you do?"

"I'm a lawyer, by trade, but I do much more." He winked. Everything he said had subtext. His charisma made him attractive, as did his stunning looks.

"You have a case here?" she asked.

"I'm handling affairs for clients. I solve problems. Do I detect a Persian accent?"

He saw through her. Could he also sense her attraction? "I'm from Tehran."

"A beautiful city."

"You've been?"

"Many times," he said. "I've traveled widely throughout the Middle East and Central Asia. Iranian women are the most beautiful."

Leila blushed. She hadn't been with a man since fleeing her husband, and her old feelings returned. Physical attraction, for sure, but more than that. Men and women belonged together, each bringing unique strengths. Something about this man—confidence or strength—made her feel safe. She missed that security. She'd had it with her husband at the beginning, but he'd beaten it out of her, until she and Ri had no sanctuary. At least she'd drawn her husband's wrath and he'd left Ri mostly unscathed.

She shook away memories of domestic terror and concentrated on the handsome man before her. "That's very kind. Persian people are wonderful."

"I'd prepared to dine alone, and now I'm in the presence of a remarkable woman. How fortunate."

She smiled demurely. Why had he taken an interest in her? Since assuming Fadel's assignments—*poor Fadel*—her self-esteem had improved. Maybe Lucas sensed her newfound confidence.

"Do you live in New York?" she asked.

"Here, there, everywhere. I have homes in New York and Paris, but I frequently travel."

"I see." A flicker of disappointment dimmed her enthusiasm. If they became involved, he wouldn't be around much. That sucked. Or maybe it was perfect. She had needs, but also responsibilities.

"You must have fascinating cases," he said.

"I just started."

"The world's worst criminals enter this courthouse, like those behind that slaughter at the airport. Are you assigned to that?"

Excitement crackled in her chest. She'd never been involved with anything significant before, and now, this gorgeous man had taken an interest. She couldn't contain herself. "I'm part of that case." She blushed. "But I'm not allowed to talk about it."

He beamed. "I knew you were special. Have you spoken to the first officer?"

"I can't say." Guilt gnawed at her for admitting her involvement.

"I understand, but you must have incredible insight. I imagine you hear all sides of a case."

"That's true. It's fascinating."

"Your position is quite unique," he continued. "You alone are present for conversations between defense attorneys and their clients, and between prosecutors and witnesses. You meet agents and have a front row seat to observe investigations coming together. Utterly astonishing."

She nodded, feeling uncomfortable. "And your work? Do you solve interesting problems?"

"Nothing as intriguing as what you do." He cocked his head. "You know, your unique analysis has real worth."

"They pay well."

"I mean, value outside the court."

Her unease grew. She should change the subject. "You didn't say exactly what you did. Tell me about your job."

"I fix things. Correct wrongs. I help people find justice, and you could be a great help to me. Like in that case with those dead passengers."

"I shouldn't have said anything."

"Your inside knowledge carries intrinsic market value. I could make it worth your while."

Fear pierced her. Lucas wanted confidential information. She stiffened. "I'm not sure what you're asking, but I can't talk about it."

"It could be worth tens of thousands of dollars to you."

"I can't sell information."

"Think about Darius. And your mother."

Her body turned to ice. "I didn't tell you my son's name." Fear amplified her voice.

"Don't yell." He glanced around, then leaned close. "I'm offering you a tremendous sum of money for your perspective."

"I can't."

"It's nothing improper. I am not a criminal. People want information. Newspapers, for example."

Panic rose inside her, and she looked at the exit. "I'd lose my job."

"We'd never divulge your name."

We.

"Who employs you?"

"People who want to help you. Serious people."

"I won't betray my oath."

He stared. "I see that I've upset you. I'm sorry, but this is time sensitive."

"My answer is no." She stood. "I won't discuss this again."

She staggered away, her head spinning.

19

Mustache bolted down the alley across the street.

"We've got a runner," Nathan transmitted.

Nathan leaped off the curb and glanced up the street as he landed hard on the pavement. A bus barreled toward him. He contracted his muscles and planted his other foot to stop himself.

A passenger bus's brakes squeaked as it lumbered past, inches away. He flailed his arms to maintain his balance and stumbled back. He'd violated rule number one—always be aware of your surroundings.

Nathan raised his hands to stop traffic as he weaved across the street. Mustache disappeared behind the building.

Russell gawked. The kid seemed frozen with indecision, or maybe embarrassment. He'd blown the surveillance. The sound of Ali's dress shoes slapping against the pavement echoed off the buildings.

"Target fled down the alley. Somebody cover 71st," Nathan transmitted.

Nathan careened into the alley, then stopped. He backtracked and hustled down the sidewalk, almost colliding with Russell. Nathan blew past him and continued eastbound, paralleling Ali.

Losing sight of a suspect often meant losing him for good, but with Ali's lead, chasing from behind wouldn't work. Nathan needed to head him off. Right-handed suspects tended to take right turns, which would bring Ali back to him. Unless Ali was left-handed, or had an escape route pre-planned, or a dozen other variables.

Sometimes cops needed luck.

Nathan sprinted to the corner and turned up 71st Street. Shadows flickered across the alley's entrance behind a medical supply store. Ali was portly and slower than Nathan, but he should appear any second. Nathan slowed and made a fist as he swung into the alley.

Ali charged at him.

Nathan used his momentum and swung his arm like a golf club. Ali's eyes widened, and he raised his hands in defense—but too late.

Nathan's forearm caught Ali under his chin. Ali's head snapped back, and his legs flew out from under him. Nathan stumbled from the impact as Ali landed on his back, and his head thudded against the concrete.

Nathan drew his Glock. Ali's arms extended out, a sign of concussion.

Nathan keyed his radio. "Oh-Two, I've got him at gunpoint off 71st, just north of the boulevard."

Shoes pounded on the concrete behind him. Russell rushed up the alley at full speed, showing no signs of physical discomfort. Ah, youth.

Nathan aimed at Ali. Russell stopped beside him, looked at Nathan's Glock, and then drew his own. Riding a desk erased muscle memory and forced agents to think through every action.

"Cover me," Nathan said.

Nathan holstered and knelt beside their suspect. He grabbed Ali's wrist, twisted his elbow behind him, and rolled him onto his stomach. Nathan pulled Ali's other arm back, then whipped out his handcuffs and snapped them on.

Ali groaned as Nathan patted him down. Nathan removed the contents of his pockets, tossing a wallet, keys, and cell phone on the ground beside him. A flicker of doubt tickled the base of Nathan's skull. What if Ali wasn't the ambulance driver, and Nathan had just injured an innocent man? If he'd been mistaken, Ali would sue and Nathan would get days on the beach.

But Ali had fled, and innocent people didn't do that.

"Nathan Burke, FBI. Where were you running, Mr. Mohammed?"

Ali looked up at him and blinked. He was dazed, but his color was normal and he wasn't bleeding. He could be concussed.

"Oh-Two," Nathan transmitted. "Role a bus. Subject bumped his head."

"Copy," Rahimya responded.

"Who's covering the business?" Nathan asked Russell.

"Three-Balls."

"Make sure we've got eyes on the alley too."

"Copy."

Nathan tried to control too much, which, if he was honest, was his tendency, but there was no room for error. Not during an operation.

A car screeched up beside them with its red dash light flashing. FBI agents and police used red emergency lights in New York City, an oddity for American law enforcement. Two agents jumped out and approached.

Nathan looked at Russell. "Stay with our suspect. Have EMS clear him, then transport him back to our office for processing. If he needs to be admitted, go with him, and never leave him alone. You got this?"

Russell nodded.

Nathan clambered to his feet and headed to the sidewalk. He stopped and turned back to Russell. "And don't forget my handcuffs." Ironically, cops stole handcuffs all the time.

Nathan raised his radio to his mouth. "Oh-One, Oh-Two, let's hit the business and figure out why he ran."

"We don't have enough for a search warrant," Rahimya said.

"We'll secure it, and apply for a warrant, or get consent. Maybe we'll get lucky and find Yemeni inside."

"Go easy," Rahimya said.

Three-Balls and two other agents lined up beside the entrance with drawn handguns. Nathan approached from the opposite side and held his Glock against his leg as he passed the window. He paused beside the door, and Three-Balls nodded. They were ready.

Nathan threw open the door and raised his gun as he entered. He pivoted through the threshold and scanned the room over his Glock's sights. Persian rugs covered the floor, and dozens more were rolled and stacked against the walls. An olive-skinned man gawked from behind a glass counter.

"FBI," Nathan shouted as he pointed his gun at the man.

The clerk raised his hands. Three-Balls and the other agents' footsteps thumped behind him, then they entered his peripheral vision. The room reeked of wool and textiles. The agents moved across the room, and Nathan posted beside a hanging blanket that covered the entrance into a back room.

"Get down," Three-Balls commanded.

Nathan waited for them to handcuff the clerk, then Three-Balls lined up behind Nathan and nudged him.

Nathan swept back the curtain, and they flooded into the rear. An old man with a flowing white beard and a black taqiyah sat on a stool beside a desk and scowled at Nathan. Piles of ledgers surrounded him.

Nathan covered him while Three-Balls eased him off the stool and handcuffed him. That wasn't procedure, but the guy looked like he was one hundred years old, and they had only reasonable suspicion, not charges. Injuring an old man based on flimsy evidence could create a massive scandal—if they were wrong.

"FBI," Nathan said. "What are you doing back here?"

"*La'afham ma taool,*" he said in Arabic.

Nathan flashed his badge and credentials. The man's eyes dropped to it, and his face hardened.

"This place is overflowing with paperwork for a carpet store that can't do much business," Three-Balls said. "What are they doing back here?"

Nathan edged around the desk. Without a search warrant, he couldn't open drawers or dig into anything. He could, but they'd lose any evidence he discovered. He looked at an open book—a ledger. The names were Arabic, and the numbers showed money flowing in and out, but more importantly, each entry was assigned and eight-digit code in ascending order.

"It's a sarafi shop," Nathan said. "This guy's a hawala dealer."

"Money?"

"Informal banking. He's moving huge sums of money around the world and avoiding the banking system."

"Think that's what our guy was doing here?"

Nathan scratched his chin. "Maybe." He glanced into the trash bin. *There.* He looked at Three-Balls. "Time to get a search warrant."

"What you got?"

Nathan reached down and lifted the wastepaper basket.

Three-Balls pinched his eyebrows together. "What are you—"

Nathan took out his phone and snapped a picture, then he inverted the wastepaper basket over the desk and dumped out its contents. Papers and tangerine rinds scattered across the wooden surface. Nathan reached into it and removed an airline ticket receipt.

"This was in plain view," Nathan said.

Three-Balls moved around the desk. "Lemme see."

"It's a travel itinerary for one-way passage from New York to Entebbe," Nathan said. "For a passenger named Said Mahdi."

"Our guy?"

Nathan pointed at a crumpled photocopied passport with an EU visa. The photo showed their target—Omar Yemeni. "The first leg is from JFK to Charles de Gaulle."

"When does it leave?"

Nathan's shoulders sagged. "Past tense. It departed at eight o'clock last night. We missed him. Yemeni's in the wind."

20

Leila stumbled out of the courthouse cafeteria as fast as she could go. She wanted to put distance between herself and Lucas. What had happened? Who was he? She'd been flattered and attracted until he solicited her to break every rule she'd been trained to follow. She'd get fired if she gave up information.

She fell in behind a group of women in the crowded hallway, but she couldn't shake her disorientation. It wasn't just the request to break her oath, but how it had happened. He'd lured her in like an online hacker, only with perfect teeth and hair.

She reached the elevator bank. A bell dinged, and she entered the first open car. She just wanted to get out of there.

"Hold the door," a man yelled.

Federico Massimi slipped between the closing doors.

"Mrs. Kabiri," he said.

She hated when people called her that. "Good afternoon."

He hadn't been in the cafeteria, so he must have come from elsewhere on the floor. Should she tell him what happened, or keep it secret and hope she never saw Lucas again?

She sighed. She needed to report this.

"May I speak to you for a moment?" she asked. The elevator stopped, and a man and woman got on.

"What's on your mind?" Massimi asked.

"Can we go somewhere private?"

He nodded and didn't seem surprised. "Follow me."

Was he aggravated with her?

They exited on the next floor, and he led her down the hall and into a break room with a candy machine. "What's the trouble now?"

Now. He must still be annoyed at her from their last encounter.

"A man approached me in the cafeteria and asked for information about the terrorism case."

He tilted his head as if mulling over her words in a balloon above her head. "What information?"

"Uh, nothing specific. He said he wanted to know about the case."

"That's not . . . everyone associated with these big cases has press asking for quotes. You didn't say anything, did you?"

"He wasn't a journalist. He said he was some kind of problem solver. I got scared."

"Scared?" Massimi sounded incredulous. "Did he threaten you?"

"Nothing like that. But he was serious, and he felt dangerous."

Suddenly, her decision to report the encounter seemed less prudent. But she'd been right to tell him, because if it came out later, she'd look complicit. She'd done nothing wrong. Not really.

"Will we keep having problems?"

"What do you mean?"

"Last time, you argued with me and refused to answer my questions."

"I didn't argue, I complied with my training, and I told you what happened."

"Reluctantly. This is your first week, and we're already having trouble."

Her temples throbbed as a headache formed in her frontal lobe. "There's no problem. I recounted a social engineering incident, like they warned us about in training."

"Are you paranoid?"

"No."

"But you see my point?"

She replayed the encounter with Lucas in her mind. She'd gone from stimulated to terrified in seconds. Was she being too suspicious? She had been under stress and—no. Lucas had offered to pay her for information, and he knew Darius's name. That contemptible bastard had brought her son into this. Her protective instincts filled her with energy, like a lion.

"I'm not imagining this, and if you won't take it seriously, I'll report it to the judge." Her pulse pounded and her vision narrowed. She'd threatened her boss, and she couldn't take it back. He'd hate her forever.

He lowered his gaze, and something flared behind his eyes—something dangerous. "You'd be well advised to think about what's good for you . . . and your family."

"What does my family have to do with this?"

He stepped back and smiled. "Nothing at all. I'm suggesting you do your job and stop creating drama. Be a team player."

He stormed out of the break room. She stared after him with her intestines tied in knots.

What just happened?

21

Nathan's shoes squished over thick carpets covering the floor in the shop on Northern Avenue. The business owner, Khalid al-Haddad, sat hand-cuffed across from him, and two young agents stood nearby.

Three-Balls had gone to JFK to meet José García to confirm Yemeni's flight departed, and also to collect video evidence to prove he'd boarded the plane. They'd contacted French authorities and the FBI liaison at the US Embassy in Paris, who'd searched Paris-Charles de Gaulle Airport on the off chance Yemeni was still there. It was all standard procedure, but it didn't alter the truth.

Yemeni had escaped again.

Nathan looked at Khalid. "What's the imam doing in Paris?"

Khalid curled his lip and shrugged.

"I know you speak English," Nathan said. "Your cousin out front told us. Saleh's cooperating, so you better too."

Khalid scowled. "I understand little."

"Let's not start on a lie," Nathan said. "You're looking at three years in a federal penitentiary for harboring a fugitive. Cooperate, and I can help you."

He shrugged again. "I did not break the law."

"Keep saying that, and we'll prosecute you. Federal statute 18 USC 1072 makes it a crime to harbor an escaped federal prisoner, and if Yemeni kills again, we'll charge you as a co-conspirator. If people die, conspiracy to commit terrorism will put you away forever."

Khalid nodded. "We all die."

Nathan hardened. "Some sooner than others."

Another shrug.

A forensic tech entered and dusted the desk for latent prints. They needed further evidence to prove Yemeni had been there, because only the ticket stub and photocopied passport with Yemeni's face tied him to the location.

"You're a hawala dealer, right?"

"An ancient and revered profession."

"It's illegal in the US."

Hawala's informal banking system allowed money to move around the world without a digital trail. A customer would go to a sarafi market and give cash to a hawala dealer, who'd provide the customer a code to pass to the intended recipient. The hawaladar would pass the number to another trusted hawaladar wherever the recipient wanted the cash, and the recipient would give the code to the second hawaladar and get paid. The money wouldn't physically move until the hawaladars reconciled their ledgers later. The system relied on trust, which was why most hawaladars were related.

Khalid glowered. "It is our custom. Everyone in the Middle East moves money through sarafi markets."

"That doesn't make it legal here," Nathan said. "Hawala operates outside regulations and is hard to track. You violated the bank secrecy act and a dozen other laws."

Khalid smirked. "I thought this is the land of the free? How can one citizen giving money to another be illegal?"

"You're a citizen?"

"Green card."

"Not for long, if you keep lying," Nathan said. "How much money do you move per month?"

Khalid looked down and said nothing.

"My answer is in your ledgers," Nathan said. "Numbers don't lie."

"Four hundred thousand," Khalid said. "Sometimes more."

Nathan inhaled. Khalid transferred five million a year with no official oversight. The funds were essentially untraceable—a money launderer's dream and the bane of law enforcement.

Rahimya entered. "May I speak with you outside?"

Nathan gestured at the agents in the corner. "Keep your eye on Santa Claus." Nathan followed her out onto the sidewalk. NYPD cars had parked out front, and officers directed pedestrians away from the crime scene.

Rahimya stopped. "What's the plan?"

"To catch Yemeni."

She frowned. "We confirmed Yemeni boarded the plane, so we'll move the manhunt to France. What do we do with these guys?"

"Arrest them."

"For harboring?"

"They're terrorists, or at least supporting terrorism. We can charge them with harboring a fugitive for now but—"

"What's your evidence?" she asked. "A discarded passport photocopy that may be our fugitive?"

"And Ali Mohammed."

"You couldn't finger him as Yemeni's driver."

"I'm certain now." Memory was funny that way. With corroboration Ali was connected to Yemeni, his mind put the pieces together, and those blurry images of the driver transformed into Ali's face. It was circumstantial, but enough to seek a conviction at trial.

"It's thin," she said. "We need to prove Khalid and Saleh new Yemeni was a fugitive and took affirmative steps to conceal him."

"They're money launderers," Nathan said. "Yemeni came here to collect money and receive fake documents."

"He's only been fleeing for a couple days. That's fast to have a fake passport made."

"Unless he had his escape pre-planned."

"And we require more evidence to prove money laundering. Is Yemeni in the ledgers?"

Good question. "It'll take time to analyze. I want to hold them on whatever charge will stick, then examine the ledgers to determine who paid Yemeni."

"Think they'll flip?"

"Only if they're not true believers. They move money, so profit motivates them, but they could be jihadists."

"Call the AUSA and have him sign off on it," Rahimya said.

"We may have stumbled on a treasure trove. These ledgers could contain dozens of terrorists, drug dealers, and other criminals."

"Be careful with them. If the charges fall through, we'll need to return everything, and even if they're engaged in criminal activity, there must be thousands of legitimate transfers from law-abiding citizens in them."

"Hawala's still illegal, but that's not what worries me."

Rahimya raised her eyebrows. "Do tell."

"What was Yemeni doing in the US?"

"We brought him."

"But did he allow it to happen? What if he orchestrated his arrest to come back to America? And what's his connection to this hawala dealer? What are we missing?"

22

———

Leila rushed around her apartment to prepare for another assignment that had come without warning. Massimi had texted her as she'd prepared dinner for Ri and Shirin.

"How can they call you during dinner?" Shirin asked.

"It's a proffer, er, a last-minute meeting."

"A woman shouldn't go out alone after dark."

"I'll take a taxi. There's no time for the subway."

Her apartment vibrated from the rumble of an unseen truck on Saint Nicholas Avenue. They lived on the fifth floor, an inconvenience in an old building with unreliable elevators, but it was safer than a first-floor apartment. Washington Heights was known as a little Dominican Republic, though low-income residents from every ethnicity occupied her building. Only the Yeshiva University campus, a few blocks away, felt safe. New York City was a melting pot.

"It's too late," Shirin said. "What job forces you to leave your family at this hour?"

"It's important. This case is . . ." Leila hesitated. After her incident with Lucas, she censored herself more.

"What?" Shirin asked.

"I'm doing important work."

"Nothing's more important than being a mother."

"I don't have time for this."

Leila grabbed her purse and kissed Ri on his head.

"Where are you going?" he asked.

"To the office."

"But it's dinnertime."

"It's an emergency," Leila said. "It won't take long, and I'll be home in a couple of hours."

Ri inspected his watch, a gift she'd given him because of his obsessive-compulsive adherence to schedules. The Timex had only cost her a few rials in Tehran, yet it had become his most cherished possession—a necessary tool to survive.

"It's six o'clock, and that's when we eat dinner."

His logic was impeccable, and childish. Worse, it was a window into his neurodivergent tendencies that infused every moment of his waking life. His noting the time was a harbinger of impending panic. Her job was to avert a complete meltdown.

"I made dinner, and Shirin will feed you."

Ri tucked his knees into his chest and rocked.

"*Siktir.* You'll have dinner on time, and I'll be home to say goodnight. Work with me."

He stared forward as he swayed. He was a good kid. Brilliant. His obsession with time and superhuman ability to recognize patterns had helped him create structure. He counted everything and broke life into tiny time increments. He'd battled internal demons all his life.

She patted his head. "I'll return soon." She slipped out and locked both the door and deadbolt. She tugged the knob to confirm she'd secured it.

Uneasiness blew through her. She hated leaving them alone in a sketchy neighborhood, but if she didn't work, they'd go broke. They already lived paycheck to paycheck, and real poverty lurked close. She must leave them to protect them. The irony wasn't lost on her.

Washington Heights had transformed from its high-crime days in the eighties and nineties, but parts of the neighborhood remained violent. Its legacy of drug trafficking had been driven by poverty, unemployment, and proximity to the George Washington Bridge, a major entry point into the city. The Dominican Republic served as a transshipment point for drugs coming from South America into the United States, and its citizens dominated the neighborhood. Leila had researched this when they fled Iran, but they couldn't afford Park Avenue. Anything was better than her husband's beatings, and America was still the land of opportunity, where hard work could raise them out of poverty.

She hoped.

Leila trudged down the hallway, a dismal corridor with stained carpeting and a flickering overhead light. She picked up her pace as she passed an apartment belonging to a twenty-something-year-old man who dealt drugs. People visited his apartment at all hours of the night, like a contraband convenience store.

She pressed the button for the elevator. It didn't illuminate.

Dammit.

Everything in the building malfunctioned, from the elevators to the washing machines. But that's why she worked. If she kept her nose down and performed, it would pay off. Eventually.

She stabbed the button a couple more times. No sound from the elevator. Even Tehran had more reliable lifts. Leila didn't have time to screw around.

She strode down the corridor to the stairwell. She shoved open the fire door and stared into darkness. The stairwell lights were out too. This kept getting worse, but what choice did she have?

She stepped onto the landing, and the door slammed behind her. Leila dug out her phone and used the flashlight to illuminate the stairs below. Fast-food wrappers, cigarette butts, and a discarded syringe littered the floor. Leila inhaled a breath of courage and plodded down. She hadn't heard of anyone being attacked inside her building. Maybe living with drug dealers brought an element of security to the neighbors.

She reached the next landing and turned down the next flight.

A man stared up at her.

23

Leila gasped and stumbled back. Shadows flickered on the walls.

"Don't be alarmed, Mrs. Kabiri."

Terror shocked her like a live wire, and her body numbed. She couldn't speak. She glanced back up the steps. She could run to the next floor and scream for help, but if he—

"My name is Gharagöz," he said in a calm, almost reassuring tone.

Would a rapist sound like that?

"I was coming up to see you," he said. "I'm sorry to startle you." His staid demeanor made his words sound rehearsed.

"I need to get to work."

"Yes, I know. I wanted to speak with you about that."

Alarm bells rang in her head. How could he know about the last-minute proffer? Who was he? "I can't discuss my work."

"You are from the Zaferanieh neighborhood in Tehran, yes?"

The flowering parks in her Tehran neighborhood flashed in her mind. She'd lived well with her husband. Except for the whippings.

"How do you know that?"

"I know much about you, but don't be alarmed, I'm a friend."

"Excuse me. I'm running late." She stepped around him.

He put his hand against the wall, blocking her. His face darkened in the shifting shadows. That must be her imagination.

"Where does your loyalty lie?" he asked.

Loyalty? What was this? "Please, I'm late." She eased forward.

He didn't budge. "You're Iranian."

"I'm Persian." The distinction meant everything to her. She was Muslim, but not a puppet of the ayatollah or the radical mullahs who'd brought their country to the brink of destruction.

"You abandoned your husband and nation to live with infidels, but you can't run from yourself."

How dare he mention her husband? What did this stranger know about the abuse he'd heaped on her, first psychological and then physical, and all of it painful.

She turned to flee. He grabbed her arm. She tried to pull away, and he shoved her into the wall.

"You forget who you are, but the regime hasn't forgotten you."

She trembled with terror. Would he kill her? "What do you want?"

He sneered and loosened his grip. Her arm ached where his fingers had dug into her flesh.

"Information."

Her case. He wanted insider knowledge, like Lucas. But this was different. Gharagöz had discovered where she lived and ambushed her. Had he broken the elevator? And he'd put his hands on her. A battery. She stared into his cold, dead eyes. This man understood violence. He'd hurt people.

"What information?"

"Don't be stupid. You'll tell us everything about your meetings."

She had to stall. Maybe another tenant would come. "Which meetings?"

He slapped her hard across the face.

She staggered back. Her skin stung, and her eyes teared. She stifled a sob.

"Who's cooperating, and what they are saying."

"I can't."

He raised his hand again, and she flinched. He smiled. "You're a vassal of the state, a soldier in Allah's army. You'll do as you're told, or you'll be martyred."

Ri's face flickered behind her eyes, then it dissolved. Her resolve faded with it. She couldn't orphan her boy. She'd dragged her family to this strange country, and now evil men pressured her. She couldn't resist.

But she refused to capitulate.

"What specifically?" she asked.

"What did Sameer Khan say?"

"Witness communication is privileged."

"What do you care about that donkey? Answer me."

This was a moment of truth. If she defied him, he'd kill her. She had no doubt. What if she gave him what he sought? The glimmer of an idea lightened her. She had little to tell, at least not yet. Khan hadn't said much. Maybe she could thread the needle.

"Khan met the prosecutor again, but he's in jail and had nothing to share."

"Did he agree to help?"

Technically, he didn't, since he'd already become a cooperator. Gharagöz didn't seem to know that, and his lack of knowledge gave her confidence. "They didn't sign anything during my meeting."

"Did Malik Dassi cooperate?"

"Who?"

The man's face hardened. "The first officer."

"He hasn't . . . I don't know."

He remained still.

"But I'm assigned to the case, and I'll know what happens." She had to retain her value to him.

He nodded. "Good, very good. You will report everything to me."

She fought to keep relief off her face. "Give me your telephone number." The FBI could use his phone to track him—if she dared involve them.

"We will meet in person, so I can look into your eyes."

Had she capitulated too quickly, and he suspected she wasn't sincere? She should push back.

"Not here. Not around my family. If you want information, meet me at the café across from the courthouse."

His eyes penetrated hers, searching her soul for the truth. Her body weakened under his gaze, but she needed to stay strong for her family. Monsters came for them, and only she could stop them.

Gharagöz leaned close. "We're in an existential battle with non-believers. All will be decided when the Twelfth Imam arrives. Those who fought for Allah will be rewarded. And those who resist will pay with their lives."

Terror seeped into her bones. She didn't speak.

The man turned and slithered away into darkness. She didn't move as his footsteps faded. The lobby door slammed shut far below. She breathed again. A thin film of sweat coated her body.

Should she call NYPD or the FBI? If she did, these men would kill her. Could the police protect her? Could anyone? But if she divulged sensitive information, would Gharagöz use it to kill others?

She sank against the wall. How could she escape this trap?

Nathan met Bridget in the hallway on the sixth floor of the US Attorney's Office. She fidgeted with her hands in front of the interview room's closed door.

"Defendant inside?" Nathan asked.

"Three-Balls and Russell are bringing him up."

Malik Dassi, the doomed flight's first officer, had been the only other survivor—making him the prime suspect in Yemeni's escape. Circumstantial evidence, bolstered by the recovered respirator, gave them enough to charge him. He'd been arraigned that morning for aiding and abetting.

"Sam here?" Nathan asked.

More fidgeting, and her eyes flittered around. "He's chatting up defense counsel away from the defendant."

"Good. We need Dassi to cooperate."

"Not gonna be easy," she said. "If he cops to helping Yemeni, he'll own mass murder, and they'll bury him under the prison."

"He'll never get out, but he can avoid the death penalty, and we can make his life easier on the inside."

Her eyes dulled. He felt it too. The weight of so much death smothered them, and capturing and convicting Yemeni wouldn't resurrect those lost souls. Death was eternal. So was the unending struggle between good and evil. That sounded simplistic, almost cartoonish, to most people—but not to cops and soldiers or the victims who faced unadulterated evil. That knowledge was the root of Nathan's calling.

But they could save the living.

"How'd it go with Khalid?" Bridget asked. They'd arrested the hawaladar for harboring a fugitive, but she hadn't been present for his interview.

"He did an impression of an Easter Island statue. He pulled an experienced public defender, and we stepped out three times to let them talk privately, but Khalid wouldn't budge."

"We got enough to convict that asshole?"

"Sam agreed to indict, but mostly to force cooperation. He's guilty, but he can come up with a million excuses for having the photocopy of Yemeni's passport. The ID was under an alias, so Khalid can claim he didn't recognize him."

"Think his buddy will flip?"

"He's younger and seems less radical, so maybe. He's got a long life ahead of him, and he probably doesn't want to spend years in jail. When a jury sees photos from the plane, they'll throw the book at him."

She snorted. "Yemeni may not be finished. We've got to catch that tool."

She was right, but finding Yemeni in Europe would be difficult. Radical Muslim refugees had flooded the continent. In Islamic jurisprudence, *hijra* referred to invasion through immigration. The Muslim brotherhood openly discussed the strategy in Arabic, but messaging for Western, English-speaking audiences focused on diversity and opportunity. Westerners needed to hear what Islamists admitted in their native tongues, but the media and politicians branded anyone who opposed un-vetted immigration from Muslim countries as racists and xenophobic.

"Look who decided to join us," Three-Balls said as he and Russell rounded the corner. Russell held Dassi's arm at the elbow and wrist, like Quantico trained them, but Three-Balls carried a notebook in one hand and a phone in the other. Good tactics deteriorated over time.

Nathan didn't respond. This wasn't the time for busting balls. They needed to build tension, because if Dassi didn't understand the gravity of his situation, he couldn't be manipulated into cooperating.

"Take him inside," Nathan said. "We'll bring his attorney."

Three-Balls smirked. "Yes, boss man."

Nathan didn't take the bait. "Keep an eye on him. We don't want him slitting his wrists to avoid what's coming next."

They led Dassi into the interview room.

"He gonna flip?" Bridget asked.

"Doesn't have much choice, but I've caught defendants on video, and they still went to trial."

"They're morons."

"Some are low IQ, but most are cunning. It's more an inability to accept their dire situation. I call it ostrich syndrome."

"He's fucked if he doesn't get on board," Bridget said.

"We'll know soon."

Sam approached with a woman. "Bridget, Nathan," Sam said. "This is Chelsea Madison, Mr. Dassi's counsel."

Nathan extended his hand. Chelsea would be the opposition, if they went to trial, but she must know cooperation was in her client's interest. For this proffer, their interests aligned.

"Does he understand what he's facing?" Nathan asked.

"Mr. Dassi knows the situation," Chelsea said.

"He interested in joining team America?"

"Ask your questions, but honestly, I don't know if he's ready to leap."

Not great news.

"Let's begin," Sam said.

Bridget's phone rang as they filed into the room. "I'll be there in a sec."

Dassi fumed in handcuffs behind a coffee-stained table as Russell and Three-Balls watched him from the corner. Leila sat beside Dassi and looked more confident than the first time. She wore a white blouse and black skirt, both clean and ironed, and she'd applied her makeup perfectly. Hopefully, her attention to detail extended to her craft, because while Dassi spoke English, his command of the language outside of aeronautical jargon wasn't great. They'd need Leila to convey nuance and tone.

Sam positioned himself opposite Dassi, and Nathan took the chair beside Sam. The pressure of having Yemeni on the run elevated his blood pressure and inflated his head like a balloon. Law enforcement couldn't be good for his health.

"Want us in here?" Three-Balls asked.

"We're good," Nathan said. "But stay close. I'll call when we're done."

Three-Balls grunted and left with Russell.

Chelsea settled beside her client. "Mr. Dassi, this is Sam White, the assistant United States attorney. He'll ask questions, but pause before you reply in case I don't want you to answer."

Leila simultaneously interpreted Chelsea's statements. She spoke at low volume so as not to drown out Chelsea's words. She was better than Tarek had been—assuming she interpreted accurately.

"Mr. Dassi," Sam said, "the interpreter will read our proffer agreement for you. We're here to explore the possibility of you cooperating as a witness. Let us know if you understand."

Sam slid a paper to Chelsea, who glanced at it and gave it to Leila. Leila scanned it, then leaned close to Dassi and interpreted it into Arabic.

The door opened, and Bridget motioned for Nathan to come out.

"Be right back," Nathan said. He joined her in the hallway.

"That was Rahimya," Bridget said. "We caught that fucker on multiple airport surveillance cameras."

"She sure it's him?" Nathan asked.

"He wore a cap and sunglasses, but he couldn't hide that beard. Here's the shot of him in the parking garage." She held up her phone. The image had been enlarged, but the quality was decent. "Clear as day. That's our boy."

"Run the footage through facial recognition, just to be sure."

"Rahimya did that. It's confirmed with sixty-eight percent probability. The glasses throw it off, but I'm telling you—it's him."

Nathan nodded. The crumpled photocopy of Yemeni's passport in the hawaladar's office had erased all doubt in his mind. The man in this photo who climbed aboard the flight to Charles de Gaulle Airport was Yemeni.

"We need to go to France and follow the trail while it's still warm," Nathan said. "The longer we wait, the lower our chance of catching him. A free terrorist is a dangerous one. God knows what he's planning."

"Already on it. Rahimya approved our travel. We're wheels up for Paris in three hours."

Nathan checked his watch. Not much time. "Let's see if this psychopath wants to save himself."

25

Leila focused on AUSA White, employing every physiological tool to discern not just what he said but how he said it. She had to convey meaning. She repeated his words seconds after he spoke them, and fell into a familiar rhythm, almost on autopilot. Gharagöz's ambush replayed in her mind. Who was he, and who sent him? What would've happened to Ri if Gharagöz had killed her? Her job had put Ri in jeopardy, which meant she'd failed as a mother.

She became acutely aware of the silence in the room. Her concentration had drifted, and she missed the last thing White said.

"Sorry, please repeat that."

He nodded, looking annoyed.

"I asked if anyone approached him asking for details about the flight carrying Imam Yemeni."

Leila translated. White couldn't know the terror she'd just experienced, and he probably found her incompetent, though she'd performed well until that moment.

"Nothing unusual," Dassi said.

"Did you or anyone you know have contact with Omar Yemeni or anyone associated with him prior to his boarding the flight?" White asked.

"No."

Leila translated seamlessly. Her confidence had returned when she received this assignment. Maybe Massimi had thought better of punishing her for following the rules. Or it took time to replace her. She covered for the recently deceased Fadel, but that didn't guarantee a permanent position. If Massimi had another option, he would've taken it. Perhaps if she kept her head down and her mouth shut, and delivered outstanding work, she'd have a chance to continue.

"How is it you were the only survivor?" White asked.

"Efron, the pilot, passed out. I smelled an odor of almonds and put on my mask."

White stared for a moment. "That's not possible. If you smelled the gas, you would've succumbed to it."

Dassi bit his lip and stayed silent. He looked away.

"We discovered tanks of hydrogen cyanide on board," White said.

Chelsea raised an eyebrow. "They confirmed that, or you're speculating?"

"Confirmed. The first thought was an accidental carbon monoxide leak, but with a fugitive missing, focus shifted to terrorism. Passengers stayed seated, so it was a fast-acting agent, like hydrogen cyanide or nitrogen oxide. They tested the surfaces and discovered cyanide salt residue around the vents and on passengers' skin. When hydrogen cyanide interacts with moisture, it creates hydrocyanic acid. The salt is what's left when it dries."

"Hold on," Chelsea said. She unlocked her phone, tapped on the screen, and searched something.

Agent Burke checked his watch again. He seemed impatient. What could be more important than an interview with a terrorism suspect?

"May we proceed?" White asked.

Chelsea looked up. "It says here, hydrogen cyanide can take minutes to incapacitate someone."

"It depends on dosage."

"Then this is speculation," Chelsea said.

Burke sighed, and Chelsea scowled at him.

"At three hundred parts per million, incapacitation is immediate, or close to it," White said.

"A Boeing 777's cabin is enormous," she said.

"I told you we established the cause and identified the gas," White said. "One hundred thirty liters of HCN would do the trick, and we located three sixty-liter canisters attached to the air-conditioning packs beneath the cabin floor."

Chelsea pursed her lips. "How would they even get inside—"

"Exterior maintenance panels lead to the pack bay. Maintenance could have accessed them without entering the cabin."

Chelsea stilled. "Still, we can't be certain Mr. Dassi didn't smell it and get his mask on."

"Certain enough," White said. "We can let a jury decide."

"My client came to discuss cooperation."

"Then he needs to be honest." White looked at Dassi.

"I'm telling you the truth," Dassi said.

"Where did the oxygen cylinder we found near your seat come from?"

Dassi looked at Leila. "What cylinder?"

They wouldn't like that answer. Leila's stomach tightened as she interpreted.

"Let's cut the bullshit," Nathan said. "Either you cooperate or an executioner will stick a needle in your arm and pump you full of pentobarbital."

Chelsea frowned. "Hey—"

"Yemeni murdered hundreds," Nathan said, ignoring her. "You helped him, and you're on the hook for every death. We'll convict you for charges from terrorism to homicide, and then we'll execute you. Work with us and maybe you can avoid death."

Leila interpreted, then paused to breathe. Her heart beat fast. The stakes here were incredibly high for the defendant and the government, and if these terrorists weren't stopped, more people would die.

Dassi slumped low. He opened his mouth, then smacked dry lips.

Chelsea touched his shoulder to stop him from speaking. "There's a moratorium on the Federal Death Penalty Act," she said. "Even if you convict, he won't be executed."

Leila interpreted for Dassi, then looked at Agent Burke.

"That a chance you want to take, Mr. Dassi?"

Dassi sighed, long and hard, then he rested his elbows on the table and mumbled something.

Leila leaned in. He was talking, but she couldn't hear. She got out of her chair, placed her hand on his shoulder, and moved her face close to his. In her peripheral vision, Nathan tensed.

"He's gone back to Africa," Dassi said.

26

———————

Nathan plopped a forty-liter backpack onto his mattress and stuffed clothes into it. The bag was a civilian model that wouldn't flag him at airports. He hurriedly added essentials based more on muscle memory than thought. Excitement over tracking their fugitive was tempered by the stress of the last-minute trip. He checked off a mental list of what needed attention. Reagan watching Bruno and Amelia, check. His neighbor Betty watching the condo, check. He could pay his bills electronically from—

"Da-ad, you're leaving again?" Amelia asked. She stood in the doorway and watched him with sorrowful eyes and a quivering bottom lip—her face a billboard of emotion.

Guilt and regret imploded his heart. "Sorry, Patootie. It's unavoidable."

"How long this time?" She looked away, pretending not to care. But she did.

"I don't know." He'd had this conversation with Amelia and Reagan hundreds of times.

"I'll stay with Mom?"

"Just until I get back."

Did his constant absences damage her young psyche? He'd grown up in a stable environment and hadn't experienced the pain of an absentee parent. Or divorce. His time away could force Amelia to self soothe and become independent, or she could fall victim to a host of unintended outcomes.

Children needed parents, and not just for guidance, protection, and teaching, but to know they were loved. She shouldn't be in this position—but he'd put her there.

"When's she coming?" Amelia asked.

"Any minute, but I may leave before she arrives, so pack now."

"What-evs. I have everything I need at Vince's."

Ouch. He wasn't just abandoning his daughter, he thrust her into the arms of her stepfather. Nathan zipped up his backpack. "I'll call you when I land. I'll miss you."

She didn't respond.

He turned to the doorway. She'd gone.

Nathan stared at the spot where she'd been. Prioritizing work over family had damaged their relationship and destroyed his family.

He sat on his bed and leaned against his overstuffed pack. His cases had saved hundreds, maybe thousands of lives by stopping killers like the Phantoms. A glimmer of hope washed over him. His work protected Amelia too. How happy would she be living under constant peril? He preserved their way of life. Didn't that count for something?

Cognitive dissonance whirled inside him. The inherent fallacy in his thoughts congealed in his chest like lead and anchored him to the truth. He fought for the country, but he also did it for himself. He'd become a cop not just to improve the world but for the adventure. He'd wanted to be part of something bigger than himself, but he craved the emotional and intellectual stimulation of chasing nefarious characters around the world. And to be honest, he enjoyed the accolades and praise. He didn't do this to be a hero. Or did he? How much did his genetics drive him to protect the tribe?

This internal struggle felt familiar, like in nagging injury that wouldn't heal. He'd ruminated over his motivations after Reagan left him. Back then, he'd chosen his career over their marriage, and that had pushed her into the arms of another man. That decision had cost him his wife and stolen Amelia's mother.

Amelia.

This was about her. He had to do what was best for his daughter, even if that meant depriving himself of satisfaction. But would he regret taking a boring assignment with normal hours? Would he resent her? Would giving up his career make him miserable, and would his subsequent unhappiness soil his interactions with Amelia?

Tension between caring for his family and excelling at his profession shredded him. He wasn't a stockbroker balancing profit and home life. His investigations mattered, and not just to him, but to the world. Humans possessed both good and evil, and the eternal struggle could end in darkness. Monsters lived among them, and the world needed people like Nathan to stop them.

Nathan slipped on his backpack, checked for his wallet and credentials, and walked down the hall to Amelia's room. She'd piled her laptop, phone, and a book on her bureau. She padded across the room in socks with pink ladybugs on them. She wore a tee shirt with a picture of Enola Holmes, Sherlock Holmes's younger sister. If Amelia admired the detective, maybe she respected his work too. Did she want to emulate him?

Nathan rubbed his chin. All his dedication and hard work—all his success—must've made an impression on her. Perhaps it wasn't all bad. If he instilled in her a strong work ethic and the values of duty and honor, his constant absences could be worth it.

Or was he rationalizing this so he could keep pursuing the career that he loved?

She turned to him. "Be careful."

His heart melted. "I always am."

Nathan stared across the Grand-Place's expansive plaza in Brussels' historic Old Town section. The Dutch called the square the Grote Markt, and the Baroque architecture of Brussels' Town Hall and surrounding buildings dated back to the fourteenth century, making the UNESCO World Heritage Site a popular tourist destination. Hundreds of people traipsed across the stone. Bridget and First Inspector Noah Peeters from the Belgium Police's Directorate of Special Units stood beside Nathan and surveyed the crowd.

"How we gonna find this prick?" Bridget asked.

"Any hits on the box?" Nathan asked Peeters. The box referred to Digital Receiver Technology known as a dirt box, a device that simulated a cell phone repeater and identified every cell phone within range.

Peeters depressed his lapel microphone and spoke in Flemish. He touched his earpiece, getting the answer. "The phone is within 150 meters. The tracking team is closing in."

Nathan scanned the crowd. Yemeni could be hiding in the swarming mass of humanity.

First Officer Malik Dassi had confessed to his role in Yemeni's escape and mass murder, though he swore he'd thought the gas would only incapacitate passengers. Even if true, he'd be a co-conspirator. He'd started sweating the moment Nathan mentioned lethal injection, and his fear of the needle had overcome his hope of winning at trial.

Dassi had given up Pierre Laurent, a French national working for Yemeni in Paris. Quick cooperation from the French General Directorate for Internal Security had identified Laurent, and the National Gendarmerie Intervention Group, known as the GIGN, had tracked him to Charles de Gaulle Airport. Surveillance video revealed Laurent in the company of Yemeni. The GIGN team tracked them to a Eurostar train destined for Brussels. The two-hour trip had allowed pursuers to scramble, but coordination with Belgium took time, and they hadn't intercepted them at Bruxelles-Midi station.

They'd tracked Laurent and Yemeni through video from public surveillance cameras and lost them momentarily before picking them up again as they exited the Bruxelles-Central train station near the Grand-Place.

Peeters touched his ear again. "Laurent's there, to the north."

"Has he made any calls?" Nathan asked.

"Laurent carries the phone but hasn't used it."

The DRT box, a mobile wire intercept platform, allowed agents to listen to conversations. An increasingly totalitarian Europe monitored its citizens' speech, an offense to liberty, but it came in handy when tracking terrorists.

Nathan scanned the faces of the people sitting at a café along the western edge of the plaza. Would Yemeni expose himself in public? He'd come to Brussels for a purpose, and sipping espresso at a tourist site wasn't it.

"He's to the north, outside the plaza," Peeters said.

"Let's go," Nathan said.

They headed across the plaza at a determined pace. Nathan inspected the faces around them, not just looking for Yemeni or Laurent, but anyone acting suspicious. The continent hosted a large Islamic population, and Yemeni could control a countersurveillance team. If Nathan had been in his position, he'd have a security perimeter.

Bridget and Peeters kept pace, and her heels clicked against the bricks. Peeters cocked his head as he received incoming transmissions. He couldn't be more obvious as they exited the northeast corner of the plaza onto Rue de la Beurree.

Nathan weaved through the crowd and reached a Baroque façade with intricate stone statues and gold appointments. Buildings around the Town Hall and King's House included old halls once used by Brussels' guilds. The city bristled with history and elegance.

He moved north through heavy pedestrian traffic between rising buildings on both sides and cargo trucks parked beneath windows secured with iron grates. He peeked into each cab, trying to be discreet. Ever since serving in Afghanistan, unattended vehicles raised gooseflesh. He'd seen firsthand the damage vehicle-borne improvised explosive devices could do. If Yemeni intended to detonate a VBIED in Brussels, attacking the plaza would ensure a high casualty count.

"Up ahead," Peeters said.

"Where are your men?" Nathan asked.

"Two teams in vehicles. They're trying to triangulate, but they're stuck in traffic."

A half dozen bicycle and patrol officers loitered on the next block outside the wooden doors to the Division Central de Police. Among them were men in civilian clothes who sported bald heads and close-cropped haircuts like military recruits.

"Yemeni wouldn't hang around a police station, unless that's the target," Nathan said.

Peeters touched his earpiece, then pointed down the street. "That way, fifty meters."

Nathan picked up his pace, not bothering to chastise Peeters for telegraphing his intentions and exposing them as surveillance agents.

The road intersected with Rue du Marché au Charbon, where outdoor cafés bordered the square. Europeans knew how to create inviting public spaces. The road snaked to the northeast, and Nathan's pulse thumped as he sped up. He was unarmed, because his role was to observe, report, and provide guidance—not act. The Mansfield amendment prohibited it, which handcuffed aggressive agents working overseas.

They followed the bend to another intersection with more cafés. Peeters grabbed Nathan's arm and jerked his chin up the street at a Peugeot minivan. "That is my team."

"Where's the signal?" Nathan asked. Hesitating in the street would expose them, and warning jitters tingled through him.

"Between us," Peeters said.

Nathan looked around frantically. "Any of these buildings could—"

There. Laurent sat at a café table and stared at the van. He sipped an espresso alone at the table and looked calm.

"That's our target," Nathan said. "Third table from the right."

"Where's Yemeni?" Bridget asked.

"Not there," Nathan said. "Peeters, have your men hit the café and search it."

"Shouldn't we wait and watch—"

"We're too late," Nathan said. "They came together, and now Yemeni's gone."

"We must wait for our action team," Peeters said.

"We can't waste time," Nathan said.

"But—"

"Hit it."

The beginnings of a migraine pierced Leila's temples. She collapsed onto her couch and curled her legs beneath her like a cat. The paisley fabric had worn down, rendering it practically invisible, and threads unraveled at the seams. What did she expect for fifty dollars? Shirin glared at her from their overstuffed armchair. Her mother found comfort in outrage. The furniture didn't match. Was eclectic interior design fashionable if she'd done it without intention? She snorted.

Fleeing Tehran in the dead of night had left her with dwindling reserves. She'd planned to leave her husband after he'd beaten her unconscious for the crime of having another man smile at her. Jealousy, she could tolerate, but a loose front tooth was too much. She'd stashed away money by stealing from her weekly grocery allowance. Human traffickers cost a fortune, but they'd smuggled them out of Iran into Turkey. They slipped into Greece, where she worked as a waitress for months, garnering slave wages. She applied for asylum in the US while landing a temporary linguist position with Med Corp, an international conglomerate that sold medical devices across North America, Europe, and the Middle East. Being multilingual was her only marketable human capital, and it saved them from destitution.

"We are not safe here," Shirin said.

"He didn't hurt me."

Leila had told her mother she'd been accosted in the stairwell, but she'd been smart enough not to mention that the man pressured her to divulge confidential information. She'd also failed to relate the earlier bribery attempt.

"Criminals infest this city like rats," Shirin said.

"All cities are dangerous."

"We were safe in Tehran."

"You weren't the one getting abused."

Rage flared inside her, and acid burned her stomach. Her mother, the woman who gave her life, was supposed to protect her. Why did she always take her ex-husband's side? That's how she thought of him, her *ex*, because saying *husband* invited feelings of hate and regret. She'd let him dominate her for too long. Mother never acknowledged her feelings or the damage her husband had done. Leila had done nothing to incur her ex's wrath, and fleeing his abuse had been her only choice. But Mother never missed an opportunity to bring it up.

Leila pinched her lips together to stop from speaking out, a trick she learned in Iran. Her fury would pass in time, as would her mother's condemnation. But if she fought back, a lifetime of antagonism would boil up and infect everything.

"Maman?" Ri's voice doused her anger like cold water.

Ri peeked around the hallway corner.

"It's past your bedtime," Leila said.

"You didn't shut off the hallway lights."

Leila sighed. "The switch is right beside you. Turn it off and go to bed."

"Come say goodnight first."

Leila's body sank deeper into the couch. How many times would she have these conversations?

"I did that already."

"But not in the right order. After you tell me goodnight, you close the door, and turn off the hall light."

"Please go to sleep."

"We have to start over."

"I'm begging you. I'll be in later. Your grandmother and I have to talk."

"About the criminal?"

She jolted. How much had he heard? "Everything's fine. Go to bed."

"Will the bad men find us here?"

She hadn't wanted to scare him when he was younger, but she'd needed to warn him about the mullah's secret police, and evil men who worked with his father. If he didn't know the danger, he could say the wrong thing, or let on that his mother was unhappy—and either of those could have landed her in a sanitarium. Or worse.

"No one's coming to hurt you. We're in America now. You're safe."

"But I heard you talk about the stranger on the stairs."

Her mother's glare intensified with the heat of the sun.

"We must be careful here, like everywhere, and that means not going out alone and being aware of our surroundings. Don't let strangers approach you, and never go downstairs without me."

"That doesn't sound safe," her mother said.

"I'll go to sleep after you come say goodnight," Ri said.

Leila looked from one to the other, then rubbed her eyes with the palms of her hands. Her migraine had returned.

29

Nathan had battled risk-averse bureaucrats and bad policies for his entire career, but cowardice cost lives. Yemeni was on the loose, leaving a trail of bodies in his wake, and the closest connection to him sat at a table twenty yards away. The Belgian action team would arrive soon, but their chances of apprehending Yemeni diminished with every second.

Nathan was unarmed, but the fire inside him wouldn't be extinguished by rule-following administrators or that smug, terrorist prick who sipped coffee while families mourned in New York.

Nathan headed across the plaza.

"What are you doing?" Peeters asked behind him.

Nathan ignored him and moved toward the café. He aimed for the front door to avoid alerting Laurent.

Footsteps clacked on the bricks behind him, and then Bridget was at his side. She looped her arm through his, as if they were lovers, a clever surveillance trick. She'd grown as an agent since they'd first partnered together. He smiled at her, in case anyone watched.

Nathan's eyes flittered over the street, hoping to catch sight of the action team bearing down on the café, but there was no sign of them. If they were close, he and Bridget could watch Laurent to ensure he didn't escape, and if the police failed to show . . . well, Nathan had never been good at following rules.

An elderly couple drank tea along the railing surrounding the patio, and behind them, three teenage girls laughed and spoke in German. Laurent sat alone on the far end. A few diners inside were visible through large windows, but none were Yemeni. He hadn't come to Brussels to chat at a café with Laurent. Their business had concluded, and Yemeni was gone.

Nathan led Bridget onto the patio. Nathan didn't look at Laurent, and he prayed Bridget didn't either. Nathan stopped at a table near the window and pulled out a chair for Bridget. The chair's iron legs scraped against the stone. From Bridget's expression, she didn't appreciate being treated like the fairer sex. He sat beside her.

Laurent's back was to them. He ignored his tea and scanned the plaza. Nathan followed his stare, but nothing stood out. No marauding jihadists or Belgian SWAT team.

Peeters stood in the street with his hand over his earpiece. *Dammit.* What was wrong with him? Even the most green countersurveillance agent would spot him. Peeters spoke to no one with his palm cupped over his ear.

Laurent stared at Peeters. The inspector was blown.

Laurent stood.

"Fuck this," Nathan said.

"Don't do what I think you're about to do," Bridget said.

Laurent looked down the street from the direction Bridget, Nathan, and Peeters had come. Was he searching for more surveillance agents, or had they been right that the police station was a target?

Laurent looked at his watch, then tossed a few euros onto the table and strolled across the patio. Peeters looked away and continued to update his team, unaware his target was on the move.

Laurent slipped through the railing onto the street and turned right. Peeters continued speaking with the invisible agent in his earpiece.

How did Nathan always end up in these situations where he had to intervene?

"Wait for SWAT," Bridget said.

"We're taking him."

"No, I said—"

Nathan sprang from his seat and hurried onto the street. Laurent was ten yards ahead. Nathan swiveled his head as he moved, but nobody in the sparse crowd stood out as a threat.

Laurent glanced back at Peeters.

Nathan gazed up at the buildings like a tourist, and Laurent didn't appear to notice him—but a trained professional wouldn't react.

Laurent reached the corner and veered down the intersecting street.

Screw it.

Nathan bolted after him, and his shoes slapped against the brick. Laurent turned as he approached.

Nathan didn't slow. He bent his knees and lunged. He plowed into Laurent like a blitzing safety. His shoulder caught Laurent below his ribs. Laurent grunted and lost his footing. Nathan drove through him, and they flew through the air. Nathan tensed as they crashed hard on the ground. Something popped in Laurent's ribs.

"Ay," Laurent cried.

They rolled across the rough surface, and Nathan's knuckles burned beneath Laurent, where the sharp brick had abraded them. Nathan pushed off Laurent and mounted him like a horse.

Laurent reached inside his vest.

Nathan grabbed his wrist and delivered a hard right cross. He connected with Laurent's chin, and the man's head snapped back. Laurent's eyes dulled, and he groaned.

Nathan shimmied up and rested his weight onto Laurent's chest as he pinned his arms against the street with his knees.

Bridget came around and grabbed Laurent's arm.

"He went for something in his vest," Nathan said.

Bridget dug into Laurent's jacket and removed a cell phone. Stress contorted her face. They'd used physical force against a foreign national in Belgium without authority.

Footsteps pounded behind them and Peeters arrived, red-faced and breathless. "What have you done?"

"He was getting away," Nathan said.

"You are not allowed," Peeters said.

"He reached for something, and I had to act." Nathan didn't mention he'd already tackled him.

"You've killed him."

"He's fine."

Laurent wriggled beneath him, then he turned his head and spit out blood.

"I ordered you to wait for—"

Tires screeched on the pavement. Nathan turned as a van skidded to a stop. Four men wearing black fatigues, ballistic vests, and balaclavas leaped out and raced toward them pointing Heckler & Koch MP5s.

Nathan had no time to flee. If these men were terrorists, they were finished.

"*Doorzoek het café*," Peeters yelled.

One officer covered Laurent, while the others burst into the café. There was little chance Yemeni was inside, but they had to check.

Laurent glowered with hateful eyes. No, more than hate. Laurent looked scared.

"Where's Yemeni?" Nathan asked.

"We must go," Laurent said in accented English.

"You're not giving the orders," Nathan said. "Tell me where Yemeni's hiding."

Laurent craned his neck and looked past Nathan at the café. "You don't understand. The bomb detonates in two minutes."

30

The explosives Yemeni's men planted in the café would detonate in under two minutes, but they had no time to find it and no demolition expert to defuse it. Their only play was to run—but not before they evacuated civilians. Nathan held the café door open while Peeters screamed for guests to flee, and tactical officers dragged people out of their seats. Bridget pinned Laurent to the sidewalk, and the fear Nathan had seen in Laurent's eyes proved he told the truth.

The stopwatch in Nathan's mind ticked down.

"I've got to warn the kitchen staff," Nathan said.

"No." Peeters blocked his path. "I'll do it. They won't speak English."

Maybe Nathan had been wrong about him. "Take them out the back."

A woman clutching a baby scurried toward the front door. Peeters sidestepped around them and raced through the restaurant. He ran behind the counter and disappeared through a swinging double-acting door into the kitchen.

Seconds melted away.

Nathan stepped aside and let the last tactical officer escort an elderly man out. Nathan poked his head inside, and fear surged through him as if he'd stuck his head inside the bomb itself.

Alarm bells clanged in his mind, and hair rose on his body. Instinct implored him to flee.

"Time's up, Peeters. Are you clear?"

No response.

Nathan pivoted and sprinted across the patio. He leaped over the railing like an Olympian and hit the ground in stride. He should grab Bridget and—

Whump.

The world lit up. A pressure wave knocked the air from his lungs and propelled him forward.

Nathan lost his footing and fell. He swung out his hands to avoid face-planting and crashed hard onto the stone.

The explosion plugged his ears, and he struggled to breathe. Particles of glass shattered around him. Detritus and ash danced in the air, and acrid smoke clouded the sky.

Nathan protected his neck and head with his hands and kept his face down to keep flotsam out of his eyes. His palms stung, and his body ached. He relaxed his chest and let his lungs refill.

His breath returned, and he rolled onto his side and looked back. Only a skeleton of the façade remained. The café's windows and door had disappeared, and the patio furniture had migrated into the street. Flames gushed out of the windows, and black smoke billowed from the collapsed roof.

Everyone inside would have died.

People screamed on the street. Nathan's head throbbed. He closed his eyes and focused. No concussion, at least nothing serious.

"Are you shitting me?" Bridget said. She stood beside him, gawking at the café.

Nathan looked back at Laurent. Two tactical officers had him in handcuffs.

"You okay?" she asked.

"Did Peeters get out?"

Bridget smiled and pointed as Peeters emerged from the alley that ran beside the café. His face had been blackened by soot, and a wisp of smoke rose out of his hair. Two young men from the kitchen stumbled behind him, both in shock. Peeters joined them.

"I apologize," Peeters said.

"For what?" Nathan asked. "You saved those people."

"Only because you stopped Laurent. Another few minutes and . . ." His voice trailed off.

"We caught him, and you showed real balls running into that restaurant. You almost ended up as the daily special."

Sirens wailed nearby in that looping, phantasmal meter unique to Brussels.

"What the hell is that sound?" Bridget asked.

"Ambulances," Nathan said. "They're eerie."

"*Scooby Doo* meets the *Addams Family*."

He laughed, but his body ached. "I feel like the Forrest Gump of law enforcement. I'm present at too many attacks."

"That's because you're aggressive and tracking these a-holes," Bridget said. "Why isn't Yemeni on the run? He must know we're on his heels."

"Exactly," Nathan said. "Dassi told us he's returning to Africa for an operation. Maybe he's creating chaos to cover his trail."

"An operation we know nothing about," Bridget said.

"The unknown is more dangerous. We've gotta catch him before more innocent people die."

Peeters shook his head. "It is easier to say than to accomplish. This man is a devil."

"Or working for him. I want a word with Laurent."

"Quickly, then."

Peeters extended his hand, and Nathan took it and struggled to his feet. Everything hurt. They walked across a black coating of ash to Laurent. Ambulances and police cars filled the street.

Nathan hovered over Laurent, and despite the failed attack, Nathan fought the urge to punch him. "Why did you do this?"

"I did not do—"

"Save it," Nathan said. "We've got video of you with Yemeni. You'll go to prison forever."

"But I—"

"My American friend is correct," Peeters said. "I will charge you with participation in the activities of a terrorist group, causing large-scale destruction and endangerment, aggravated battery, and attempted murder. Use of explosives will add years to your sentence."

Saving lives and almost dying had transformed Peeters. He'd become bold and confident. Aggressive. An improved version of his former self. Combat did that to men, and near-death experiences in civilian life had the same effect.

"I admit nothing," Laurent said.

Bridget picked up Laurent's satchel and opened the flap. A stack of papers poked out, including the unmistakable shape of a passport. She leafed through the entry and exit stamps, then examined the papers.

"Laurent just returned from Uganda," Bridget said.

Nathan's chest tightened. "That's where Yemeni was headed when we grabbed him in Harare. I'd think that would be the last place on earth he'd travel."

"Maybe that *fukah*'s support team is there, or he left something he needs to collect."

A familiar dread clawed at Nathan's guts. "Or he's planning an action in Africa."

"What could he do in Uganda?" Bridget asked.

"We don't know he's going there for certain. I'm calling Rahimya." He and Bridget walked out of Laurent's earshot, and he dialed his cell phone.

"It's early," Rahimya said, her voice full of sleep.

"We tracked him to Brussels. He blew up a café."

"Shit. How many casualties?"

"None serious. We caught his contact and got people out in time."

The line was silent.

"You there?" he asked.

"Sorry, I'm still waking up. I'll need a full report to brief the SAC."

"We've got a lead from his contact's pocket liter, and it corroborates the info Yemeni's codefendant gave us. We think he's headed back to Africa. We've got to alert the airport."

"Every airport," Bridget said. "He's a train or car ride away from half of Europe."

"They'll need you as witnesses in Brussels," Rahimya said.

"This guy can't hurt us anymore," Nathan said, "but Yemeni can."

"What should we do?" Bridget asked.

Nathan cringed. Better to do what they thought was right, and deal with the consequences later, than to ask the question and be forced to violate a direct order. He didn't breathe.

"Find Yemeni and take him into custody," Rahimya said.

Nathan was starting to like her.

31

———

Something was bothering Maman. She trudged through their living room with that stiff movement she had before she started yelling at someone. Maman picked a piece of lint off the couch. She moved a pillow and then replaced it in the same spot. She patted it with her hand.

He never knew what she was thinking, but this was a pattern he'd seen before. When she limped around the house after Father beat her, she'd often adjust the figurines on the shelf above the stove, turning them and putting them back, and then moving into the other rooms to tidy up a nonexistent mess. The order brought him happiness. Maybe it did the same for her, but that was a mystery he'd never solve. What he recognized was the pattern. When Mother was in pain, she'd clean things that didn't need it. And that's what she was doing now.

Darius perched at the table, drawing concentric circles on a piece of paper with a pencil. The spacing had to be perfect between them, and the smaller they got, the harder it was to make everything even. They had to be even and perfectly round.

"Why are you sad, Mother?"

She looked at him.

"Are you angry about something?"

She canted her head, the way people often did after he'd said something. Was he a mystery to her too?

She tussled his hair. "Nothing's wrong, Habibi."

"Nothing's wrong, nothing's wrong, nothing's wrong," Darius said.

She flashed that familiar sad smile. Was she disappointed in him? Had he done something wrong?

"Why does he always talk like that?" Bibi asked.

"Stop it," Maman said. "You know why. It calms him." She lifted a doily off the chair, shook it, then held it up and inspected it in the light. She placed it back on the headrest and flattened it with her palm.

Darius drew another circle inside the last one.

"Please stop that," Bibi said. She stormed into the room in a huff.

Mother looked at her. "Stop what?"

"You're incessant cleaning. You're making me nervous."

"Then don't watch me."

Bibi glared at Maman.

Something was wrong with Maman, between her and Bibi too. They'd been snapping at each other for days.

And he'd heard Maman crying in the bathroom. He watched her now, unable to tear his eyes away from her face. She'd always been strong, but she did things that surprised him. Unexpected things. The disorder created pressure in his head. It rolled like a ball from the base of his skull to the top and then back down. Things were not as they should be, but what was wrong, he didn't know. And Maman would never tell him.

Maman walked into the kitchen, and Bibi glared after her, then she stormed into the bedroom. Darius looked back down at his circles. The last one he'd drawn wasn't round. He'd almost finished, but that wasn't right. Darius lifted the paper with dozens of circles and frowned. He crushed the paper in a tiny ball and pushed it aside. He grabbed another paper and started over.

32

Nathan opened the door to his hotel room and held it for Bridget to enter. A plane roared overhead, and the vibration rattled the window. They'd taken adjoining hotel rooms in a shabby three-star hotel in the Zaventem neighborhood in the Flemish Brabant province. The accommodations weren't great, but the hotel's proximity to the airport and major thoroughfares made it a tactical place to stage while Belgian police searched for Yemeni.

"You were quiet during dinner," Bridget said.

"I'm tired."

"That it?"

He nodded. After the adrenaline from almost getting blown up had dissipated, a deep fatigue settled into his muscles. Normally, he'd be on edge waiting while Yemeni put distance between them, but his thoughts moved to Amelia. When he'd called Reagan to check on her, Amelia hadn't come to the phone. She didn't like his abandoning her, and he couldn't blame her.

"May I?" Bridget said as she took a water bottle off his bed stand.

"Have at it."

She twisted off the cap. "I've known you long enough to know when something's—"

"Had you already opened that bottle?" Nathan asked.

"Huh?"

"The bottle. Did you just open it?"

"Do you want it? I can get another one."

"It didn't make a sound." Nathan's senses heightened, and he strode across the room to her.

She narrowed her eyes. "You feeling okay?"

"Let me see it."

"What's going on?"

He held out his hand, and she handed him the bottle. He lifted the bottle to his nose and sniffed. No odor.

"You're freaking me out," she said. "Should I call a psychologist?"

"The plastic caps on these bottles are machine sealed. They snap when opened, but I didn't hear a sound."

"I wasn't paying attention," she said. "Maybe it did, and you just didn't hear it."

"I drank a bottle earlier, and it took a little pressure to open it. Did you feel any resistance?"

She looked down and bit her lip. "No, er, I didn't notice. You're saying the bottle was open?"

"Or someone opened it."

"We're both tired," she said. "I haven't had a good night's sleep since we saw those bodies in the plane."

"I'm not tired."

"Jet-lagged."

Nathan examined the bottle. The label looked legitimate, as did the plastic cap.

"No audible pop."

"You sound a little crazy," she said.

"A little crazy can be a good thing."

In the past, he'd battled with mild obsessive-compulsive disorder, a natural reaction to living in places like Afghanistan where bacteria, viruses, and diseases spread like wildfire. He had it under control at home, but when he traveled, his awareness of germs heightened as a defense mechanism.

"You think someone broke into your hotel room and opened my bottle of water? Why the hell would anyone do that?"

"To poison you." He hesitated. If someone had targeted them, he or she would have tampered with the water in her room too. He'd need to check that.

"You know how this sounds, right? This is how people act before they get institutionalized."

He held the bottle closer to the light. No discoloration or foreign objects inside.

Was he paranoid? People wanted him dead, and he was chasing a terrorist who just murdered hundreds of people. Was his concern rational or an extension of mental illness?

Nathan walked into the bathroom, and the automatic lights flipped on as he moved to the sink. He hovered the bottle over the porcelain. He leaned over it and poured out a thin stream of water.

"Whatcha doing?" Bridget asked.

"Checking."

He inspected the trickle for impurities. He sniffed, but not too deeply, just in case.

"You're a whack job," Bridget said. "Maybe I should call—"

Nathan looked up. "What's wrong?"

Bridget scrunched her nose. "Do you smell almonds?"

"Almonds? What are you—"

The water.

Nathan watched the liquid swirl around the drain. He set the bottle down and backed away.

"Out of the bathroom," Nathan said. "Now."

"You're freaking me out," Bridget said. She trailed him into the living area. "What's happening?"

"I think someone poisoned it."

"That's friggin crazy."

He picked up his phone, opened the AI browser, and typed a prompt.

Which poisons are odorless, tasteless, invisible, but can sometimes smell like almonds?

He read the response and stared at her.

"What's going on?" she asked.

"Someone poisoned your water with an odorless and colorless toxin that produced that almond smell when it interacted with drain cleaner. There must've been cleaning residue in the pipe."

"That's batshit nutso. What would do that?"

"Cyanide."

33

Bridget and Nathan waited in an interview room inside the Coordination Unit for Threat Analysis, the Belgian team that assessed terrorism threats. Peeters had picked them up at the hotel and dropped them there for their safety while he took the bottle of suspect water to the National Institute of Criminalistics and Criminology's laboratory for priority testing.

"If there's nothing in that bottle, we're gonna look like jerk-offs," Bridget said.

"Better a little embarrassment than an agonizing death."

"I shoulda joined Boston PD with my brothers."

"I'm glad you didn't."

She smiled, and he looked away.

"You still look like garbage," she said.

"Thanks."

"Do I gotta drag it out of you?"

He sighed. "I'm worried about screwing up Amelia. I'm gone all the time, and I know she worries about me."

"You're a good papa bear, and you're doing important work."

"Being there is a big part of parenting," Nathan said, "and I'm not home. I'm failing at the most basic function."

"Amelia knows you love her. You don't have to be there for her to feel your presence."

Nathan shifted uncomfortably. "How can she feel protected when I'm gone? I spend half of my time flying around the world."

"You talk to her every day. You call, email, and text, and you do more video calls than any father I know."

"How many fathers are overseas hunting terrorists? I've chased down criminals on every continent except Antarctica."

Bridget put her hand on his. "Our job is a calling. You told me you feel like that. It's important, and jobs like ours take a toll. They require us to be present too. And you parent from afar, whether you're sitting on the couch next to her or five thousand miles away."

"But am I even doing that right? I've never parented before, and God knows I've made mistakes in my life. Am I helping her reach her full potential? What if I'm holding her back?"

"Listen." Her voice softened. "That you think about these things means you're doing your best."

"What if that isn't good enough?"

"I never met your parents, but I'm sure they screwed things up. Mine sure did. But you're trying. You've learned from your experience, and you can help her avoid the same mistakes."

"I didn't turn out so great either," Nathan said. "I'm a middle-aged divorced guy, and my girlfriend's ghosting me."

She lowered her gaze. "You're halfway around the world hunting the biggest fugitive since Osama Bin Laden, and your stomach's in knots worrying about Amelia. That's good parenting, and for the record, I think you came out pretty good."

His cell phone rang, and he answered. "Burke."

"We got a hit," Peeters said.

Nathan inflated. He put the call on speaker. "Talk to us."

"They tested positive for a cyanide salt—bottles from both your rooms. They suspect potassium cyanide, but they require further analysis."

"No freaking way," Bridget said.

"I must ask," Peeters said. "How did you know?"

"The bottle didn't click."

"Unbelievable," he said. "I'm getting a call from my team. I'll call back if there's news."

Nathan hung up and shrugged at Bridget.

"You're abnormal," Bridget said. "You got some high-level paranoia going on."

She was right. OCD and germophobia were abnormal by definition, though they only classified as mental illness if they interfered with his life. In this case, they'd saved him.

"I'm hyperaware of germs and things out of order," Nathan said.

"Where does that come from?"

"Afghanistan."

He'd been paranoid overseas, and angry too, but when he was back home, he moderated the behavior. But his germophobia returned whenever he traveled.

"You've got a friggin superpower."

"It's like when I'm in a war zone and always monitoring the road for IEDs. The behavior's ingrained. I do it without conscious thought."

"You wore a hazmat suit in Philly."

"I've got it under control . . . mostly."

Bridget rolled her eyes. "Coulda fooled me. But whatever the hell it is, thanks for saving my life."

"Our lives."

Bridget opened the door and peered into the hall. "Yemeni isn't fucking around. I mean, the guy's good."

Tension tightened Nathan's chest, the way it did whenever facts didn't compute. Attempted murder, especially through poisoning, created cognitive dissonance. He paced to release his nervous energy.

"You okay?" Bridget asked.

"How would Yemeni know where to find us?"

"Fifty people watched us arrest Laurent. He knows we're tracking him."

"I mean, how did he know our hotel?" he said.

"We checked in under our real names."

"That would mean he has official support."

"A mole inside the police?" she asked.

"Maybe. And he's on the run. Why stop to take us out instead of getting out of Dodge?"

"He probably ordered one of his guys to do it. He came to Brussels to meet Laurent, so it makes sense he has other contacts here. Yemeni probably thought he'd kill us, but if it didn't work, he might injure us or tie us up looking for the attempted assassin."

"Maybe," Nathan said. "Or . . ."

"Or what?"

"Yemeni wasn't the one who tried to kill us."

"Then who?"

His cell phone rang again, and he answered.

"We got a hit on him," Peeters said.

"Yemeni?"

"Facial recognition confirmation. He boarded a flight yesterday afternoon, two hours after we arrested Laurent."

"Headed where?"

"Malta."

34

Nathan and Bridget waited outside Malta International Airport, where Yemeni had landed almost twenty-four hours before them. He'd departed Brussels for the Republic of Malta on a Turkish Airlines flight, according to security camera photographs in Brussels. Malta's Police Counterterrorism Unit was checking the records and surveillance footage to confirm Yemeni had disembarked.

"What's this prick doing in Malta?" Bridget asked.

"Malta's a hundred square miles and a half million people. If he's here, we'll find him."

"What do you mean, *if*?" Bridget asked.

"He could've continued on to Uganda."

"Then why not fly direct from Brussels?" Bridget asked.

"He's the world's most notorious criminal, and he knows we'll use every resource to find him. Maybe he's taking a circuitous route to throw us off. He must know we'll catch him, eventually."

"He knows and doesn't give a crap."

"Running thousands of hours of video through facial recognition software takes time. He's probably counting on that."

"But we'll still find his destination."

"Maybe he doesn't need too much of a lead to accomplish whatever he's planning."

"That fucker."

Inspector Ganni Farrugia from Malta's Police Counter Terrorism Unit exited through the terminal doors and slipped his cell phone into his pocket as he joined them. A shadow of gray stubble darkened his chin, and he wore a tailored linen suit and Gucci oxfords.

"Wacha got?" Bridget asked.

"*Ta*, it is confirmed," Farrugia said. "The man matching your fugitive's description arrived on flight TK1943 from Brussels under the name Osman Turkoglu."

"That's our guy," Bridget said.

"He disembarked, and our surveillance cameras recorded him exiting the airport terminal. He entered a blue Toyota Yaris. He joined another passenger in the backseat, and they headed north on Route 1."

"Then we should be able to track them," Bridget said. "Can you put out an all-points bulletin for the car?"

The inspector smiled, exhibiting none of the chauvinism or bristling cops often had when talking to a female FBI agent. Equality thrived in Malta. "*Mela.* I have already issued the notice, but the Toyota Yaris is a common vehicle in Malta."

Bridget scowled. "Can't they—"

"My men do not need advice on how to track a terrorist."

"We trust you," Nathan said. "Where did the car go?"

"The cities of Sliema or Valletta on the North Shore, but Route 1 continues to Marfa, where he could catch a ferry to Comino."

"Malta has multiple islands?"

"Eight, but five are tiny and uninhabited."

"Sounds like a clever place for a fugitive to hide," Bridget said.

The inspector waved his hand. "He would stand out, but I can have my people overfly them."

"He could travel to Africa by boat," Bridget said. "How long would that take him?"

"The African coast is 320 miles due south," Farrugia said.

"He'd have to take a small boat," Nathan said, "either something pre-staged by his people or a rental."

"Many have drowned making the trip between Malta and Africa," the inspector said.

"Assuming that's his plan, and he averages eight knots, that would be . . ." Nathan looked up and did the math. "Forty hours at sea."

Bridget's eyes brightened. "That gives us time to catch up."

Farrugia smirked. "The Mediterranean is a big place, and he could land anywhere on the northern coast of Africa. Tunisia is closest."

"He could also be headed north to Sicily, or east to Cyprus, or anywhere else," Nathan said. "He could have changed disguises and boarded a flight back to Europe."

Bridget's lightness disappeared. "You're a real ray of sunshine."

"There's no place for optimism when dealing with Islamists who don't value life. The Shia sect of Islam seeks the end of times, and both fundamentalist Shias and Sunnis praise martyrdom. Dealing with radicals who believe in sacrificing infidels for their theo-political supremacist ideology leaves every horrific endgame on the table."

"You're a *worst-case* kind of guy."

"If we prepare for the worst, we'll handle anything that comes our way."

Farrugia snorted. "I very much doubt your man came to Malta to throw you off the scent. He's here to do something, and I only hope it is not an attack."

"We're on the same team," Bridget said.

"Our rapid intervention unit is on standby and ready to take him into custody."

"That won't be as easy as you think," Bridget said. "This nut-bag is dangerous."

"So are my men," Farrugia said. "We'll have him, dead or alive. It makes no matter to me. We do not tolerate Islamic extremism in Malta."

"Sometimes that's not up to you," Nathan said.

"Malta has been ruled by Phoenicians, Carthaginians, Romans, and Byzantines, but we've only been conquered once by the Arabs in the Year of our Lord 870. The Normans threw them out in 1091, and we've been a Christian nation ever since."

"Maltese are Christian?" Bridget asked.

"We've resisted Islam aggression since the Knights Hospitaller repelled the Ottoman Empire during the Great Siege of Malta, and we remained Catholic through French and British occupations. We crushed invaders like your fugitive for hundreds of years before your country existed."

"We're in your house," Nathan said. "What's our play?"

"*Grazzi*," Farrugia said. "We go to Sliema and wait. Your boy will be there or in Valletta."

"Think he's at a marina?" Bridget asked.

"He has come to Malta for a purpose. I don't need to find him, just the men who retrieved him from the airport."

Muffled Maltese crackled from a radio inside Farrugia's jacket, and he unclipped a Motorola handheld from his belt. He spoke into it, then waved at someone down the driveway.

"We may have found the Yaris," Farrugia said. "Airport surveillance video captured a partial license plate, and then three of our twenty-seven traffic cameras filmed the car."

"Where?" Bridget asked.

"Headed toward Valletta, as I suspected. Three hours later, a camera spotted the vehicle continuing along Route 1. They did not stay in either Sliema or Valletta."

"Did the camera confirm our target inside the car?" Nathan asked.

"Unclear. It traveled past St. Julian's but didn't pass the checkpoint camera near Fort Madliena, which means they may have entered the interior. My men are searching the Tal-Ibraġ and Il-Mensija neighborhoods."

A SsangYong Musso driven by a man in plainclothes pulled from the curb beside them. The four-door vehicle sported an open bed, making it a hybrid pickup truck.

"Get in," Farrugia said. "We will hunt the buzzard down and trap him in our clapnet."

35

Leila needed help, but where should she turn? She could tell Massimi what happened, but after the way he reacted the last time, she'd only infuriate him. He didn't believe Lucas had tried to socially engineer their conversation in the cafeteria. Massimi had asked for proof of bribery, which she didn't have, and now, she had only her word Gharagöz had threatened her.

She could inform the police about her encounter in the dark hallway, but what could they do? She didn't know if Gharagöz was her tormentor's real name. And a police report would prove she'd reported the Iranian spy, or criminal, or terrorist, or whoever he represented. It didn't matter if the mullahs or the Phantoms had sent him. They'd all murder her without hesitation once she ceased being useful. That was the key. She must play along until she could figure a way out.

She needed to confide in someone.

The courtroom doors opened, and two female attorneys she'd seen around the courthouse exited. Khalil Monsour came out behind them and smiled when he saw her. The Lebanese interpreter had become her only friend in the unit, and based on their brief conversation over coffee, he harbored distaste for the Iranian government and outright hatred for Hezbollah. That Iranian proxy had ruined his country, and he hadn't been shy about expressing it.

"Good afternoon, Ms. Kabiri."

She attempted a smile, but her mouth didn't respond. Emotion welled up inside her.

"Is something wrong?"

"May we speak in private?"

He glanced around, then stared at her. This was a man who understood secrets. And danger. "Let's slip into the witness room." He led her through the courtroom's anteroom and into a tiny room with a square table and three plastic chairs.

She closed the door, and he waited for her to begin.

Should she trust him? She'd already decided to come clean, so why second-guess herself? Khalil was a Maronite Christian, which lessened the chance he was an Iranian operative, though his bluster about Iran could be a cover. Iranian agents were everywhere.

She summoned her courage. "People are pressuring me to disclose information about my work."

Khalil raised an eyebrow. "People?"

"I think the Iranian government sent them. Or they're affiliated with Imam Yemeni's terrorist group."

He scowled, and he looked at the door. "You reported this?"

"I told Mr. Massimi about the bribery attempt, but he didn't believe me. Or they've compromised him too. He insinuated I should do what's right for my family."

Khalil twirled the ends of his mustache. "This is bad."

"And another man intimidated me in my apartment building. He said they'd eliminate anyone who stood in their way, or words to that effect." Her words came faster with the relief of telling someone.

"This is very dangerous," Khalil said. "Extreme peril. I've seen this sort of thing before. If they are from Iran, and you oppose them, they will kill you."

"I know."

"And your family."

Icicles pierced her nerves, and terror spread through her. "This has happened to another interpreter?"

"In Beirut. Those who oppose the Iranians' puppets go missing."

"I should hide my family, move to a new apartment."

"It's not just them. You are from Tehran, right?"

"Yes."

"Any relatives you left behind can be imprisoned and tortured. They'll use them as leverage against you."

"There's no one. My husband . . . but they'd be doing me a favor."

Khalil flashed his kind smile. "I see."

"What should I do?"

His smile faded. "It is a difficult choice. You can report this to the judge or the police."

"How will they respond?"

"They'll remove you from the case immediately."

"Then these men will know I reported them."

"Yes."

"Maybe if I'm not involved with the case, they'll leave me alone. I can't help them if I don't have information."

He looked sad. "Once they have their hooks in you, they won't let go. If you report them, they'll murder you and everyone you love."

36

____

Farrugia's driver trolled Malta's narrow streets as they waited for someone to spot Yemeni or the Yaris. Bridget and Nathan sat in back. Farrugia perched in the front passenger seat, and his eyes darted back and forth, scanning like a robot. He gave the impression he saw everything. Eternal vigilance.

"The structures here look ancient," Bridget said.

"They are," Nathan said.

"That guy outside Starbucks is playing on his iPhone," Bridget said.

"Ah, yes," Farrugia said. "You see the contradictions in our society, the complexity of Malta. We have prehistoric ruins that date to 6000 BC and the comforts of the modern world."

Static hissed out of the radio, then a transmission in Maltese.

"*Ajma*," Farrugia said.

"That didn't sound like good news," Nathan said.

"They've not found it, but a Malta Post courier said he spotted a blue Yaris near St. Helen's Basilica. They're driving by the residences, but most have walls and gated awtostrada."

"What?"

"Car parks. We will join them." He uttered something in Maltese, and the driver turned at the next intersection.

Nathan's cell phone rang, and Amelia's number showed on the screen. Alarm jolted Nathan. He answered. "What's wrong?"

"I had a bad dream," Amelia said.

"The cemetery again?"

"Yeah."

Her voice sounded so tiny it made his heart ache. They'd almost been murdered in the congressional cemetery two years before, and their near-death experience had left deep emotional scars. Amelia seemed fine most of the time, but occasionally, she'd awaken screaming. Sometimes Nathan would check on her and find her crying in her sleep. That was worse.

"Is your mom there?"

"Bet."

"Why don't you sleep with her and—"

"Vince is back from the Dominican Republic. I don't feel comfortable going in there."

Nathan's stomach twisted. He turned to steel and lowered his voice. "There's nothing . . . I mean, has he acted inappropriately—"

"Da-ad, gross. Nothing like that. I just don't wanna go in when he's home. Who knows what they're doing?"

Her personality infected her voice. Nathan's misunderstanding had made her think about her mother with Vince, and that had snapped her out of her mood. Sometimes, parenting worked like that. Mistakes had unintended outcomes, and they weren't always bad.

"Want to tell me about the dream?"

She sniffled, and Nathan's heart cracked again. "I'm fine. I just wanted to hear your voice."

"It's late. Go back to sleep."

"Okay."

"Call me anytime."

The line was quiet.

"Amelia?"

"Yeah, I'm here."

"What is it?"

"I'm good now. Thanks, Dad."

She hung up.

"Everything good on the home front?" Bridget asked.

"Just great." His daughter stayed with his ex-wife and her prick of a husband, while Nathan tried to act like a parent from halfway around the world. And he was *acting*. A real parent would be home holding her hand and telling her everything would be okay.

"Hope so." Bridget didn't look convinced.

"How much farther?" Nathan asked.

"The neighborhood where they spotted the vehicle is close," Farrugia said.

The sun beat off the pavement as they rolled up a long hill past two- and three-story residences built from white stone. Most had lofty walls with iron gates and balconies that faced the sea. Even the homes in disrepair looked like medieval castles that must be five hundred years old. Above Valletta's skyline, the Mediterranean shimmered in the distance.

"It reminds me of Aruba," Nathan said.

"When were you in Aruba?" Bridget asked.

"On my honeymoon with Reagan. Damn, that feels like another lifetime."

"Were you chasing a terrorist then? Knowing you, it wouldn't surprise me."

"I mean the terrain and climate. It's arid, sandy, scorching hot."

The population density decreased as they followed an elevated road into the island's interior. The sun glared off blue water in every direction. Sprawling residences constructed of ancient stone, and the occasional turret, nestled among the hills. Northern California in the Middle Ages.

"These houses are frigging old," Bridget said.

"The climate is kind to our structures," Farrugia said.

"It's a scorcha," Bridget said. "Let's do our next case in Antarctica. What if we—"

"Up there." Farrugia pointed at police cars parked outside a palatial complex atop the next hill.

A ten-foot stone wall surrounded the residence, rising and falling with the contours of the rolling terrain. The four-story main building was bracketed by two-story wings. The entire structure had been constructed from sand-colored stone blocks, weathered brown over hundreds of years by the Mediterranean wind.

"This is not good," Farrugia said. "Not good at all."

"I gave up hoping for good news a long time ago," Nathan said. "What's the problem?"

"That estate belongs to Noah Grech, a seventy-year-old billionaire who owns at least a dozen properties on our two major islands. He's a venture capitalist and financier, and he wields considerable influence."

Malta's sixty-five-member Parliament appointed a ceremonial president and a prime minister who ran the cabinet and government. Corruption plagued the administration from financial scandals to suppression of the press. If Noah Grech controlled a billion dollars and could throw around money, his influence could have no bounds.

More concerning was the connection to Yemeni.

"The Yaris came here?" Bridget asked.

"Our officers checked the drives of every house on the hill. It's parked inside the gate."

"Wonderful," Nathan said. "What's Yemeni doing in a Maltese billionaire's car?"

Farrugia snorted. "That's an answer I don't relish discovering."

Malta hosted many foreign nationals, but it remained a relatively insular community, and Farrugia would probably lose his job if he stepped on the wrong toes. He could lose much more.

"Make me the bad guy," Nathan said. "You're accommodating an official request from the United States, and you don't have to take the heat."

The bones on Farrugia's face seem to collapse as his skin folded. "A nice thought, but I doubt Mr. Grech will see it that way."

"That mansion could be packed with terrorists," Nathan said. "How do you want to handle it?"

"Crash through his gate," Bridget said.

Farrugia parked behind a patrol car. "Your fugitive has been here for twenty-four hours. I'm not sending a tactical team."

Nathan tensed. "Yemeni murdered hundreds, and he facilitated the opioid attacks two years ago. He's *dangerous*."

Farrugia sighed. "You may be correct, my American friend, but in this, even the police don't have the authority."

"Then what's our plan?"

"We knock on the door."

37

Farrugia spoke on the security phone attached to Noah Grech's front gate. Six counterterrorism officers stood behind him, a modest show of force, but Farrugia had capitulated to Nathan's request—and to common sense—and had called out eighteen members of the Rapid Intervention Unit. Half of the tactical team formed a perimeter around the fortress, and the others waited on the road in case Farrugia needed a quick response force.

Farrugia hung up and turned to Nathan and Bridget. He looked like a man who'd just been sentence to death row. "He is home, and he has agreed to receive us."

"Think Yemeni's hiding inside?" Bridget asked.

"Only God knows that," Farrugia said. "And Mr. Grech."

Two men in black linen suits and sunglasses—both the size of silverback gorillas—marched down the interior drive. One of them tugged a lever, and the gate opened with an electric hum.

"We walking into a trap, partner?" Bridget asked.

"We're on an island," Nathan said. "This guy's a billionaire with influence. He's not gonna lure a bunch of Maltese cops into his house to kill them."

"If we catch this *fuckah* with Yemeni, he's going away, no matter how many zeros he has in his bank account. That's enough motive to whack us and flee."

She wasn't wrong. If Grech was in league with Yemeni, could he have been careless enough to bring him back to his residence? Rich and powerful people rarely understood their own vulnerability. Sex scandals proved that. Every cop on earth searched for Yemeni, so Grech may have considered his home a fortress and the logical place to hide him. That would be an epic miscalculation—if they arrested Yemeni.

"Mr. Grech will receive you in the main house," the first gorilla said. He acted like they'd come for afternoon tea. Was an unannounced visit by armed police a regular occurrence? Grech was a cool customer.

"Very well," Farrugia said. He seemed resigned to play this out and accept his fate.

Farrugia, Bridget, Nathan, and six officers followed the guards up the hard-packed earth driveway, and shells crunched beneath their boots. They walked up a sandstone path to a thirty-foot-wide arched entryway. Nude sculptures bracketed thick mahogany doors with iron bracing and Baroque carvings.

The doors opened, and they entered a foyer with polished tile and nine Romanesque arches in the towering ceiling. Circular iron chandeliers with electric candles dangled from chains high above, and lantern fixtures illuminated the walls. It wasn't the warmest of rooms—more *Game of Thrones* than *Snow White*.

"You will wait here," the guard said. A statement, not a request.

Gorilla number two stood nearby and watched them. The earth's gravitational pull seemed stronger inside the lair. Castles did that. Had peasants felt the same six hundred years ago when they entered the foreboding structure? The distinction between guest and prisoner blurred.

"This place is friggin huge," Bridget whispered.

"With a thousand places to hide," Nathan said.

"I feel like we're in a *Scooby Doo* episode."

"Rut-roh, Shaggy."

The sharp clicking of heels echoed toward them, and a diminutive man with gray hair wearing a black tunic and gray pants approached. The butler, assistant, or whatever the hell he was, moved with brisk movements without wasted motion.

"Good day," he said. "I am Gorg Spiteri, Mr. Grech's assistant. He awaits in the garden."

Farrugia sighed and looked sheepishly at Nathan. They followed Spiteri. The group paraded down a long corridor between brick walls decorated with iron lanterns and oil paintings. Nathan eyed doorways as they passed.

Grech was too smart to try anything. Probably.

They rounded another corner and stepped onto an expansive patio with porticoes and iron furniture. The fifty-by-fifty courtyard featured palm trees, exotic flowers, and a massive fountain that spit water in a high arc. The group stopped, and everyone waited, stiff and awkward.

Grech sat at a long teak table before a steaming cup of tea. He didn't rise. "Inspector Farrugia, what an unexpected pleasure."

Farrugia's eyes widened, possibly surprised that Grech knew his name. He recovered and approached the billionaire with bent shoulders and head bowed, like a student called to the principal's office.

"Good afternoon, Mr. Grech," Farrugia said. "Thank you for seeing us. I'm, er, our unit is hunting a fugitive. He, uh, Omar Yemeni arrived in Luqa last night, and we believe he is somewhere on the island."

"I appreciate your hard work keeping Malta safe," Grech said. "That's why I donate so much money to the police, but I don't see how I can be of any assistance."

Farrugia cleared his throat. "We have video showing Yemeni entering a vehicle at the airport."

Grech raised an eyebrow. "I'm a busy man, Inspector."

"We tracked the vehicle through traffic cameras into Valletta. We're not sure what happened there, but, uh . . ."

Farrugia wouldn't look Grech in the eye. For an experienced investigator, he seemed cowed. His humiliation embarrassed Nathan and probably the other officers, who kept their distance from the confrontation.

"Please get to the point."

Farrugia cleared his throat again. "The vehicle is here."

"Which vehicle?" Grech asked.

"The one Yemeni entered at the airport." Farrugia seemed relieved to finally spit it out.

"Absurd."

"We have the description and partial license plate."

"Partial? Then you can't be sure you have the correct car."

"We're quite certain," Farrugia said. "We tracked it here."

"And you believe this man . . . what was his name?"

"Yemeni."

"You believe he drove here?" Grech flashed an incredulous smile.

"We, uh . . ."

"For fuck's sake," Bridget said. "That Islamist monster murdered two hundred Americans, and we chased him here. Yemeni got into one of your cars, and that car is parked in your driveway."

Grech's face clouded like a front billowing over the sea. "I'm hearing an accusation. Is that what you're doing, Miss . . . ?"

"Special Agent Bridget Quinn, FBI."

Nathan approached to draw Grech's attention. "We're not alleging you did anything. Agent Quinn just stated the facts. Your car picked up a killer, and now it's here."

"I know nothing of this matter. What is it you want?"

"Who drove your car today?"

"I own twenty vehicles."

"The Yaris sitting in your driveway," Bridget said.

Nathan cringed but kept his displeasure off his face. When interrogating suspects and witnesses, they needed to show a united front. A perpetrator could manipulate any display of dissension. At a minimum, it would make them seem to appear vulnerable.

"Assuming that person entered my vehicle, a multitude of innocent reasons could explain why one of my employees was with him."

"A second person sat in back with him," Bridget said. "The positioning seems more like a boss than an employee."

Grech's eyes flared like lasers. "What are you implying?"

"Harboring an international fugitive is a crime—both here and in the United States."

He glowered. No one spoke. The silence weighed them down.

Grech pinched his lips. "I am familiar with your American laws. I do business there, and in Europe and Asia. Wouldn't my employee have to know the person in his company was a fugitive for this to be criminal?"

"That's true," Nathan said.

"And my employee must assist this fugitive's escape to be charged, correct?"

Nathan moved closer. "Not necessarily. Any support could be considered aiding and abetting. And two people met him at the airport and drove him into Valletta. That constitutes assistance, and—"

"Assuming they knew he was wanted, yes?"

"That's up to a jury," Nathan said. "But I believe the video is prima facie evidence. And after traveling to Valletta, the car arrived here."

"We don't know if Yemeni was in the car," the inspector said.

Nathan winced. Farrugia didn't need to act as Grech's attorney. Farrugia had to play a delicate game or risk losing his career, but why give Grech ammo? Staying quiet would serve the same purpose.

"Your fugitive is not in my home," Grech said.

"We gotta confirm that," Bridget said.

There it was—the moment of truth. The whole reason they'd come.

"I'm confirming it," Grech said. "You came for an answer, and I've given it to you." All pretense of civility had dissipated.

"We'd like to search your residence," Nathan said.

"Absolutely not," Grech said. "I won't allow civil servants to invade my privacy."

"I'm not saying you're involved, but it's possible a household employee brought him inside without your knowledge. We must check this off our list."

"I won't have you pawing through my belongings."

Nathan plastered on his most sympathetic face and smiled. "I understand your reluctance. We won't damage anything, but have to say we searched."

"Then go back and tell your masters you did," Grech said.

Nathan tightened his core to restrain his visceral reaction to Grech belittling him. "We have video evidence."

"Meaningless."

"Perhaps, but unless we do a cursory search, the air of suspicion will hang over this residence, and by extension, over you."

Grech frowned. "You know nothing of Malta."

"I know I need to report to the FBI that we checked, or you'll remain under suspicion. You want this to be over, *correct*?" Nathan used the same word to stick it in like a knife. It wasn't smart, but he couldn't contain himself. He wasn't gonna let some billionaire prick push him around.

Grech turned to Farrugia. "Inspector, you may search my residence for your fugitive if it will end my time with this distasteful man, but know this —I'm displeased."

Farrugia shriveled like a deflated balloon. "Thank you for your cooperation, Mr. Grech. My men will make quick work of it."

Farrugia didn't make eye contact with Nathan. He looked at his men. "Check the residence."

Nathan and Bridget trailed them inside, where Farrugia assigned his men to sections of the house.

"Hey," Bridget whispered. "If this fucker's consenting, Yemeni's long gone."

"The odds are you're right," Nathan said. "But suspects frequently agree to searches when they're holding."

"That's because the average schlep doesn't know the law, but Grech probably knows it better than we do. He certainly understands his rights in Malta. He probably helped craft the laws."

She was right.

"People waive their rights because they think not doing so will make them look guilty. Grech wants to put this behind him."

"Waste of fucking time," she said.

"There's only one way to find out."

38

Farrugia's men formed in the central corridor with six additional officers Farrugia had called inside. Farrugia's deputy broke them into teams of four and each took a different wing of the structure.

"Bridget and I will accompany them," Nathan said. "Shout if you find anything."

"Look, but don't touch," Farrugia said.

"Which team?" Bridget asked.

Nathan jerked his chin toward the team that filed down stone steps. "Into the basement. Rats scurry into hiding when threatened."

The temperature dropped as they clomped down spiraling, narrow steps. The four officers fanned out in a long, narrow room that was dimly lit and ten degrees cooler than upstairs. Thick wooden doors, stained dark, lined both sides. Had they been prisoner cells hundreds of years before?

Did a team of Phantoms hide in the shadows?

Officers spread out to opposing sides. They flung open doors opposite each other, which wasn't tactically sound, but Nathan shouldn't interject. An officer illuminated a tiny stone room filled with old furniture. Across from them, a vacant room.

"Dry hole," Bridget said.

"Stay alert."

The officers moved to the next doors. They opened them simultaneously. Both empty. They proceeded to the following rooms.

A chill ran up Nathan's spine, as if a ghost had brushed past. What had happened down there over the centuries?

Bridget and Nathan followed them to the end. All empty. The first officer shrugged as he led them all back upstairs.

Gorg—Grech's butler, or assistant, or whatever title the minion held—waited for them in the foyer. "Satisfied?"

"The cellar's clear," Nathan said.

Farrugia hurried over with a crinkled brow. "Our search has turned up nothing."

Nathan turned to Gorg. "Take me to Mr. Grech's home office."

Farrugia looked up in alarm. "Your fugitive won't be hiding there."

Nathan's stomach hardened. Farrugia strode the line between unhelpful and obstruction. "Yemeni came here for a purpose."

Farrugia's face tightened, evoking a flicker of empathy in Nathan. The inspector was having a bad day, which would worsen if they found anything. His career depended on Grech's reaction.

"Then I'll inspect the office myself," Farrugia said.

That was an awful idea. How hard would Farrugia search? Would he snoop or take a compulsory glance around and declare the search fruitless? Politics imposed themselves on investigations in Malta the same as they did in Washington and everywhere morally weak men sought career advancement over justice.

"I understand," Nathan said. "Let's go."

"I don't know if—"

"We can put this to rest right here," Nathan said. "But we need a thorough examination."

"You're used to getting your way, aren't you, Agent Burke?" Farrugia said.

"You know Grech is hiding something."

Farrugia swallowed hard. "Touch nothing."

Nathan pointed at Gorg. "The office."

Gorg's eyes flashed to the inspector, and he nodded. Gorg turned with an athleticism belied by his stocky frame and bounded up the iron staircase to the second floor.

Nathan turned to Bridget. "Keep your eyes on Grech. I wanna know what he's doing."

"This turned into a nothing burger," Bridget mumbled over her shoulder as she headed for the patio.

Gorg led the way, followed by Farrugia and two officers with Nathan bringing up the rear. Upstairs, Renaissance oil paintings covered the corridor's walls. The artists' squiggly signatures didn't ring any bells, but the artwork looked priceless. They passed a series of doors, and Nathan paused at one and nudged it open with his elbow, revealing a spacious bedroom with a king-sized bed, Louis XIV furniture, and a plasma TV. Tacky, but probably worth a fortune.

Gorg opened the office door at the far end. Farrugia's men had already searched the floor, so why were the doors shut? Had they executed a perfunctory scan, or worse, had they failed to search at all?

Nathan followed the group into an expansive room with a mahogany desk with a green-leather writing surface, positioned across from floor-to-ceiling bookshelves. Farrugia's men spread out. Two officers moved to a closed door. The first officer flung it open, revealing a full bathroom with black-and-white checkered tile.

They flooded inside, but Nathan didn't follow. Shower rings rattled. Cabinets slammed.

Farrugia emerged, looking relieved. The man wanted to flee Grech's house. "That's it. He's not here. Time to go."

Gorg smiled. He stepped aside as they filed into the corridor. Gorg secured the door, then led them toward the stairs.

Nathan hung back. When they were halfway to the stairs, he hurried back to the office. He opened the door with an audible click. Too loud. No time to worry about that. He slipped inside.

Nathan rushed to the desk. Piles of neatly stacked papers covered the surface, except three forms laid out in front of the chair.

Footsteps pounded outside.

Nathan reached for the paper.

"That's private correspondence," Gorg said. He glared at Nathan from the doorway.

"You must have the eyesight of a falcon."

Gorg's face tightened.

Nathan snatched the papers off the desk. Gorg bolted across the floor like a free safety.

Nathan read the document—a receipt for a private boat. Eighty thousand euros for passage from Malta to Alexandria, Egypt. Dated today. The paper had been signed by someone other than Grech, but he must have paid.

A shadow crossed the paper. Gorg snatched it out of his hands. "This is private."

"Who did Mr. Grech send to Egypt this morning?"

"These papers are none of your concern."

"The inspector can be the judge of that," Nathan said.

Gorg's eyes flickered to the entrance, then he leveled his stare on Nathan. A cloud darkened in his face, as if he'd been possessed.

He reached into his tunic.

Nathan lunged forward, his body moving before he consciously understood the meaning of Gorg's action. A lifetime of life-and-death work had honed his instincts.

Gorg clutched a revolver and tried to free it from his clothing.

Nathan snatched his wrist and leaned into him. Gorg stumbled backward as he freed the gun. Nathan grasped the gun's warm steel and shoved the barrel upward.

The gun exploded.

Burning embers stung Nathan's cheek as the bullet whizzed past his face and ricocheted off the stone ceiling.

Nathan drove Gorg's arm into the air. Gorg struggled to get off another shot.

God, he's strong.

Nathan had one chance. He released the gun. Gorg aimed as Nathan swiveled his hips and cocked his arm. The gun's deadly black eye pointed at Nathan's face.

Nathan uncoiled like a spring and snapped a right jab into Gorg's face. His knuckles connected with Gorg's nose. Blood splattered the air with a sickening crack.

Gorg's head snapped back, and the gun clattered onto the floor. Nathan drove the man backward. He hooked his leg around Gorg's heel and tripped him. Gorg fell, and Nathan dove on top of him.

They crashed to the floor, and Gorg's head smacked against the cold stone. His body went rigid, he held his free arm out like a Nazi salute—a sure sign of a brain injury.

Nathan raised his elbow, ready to strike again. He stopped. Gorg didn't move.

Farrugia's men burst into the room with their guns out.

Farrugia's face widened with fear. "What have you done?"

39
_____

Eyes followed Leila, every face sinister, every shadow a monster. She walked through the courthouse with her shoulders hunched and her eyes down, afraid to look into the face of evil that must be stalking her. Every day the presence of her watchers weighed more.

Eventually, she'd snap.

Someone blocked her path, and a tremor of fear passed through her. She raised her eyes, and Khalil looked down at her. Relief washed over her.

"You look terrible," Khalil said.

"Not here."

He glanced around. "Follow me."

They moved to the elevator, then exited on the fourth floor. Khalil took her down a corridor, and they stopped on a bench.

"I feel like they're always watching," she said.

"Have they threatened you again?"

She shook her head and bit back tears.

"Just act naturally. No one knows what you're saying to me."

"I need help. Should I give them what they want?"

Khalil twirled his mustache. "This is a serious case with real consequences."

"I don't want to be involved."

"In this, you have no choice," he said.

"I'm asking for advice."

He scratched his chin. "These people are bad."

Frustration surged inside her, a mixture of anger and desperation. "Don't you think I know that? They threatened my family. I'm going to quit and walk away from the court."

He frowned. "That's not the answer."

Doubt crept into her. Was he trying to convince her to help those animals? Was he one of them? Her skepticism metastasized into an icy fear.

"Then, what?" Her voice shook. He'd been her only ally, and if he was corrupt, no one was safe.

"Interpreters have disappeared before. They told us they went on to other jobs, but I don't believe it. If you quit, then what? Someone else gets assigned, and they do the same thing to that interpreter."

She'd be putting other people in jeopardy, but her priority was to protect her family. How much moral responsibility did she shoulder for what these men would do with somebody else? She was just protecting herself.

"My family comes first. If I report this, they'll kill me, but if I quit and move to another city, I won't have the inside information they seek."

"Leila, that is your problem." He hadn't used her first name before, and his eyes softened. "Once you're no longer of use to them, your life has no value."

"If I'm unemployed, I can't assist them."

"But their efforts will continue, and you can connect them to this case."

"I wouldn't report them and endanger my child."

"Look into your heart. Do you think these people trust you won't inform the FBI? They'll eliminate you to protect themselves."

The truth of what he'd said settled into her bones. It sank into her like a dead weight. She couldn't breathe. The world darkened.

"What is it?"

"You're right, but even if I betray my oath and give them everything, when the case ends, what's stopping them from killing me anyhow."

"To cover their tracks?"

She nodded, unable to speak.

Another chin scratch. "Reporting this may be your only escape. Perhaps I can help."

"How?"

"I've interpreted in trials where police used parallel means to gather evidence and conceal sources' involvement. What if you pretend to cooperate, while I help the police catch them?"

"You'd do that for me?"

"I'd want my daughters to receive the same kindness."

"But this is more than kindness. It's perilous."

A grim smile spread across his face. "Sometimes, it's harder to live with not doing a hazardous thing than doing it. I must be able to sleep when I return to my wife."

Leila choked back a sob, but she couldn't stop her tears.

40

Nathan and Bridget stood inside the Alexandrian office of the Egyptian National Security Agency—Egypt's Homeland Security—and waited for answers.

After Farrugia had arrested Gorg, his officers had rushed to the dock where the *Zainab*, the ship they believed carried Yemeni, had been, but they missed it by twelve hours. Under Farrugia's wrath, a young dockworker had given up the ship's destination—Alexandria, Egypt.

Nathan and Bridget had flown to Alexandria hoping to catch Yemeni at the dock. Nick Dabrowski, the US Regional Security Officer, and Mark Simmons, the FBI's LEGAT, had driven up from the US Embassy in Cairo and picked them up at Borg El Arab International Airport and driven them there. Both men sat before a thick wooden desk with ornate carvings. Egyptian Brigadier General Mustafa Hassan shouted Arabic into a clunky communications box with encryption buttons.

"It sounds like they caught somebody," Simmons said.

"Yemeni?" Nathan asked.

"Not sure."

Nathan lowered his voice. "Does his general have the juice we need?"

"He's the top guy from the National Security Sector in Alexandria,"

Simmons said. "They're under the Ministry of the Interior, and they handle counterterrorism."

Bridget leaned close to Nathan. "What'll happen to Grech?"

"Gorg will probably remain in custody. Grech may sacrifice him as a fall guy."

"Will they arrest Grech?"

"Money buys influence and protection," Nathan said. "People in power have skeletons buried in their closets, and that makes them reluctant to turn on each other. The Maltese need overwhelming evidence to arrest the richest man on the island. Grech isn't an idiot. I'm certain he's insulated himself with cutouts and laundering."

"Would've been easier for Yemeni if he'd flown straight to Egypt," Bridget said.

"He must've needed things from Laurent and Grech."

Simmons turned to Nathan. "Did you catch that?"

"I don't speak Arabic," Nathan said.

Simmons flashed a derisive smirk that said, *I'm better than you.* "The general's men interdicted the boat as it prepared to return to Malta."

Nathan's pulse accelerated. "Yemeni?"

"No dice. They missed him."

"Take me to the ship," Nathan said.

"Hold on a sec," Dabrowski said. "We're guests here, and we don't have any jurisdiction. You're sitting in as a favor, so don't cause problems."

Bureaucrats always worried about causing problems.

Brigadier General Hassan hung up and inflated his chest. "We have caught the vessel, but your fugitive left four hours ago."

"You're certain?" Nathan asked.

Dabrowski shot him a dirty look.

"The boat's pilot cooperated. He will spend years in my prison for bringing a terrorist to our shore, and my men can be persuasive."

Nathan cringed. Egyptian police weren't known for subtle interrogation techniques.

Simmons cleared his throat and leaned forward, inserting himself into the conversation. "Did the prisoner say where Yemeni's headed?"

"Your fugitive had a white Toyota Land Cruiser waiting for him. We will set up a roadblock."

"He won't let you take him that way," Nathan said.

"He can't go far," Hassan said.

Nathan blew out a long stream of air. "You don't know Yemeni. He planned his escape contingencies long ago."

Hassan returned to the phone and barked orders. They had to do their due diligence, but Yemeni must've prepared for this. He could be in a car with a hidden compartment, or in disguise with fake identification, or traveling a different route. Maybe he'd remain in Alexandria until things cooled down, then continue. Or was Alexandria his final destination?

Nathan paced, and his thoughts drifted to Amelia. She had a softball game sometime this week. Was it today? What day was it? Travel across time zones jumbled up his sense of time and place.

Waves of guilt tickled the shores of his conscience. Was he a good father? Other parents drove their children to sporting events and attended PTA meetings, but Nathan traveled the world hunting sociopathic leaders of transnational criminal organizations. He led a life unrecognizable to his neighbors—a different existence.

He snorted. He shouldn't complain. The money wasn't awful, and he'd had experiences unattainable in civilian life. And he'd chosen this profession. Law enforcement was a higher calling, and he'd accepted his duty to be a sheepdog the moment he clipped on his badge. But the greater good he sought wouldn't make Amelia less lonely when she looked into the bleachers and didn't see her father.

Hassan hung up, and the phone rang. He answered and exchanged a hurried conversation in Arabic. His tone rose as he spoke.

"What is it?" Nathan asked Simmons.

The general ended the call and inflated with importance. He raised a finger toward the ceiling like a schoolmaster about to deliver a lecture. "Your fugitive is headed south."

"Where?" Nathan asked.

"Uganda."

41

Fluorescent lights reflected off inky tile inside Entebbe International Airport as Bridget and Nathan dragged their roller bags through a scrum of disembarking passengers. There'd been no direct flight from Alexandria to Uganda, forcing them to drive to Cairo International Airport and catch an Egypt Air flight to Uganda. The constant travel wore him down, and he shuffled forward. Only the urgency to catch Yemeni before he killed again kept Nathan's body in motion.

If Yemeni eluded them, they may never find him.

Conversations in English, Luganda, and Swahili floated through the terminal. Passengers dressed in colorful materials rooted in traditional fashions and carried suitcases wrapped in plastic.

A frail woman with blond hair tied in a bun held a sign with his name on it. Beside her stood a man with graying hair, cropped tight, and a three-piece suit. He was six-five and thick around the chest and arms—a mountain of a man. The FBI didn't have a permanent office in Uganda, but their legal attaché in Pretoria, South Africa, covered Uganda and fourteen other African countries. The LEGAT oversaw investigations and liaised with diplomatic personnel, and with such vast responsibilities, the LEGAT hadn't come in person. Instead, he'd sent Special Agent Emma Hart.

They approached the woman. "I'm Nathan Burke, and this is Bridget Quinn."

"Emma Hart, Pretoria Office. This is Assistant Superintendent of Police Dembe Odongo. He's our POC with the Uganda Police Force."

They shook hands.

"We're chasing a terrorist," Nathan said.

Odongo smiled. "That is why I am here. I work for Directorate of Counter Terrorism, and I'm a member of the Anti-Terrorism Police Unit and the Joint Anti-Terrorism Task Force. As a senior officer, I also have contacts within the Government Security Office and the Uganda People's Defense Forces."

"Omar Yemeni's leaving a bloody trail."

"Is he planning an attack in Kampala?" Odongo asked.

Nathan grimaced. The information from the ship's crew could be bullshit, but if Yemeni had come to Uganda, could they catch him in a country that wasn't exactly friendly to the United States?

"We don't know why he's here," Nathan said. "We're playing catch-up."

Odongo steeled his eyes. "You don't know the purpose of his entry?"

"Not yet," Nathan said. "But whatever brought him here, it can't be good for the Ugandan people."

Hart faced Odongo. "I briefed you on everything they sent us." She had an edge to her voice. Had her rushed flight to Entebbe irritated her, or the lack of Ugandan cooperation? Diplomatic relations had been strained for many years. Hart wasn't assigned there, so she wouldn't worry about keeping Odongo happy.

Odongo stared back with dead eyes, sensing her mood. "We activated our assets immediately. We are serious about terrorism."

"Did you find anything?" Nathan asked.

"We developed information that led us to a slum in Kibiri Busabala, in Kampala. We believe your man is there."

"Developed information from where?" Hart asked. Her tone hadn't warmed.

"A source."

"Human?"

"We should hurry," Odongo said. "Our task force officers have established surveillance on an apartment building, and they're preparing to make entry."

Alarm bells rang in Nathan's head. "Do you have confirmation he's inside?"

"A man matching his description entered last night. That is enough."

"We can have our Hostage Rescue Team here in forty-eight hours," Nathan said.

"In two days, I'll have your rebel swinging from a rope."

"But if we act without confirmation and miss him—"

"If you wish to be present when we arrest him, follow me." Odongo headed for the exit.

Hart rolled her eyes. "We'll follow in my rental car."

Bridget walked beside Nathan. "What would bring Yemeni to this shithole?"

"No extradition treaty for one thing," Nathan said. "Minimal cooperation with the West. A corrupt government that can be bribed to protect him. A deregulated country where he can do anything for a price."

"It's not a hotbed of Islamic terrorism."

"Uganda has a history. ISCAP has murdered civilians and assassinated officials here," Nathan said, referring to the Islamic State Central Africa Province, a wing of ISIS.

"Then why are we confident the Ugandan government will give him over to us?"

"Who said anything about being confident?"

"We shouldn't have told them anything," Bridget said. "We should've grabbed him, thrown him in a private plane, and flown him to New York."

"That's a step too far for the attorney general, and the ambo would've lost his shit. If they catch him, we'll request a judicial removal—and this time we'll handle the charter flight ourselves."

"My brothers were smart to join the Boston PD."

"Maybe Yemeni will make us kill him."

She cocked her head. "We're still cops, right?"

"Yeah, but we're fighting a war."

42

Agent Hart pulled off the road in the Kibiri Busabala locality in the Busabala Parish, Wakiso District. The capital city of Kampala lay to their north. She parked behind Odongo's Toyota Harrier SUV—a vehicle that would have been excellent for surveillance if it wasn't the most expensive car in the neighborhood. Bridget and Emma wore colorful Ugandan blouses over their clothes, and Nathan had added a white Ugandan shirt to blend in.

Nathan and Bridget exited with Hart, who continued talking to her office in Pretoria. The air reeked of charred rubber and toxic chemicals from burning trash. They met Odongo outside his vehicle, but he'd already briefed them, so there wasn't much to say.

Fitting that Yemeni had hidden out near Entebbe International Airport, the site of Operation Thunderbolt in 1976 when the Israelis had raided a hijacked plane. Half a century later, and the West still fought radical Islam. When would they learn?

"The apartment building is across from the bazaar," Odongo said. He didn't look in that direction, a credit to his professionalism and a relief to Nathan.

Hart covered the receiver of her phone with her palm. "Are your men in position?"

"My men watch the doors, and our tactical officers approach now." The muscles in his face tightened, and his laissez-faire attitude disappeared. A good sign.

Wind blew straw across the hard-packed earth and spread the acrid scent of feces through the Kibiri Trading Center Market. Poverty-stricken slums, rife with criminality, surrounded the open-air market.

Hart ended her call. "That was the LEGAT. He updated Washington, and they're briefing the AG. He wants to know how confident you are with your operational security."

"We will know soon," Odongo said.

Corruption infiltrated every aspect of Uganda's government, including police and intelligence units, and it threatened to undermine every operation, but the stakes were higher when trying to catch a high-value target. Rahimya Nawaz had notified the FBI's Hostage Rescue Team, in case things went sideways, but they'd take days to respond. Yemeni had slipped through the FBI's fingers too many times, and they must take him out.

Lives depended on it.

"It's a scorchah," Bridget whispered in a Boston accent so out of place it could've come from another planet.

Nathan glanced around to make sure no one had heard. He covered his face with a scarf as they weaved through the sparse crowd of shoppers picking through recycled garbage on dirty wooden tables. Flies buzzed around ears of roasted corn on a metal screen ten feet from a pile of garbage.

Bridget slipped around a stall made of plastic milk crates and sidled up beside him. Nathan stopped and stared across the dirt road at a three-story apartment building constructed with concrete slabs and a corrugated tin roof. Colorful clothing hung from long cords that stretched across balconies and decorated the building like a parade float. Drying clothes flapped in the breeze.

Two teenagers pushing a bicycle with no tires on the rims eyed him as they passed. The unspoken threat of violence permeated the city like the sizzling summer heat.

"He was last seen inside," Odongo said. "Our source said he only moves at night."

"What's this a-hole doing in a dump like this?" Bridget asked.

"There is a reason he stayed alive this long," Nathan said.

"Fucker is wicked smart."

"We'll see."

"My assault team has arrived," Odongo said.

Nathan followed his gaze to a group of men disembarking from dusty cars. Eight officers from the Anti-Terrorism Police Unit, all disguised in plainclothes, edged through the market toward their target. Odongo had another twelve of their elite strike team unit staged in vans on the eastern side of the market. They'd all come for one purpose—to catch the FBI's most-wanted fugitive.

Nathan's heartbeat quickened. In five minutes, they'd either have Yemeni in handcuffs or Nathan would be standing over his bullet-ridden body.

The choice was Yemeni's.

"Time to move," Odongo said. He withdrew a radio from his pocket and inserted an earpiece. He seemed unconcerned if anyone noticed.

The assault team approached the building.

Nathan faced Bridget but shifted his eyes to the complex. A teenage boy, only fifteen or sixteen, loitered outside the front entrance. He could be waiting for someone, or he could be a lookout. Yemeni had evaded his Interpol Red Notice and the best efforts of American intelligence and law enforcement for long enough to prove he was a cunning SOB. He'd have people watching the entrance. If he was inside. The FBI had thought they'd had him several times before his last arrest, and those moments of hope had punctuated the investigation only to come up empty time and time again.

Two muscular men crossed the street from the opposite direction. More operators. They positioned at the building's corners. Others would cover the rear. The plainclothes officers emerged from the market and formed a perimeter. They watched both the building and the surrounding people. These men had seen action.

Odongo touched his ear, then looked at Nathan. "Hurry now."

Vans braked hard outside the entrance, and twelve officers piled out. They wore black uniforms with berets and carried AK-47s. Their squad leaders carried Israeli-made Jericho 941 handguns. Professionals. They formed a column, and their commander led them forward.

They charged into the building.

Nathan and Bridget followed Hart and Odongo to the door. Shouts emanated from inside as anti-terrorism officers charged across the vestibule and pounded upstairs. Odongo paused for them to clear the lobby and the perimeter guards to post outside before he entered.

"We're not allowed to participate," Hart said.

"We're just monitoring." He exchanged a look with Bridget, and they entered.

"Hey," Hart said.

Nathan ignored her. Most of the lobby's lights had burned out, casting the lobby in darkness, and the odor of urine tinged the air. They followed Odongo up the staircase. The marble steps bowed in the middle where thousands of shoes had worn down the stone.

Yelling and the sound of cracking wood came from above as they approached the second floor. They moved down the hall and paused outside a shattered door where an officer stood guard.

"Wait here," Odongo ordered. He disappeared inside.

Men yelled in a back room. Bridget looked at Nathan and he shrugged. They waited.

The commander exited the apartment. *"Wazi, kutoka nje."*

"Did you find him?" Bridget asked.

The commander wagged his finger. "Not here."

Nathan deflated. "Dammit."

"How'd we miss that fuckah again?" Bridget said.

Nathan sighed. "Can we look?"

The commander said something in Swahili, and Odongo leaned into view inside the living room. Odongo responded, and the commander stepped aside.

Nathan and Bridget entered the apartment, a decrepit hovel. A film of dirt powdered the linoleum tile, and chipped green-and-blue paint covered the walls. A handcrafted table and couch both had ripped fabric and uneven legs. Nathan's belly hollowed. Had Yemeni stayed there, or had Odongo's intelligence been wrong?

A colorful teapot and mug rested on the table. Steam rose off the liquid. Whoever had been there hadn't been gone for long.

Wood scraped in the bedroom. Men shouted. Then scuffling.

"*Nenda Chini*," an officer shouted.

Nathan burst into the bedroom with Bridget behind him.

Anti-terrorism officers stood in a semicircle and pointed their guns at the open closet. Inside, someone peeked out from behind a pile of clothes. He raised his hands. An officer grabbed him by the arm and dragged him out.

Not Yemeni.

Nathan's hopes sank as the officers cuffed their suspect. He wore a business suit, out of place in the slum. He wasn't their fugitive, but he was involved. Somehow.

Nathan approached. The man glared back at him, his eyes simmering black coals.

"I'm searching for your boss," Nathan said, "and you're going to tell us where he's hiding."

43

Nathan paced on the dusty, hard-packed earth outside the Uganda Police Force building in Kibiri Busabala while Bridget lounged on a cement stoop reading something on her phone. Odongo had evicted the two regular police officers and a special police constable who manned the outpost, and those men wandered around in their mismatched uniforms.

In the rear of the building, behind a Formica counter, Odongo and his commander interrogated their prisoner in a tiny holding cell. Muffled shouting reached outside, but the prisoner hadn't given them anything—not even his name.

A door slammed inside, and Odongo exited the building, shaking his head and cursing under his breath. He stopped beside Nathan and bared his teeth.

"Went well?" Nathan asked.

Odongo snorted. "He tests my patience, but we will break him."

"How can you be sure? He's a jihadi, which means he craves death."

"We break everyone."

Bridget lumbered to her feet, probably sensing the futility of the interrogation, and joined them.

"Nothing?" she asked.

"Soon," Odongo said.

"He's tied to Yemeni," Nathan said. "Why aren't we at your head-quarters?"

Odongo's eyes narrowed. "The man you hunt was in that apartment last night. Every second he remains free lowers our chance to find him."

Bridget braced her hands on her hips. "You can interrogate this asshole anywhere. This seems pretty freaking unsecure."

"I am Ugandan," Odongo said. "My Basago Tribe has lived here since the dawn of time, so understand me when I say I love this land and my people. But I live in the real world, and I know our government has problems."

"Meaning?" Bridget asked.

"Yemeni murdered many innocents to escape. He eluded you in Europe, and you told me he has the support of the richest man in Malta."

"And?" Bridget said.

"Anyone with money has influence in Uganda," Odongo said. "If I bring Yemeni to our headquarters, someone will free him."

Corruption infected every country, but in Central Africa, its cultural legacy permeated society. It couldn't be excised without restructuring government and indoctrinating citizens with an understanding of individual liberty. That wouldn't happen soon. At least Odongo was a realist.

"So, you'll keep him here?" Nathan asked.

"Until we break him."

"And if he doesn't cooperate?"

Odongo flashed a cruel smile. "Give me two hours." He balled his fists and strode back into the building.

"We gonna let him torture that guy?" Bridget asked.

"Not up to us."

"He's our prisoner."

"No, he's not," Nathan said. "And the only thing linking him to Yemeni is Odongo's informant."

"And the papers they found inside?"

"Everything's written in Luganda, Swahili, or Arabic. We need translations."

The prisoner screamed inside, curdling Nathan's blood.

"I don't like this shit," Bridget said.

"Me neither, but it's not our show. We've got to understand our limitations. This is how business gets done in Central Africa."

The man's voice rose an octave higher, and the sound cut through Nathan like an ice-cold blade.

"But we're a part of it. We made this happen."

She was right. Odongo inflicted pain on the man inside because they'd chased their suspect there.

The Ugandan government wasn't known for temperance or human rights. Few countries in Africa, or in the world, resembled the United States' limits on police authority. He wasn't their prisoner, but they stood to gain from the torture Odongo inflicted. They may not be able to stop it, but they could try.

The prisoner loosed an inhuman wail that came from unearthly torment.

"Nathan?" Bridget asked. She raised her eyebrows.

"Okay, I'll ask him to stop."

Nathan climbed the steps toward the office. The sound of Nathan's footfalls snapped the officer standing guard out of his stupor, and he narrowed his eyes. He wore a blue camouflage uniform with his cap turned up at a radical angle. The way cops wore uniforms indicated their level of training and professionalism.

The officer stepped into the doorway and blocked Nathan, but he looked uncertain. Nathan had arrived with Odongo, and this officer didn't know Nathan's authority.

"Stand back," Nathan commanded. "I need to see Odongo."

The prisoner screamed again, then rattled off what sounded like Swahili.

Nathan bladed his body and slipped past the officer. The officer looked unhappy but did nothing. Nathan marched confidently around the front desk. Acting like he belonged granted him access to private spaces. People bowed to authority, because strong leadership could make hard lives easier. Or it could end them.

Nathan rapped on the interrogation room's door.

It cracked open and Odongo filled the space. Sweat streamed down his face. "Yes?"

"You can't torture him," Nathan said. "If you do, anything we obtain will get thrown out of an American court."

They didn't need more evidence, only to rearrest Yemeni and have him serve out his sentence. But if they could prove his role in the murdered passengers, he'd get the death penalty.

"We don't have such problems in Uganda," Odongo said. "But it doesn't matter."

"What's that mean?" Nathan asked.

"He told us where to find your fugitive."

Nathan's pulse thumped in his neck. "Where?"

Bridget entered his peripheral vision.

"He's headed for the Ekitebe kya Uganda ekya Bulimi, a wildlife preserve about a five-hour drive from here."

That stopped Nathan short. "Why would he hide there?"

"Our prisoner claimed he went to collect something."

"He could be lying."

Odongo sneered. "I assure you, he withheld nothing."

A wave of nausea unsettled in Nathan's stomach.

"And we found this." Odongo withdrew a folded map from his pocket. The displayed section detailed part of Lake Kwania in Northern Uganda.

"What's up there, besides wild animals?" Nathan asked.

"Tiny businesses and a few government facilities in villages built along the Nile," Odongo said.

"Terrorist targets?" Nathan asked.

Odongo rubbed his chin. "Not that I know of, but he's after something."

"Buried treasure?" Bridget asked.

"We can ask him when he's in handcuffs," Nathan said. "Let's set an ambush."

44

—————

Odongo reclined in the Toyota Land Cruiser's passenger seat while his driver steered with two fingers across the central plateau into northwest Uganda. They'd driven for hours and had reached a wild and mostly uninhabited area between the Murchison Falls National Park and Lake Kwania. They crossed the Victoria Nile and followed hard-packed roads over rolling hills as the undulating terrain rose higher.

Bridget squirmed in her seat.

"Problem?" Nathan asked.

"I'm a Boston girl," she said. "The jungle freaks me out."

"Cities are way more dangerous," Nathan said. "You're not gonna get attacked by a gang out here."

"Don't be so sure," Odongo said over his shoulder. "Gangs don't just infest our cities. The Aguu in Gulu is active in the northwest."

"Lovely," Bridget said.

Their tires crunched over the dirt road. They hadn't seen another vehicle in fifteen minutes. They passed a roadside shack selling bottles of Stoney Tangawizi, a popular carbonated soda that tasted like spicy ginger.

"How much business can that guy do out here?" Nathan asked.

"Many villages have grown around the lake," Odongo said. "The Nile has facilitated trade for hundreds of years, and we're approaching the preserve. He must sell to the facility's employees and visitors."

Nathan jolted. "What facility?"

"Our wildlife sanctuaries have staff to protect the animals from poachers and to facilitate safaris and guided tours. Some conduct research."

"Do they allow hunting?" Bridget asked.

"The safaris allow tourists to observe the animals. This preserve hosts many predators, so visitors must tour in caged vehicles."

Nathan leaned forward. "Fun vacation. Tell me about the research. Yemeni isn't coming for the animals."

"Agriculture."

"Meaning?"

"They're probably studying the effects of soil and plants on communities, or they're experimenting with improved food production methods. You can ask them yourself."

On their right, shea butter trees, date palms, and papyrus dotted the marsh surrounding Lake Kwania, and flashes of blue water peeked between them. They rounded a corner and passed a billboard with faded images of elephants and lions. It announced Murchison Falls National Park in Luganda, English, and Swahili.

"My team's preparing their surveillance equipment," Odongo said. "We'll set up a stationary post on the entrance and position the arrest team somewhere inside."

"We don't know when Yemeni's coming," Nathan said. "Your guys could be up here for a while, and if Yemeni gets a whiff of them, he'll disappear."

"That's why I wanted to see it first. We need to be prepared."

They turned into the driveway and stopped beside a gatehouse. A trench, ten feet deep and fifteen feet wide, paralleled the road, like a medieval moat. A towering wall constructed from concrete cylinder blocks led from the gatehouse down the driveway and into the preserve.

An overweight guard wearing a green camouflage uniform, field cap, and jungle boots sat inside the open door of the tiny guardhouse. A worn leather gun belt wrapped around his expansive waist, and the wooden pistol grip of an old revolver pressed against his love handle. He braced his hands against his knees and struggled to get off a stool. He appeared as bored as he was lazy.

"Does that wall enclose the preserve?" Nathan asked.

"That would be impossible." Odongo smiled, as if talking to a small child. "The preserve is hundreds of thousands of hectares."

"They use a trench?" Bridget asked.

"That is correct. Manual labor is cheaper than materials. The wall protects the facility."

The guard approached and rested his forearm on the open window. His horrible officer-safety technique made Nathan cringe, and a coal of irritation flared inside him.

Odongo displayed his identification. "Assistant Superintendent Dembe Odongo, Directorate of Counter Terrorism."

The guard stiffened. *"Okulwanyisa abatujju? Tuli mu kabi?"*

"I wouldn't be here if you weren't in danger," Odongo said, "and speak English. My friends don't understand Luganda. Have you seen anything suspicious?"

The guard shook his head. "No."

"How many people have entered the preserve today?"

The guard hooked his thumbs in his belt, and his eyes flittered to the road. "We have a bus with schoolgirls and our normal employees. No one else."

"How many students?"

"I did not count. Maybe fifteen."

"Employees?

"Twenty-six. The same every day."

"How many security officers are on duty today?"

The guard counted on his fingers. "One at the eastern gate, two in the lab, two rovers on the perimeter, and four rangers in the preserve. Plus Mr. Mugisha, our security chief."

"We need to speak with him. Have Mugisha meet us at the facility."

Odongo rolled up his window. The guard stepped back, unclipped a walkie-talkie from his belt, and spoke into it. The driver drove down a long dirt driveway between tall trees and the towering wall.

The road serpentined around thick trees and boulders and seemed to go on forever. The perimeter wall angled away and disappeared into the trees. Minutes later, they emerged from the jungle and entered a parking lot. A massive gate, right out of *Jurassic Park*, barred entrance to the preserve. The proximity to predators enhanced the air of danger. They passed a dozen vehicles and two coach-style buses painted green and white with "Lira Primary" stenciled on their sides.

Bridget pointed to a white-stone structure. "What's that?"

"That is the Ekitebe kya Uganda ekya Bulimi."

"I don't speak Luganda," she said.

Odongo smiled and spread his palms wide. "The Uganda Institute for Agriculture."

They parked and exited. Behind the agricultural center, the waters of Lake Kwania sparkled in the sun. The long trip had tightened Nathan's lumbar. He stretched and his back cracked. His shoulder ached too. Getting old sucked.

Odongo pointed at the gate. "This is one of twelve wildlife preserves, fifteen sanctuaries, and ten national parks run by the Uganda Wildlife Authority."

"I want a picture with a giraffe," Bridget said.

"Do not wander into the sanctuary," Odongo said. "And don't go near the water."

"I'm afraid to ask," Bridget said.

"The lake is inhabited by hippopotamuses, Cape Buffalo, Nile crocodiles, and venomous snakes. African rock pythons are the largest on the continent."

"Pythons prey on humans?" Bridget asked.

"They eat everything from crocodiles to antelope. If you see one, head the other way. And go as fast as you can." He scratched his chin. "But don't run from lions or leopards. If you act like prey, you trigger their instincts to chase you."

Bridget glanced at Nathan. "It's a real joy being partnered with you again."

Nathan smiled. "Keep your hands and feet inside the car at all times."

A diamond-shaped sign with black writing and a yellow background read, *Ebinyamaswa-Bikalubye*. "What's that mean?" Nathan asked.

"A warning about wild animals. This wildlife preserve contains lions and all kinds of predators."

"I'm more worried about the most dangerous predator," Nathan said. "Man."

Odongo's face hardened, and he nodded. This man had seen what evil men could do. "I'll brief their security chief and prepare my surveillance units. My instinct tells me Yemeni will arrive soon."

Nathan had the same feeling, and it wasn't a good one.

45

The facility's front doors swung open, and out stepped a muscular man wearing khaki pants, a wide-brimmed hat, and a tan polo shirt with the preserve's logo embroidered on it. He scowled as he hurried down the steps and trotted over to them.

"Don't give him too much information," Nathan whispered to Odongo.

"We cannot set a trap without his cooperation."

"But the corruption—"

"We will confide in him, and only him," Odongo said. "His men don't need details, but they must be ready to fight."

"If they act differently, they'll burn the surveillance and—" Nathan stopped as the man approached.

"Kaikara Mugisha, chief of security. What is the problem?"

"Dembe Odongo, assistant superintendent." He presented his identification. "We tracked a Mohammedan militant to the City of Seven Hills, and we believe he's headed here."

"We've had no breaches," Mugisha said.

"Anything suspicious?" Odongo asked.

"School girls." He smirked.

Odongo leveled his gaze on him. "Why would an Islamic terrorist come here?"

Mugisha's smile evaporated. "I ask you the same question."

"What is of value here?"

"In the preserve? Nothing, unless your terrorist wants to steal an endangered animal, or perhaps kill one for its hide. The pelts and teeth can fetch a fortune in the black market."

"And inside the laboratory? What kind of equipment or specimens have resale value?"

Darkness settled over Mugisha's face. "You will have to speak to Dr. Opio about specifics. My job is to protect the preserve and make sure our employees don't steal."

Odongo scratched his chin, a habit he displayed when something tickled his curiosity. "What about the personnel? Are any of your scientists from monied families?"

"You're thinking kidnapping?" Nathan asked.

Odongo shrugged.

"They are all first class and educated," Mugisha said. "They have money, at least more than my men possess."

How much did class warfare intervene in the daily workings of the preserve? Did a rift between the educated and uneducated or rich and poor motivate employees with nefarious intentions?

Two guards stood by the far end of the building watching them. Both wore camouflaged uniforms and carried older revolvers in holsters. Civilians often lumped agents, cops, and security guards into one group, but stark differences existed between security and law enforcement. One was a reactive job protecting physical structures and people, while the other involved proactive investigation.

"You have six officers on duty today?" Nathan asked.

Mugisha's eyes slid to Nathan like a snake. He regarded him for a moment. "You are counterterrorism?"

"Agents Burke and Quinn, Federal Bureau of Investigation."

Mugisha's expression didn't change. "Six, plus two rangers patrolling the preserve today and tomorrow."

"Are they armed with anything more powerful than revolvers?"

"Tranquilizer guns for the animals and Lee Enfield .303 rifles for poachers."

"Bolt action?" Nathan asked.

"I have two AK-47s locked in my office," Mugisha said. "We've arrested six trespassers this year. We can handle ourselves."

"Our target is a terrorist mastermind, not a smuggler. He kills without mercy. I suggest you retrieve those carbines while Odongo organizes his surveillance and arrest operation."

Mugisha shifted, digging in his feet like an offensive lineman. This guy didn't like people intruding on his territory, especially Americans.

"If you worry about this suspect, why didn't you bring more officers?"

"If he's coming here, a big footprint would scare him off," Odongo said. "So we must—"

"*If?*" Mugisha raised an eyebrow.

"We learned his destination, but not the timeframe. As we speak, my teams are setting up surveillance on the primary route. I've alerted our tactical team, so if surveillance spots him, they'll launch and make the arrest."

Mugisha smirked. "All this for one man. We can arrest him ourselves, without Kampala's help."

"Absolutely not," Odongo said. "This is a counterterrorism operation."

"My rangers have authority here."

"I'll stop your jurisdictional pissing contest," Nathan said. "Our suspect is responsible for hundreds of deaths, and he's eluded capture a dozen times. We're letting the tactical team capture him."

"You have the least authority here," Mugisha said.

"He's our terrorist," Bridget said.

Mugisha flashed that condescending smirk again. "Then why don't you have him in custody?"

"Enough," Odongo said. "The Counterterrorism Directorate trumps local jurisdiction. This isn't about preserving wildlife, it's about capturing a murderer."

"The beasts we protect are far more dangerous."

"I interrogated his assistant, and when I looked into his eyes, I saw more than hate. He was afraid. This terrorist we seek is a vicious killer."

Mugisha seemed to tire of the argument. He must know he couldn't override a counterterrorism deputy superintendent. Overstepping his bounds would cause him problems, and if his intervention allowed Yemeni to escape, Mugisha's future wouldn't be bright.

"Very well. Tell me what you need."

"Who's in charge?" Nathan asked. "Our target is coming for a reason, and we need to know why."

46

Mugisha radioed for the chief scientist to join them, then he led Bridget, Nathan, and Odongo into the building's expansive lobby. Light flooded through the windows and shimmered on the rose-colored tile and stark-white walls. It had the charm of a medical building.

A giant statue in the corner portrayed a lion standing on its hind legs with its front paws raised and baring its teeth. Mugisha paused at a long reception desk beside a young woman in a crisp ivory blouse. A security guard in camouflage watched them. A dirty Makarov semi-automatic handgun stuck out of his leather holster.

"They founded the institute forty years ago," Mugisha said. "Behind reception, we have offices for administration, public relations, government affairs, and scientists, as well as conference facilities. Staff can tele-conference around the world with encrypted communications." Mugisha's voice had morphed into that of a tour guide. How many visitors had he hosted? The lab had probably cost tens of millions, which would bring scrutiny from the Ugandan government—especially from corrupt officials.

"The west wing contains the Level 1 and Level 2 laboratories, and Levels 3 and 4 are in the east."

"I'd like to see Level 4," Nathan said.

Mugisha raised his hand and wagged his finger like a schoolmaster at a student. "That is not for you. Access is strictly limited."

"But I—"

A group of girls skipped by, all wearing green, high-waisted, pleated skirts with white blouses and dusty shoes. They appeared to be middle schoolers, or the Ugandan equivalent. Was public education the same way in Uganda? Nathan's total lack of knowledge about Central Africa became more and more obvious. He chased a few terrorists through Africa, but mainly Al-Shabab in Somalia and al-Qaeda in the Islamic Maghreb.

"Why are students here?" Bridget asked.

"A scheduled tour," Mugisha said. "They're going to the auditorium for a lecture."

Two girls hung back from the group and huddled together, whispering as if to avoid their headmaster. Teenagers hung at the threshold of life preparing to embark on untold adventures—happy and tragic—in a world that was both incomprehensible and full of wonder. Their intense gossip made them appear much younger.

An image of Amelia popped into his consciousness. He frowned. He'd been watching the students with fatherly awe, but his own daughter, half a world away, went about her life without him. Law enforcement was his calling, but his career came with sacrifice—and not just for him. How many birthdays, school plays, and softball games had he missed because he chased some criminal around the world? Had his absence created psychological problems for Amelia? Had he deprived her of the happiness he'd experienced as a child? Self-doubt and insecurity clawed at him.

Am I a good father?

A woman with braided hair and an Afro puff whisked across the lobby toward them. The tail of her lab coat flapped behind her. A ball of energy.

"This is Dr. Lucy Opio," Mugisha said.

She smiled. "We don't receive many Western visitors. Welcome to our facility."

"Who are the schoolchildren?" Nathan asked.

Opio turned her attention on him, and her energy infected him. "Students from Lira Primary, my daughter's school. I arranged their travel to show them what we do."

"What do you study here?" Bridget asked.

A young girl in a school uniform strode up and stood beside Opio. She brimmed with confidence but didn't interrupt. She'd woven red, yellow, and green beads into her cornrows, and she watched Bridget with the same expression Opio wore.

Opio smiled at her. "This is my daughter, Laker."

Laker beamed at Nathan with intelligent eyes that seemed to take in everything.

Nathan smiled. "Hello."

"*Itye nining, ladit?*" Laker shook his hand with a soft grip. She turned to Bridget. "*Itye nining, layot?*"

Bridget cocked her head.

Laker grinned like her mother. "That's Leb Acholiello for 'How are you?' It's the native language of our Acholi tribe."

"It's nice to meet you," Nathan said.

"Why are you interested in Mother's laboratory?"

"Laker, it's impolite to inquire about their business," Opio said.

"Sorry, *Min*," Laker said.

"No, it's a good question," Nathan said. "I'm sure you don't see many Americans here. We're here on business."

Three giggling girls raced past, and Laker's eyes followed them. Her question had been rooted more in politeness than genuine curiosity.

"Run along," Opio said, "and let us conduct our affairs."

"We're going outside and see the animals," Laker said.

"That's not safe," Opio said.

Laker's face wrinkled into a frown. Amelia did that too when she protested. Laker mirrored Amelia in many ways. God, he missed his daughter. Laker opened her mouth to speak, then her shoulders sagged. "*Tye kakare.*"

Tantrum averted.

"Go now," Opio said.

Laker skipped across the tile after her friends.

"Please excuse her," Opio said. "She's more at home in the jungle than inside a laboratory. She sneaks away to hunt whenever she can. I think she prefers spending time with animals."

"Which animals are here?" Bridget asked.

"A lion pride has been stalking prey near the fence. The sanctuary runs along the northern shore of Lake Kwania."

"Isn't this an odd place for a research facility?" Bridget asked.

"Quite the opposite," Opio said. "Our institute was founded to study bacteria and parasites that inhibit agriculture. Years ago, we had pens filled with livestock, and proximity to the preserve provides opportunities to trap animals we wish to study."

"You say years ago," Bridget said. "What's changed?"

"Our success brought more donor dollars and government financing, and we expanded our research into the study of jungle viruses. Basing here puts us close to the nature we're examining and creates a buffer between us and more-populated areas."

"Why do you need a buffer?" Nathan asked.

"In case there's a leak or exposure."

Nathan's blood cooled. "What kind of leak?"

She squinted at his question. He had that effect on people. "We study harmful bacteria in the soil and deadly contagions."

Uh-oh. "Which contagions?"

"Pathogens that spread pandemics."

A cool wind blew through Nathan's core. Lethal viruses and terrorists didn't mix. The Phantom's carfentanil attacks had killed thousands, but a pandemic could affect millions.

A girl screamed.

Nathan spun around. Six students laughed as a tall classmate chased them. Horseplay.

Nathan watched the girls and saw the laboratory through their eyes. Their exuberance was infectious. Hopefully, that was the only thing he'd catch from them.

Contagions. The mention of pathogens put him on edge.

"You look like you just saw a ghost," Bridget said.

"It's not *who's* in the lab, it's *what's* held here. Yemeni isn't coming to kidnap schoolgirls. He wants the pathogens."

47

Dread electrified Nathan. Yemeni wasn't headed to the wildlife preserve to hide or meet another benefactor. He sought deadly diseases. Bridget gawked at Nathan, but Odongo narrowed his eyes and set his jaw, as if he'd reached the same conclusion long ago. He could've said something.

Bridget raised a finger. "Hang on, he's—"

"Yemeni was the Phantom's facilitator," Nathan said. "He provided Zabihullah al-Afghani with direction, funding, and manpower to execute operations. Thousands died, but those attacks may have been a precursor to biological warfare."

"From here?" Bridget asked.

"What better place to steal deadly pathogens then a lab in Central Africa?"

"Is that why Yemeni was in Zimbabwe?"

"I don't know."

"That's a problem," Bridget said. "He could just be evading capture. We're making big assumptions."

"Maybe I'm wrong," Nathan said. "But Odongo's source has him headed here, so let's prepare for the worst. We need to set the trap before he arrives."

"Assuming you're right," Bridget said, "How would Yemeni steal a sample?"

"Perhaps," Odongo said, "he has someone on the inside."

Everyone looked at Opio.

Her face bunched into a ball. "Everything is controlled. The specimens we test are dangerous and highly contagious. We have protocols—"

"Doctor," Odongo interrupted, "provide us with a list of employees who have access to hazardous materials." He told her, instead of asking, and he'd used her title to formalize their interaction. Odongo took this seriously.

"I think it's time for us to see the facility," Nathan said.

Opio tightened her lips. She glanced across the lobby at the girls, then met Nathan's eyes. "Everything is secure, and we have armed guards."

"Indulge us," Odongo said.

"Of course." She pointed at the western corridor. "Down there are the lowest threat levels, where we research bacterial blight, black rot, and other pathogens that destroy crops. We—"

"Our suspect isn't coming to steal bacteria to destroy Ugandan farming," Nathan said. He pointed to the eastern wing. "We need to see what's down there."

"That's Level 3 and Level 4 containment," Opio said. "We don't allow tours in those areas."

"We're interested in your most dangerous viruses, anything that could be used as a weapon."

"But—"

"Doctor," Odongo said, "you will take us there now."

Opio stared at Mugisha, then turned and led them down a hallway with glass doors on both sides and into the eastern wing. She withdrew a lanyard from her lab coat and pressed it against a wall-mounted card reader. A thick door opened inward. They followed her into an oval room with a wraparound console, digital monitors, and flashing lights.

"Welcome to our command center," Opio said. She pointed at floor-to-ceiling windows with a view of interior laboratories. "We can monitor biosafety level 3 from here. The laboratory was built with concentric circles."

"Where are your most dangerous materials?" Nathan asked.

"In the center. We must transverse multiple airlocks with negative pressure to reach them."

"Show me."

"The three innermost labs are Level 4, and they contain our deadliest contagions. To enter, we require full-body, positive-pressure, Level A hazmat suits, and decontamination protocols."

"What do you study in Level 4?" Nathan asked. His heart sank as his worst fears materialized.

"The most infectious pathogens. Our most recent outbreak was from the Sudan Virus Disease, so our efforts have tilted in that direction over the past few years."

"Sudan Virus?"

"SVD is a viral hemorrhagic fever, an Ebola variant."

Nathan's pulse increased. "You keep Ebola here?"

"Of course. We test Sudan Virus Disease and other common Ebola variants from across the continent."

Outside the room, a girl's raucous laughter penetrated the walls. This was a soft target filled with civilians, and from the looks of it, Mugisha's men didn't have experience catching criminals, never mind terrorists. It took courage to face a charging rhino, but wild animals didn't possess human cunning, and Nathan hunted the most lethal beast—man. They needed to arrest Yemeni outside the lab to avoid collateral damage.

"Which other diseases do you study?" Bridget asked.

"In Level 4, we focus on anything that can cause a pandemic. We study dengue, Crimean-Congo hemorrhagic fever, yellow fever, Rift Valley fever, tuberculosis, malaria, monkeypox, Colorado, and dozens of neglected tropical diseases."

"What are those?" Bridget asked.

"Endemic diseases from leprosy to river blindness. We keep samples of everything. We also do work on measles, rotavirus, and other diseases we're suppressing with vaccines. We've seen an increase in acute febrile illnesses, like arboviruses and Zika."

Nathan's breathing became shallow and rapid. Perspiration cooled his skin. "Tell me they're secure."

"We have decades of experience studying infectious substances," Opio said. "Our entire facility was constructed at a biosafety level 2 rating, and a couple years ago, we upgraded to BSL-3 to handle inhalation risks like SARS and COVID. We recently added tiny BSL-4 for advanced research on Ebola and Marburg."

"That's what he's after," Nathan said.

"This man you're chasing?"

"Imam Omar Yemeni, a radical Islamist who kills without hesitation. He's in Uganda."

Her brow furrowed, and her professional mask slipped as a flash of fear crossed her face. "What does he want?"

"I don't know exactly, but your pathogens are like gold to terrorists seeking to destroy Western civilization."

A girl screamed again. Why wouldn't their teachers force them to behave while they were in a professional setting? Didn't they—

Bang.

A gunshot.

48

Leila needed Khalil to set up a meeting with the judge. The pressure was too much, and she couldn't stall her tormentors for long before they'd know she wasn't cooperating. What would they do then? They could harm her family or disappear her and take their chance with whoever replaced her. Their bribes might entice someone who didn't care what happened to others, but she couldn't do that. Harming innocents would stain her ephemeral soul and haunt her forever.

She hurried into the courthouse and badged her way through the employees' metal detectors. Every movement seemed an effort, as if she'd strapped weights around her ankles. Stress filled her with damaging hormones that had taken a toll.

She passed attorneys and court personnel, but the building didn't feel the same as it had on her first day. Who else had been co-opted? Who'd been tasked to watch her. She operated in a fishbowl, and one wrong move could mean death for her family. Should she have stayed in Iran and suffered the abuse and oppression? At least Ri would've been safe. Self-preservation urged her to capitulate to her tormentors, but beyond the ethical implications, she knew deep in her bones that they'd kill her when they were finished.

Her only choice was to seek help.

Agent Burke seemed like a straight shooter, and he'd shown no fear in the face of terrorism. Anyone could talk tough during a proffer, but he'd been in shootouts with terrorists. His battle with the Phantoms had made him famous, for a time. But fame faded, like everything else, and so did the public's memory of the peril. But not hers. Demons had exposed themselves, and her life hung by a thread.

She entered room 270. No Khalil. He should be there. She checked her phone. No messages.

She dialed. His phone rang four times and connected to voicemail. A robotic voice asked her to leave a message.

"It's me," she said. "Where are you? Call me." She hung up, feeling silly for not leaving her name. They were colleagues, and her calling him didn't mean they conspired to overthrow the criminal organization. She could've been asking for advice on a case or just for coffee.

But that wasn't true.

Around her, administrative personnel shuffled papers, and an interpreter scribbled something in a notebook. Was she noting Leila's comings and goings?

Leila started forward, then stopped. She needed to resolve this before something bad happened.

Khalil had said he'd approach a friendly court officer in Judge Baron's courtroom and ask his advice. If the officer agreed, he'd arrange an off-the-books meeting with the judge. She'd agreed to have him speak with his friend, but not approach the judge yet, because any conversation she had with him would be shared with the defense attorney and prosecutor. Once the coercion attempts became public, they'd kill her family.

But her conservative approach hadn't worked, and water boiled in the pot around her. Something had to change. It was time to ask the judge for help.

She approached the assignments desk, where a scrawny male administrative assistant sat. He'd always responded to her kindness with snide looks, and he seemed offended by her presence. That happened sometimes. Some men were attracted and solicitous to pretty women, while others seemed to resent them.

"Excuse me," Leila said. "Do you know where Khalil Mansoor is working this morning?"

He looked up at her, startled. "Didn't you hear?"

Leila's blood turned to ice. "What?"

He glanced around the room, then swirled his tongue around in his mouth, as if savoring a tasty morsel. Men like him lived on gossip. She'd seen it before.

"Tell me," she said.

He leaned forward. "There was an accident. He left his house this morning, and a car hit him."

Leila gasped.

Thoughts swirled in her mind like debris sucked into a tornado. Was this an accident or had she put a target on Khalil's back too? This might be her fault. She had to go to him.

"Is he in the hospital? Where did they take him?"

He licked his lips and vibrated with anticipation. Khalil was hurt, and this asshole was excited about being able to share dramatic news. His eyes widened.

"He's dead."

49

The rifle shot echoed through the command center. Opio and Mugisha stared at the closed door with alarm. Odongo remained still as a statue.

Nathan darted for the door before cognitively processing what happened. He grabbed his hip, where his gun should be—if he'd been allowed to carry in Uganda—and his fingers touched an empty belt. He stopped in the threshold and leaned toward the window.

Then Bridget was beside him. Cops did that. They moved to contact.

"What was that?" Opio asked.

"Gunshot," Bridget said.

Nathan peered through the window's wire-reinforced glass.

Fluorescent lights glared off the hallway tile, and at the end, a sliver of visible lobby was vacant.

Nathan canted his head for a better angle.

"What you got?" Bridget asked.

"Nothing."

Behind him, a radio chirped, and Mugisha barked orders in Swahili. Odongo pressed a cell phone against his ear.

Crack.

Another discharge from an AK-47, followed by two fainter shots. The guards had returned fire.

"What's happening?" Opio asked.

"We had this backward," Nathan said.

"Huh?"

"We came here to catch a murderous terrorist, but now we're the ones trapped."

Someone had taken a shot outside, and there were civilians inside the building. He couldn't sit still while students were in danger. He turned the handle, and the locking mechanism clicked.

"Perhaps it's a mistake to go out there," Odongo said.

"Schoolgirls are in danger," Nathan said.

"My daughter," Opio said, her voice frail and frightened.

"They're coming for your samples, not your daughter," Nathan said.

Bridget's eyes locked on the hallway.

"Can you reach your tactical team?" Nathan asked Odongo.

"No service," Odongo said.

"The building's structure is shielded inside the laboratories," Mugisha said. "It's part of the containment protocols. We have Wi-Fi outside the labs, but inside, we're restricted to wired telephones or our radios."

"Let's go." Nathan opened the door. It whooshed with escaping air, and the speaker above it chirped as a light turned green.

"My men aren't answering," Mugisha called out from behind him.

Nathan slipped out and scanned the corridor. Girls screamed in the distance. Nathan moved toward the lobby with Bridget beside him.

"I wish I had my Glock," Bridget said.

"No kidding."

Being unarmed was a bad feeling, and one he'd experienced too often. If they survived this, he'd start carrying a handgun overseas and the rules be damned. The terrorist they chased didn't worry about the legality of carrying firearms, so why should he? If the FBI allowed him to work with foreign police, they should recognize the danger and hammer out carry protocols when they accompanied foreign police on operations.

Nathan glanced back. "Mugisha, you gonna bring that handgun up here?"

Mugisha followed. He should be worried about his officers fighting for their lives, but he seemed hesitant. The psychological chasm between security officers and cops made them different species. One was a rule follower, and the other a predator.

Mugisha sidestepped around Bridget with his revolver drawn. He flagged them as he approached the lobby. If the situation weren't dire, Nathan would've berated him for his reckless technique.

Crack.

Another handgun fired outside. At least all the security officers weren't dead—a surprising outcome. Nathan had expected Yemeni to accept a sample from a corrupt employee, not launch an armed attack.

Mugisha stepped into the lobby without checking for armed assailants. How had he lasted this long?

Nathan and Bridget paused behind him and made eye contact. They peeked out simultaneously and checked the corners. All clear, which explained why Mugisha hadn't fallen under a hail of bullets. The receptionist had vanished, but two students huddled beside the lion statue.

Mugisha marched across the lobby to the front door.

"Get those girls behind cover," Nathan told Bridget.

"Roger."

Mugisha opened the entrance door without hesitation. Did he have a death wish?

Nathan jogged after him, avoiding the windows. He paused at the front and looked out.

One of the security guards lay prone on the steps, not moving. A pool of blood grew beneath him. Mugisha stood over him, gaping as if he couldn't believe what had happened. An ambulance parked opposite the entrance with its doors ajar.

The other officer—a ranger named Lubega—crouched behind a modern art sculpture and used the grotesque stack of blue-and-aqua-colored tiles as cover. He knelt and leaned around it. He held his gun with both hands and stared over its sights. His technique revealed a higher level of training than the other guards, but he remained one man against six, and his handgun was little match against AK-47s.

The ambulance driver had parked close, without apparent concern, as if the jihadists assumed their show of strength would force surrender. Or they were incompetent. Either way, the bloody body on the steps indicated their willingness to take lives without remorse—and innocent schoolgirls hid inside.

Lubega fired at a jihadist, and his round clanged against the vehicle's engine. Even a trained shooter had limited capability with an older revolver.

His target ducked behind the ambulance. The two insurgents in back raised their weapons and fired. Rounds shattered tile in front of Lubega and ricocheted into the air. At close quarters, the jihadists should be able to take him out, but their marksmanship sucked. Nathan had witnessed Taliban firing from the hip without looking. Their lack of precision made them less lethal but didn't lessen the hatred in their hearts.

"Stop shooting," Mugisha hollered across the space.

A jihadist gestured at him and rattled off guttural Swahili. Did they think they could negotiate a surrender? They'd already shot one officer, making the rest less likely to give up. The body bleeding out on the concrete upped the stakes, and there was no going back.

The terrorist stared at Mugisha. Why didn't they shoot at him too?

"*Tosha vurugu*," Mugisha shouted in Swahili.

Lubega fired two rounds at the driver and two more at the men behind the ambulance. He sprinted for the entrance. Mugisha held it open, and Lubega dashed inside.

Mugisha followed without taking a shot.

Vehicle engines reverberated through the jungle. Two Land Rovers frosted with mud raced down the driveway and skidded to a stop.

A glimmer of optimism lightened Nathan's chest. Was this Odongo's Quick Response Force? Had help arrived?

The doors sprung open, and more jihadists piled out. Another eight opponents.

Shit.

Nathan cast a backward glance at the ambulance. The men gestured and spoke to each other with urgency—then they fixated at the entrance.

Uh-oh.

The closest terrorist moved from behind the ambulance, and the others followed. They weren't worried about the ranger firing from inside, or if they were, they willingly took the risk.

They marched toward the facility.

50

A dozen jihadists pointed their carbines at the laboratory and advanced toward the entrance.

"Let's get the girls out," Nathan said.

Mugisha scowled, then pointed at Lubega. "Take them into the auditorium and keep them there."

"We can't stay inside," Nathan said. "Let's slip out back."

"Keep them here," Mugisha said. "It's too dangerous to enter the preserve."

"What about the viruses?" Nathan asked. "They're coming for pathogens."

"That is my concern."

Lubega raised his gun and cracked open the front door. He aimed outside.

"Don't shoot," Mugisha said. "Help them with the children."

"But—"

"Do it now. Go."

Nathan jogged across the lobby with the ranger. Odongo and Opio remained in the command center, which meant Mugisha would have to fend off the attackers himself. Not a good situation.

Nathan sprinted past the reception desk and turned the corner. Ten girls huddled against the wall with terror plastered on their faces. Tears stream down cheeks. Bridget raised her arms in defense—a lion protecting her cubs.

"They're coming," Nathan said.

Lubega pointed at double doors leading to the auditorium. "Go there."

"We'll be sitting ducks," Nathan said. Down the hallway, an exit sign glowed red. "That way. Get everyone outside."

"Not good," the ranger said. "Very dangerous."

"So are bloodthirsty jihadists."

"Up, girls," Bridget said. "Everyone outside."

A flicker of doubt tightened Nathan's chest. Was he putting the children in greater jeopardy? Anything had to be better than zealots with carbines. Mugisha had been clear about where to secure the children, but his directions made no sense. Neither did that scene outside. What was happening?

"Ticktock," Nathan said.

Bridget whisked down the row of girls, motioning for them to follow. She yanked up a girl who'd frozen from fear. Nathan followed, shielding them with his body. He wasn't armed, but he'd use his flesh to catch bullets. He glanced back. The ranger posted outside the auditorium. He didn't look happy.

"You coming?" Nathan asked.

Lubega glared. Violating Mugisha's orders didn't sit well with him, but he must see the futility of resistance. Nathan was taking those girls out, and the ranger could do nothing to stop them, short of shooting.

Bridget opened the exit door, revealing the dark-green canopy surrounding the property. The tops of towering trees poked up from behind the chain-link fence, and vines crept over and through the wire. The barrier rose thirty feet, high enough to prevent animals from jumping over, but it didn't look sturdy enough to stop a charging rhino or whatever giant beasts lurked in the preserve.

Bridget held the door, and the girls filed out. They'd been frozen with fear, but their innate desire to survive propelled them forward, and they sped up as the thought of escape imbued them with hope. A few whispered, but their terror kept most of them quiet. Nathan followed and closed the exit behind them.

"Where to?" Bridget asked.

"Anywhere with concealment," Nathan said.

Caged enclosures lay nearby. Whatever animals they kept for testing wouldn't make good roommates. Two outbuildings near the fence looked like maintenance or supply sheds. The fence had a giant gate, wide enough for large animals to pass through, and a human-sized door built into it for preserve access—but everyone had been clear about the danger. On the far side, Lake Kwania's water shimmered through the trees. That was perilous too. Everything on this continent seemed lethal.

Halfway down the building, cement stairs led to a lower level.

"Head for the steps," Nathan said.

"Everyone follow me," Bridget said. She took a girl's hand and jogged toward the stairs.

"Wait," Nathan said. "Do we have everyone?"

Bridget bit her lip and counted. Nathan scanned their faces. Where was Laker? The guard had estimated fifteen students. He did a quick head-count. Twelve.

"Where are the rest?"

"No friggin idea," Bridget said.

Another gunshot, this time from inside. Everyone stared at the building.

Men's voices emanated from near the building, their foreign words filled with venom.

"Hurry," Nathan said.

Metal creaked, and Nathan jerked his head around. The smaller door built into the massive gate opened. Adrenaline surged through his veins.

A jihadi stepped through the door, followed by another, both with carbines slung over their shoulders. They carried heavy plastic containers filled with liquid that had devices attached with black tape. Explosives. They planned to destroy the laboratory.

Nathan turned to Lubega, but he already had his revolver up.

Crack, crack. He loosed rounds at each.

Click.

Lubega's hammer fell on an empty chamber. The sound seemed to startle him, and he flipped open the cylinder and shook out the casings as he reached for a speed loader on his belt.

Both jihadists fell, and their explosives toppled onto the ground beside them. The ranger's rounds had found their marks.

Nathan raced toward them. Getting shot didn't take people out of a fight, even if they'd received lethal wounds. The men had gone down, because either a round had hit their cerebral cortex or other vital organs, or more likely, the pain had shocked them. They hadn't trained to fight through their agony.

Nathan closed the distance. One man lay on his back with his mouth open and blood streaming from his forehead. A headshot. Bull's-eye. The other held his side, and blood seeped through his fingers. If the round pierced his liver, he could bleed out fast, but he was still a threat.

He looked up as Nathan neared. His AK-47 had slipped off his shoulder, and he'd fallen on it. He rolled off, still holding his side, and grabbed the carbine.

Nathan was too close to do anything but attack.

He took three long strides and leaped as the terrorist swung around the carbine muzzle. The man's bloody fingers fumbled with the safety.

Nathan crashed into him and drove his knee into his chest.

The terrorist grunted.

Nathan's momentum carried him forward, and he swung his elbow into the man's face. His bone connected with the man's cheek.

The man's head banged against the ground with a thud, and his eyes went white. The AK-47 flew out of his grasp and landed in the dirt.

Nathan coiled to throw a punch, but the man was unconscious. Nathan snatched the AK-47.

The man groaned, and blood poured from his abdomen.

Nathan snapped off the AK-47's safety and aimed at his chest. His finger found the trigger, and he applied slight pressure. Was the gun even loaded? Using an enemy combatant weapon brought risk.

The man looked up at him. He coughed, and dark liquid coated his chin. Arterial blood. The bullet had done serious damage ricocheting inside. The man coughed up more blood. His eyes rolled back, and he collapsed. He was finished.

The gate the men had entered through remained open. Nathan glanced at it. Should he corral the girls and run into the preserve? Were dangerous predators close? The staff had lured them close to the lab to capture and study them. Did they dump garbage or food to keep them close? Maybe he should secure the—

The lab's back door burst open, and an Islamist exited with his AK-47 pointed forward.

Nathan raised the carbine and lowered its front post to the man's chest. No time to aim. He pulled the trigger and hoped for the best. The weapon bucked as a 7.62 mm round flew out of the barrel at two thousand feet per second.

The round struck the man on his right side, and the impact spun him around. Nathan lined up his sights and squeezed off two quick rounds.

The man arched his back as lead penetrated him. He dropped his carbine and tumbled backward down the steps. He lay prone. His foot twitched, then he didn't move.

Nathan retrieved the carbine off the second corpse and returned to the group. One girl wept uncontrollably.

Nathan handed the carbine to Lubega, who took it and holstered his pistol. He pulled back the slide and checked the chamber. He had training.

"Hide them downstairs," Nathan said.

"Where are you going?" Bridget asked.

"Back inside to find the other girls."

51

Leila sat at home with stacks of paper and manila folders spread out on the kitchen table. She'd copied the files for the court cases on which she'd assisted. The files contained logs, contacts, and pay sheets—the administrative red tape that accompanied any government adventure. She flipped through the documents hoping to find some clue. What were her extorters after, and who cooperated with them?

Ri watched some mindless sitcom on television. She couldn't concentrate enough to tell which show it was, but the laugh track grated on her nerves like fingers on a chalkboard. Her mother clattered around in the kitchen, putting away dishes from dinner while she listened to "Morgh-e Sahar," a classical Persian song.

Khalil's death made everything real. A fatal accident on the day he contacted his friend to request a secret meeting with the judge was too coincidental. These monsters were real. Khalil's death hung around her neck like an iron shackle. She forced herself through routine motions, and her thoughts never strayed from her predicament. Khalil had warned her that these men could kill, and he'd been right, though he'd probably never worried he'd be their victim. Murdering a fifteen-year veteran of the court showed that they wouldn't hesitate to take an innocent life. Her family was in grave danger.

"Poor Khalil."

"What's that?" Ri asked.

Leila jolted, not realizing she'd spoken aloud. "Nothing, Habibi. I was just thinking."

"Who's Khalil?" Ri asked without looking away from the screen.

"Someone at work."

Her eyes burned, and a lump formed in her throat. She swallowed to hold back the tears. She hadn't told her family about Khalil, because Shirin didn't need encouragement to pack up and return to Iran. Mother hated New York and would leave tonight, despite Leila's abusive husband and the secret police, who'd arrest them for immigrating without permission.

And Shirin didn't know the half of it.

Khalil had three young daughters, and a wife he seemed to care about, all of which compounded the tragedy. One life snuffed out too early was a significant loss, but a spouse left to fend for herself, and children abandoned to grow up without their father, was too much to bear.

Everything was Leila's fault.

They were in real jeopardy, and every option involved likely negative outcomes. But she couldn't fight reality and had to choose among terrible options. Nothing good would come of this.

But she must act and do it now, before all three of them ended up in boxes buried underground.

52

***

Nathan watched the lab's open back door. The third terrorist he'd shot lay dead at the bottom of the stairs, but how long would it take for more to come, and how many were there?

"Stay with the girls," Nathan told the ranger.

Lubega cocked his head.

Nathan gestured at the group. "The girls. Protect the girls."

"Ah," he said. He jogged after them.

Nathan covered the exit door and walked heel-to-toe to steady his shooting platform. As he approached, he sliced the pie, visually clearing the entry from a distance. The hallway was empty.

Hurry.

Nathan bounded up the steps into the facility. He closed the door behind him to avoid telegraphing his location. When the terrorists found their dead colleagues outside, maybe they'd assume the children fled into the jungle.

He traveled down the corridor on the balls of his feet to minimize noise. The doors leading into the auditorium remain closed, as did the office doors opposite them. How many girls were still hiding inside the building? And where were they?

Nathan paused, and without looking, he thumbed the magazine release and pulled it out. He pressed down on the bullets, and they offered little resistance. Less than half full, maybe ten rounds. He reinserted it and slapped the bottom. An improperly seated magazine would fall out the moment he fired and end with his death.

Nathan advanced and peered into the tiny window in the first office door. The darkened room contained a desk cluttered with paperwork. If girls hid under the desk or in a closet, he'd never find them in time. Terrorists could flood the corridor at any minute. He must move fast.

Nathan followed the curving hallway and peeked into each administrative office as he passed, then he stopped short of the lobby. He shuffled forward, careful not to stick out his barrel, and inched around the corner. He scanned the lobby.

Mugisha strode across the tile with his handgun holstered. What was he doing? Even for a security officer who'd seen little action, he seemed tactically incompetent.

No one else was in the lobby. At least the missing girls had been smart enough to seek shelter. Where were Mugisha's other men? The first security guard they'd met was likely dead, and Lubega protected the kids, which left three more armed officers. They were outgunned, but at least Nathan and Lubega had AK-47s.

Nathan leaned out farther. Through the windows, gun-toting terrorists climbed the steps. Mugisha stood just inside the entrance. They'd mow him down in a second. Nathan opened his mouth to call a warning, then stopped.

Mugisha unlatched the door and let them inside.

Treasonous son of a bitch.

Mugisha had either been bribed, or they'd scared him into surrendering. But a coward would've run and not welcomed them with open arms.

Nathan had to act. He could hit one or two, but eight more followed, and more could be coming. He'd get pinned down, and they'd surround him, preventing him from accomplishing his mission—save the girls and keep deadly pathogens away from suicidal killers.

Nathan backtracked and slipped into the hallway behind reception. He didn't have time to search every room looking for the missing children, but he could get to Odongo in the eastern lab and maybe even find the girls on his way.

He moved past offices with conference tables and a break room with vending machines. Nathan glanced into a room with coffeepots running along the counter, then turned to go. He stopped. Something had caught his eye.

Nathan looked back into the room. A shadow on the back wall. Something moved inside, and terrorists didn't hide.

Nathan turned the handle and entered.

"Girls?"

A head popped up behind a table. Then two more.

Laker.

"We've got to go. Follow me and stay quiet."

He checked the hall. All clear. He waved, and the girls followed.

Men spoke in the lobby in a language he didn't understand, but they'd search the building and capture or kill everyone inside. Then seize their prize.

Nathan couldn't let that happen.

He mounted his AK-47 and depressed the barrel as he moved toward the hallway intersection. The girls trailed behind him like ducklings after their mother. To their credit, they were quiet, despite the tears that streamed down their cheeks. These situations were fraught for a trained agent, but for teenage girls, it must topple their world.

He stopped at the intersection and glanced out. To the left, an empty corridor with closed office doors. To his right, the hallway emptied into the lobby. Opposite them, the eastern laboratory entrance remained secured. But not for long.

"I need to protect the lab where the dangerous viruses are kept," he said. "Move down the hallway to our left as quietly as you can and slip out the exit door into the field behind the facility."

"No," Laker whispered, her voice desperate and pleading.

"When you get outside, head for the stairs leading to the basement. Bridget is down there with a ranger and your classmates."

"Don't leave us," Laker said. "Please."

Her face morphed almost into Amelia's. She was the same age, and she had the same confidence . . . and the same fear. He shook away the thought.

"There's no choice," Nathan said, "or time to debate. More bad guys are coming this way. Are more students hiding inside?"

"I don't know," Laker said. "People started shooting, and we ran."

This would get ugly. "When you reach the basement, announce yourself so they don't shoot you by accident."

Laker nodded. Smart girl.

"Go now and stay quiet."

Laker led the girls toward the fire exit. Nathan stepped out and shielded them. More voices in the lobby.

What followed would be chaotic and violent. Gunfights always were.

Nathan peeked into the lobby. A jihadi stepped through the threshold holding a severed eyeball.

Bile rose in Nathan's throat, and he swallowed it. He looked back at the girls.

"Run."

53

Nathan glanced back and confirmed the girls exited the building. He faced forward and adjusted his fingers on the grip. He extended his support hand farther down the handguard and pulled the stock against his shoulder. Any second, the front doors would open, and more jihadists filled with blood-lust and hate would storm inside. The odds sucked, but victory went to the bold, and first aggression often won.

Nathan sidestepped around the corner, careful not to cross his feet. He kept his barrel level and his grip firm as he looked over his sights. He kept both eyes open and didn't line up his iron sights. What came next would be less about marksmanship and more about speed and reflexes.

He moved in a semicircle, and the lobby came into view—the tile floor, the windows, the glass doors. The front door remained closed. A good sign.

He took another step. Mugisha and two terrorists stood beside reception and stared down the hallway.

Nathan didn't hesitate. He lowered his sight onto the first terrorist's back, inhaled, and squeezed the trigger.

Bang.

The man jerked as a bullet exploded through his torso.

Nathan fired again, then aimed at the other terrorist. The man turned as Nathan double tapped. The AK-47's weight kept his sight on target.

The man spun, and the second round caught him in the face and shattered his jaw. Blood sprayed high into the air.

Mugisha gawked, as if he hadn't considered Nathan a threat. There was no need for a court of law. The security chief had let the terrorists inside. He was the enemy.

Nathan dropped his sights onto Mugisha's chest and fired. The traitor stumbled and fell onto his back.

Men shouted outside as more terrorists raced up the steps. Nathan didn't wait around to engage. He ran down the hallway into the eastern lab.

The front door opened behind him as he reached the air-locked door. He banged on the steel and peered through the glass. Odongo stared back at him.

"Let me in," Nathan shouted.

Odongo hurried to the door, revealing Opio behind him. He'd been shielding her with his body. Good man.

The green light flashed, and the changing air pressure whooshed as Odongo opened the door. Nathan slipped inside and yanked it shut behind him. The light glowed red. He looked out. No sign of the terrorists. They'd entered the building, but they took their time, avoiding the same fate as their comrades.

"What's happening?" Odongo asked.

"Mugisha turned on us. He let them in."

"That *busha*," Odongo said. "I'll stand him before a firing squad if we escape."

"That won't be necessary. He's dead."

Odongo narrowed his eyes. "You?"

Nathan nodded. Would he end up in front of a firing squad too?

Odongo shook his head. "You took that joy from me. Mugisha is lucky. His life ended with too little pain."

Opio stepped between them, clutching her trembling hands. "My daughter?"

"She's safe," Nathan said. "For now."

Opio's shoulders sagged. "Where?"

"I sent them to the basement."

"She's in danger," Opio said. She wouldn't accept the hope Nathan had offered.

"Bridget and a ranger are with them." He turned to Odongo. "Launch your QRF."

Odongo pointed to his pocket. "No service."

"Use the landline," Opio said. "Dial zero for the operator and ask for an outside line."

Odongo moved to the control bank. Opio turned to follow.

"Hold on," Nathan said.

She stopped, her face a mask of conflict.

"I only have ten rounds left," Nathan said. "I can't hold them off for long, and if they enter before the QRF arrives, they'll steal some terrifying stuff. We've got to stop them, or many people will die."

Her face hardened. "We destroy samples after testing. There isn't much here."

"Which pathogens?"

"We study dozens of diseases that —"

"I'm talking about viruses used for biological weapons. Specimens that can be spread without too much engineering. Yemeni won't have access to sophisticated laboratories and scientists. They'll want contagions that can trigger a pandemic."

Men shouted in the lobby, massing for an attack. He needed a plan. His presence—an FBI agent with an AK-47 guarding the lab—must be a wrinkle they never expected. The disruption gave him time.

But not much.

"The highest mortality rates come from Marburg virus, the Zaire Ebola virus, and then Crimean-Congo hemorrhagic fever, but those are mostly transmitted through contact with bodily fluids."

"The Phantoms perfected chemical warfare when they sprayed people with carfentanil, so I'm confident they'll know how to sustain the virus in a fluid."

"Level 4 containment also holds Nipah virus and hantavirus, both respiratory diseases that can be aerosolized."

"Damn."

"We also have a sample of the DRC Mystery Fever that spread in the Congo in 2025. It's a nascent hemorrhagic fever."

"This keeps getting better and better."

"We have others to, but those are the worst."

"If any fall into Yemeni's hands, it'll be a disaster."

"They'll head for Level 4," Opio said. "They want the Marburg virus."

"How can you be certain?" Nathan asked.

She shed a tear. "I just know. Marburg has a long and deadly history here. It'll cause fear. And death."

Odongo faced them. "I can't reach the operator."

"Dial zero," Opio said.

"They've cut the line. I need to go outside and use my cell phone."

Movement outside caught Nathan's eye, and he stuck his face back in the window.

A man in black fatigues carried an AK-47 across the lobby. He wore a headband with symbols Nathan had seen before. ISIS.

"ISIS joined the party," Nathan said. "Yemeni keeps bad company."

The man entered the hallway and stared at Nathan. Nathan jerked back from the window, but too late.

"He saw me."

Nathan looked out. Another terrorist joined the first in the hallway. They hugged the walls and pointed AK-47s forward. Two more covered them from the lobby. These guys had training.

Time was up.

54

Something troubled Mother. Darius watched her make his oatmeal, as if he was a referee at a football match. She'd added exactly forty grams of oatmeal, and a dollop of milk would come next, right in the center. Not mixed in with the grain, but a tiny puddle on top. That's how it should be done. That's how it must be done.

She retrieved the milk carton from the refrigerator and poured it into a spoon. She did the right things, but her movements were stiff. Darius couldn't read facial expressions or understand sarcasm or pick up on any of the external clues that mother said revealed what people were thinking. He tried. Oh, man, he'd tried. But watching someone's face when they spoke and trying to figure out what they meant was like reading a foreign language. Their expressions had no meaning.

She hovered the spoon over the oatmeal, then poured into the indentation she'd made with the spoon. Perfect.

Yet she wasn't herself.

"How is work, Mother?"

Her face contorted into an expression he hadn't seen before. But it was as meaningless as her others.

"Work is work."

"You've been gone a lot this week."

"That's important for us. When I'm at work, I'm making money, so I can buy things, like your oatmeal."

"I know what money's for, but I don't enjoy being alone with Bibi."

Her expression changed. She looked . . . softer? What did that mean?

"But I make it home for dinner, and I'm always thinking about you."

"When do I start school?"

"We need to identify the right one for your . . ."

"My what?"

"A place that recognizes your superpower and can help you get stronger."

Mother always called it his superpower. He was different from other kids, he knew that, but it didn't feel like a superpower. It caused problems. He didn't have many friends, and whenever he got to know anyone, like Reza in Tehran, he'd end up saying something that made people look at him funny. If he must have a superpower, why couldn't he fly or be strong like Rostam?

"Will there be kids my age?"

"Of course."

"Kids like . . ." He inspected the tabletop. ". . . like me?"

She bit her lip. Something was wrong. "There aren't any children as magnificent as you. But of course there'll be other kids in school."

He filled with optimism. "I'd like to make a friend here."

His mother's eyes teared. Whatever was bothering her seemed to get worse.

"You'll have friends here, my little darling, I promise."

He hated it when she called him her *little darling*. He was practically a man, and now he'd lived in two countries. How many little children could say that? And father was no longer there, which made him the man of the house.

Darius's appetite returned. He grabbed his spoon and dug into the oatmeal, careful not to disturb the milk in the center. He had to eat that with the final bite. That's how it worked.

55

Nathan ducked beneath the door's window. The steel would stop 7.62 mm rounds, but those projectiles would pierce safety glass. He turned to Odongo and Opio.

"They're coming."

"What's our plan, Mr. Agent Man?" Odongo asked.

"Destroy the viruses," Nathan said.

"Too dangerous," Opio said.

"You told us you destroy samples after you record the data," Nathan said. "How's that done?"

"We use an autoclave to incinerate biological samples, and animal carcasses from testing are burned in an enclosed facility out back. But there are many samples and little time. We'd need hazmat suits and decontamination."

Metal scraped in the hallway.

"I'm afraid time is up," Odongo said.

He was right. "Then I'll buy us some more," Nathan said. He knelt and touched his muzzle against the doorframe. He pushed the door and punched his muzzle through the opening.

An incoming round smacked the metal like a thunderbolt.

Nathan fired. His ears rang and his hearing shut down. He feathered the trigger and unleashed three rounds. The carbine jerked in his hands. He adjusted his aim and shot twice more. He kicked the door closed.

Odongo grimaced, and Opio covered her ears like a child.

"Annihilate those viruses," Nathan said. "I'll keep them at bay."

Odongo wagged his finger. "I am not afraid of terrorists, but I won't enter a lab with those devilish monstrosities. Give me your weapon. I will hold them back."

"This won't be easy," Nathan said. "They have overwhelming firepower, and they'll breach the lab, eventually."

"Then I will die," Odongo said. "I would rather get shot than have an invisible creature devour my organs."

Nathan wanted to argue, but there wasn't time. He handed his carbine to Odongo and met his eyes. "Godspeed."

Odongo nodded. He tugged back the charging handle to confirm a round was in the chamber and posted at the door.

Nathan hurried across the room. "Let's go, Doctor."

"It'll take hours to destroy every specimen."

"We don't need to burn everything, just the most dangerous. We'll skip Level 3."

"I don't see—"

"It wasn't a question," Nathan said. "Get moving."

Opio scowled as she pressed her key badge against the security pad. The interior door whooshed open. Nathan followed her into an anteroom with hazmat suits hanging in cubbies.

"These BSL-4 positive-pressure suits are required for Ebola and Marburg."

An image of hundreds of corpses inside the Wells Fargo Center flashed in Nathan's mind. "I've used them."

"If we enter without them, we're dead. I've watched victims bleed out from hemorrhagic fever as their organs disintegrated. Catastrophic system failure is horrifying."

"I'm not arguing."

"We're supposed to inspect the suits for damage and test the pressure system," Opio said, "but that takes too long." She removed a suit from its hook. She flung her lab coat onto the ground and unbuttoned her blouse.

Muffled gunfire thumped behind them. Odongo should wait until Yemeni's men breached the threshold.

Opio stripped down to a tee shirt and underwear. She showed no embarrassment. She slipped on green scrubs and stepped into her hazmat suit. Nathan ripped off his shirt, kicked off his shoes, and dropped his pants. He put on scrubs too and glanced at her as she dressed, making sure he emulated her procedure for zipping up seams, connecting hoses, and sealing the suit. She moved with speed and efficiency, and he rushed to keep up. He had to be ready to move when she finished, but one mistake could lead to an ugly death.

"Help me with the hood," she said. He lifted it and followed her instructions, sealing, snapping, and zipping. She flashed a thumbs-up.

She plugged into a wall connector and flicked a switch. An engine throbbed and her suit ballooned as it inflated. A green light illuminated on her wrist monitor. She just disconnected the hose and monitored her instruments.

She looked at him through her face shield. "Now you."

She helped Nathan into his suit, and despite having received hazmat training for clandestine laboratories, claustrophobia tightened around him. He shut his eyes and breathed deeply until it lessened. Phobias existed in the mind—but real danger birthed them.

She checked him over. Her lips moved, but he couldn't hear. He tapped his ears, signaling she wasn't getting through. Her eyes widened with understanding, and she clicked a switch on his helmet. Static filled his ears.

"Hear me?" she asked.

"Yes."

"Ready?"

"No choice."

She'd wrapped her lanyard around her wrist, then pressed the badge against the access control plate. The interior door wheezed open, and they entered a short tube with fans on the ceiling and circular openings in the walls. She held up her finger for him to wait, then she pressed a button on the wall, and fans whirred to life. The outer layer of their hazmat suits fluttered until the fans stopped. She led him into the next section. The door sealed behind them and she hit a switch. Liquid poured out of showerheads in the ceiling, and clouds of yellow mist filled the room.

"We're decontaminating," she said, "so we don't interfere with experiments or drag anything deadly out into the world."

"We're nuking everything in Level 4."

"Force of habit." She slapped a button, and the mist cleared. She used her fob again, beneath a Level 3 sign, and they entered another corridor. Stainless steel doors with thick gaskets around safety glass windows lined the wall.

"Skip Level 3," Nathan said. "Yemeni will go for the worst of it."

"Follow me."

She led him down the corridor, and motion-activated ceiling lights illuminated as stark light flickered on inside each lab. Nathan peeked through a window. Vials and electronic testing equipment filled glass cabinets and steel counters. These labs contained every advancement he'd find in a Western laboratory.

She stopped before a sign for Level 4. She touched her key card against the pad and led him through double-sealed doors into another decontamination area. The door latched behind them and she hit the button, dowsing them with wind and decontamination chemicals. When it stopped, she faced him.

"Be careful in here," she said. "Don't touch anything unless I tell you."

"You don't need to say that twice."

She stared, as if about to speak, then she deactivated the lock with her key.

The chamber opened, and they entered the hot zone.

56

Level 4 was almost identical, except it only housed three labs. The incinerator room was at the end of the hall. They stopped at the first lab. Through the window, gleaming surfaces reflected bright fluorescent lights, everything germ-free and sterile.

Except the deadly pathogens stored inside.

Fine hair rose on Nathan's body. These viruses were the deadliest life-forms on earth. His parents had wanted him to be a lawyer. Maybe they'd been right.

"We'll retrieve the specimens and then incinerate them," she said.

He nodded. Sweat ran down his face and dripped down his back. His encapsulated suit had warmed, but his perspiration came from something else—fear.

She pressed the button, and they entered. She moved to a large tank with a plexiglass enclosure and openings with gloves on the inside for scientists to manipulate specimens without exposing them to the room. The interior of the machine was empty.

Opio pressed her key card against an access plate on a refrigeration unit. It clicked, and she opened it. Cold vapor puffed out. A chill ran up his spine. Glass vials and sealed metal containers packed the shelves, each marked with dates and descriptions. Nathan leaned close.

Ebola.

Nathan licked his lips, but the moisture had gone from his mouth.

Opio unclipped a pouch from inside the refrigeration and unzipped it.

"How do we do this?" he asked.

"I'll hold open the double-sealed bag, and you fill it with vials."

Nathan swallowed hard. There was no other option. He reached inside with a gloved hand, careful to not knock over vials filled with colored liquids. He grasped a glass container. Rubber ridges covered his glove's fingertips, but he couldn't feel it. What would happen if he dropped something? He shook off the fear.

He laid the first vial on the bottom of the bag. The refrigerator contained dozens of vials, and this was only one of three Level 4 labs. He must move faster. He grabbed two more and set them inside the bag. The vials clinked, but he kept going.

Thump. Thump. In the distance, more AK-47s fired.

Once terrorists captured the command center, it wouldn't take long for them to enter the lab. They probably didn't have access codes, but they could break in, and they'd planned enough to co-op Mugisha, so they may possess key cards. They'd enter Level 4 soon.

Nathan placed the last of the Ebola samples into the bag. "That's it."

"Got it," Opio said. She zipped the bag closed, then surveyed the laboratory.

"Anything else?"

"Other compounds, but no viruses."

"Let's go."

She hit a red plastic button, and the door opened, a keyless exit. They hurried past the next lab.

"What's in this one?" he asked.

"More viruses," she said, "but we've got to incinerate them individually. The primary chamber isn't large."

They continued to the end of the hall, and she keyed them into an incinerator room. He shut the door, sealing them into the tiny space. She tapped a button on a control panel built into the wall, powered up the machine, and typed in a code. A metal cover slid open, revealing a compartment. She unsealed the bag and removed a single vial.

"No time," Nathan said. "Dump everything in there."

"If we shatter a vial, we'll contaminate the lab—and ourselves."

Nathan pulled the bag from her grip. "We have minutes, best case." He shoved the entire bag into the compartment.

She nodded and typed numbers into the keypad. The metal door slid shut with a click. The machine beeped, and an indicator light glowed green. She pressed a red button, and warning lights flickered. The machine hummed and glass clinked inside a chute behind the closed door. The incinerator groaned and vibrated.

"It reaches two thousand degrees," she said, "hot enough to kill any virus or bacteria."

"What happens to the ash?"

"There isn't much left, but it's automatically sealed in containers. The boxes of ash go into a containment box that's retrieved once a month."

"And then?"

"We bury the containers in a cement depository, so they won't rise to the surface over time. None of the viruses could survive the flame."

"Next."

He hit the red button, and they made for the second lab. Gunshots whomped behind them, louder than before. Had the terrorists breached the door? Opio accessed the lab.

"Anything happens to you," he said, "I'm stuck in here."

"You can exit without a key and leave through the command center."

"Is there another way out?"

"That's the only way."

"What about fire exit?"

"We have fire suppression and safety equipment, but it's designed to contain biohazards. If something goes wrong in here, fire is the least of our problems."

She opened a horizontal refrigerator, like the one his parents had used to store popsicles and frozen steaks in their basement, but this one contained a different treat.

Opio unhooked another double-containment bag and opened the refrigerator. Nathan reached in and removed vials, repeating the process. This chest contained fewer samples, and he emptied it briskly.

Sustained gunfire erupted outside. Odongo must be fighting for his life. The urge to race back and help tensed Nathan's muscles and filled him with adrenaline. He tamped it down. He must prevent the viruses from falling into Yemeni's hands.

He slapped the exit button and bounded down the hall. She followed with the sack, and he took it from her as she tapped in her code and entered. She opened the incinerator, and Nathan crammed the bag inside. She dialed in the code, and as the machinery hummed again, Nathan hit the exit button—but this time, the door didn't open.

"What's wrong?" he asked.

"We can't exit until it's finished. Safety protocol."

"That's a procedure that can end in thousands of deaths."

The process completed, and the door opened. He shuffled down the hallway, clumsy in his bulky suit. They stopped outside the final room.

"What's in here?"

"Marburg."

The name of that deadly virus chilled him.

The gunfire stopped—a bad sign. Odongo could have run out of ammunition and given up, or the terrorists had regrouped, but the likelihood was darker.

Odongo was dead.

Thumping echoed down the hallway. Someone banged on a door to Level 3. They'd broken through.

They were coming.

57

Opio unlocked the third and final lab, and they slipped inside. It resembled the others, but it contained a slim refrigerator nestled between freestanding microscopes. She unlocked it, and Nathan moved beside her, ready to empty the vials. They'd fallen into a rhythm, as the stress and stakes of their situation molded them into an efficient team. Pounding came from the hall as terrorists tried to break down the door in Level 3.

Opio stared into the refrigerator. The hook didn't hold a double-sealed bag. She looked around the room, then moved to a cabinet without a word. She unlocked it and dug out a thick plastic bag with a bulky clip that looked like an industrial sandwich bag.

"Use this."

"Shouldn't we find the right bag to transport—"

"It's not here. Someone moved it. I can go—"

Glass shattered outside, and they both looked at the door.

"No time," Nathan said. "They're in Level 3, and we're next."

He wrapped his thick gloves around two metal containers with glass tops, different from the others. Did that make them more secure for Marburg? Everything in Level 4 could kill them, and if the viruses escaped, thousands of people. The mortality rate for Marburg was somewhere north of ninety percent, which prevented the nasty virus from wiping out humanity. Victims died fast, before the virus could spread. A longer incubation period with less observable symptoms would have caused a global pandemic.

Opio held the bag, and Nathan lowered a container into it, but the narrow opening made it challenging. She squeezed the ends to expand the center, but his gloves prevented him from reaching the bottom.

He let the container drop. It thudded against the bottom. He grabbed another and aimed for the spot beside the first. It landed safely. They needed to move faster. Nathan dropped two more into the bag, and the containers clinked against the others.

An electrical shock of terror crackled through him.

She peered inside. "It's okay. Keep going."

Loud bangs came from outside. Islamists tried to break into Level 4, and they'd breach the door soon.

Sweat dripped into his eyes as Nathan stretched to reach a glass vial at the rear of the top shelf.

Got it.

He retracted the container with his gloved fingertips. He turned to drop it into the bag.

It slipped out of his grasp.

A jolt of adrenaline flashed through him as he lunged for it. It bounced off his glove and twirled in the air—out of his reach.

Horror spread through him—a deep, primal fear of the invisible disease.

The beaker clinked against the floor, bounced once, then rolled across the smooth surface. It came to rest against the wheel of a portable microscope stand.

Nathan froze. He didn't breathe. His heart pounded. "Did it break?"

Opio's face twisted into a mask of terror, transforming her from brilliant scientist to terrified schoolgirl.

He approached the microscope.

"Be careful," she said. "If it's compromised . . ."

She didn't finish her sentence. If they'd unleashed Marburg, it would contaminate everything in the room. And if either of their suits had ripped, or they hadn't sealed them properly . . .

Shit. Bleeding out from a hemorrhagic fever would be a nightmare.

Nathan stopped a few feet away, afraid, as if it might bite him. Its venom would deliver an agonizing death. Perspiration dripped down his face and back—cold sweat driven by dread. He leaned forward.

A crack split the vessel.

Nathan's pulse drubbed in his temples. His breathing came shallow and fast, and his vision tunneled until he only saw the crack.

"What?" Opio asked.

"It broke."

Opio stood beside him. "It's exposed?"

"Yeah."

She knelt beside it, and her courage shamed him. Their self-contained, pressurized suits should protect them, but Marburg—perhaps the deadliest pathogen known to man—could be floating around him.

His skin crawled. A tickle ran up his spine. The sweat on his forehead cooled. He'd been in gunfights and wrestled terrorists, yet airborne hemorrhagic fever triggered terror in ways criminals couldn't. This life-form could kill any mammal—deadly and unseen.

The room wobbled, and he reached for the wall. He stumbled and caught his balance. He shuffled to a chair and sat.

"What's wrong?" she asked.

"Is it out?"

"You're safe, as long as your suit isn't compromised."

"What do we do?"

"Our procedure is to contain the spill, clean up the substance, and incinerate everything that could've been affected. Then we decontaminate ourselves."

More banging from the hall.

"They'll be here any minute," Nathan said. "How long will this take?"

"Half an hour, at least."

"We can't wait."

"Anyone who enters will be exposed," she said.

"I'm not worried about them."

"One infected person can cause a pandemic. A terrorist spreading Marburg in Kampala would be a disaster."

Glass shattered outside.

"It's too late," Nathan said. "They're here."

58

Nathan and Opio stared at the door to their Level 4 lab. Yemeni's men had broken the glass in the containment door, which meant they were about to enter the corridor.

"We can't let them get exposed," Opio said. "Let's seal the room. We can clean it up whenever this incident resolves."

"They're coming for the virus," Nathan said. "That's the point of their operation."

"We can warn them . . . tell them of the danger."

"The virus could shield us," Nathan said as a flicker of hope bolstered his resolve. "Unless their lives don't matter to them."

"I don't understand," she said.

"True believers will sacrifice themselves to get the samples."

"Who would knowingly expose themselves to hemorrhagic fever?"

"Islamists crave death. Sacrificing themselves during jihad is their endgame. They belong to a death cult."

"You're saying they'd enter knowing they had a ninety percent chance of a horrific death?"

"It depends on their level of commitment," he said. "Let's hope they're mercenaries and not fundamentalists."

"What do you suggest?"

"Let's test them."

Nathan moved to the counter and scooped an empty beaker out of its ring stand. He turned on a faucet and filled it with water, then he hurried to the door.

"What are you—"

"I'm gonna see if these guys have a shred of self-preservation. Marburg will expose their motivations."

He pressed the exit button, and she followed him inside the airlock. He pressed his mask against the window but couldn't see far enough down the hallway. He reached for the door release.

"Wait," she said.

"We need emergency decontamination."

She pulled a red lever, and liquid misted out of nozzles in the ceiling and walls. She turned beneath it and raised her arms to allow the spray from the side jets to coat her. He mirrored her movements. Their suits had been exposed, and if the chemical rinse didn't kill the virus, they could free microscopic monsters into the world.

"That enough?" he asked. "Did we kill it?"

"Theoretically," Opio said. "We have a lengthy exposure protocol, but whatever airborne microbes may have attached themselves to us are probably dead."

Probably. Nathan squirmed inside his suit. There was a reason he hadn't gone into science as a profession. That stuff freaked him out.

"Stay here." He activated the exit and peeked out.

Glass fragments covered the hallway, and the exit door stood ajar. An insurgent clothed in a hazmat suit held an AK-47. The protective suit was a good indicator he didn't want to throw his life away—unless he only planned to live long enough to capture the virus and release it into the population. The man raised his weapon.

Nathan held up the beaker and waved it in the air.

The man's eyes widened.

"This is Marburg," Nathan yelled. "We had a leak, and the laboratory is contaminated."

The man shouted something incomprehensible in Swahili.

Opio appeared beside Nathan with her hands up. She yelled something in Swahili or Luganda. The man lowered his muzzle and stepped back.

"What did you say?" Nathan asked.

"The deadly disease escaped into the air. I told him to leave and decontaminate, or he and everyone he knows would die a horrible death."

The door to the first lab opened, and two terrorists exited wearing hazmat suits. The first one shouted and aimed his AK-47.

"That guy didn't get the message," Nathan said. He held the vial up. "Marburg. We're all exposed."

The man aimed at Nathan and looked over his sights.

Nathan threw the beaker at him. It shattered on the floor, and liquid splashed. The man stumbled back. The first terrorist fired.

Nathan yanked Opio back into the decontamination chamber as the shot echoed off the walls.

Why hadn't Nathan brought a weapon into the hot zone? He had to play this out without a weapon. Again. How many times had he faced armed attackers during this investigation without the benefit of his Glock?

Nathan quick-peeked out. The terrorists had retreated into the airlock leading to Level 3.

"It worked," he said. "These guys are hired guns or Islamists who haven't been radicalized enough to wanna throw their lives away. Sometimes, fear of death triumphs."

"They're from Uganda," Opio said. "They understand Marburg. Our people have suffered from these outbreaks many times before. Dread of the virus lives deep within us."

"We bought a little time. They won't enter the contaminated hallway."

"But we can't get out," Opio said. "We're trapped."

59

Nathan leaned against the airlock door and scanned the hallway through the safety glass to make sure the terrorists weren't preparing to assault—not that he could do anything to stop them. Opio stood beside him, and behind her face shield, a vein pulsed in her temple. The sign of fear humanized her.

"We need to destroy the Marburg," Nathan said. "Let's clean up that broken vial and incinerate the last of it."

"A BSL-4 exposure requires a biohazard remediation team, so we need to wait for authorities to liberate the lab."

"A rescue team may not arrive before those jihadists kill us and recover whatever virus is left. If Yemeni's out there, he'll know who to send."

"You think they'll risk contagion?"

"I know it. They're out there planning right now. They entered the first lab, so they know we removed the viruses. Eventually, they'll conclude this lab is their last chance to recover Marburg. Yemeni will send someone in to check."

"Even if we incinerate the last samples, they've taken the command center, and we can't get past them."

Odongo's face flashed behind Nathan's eyes. He shook the thought away. Emotions weakened resolve, and he needed to stay professional and act with logic and reason. Any wrong decision could end their lives.

"There must be another way out," Nathan said. "Don't you have codes that require multiple exits?"

"They both filter past the command center."

"That's insane."

"We study the deadliest organisms in BSL-4. We exist to prevent a pandemic."

"One problem at a time," Nathan said. "Let's finish the job."

She activated the door, and they entered the lab. His cool sweat returned. Confronting fear should make his terror subside over time, but an invisible enemy floated around him, trying to penetrate his protective layers and burrow into his organs. That was too dark and primal for him to ignore. He'd been labeled a hero for his shootout with terrorists—but scientists who faced hemorrhagic fever displayed a level of courage he didn't possess.

Opio hurried to the broken vial, while Nathan returned to the refrigerator. He held open the bag with one gloved hand while he filled it with beakers. He moved fast, with little caution, because the worst had already happened. Adding more Marburg into the air wouldn't be much worse. He'd either been exposed or he hadn't.

Opio scooped up the cracked container off the floor, put it in another bag and sealed it. She sprayed bleach on the floor.

"It's in the air," Nathan said. "Why are you cleaning the spill?"

"It must be done, and . . . I don't know. Force of habit."

Nathan placed the final container inside and sealed the container. "Ready."

She followed him with the bag containing the compromised sample, and they exited into the airlock. She activated the system, and decontaminant doused them. Nathan turned the bag to let the disinfectant coat it. The spray stopped, and the green light blinked.

"One more cycle," Opio said. "We're violating so many protocols."

"Terrorists shooting in here violates policy too. Let's find a way out." He unlatched the door and peeked out. Movement flashed behind the shattered window at the end. At least one terrorist remained inside the chamber to monitor them.

"We have an opportunity," Nathan said. "Hug the wall and hurry."

They entered the corridor and made for the incinerator. Nathan moved fast and tried to keep quiet. It wouldn't take much for that jihadist to stick out a barrel and shoot down the hallway.

Opio stayed close, and they reached the incinerator. She keyed open the door, and they slipped inside. She activated the machine as before and packed the bag inside. She triggered the heat and destroyed the last of the Marburg—or at least they hoped she did. The disease could exist somewhere in that last lab, stuck in a crack, floating in the ventilation system, or hiding—

Wait. That was the answer.

"The exits leading past the command center aren't the only connection to outside," Nathan said.

"I told you—"

"How is the facility ventilated?"

"Through a series of boxing systems with layers of HEPA filters, and—"

"I mean, is it recycled air, or does the intake draw from outside?"

She cocked her head. "All BSL-4s use fresh air. Recycling could spread a spill and contaminate the atmosphere throughout the lab. Each room has an individual, isolated system. It sucks air from outside through a pressurized tunnel to ensure the airflow goes one way."

Hope bubbled inside him. "How wide are those vents?"

Opio's eyes widened behind her mask. She got it. "Wide enough, but we risk damaging the vent and compromising the seal."

"Leaving Islamists in charge is riskier. We can replace the filters behind us, but it's our only way out, right?"

She screwed her face tight. "Yes."

"Let's find a vent in a room that isn't compromised."

Men's voices came from Level 3. Nathan and Opio stared down the hall.

Yemeni's men had a new plan.

60

Massimi stood before Magistrate Judge Stalwart's elevated dais on the courthouse's seventeenth floor. "We've lost a dear and trusted colleague, someone who's been with us since before my tenure began here. This is a difficult time for all of us."

Leila shifted on a hard wooden bench in back. The old court room didn't have hearings scheduled, so the Court Interpreter Services human resources team had borrowed it to discuss Khalil Mansour's passing. The room was packed with interpreters, stenographers, marshals, and others who'd worked with Khalil. No attorneys were in attendance because this was an official grief counseling session and an opportunity to ask questions and put rumors to bed. They could ask whatever they wanted, but the accident remained a hit-and-run with no suspects.

The head of the unit had addressed them before Massimi took over, and a psychologist specializing in workplace trauma waited in the wings. In group events like this, blowhards always had to say a few words, as if sitting quietly with their own thoughts somehow diminished their authority.

"... and that's the latest we have on the investigation," Massimi said.

Leila looked up. She hadn't been listening. Had he shared important information the police had divulged? She scanned the surrounding faces.

Everyone looked dour, more bored than sad, but a couple of women dabbed red eyes.

Massimi cleared his throat. "Allow me to introduce Dr. Frank Bishop. He'll say a few words about coping with grief, and then he'll make himself available if anyone wants to speak with him in private. Remember, our Employee Assistance Program provides services for people experiencing trauma."

Leila couldn't take any more of this. These people weren't victims—only Khalil. And her. Monsters targeted her family, and no EAP program or psychologist could save her.

She shuffled down the row, excusing herself. Massimi looked up and scowled at her. But she didn't care. What more could they do to her? Maybe she'd get lucky and he'd fire her and end her involvement in the case that had ruined her life.

Fear jolted her.

If he terminated her, would Yemeni's men, or whoever orchestrated this, assume she'd informed police? Or would they just kill her to eliminate a potential problem? They'd thrown away Khalil's life at the drop of a hat, so they didn't value hers either. It was possible Khalil's death could have come at the hands of a random drunk driver, but that was too coincidental to believe—no matter how hard she wanted it to be true.

Allah help me.

What a horrible thought she'd had by wishing for an accident instead of a murder. Whatever the cause of death, the only person who'd offered to help her was dead.

Her tears were coming any second. She pushed through the doors and beelined toward the restroom, searching for privacy.

A man in a black suit approached her. As he strode across the marble floor, his jacket opened, displaying an NYPD detective's shield. She angled away from him, but he adjusted and intercepted her. He blocked her path.

"Miss Kabiri?"

She nodded, not trusting her voice. She teetered on the brink of hysteria and didn't want anyone to see. Just a week ago, she'd been so confident, so strong.

"How's everyone doing in there?" he asked.

"Fine, thank you." Why was this man she'd never seen before talking to her as if they were old friends? She stiffened.

"I'm very sorry to hear about Mr. Mansour."

More empty platitudes. She'd had enough of people pretending they cared about Khalil. They hadn't known the man, and with a few exceptions, their comforting words were more virtue signaling than genuine concern.

"Thank you. It's horrible." She clenched her teeth to hold her tears back.

"I know you two were close."

"It's a loss for—"

Her chest hollowed, and her heart disappeared into the chasm. How had this man—someone who didn't work in her unit—know she and Khalil had been close? Did he assume because they'd worked together they had been friends? Or did he know about the secret conversations she'd had with Khalil?

"Something wrong?" he asked.

"This is hard," she said, straining to keep suspicion off her face, "for everyone who worked with Khalil."

The compassion disappeared from his face. "What do you think happened to him?"

"I need to go to the restroom."

"Was it really an accident?"

"Excuse me." She sidestepped around him.

"Wait." He grasped her bicep, and his fingers pressed into her flesh.

"Don't touch me."

"Sudden death can be just that. Sudden. It comes without warning."

She glanced around the vacant lobby, but everyone was inside the EAP session. An icy fear crept into her.

"What are you saying?" she asked.

"I need you to understand."

"Stop talking in riddles."

"The tiniest decisions can have devastating consequences."

Fear hardened inside her and turned to anger. She yanked her arm out of his grip. "Meaning what?"

"Be careful or suffer the same fate." His fake smile returned. He pivoted and walked away.

She watched him go, and her panic returned with a vengeance.

61

Nathan and Opio slipped out of the decontamination room and hurried in the opposite direction from the access door where at least one terrorist watched and waited. The U-shaped corridor looped back around to the command center, so they had to find vent access soon.

Opio stopped when they were out of sight. "Let's shed our suits here."

Terror sliced through Nathan's chest. "We're still in Level 4."

"We'll never access the vents wearing hazmat suits, and even if we could, we'd shred them on the metal."

"But the virus . . ."

"Should be contained inside lab three."

Opio unsnapped her mask and lifted it off her head. Her face drew tight with tension. Nathan watched her, unable to follow. Was he waiting for her to collapse from an invisible enemy invading her body? Even if they'd been infected, they wouldn't exhibit symptoms for days. He grabbed the zipper beneath his chin. He'd done many things that scared him. Trepidation wasn't a weakness but a natural emotion and an evolutionary defense mechanism to preserve life. Courage was the ability to overcome fearfulness and act anyhow.

Nathan unzipped his suit and undressed.

They left their hazmat suits in a pile on the floor.

"Shouldn't we hide these?" Nathan asked.

"What's the point? They know we're here."

She was right. They had little chance of escaping before the jihadists swarmed through the lab, found them, and killed them. Their odds of survival couldn't be higher than twenty percent. But beating the odds was how Nathan had won so many cases. It's why he remained alive.

"In here," Opio said.

She stopped outside double doors with a keypad. She unlocked it and opened the doors, revealing a supply room. Shelves lined the walls, and two standing shelves filled with electronics divided the room in half.

She entered and pointed to a two-by-two vent opening in the wall. The cover was flush against the ceiling. Tiny red ribbons on the grate fluttered in the flowing air. Opio moved to an instrument panel on the wall beneath it and opened its plastic cover. A light on the panel glowed green. She typed her code into the keypad and hovered her finger over a red button.

She faced him. "If I deactivate this, the air pressure in this room goes to zero and anything inside can escape.

"Do it," Nathan said.

She pressed the stop button. A message asked for confirmation. She clenched her jaw and tapped it. The whispering hiss of air flowing through the vents disappeared, and the red strips succumbed to gravity. Now, the room's air could seep back through the vents to the HEPA filters.

Nathan moved to a plastic cargo box beside the wall and dragged it beneath the vent. He climbed onto it and inspected the vent. Screws affixed the cover. He dug out his penknife and inserted the blade onto the screw's drive slot. He twisted it, and the blade bent. The screws hadn't moved in ages. The closed ventilation system was meant to contain toxins, not act as an emergency exit.

He repositioned the blade and twisted harder. The screw turned. He loosened it and removed it with his fingers.

"I hear something in the hall," Opio said.

He glanced at the door. They had little time. He returned to the vent and took out the remaining screws. He stuck his fingers in between the louvers and tugged. The cover came off with a puff of dust.

He peered into the dark space. Light from the room leaked in and illuminated stainless steel that appeared sturdier than residential ductwork—but would it hold their weight?

Terrorists' voices echoed down the hall. They'd reentered Level 4 to search for them.

Nathan inspected the vent. Was this even possible?

"I'll climb in and help you up," he said. "Bring the cover and replace it behind you so it's not obvious where we went. The vent won't stop bullets."

"They'll see the cargo box."

"Let's hope they don't put it together. It won't matter if they bust in while we're dangling on the wall."

He grabbed the vent's lip and braced his feet against the wall like a rock climber. He had to enter feet-first so he could reach back and pull her up. The vent was too high for her to do it alone. He ascended the wall, then pushed off and fired his legs through the opening. His back slammed on the vent, and the noise echoed through the system.

The terrorists must've heard.

Nathan shimmied his butt on the metal and wiggled into the space. He hunched his shoulders and squeezed through the tiny opening.

He looked out at Opio. "Give me your hand."

She picked up the cover, then extended her arm. He grabbed her wrist. He tucked his knees beneath him, then coiled his body and pulled hard. Her sinewy body was muscular and strong, and she easily climbed to the vent.

"Hold on," he said. He rotated onto his side to give her room. "Climb in."

She squeezed beside him, and he took the cover from her.

"Move forward," he said. "Give me room."

She crawled forward and slithered by him. Her feet cleared the opening, and Nathan emplaced the cover. He couldn't screw it in from the inside, so he tugged it into the groove and prayed it would hold. He released it.

The cover didn't fall.

"Keep going and find the outside intake. Don't jostle the vent. If the cover falls, or we make too much noise, you know what will happen."

She crawled, and the vent amplified every tiny thump. He faced forward, without room to turn around, exposing the flaw in his plan. He'd need to crawl backward. At least she knew the system better than him. Everything in the lab was as alien to him as a space station.

He crept backward on his elbows and knees. The vent shifted and creaked, and he stopped.

"Coming?" she asked.

"Don't wait for me. I'll move slower, and you'll need time to remove the HEPA filter."

"If I can."

He should've brought tools. The urgency to escape hadn't allowed him time to think through their haphazard plan, and they couldn't go back.

62

The vent pinged and popped as Opio lead the way through the narrow vent. The metal shifted beneath Nathan as he slithered backward through the claustrophobic space. Sweat beaded his forehead, and his muscles ached. What if he got stuck and couldn't escape? He dismissed the endless loop of nightmare scenarios playing in his mind. Being trapped inside a stuffy ventilation system would be horrific, but making noise would invite a barrage of bullets. He tightened his core and bowed his head to avoid banging into the shaft.

Opio's sounds faded as she pulled farther away from him. His shoulders brushed the ductwork, and he stopped. Staying rigid took all his energy.

Something light and silky ran across his ear, and he flinched. A spider-web. A chill traveled down his spine. He didn't have arachnophobia, but spiders creeped him out, especially ones he couldn't see. Jungle spiders could be huge. And venomous. He tucked his shoulders around his ears and continued.

Opio's sounds stopped.

She must've reached the filter system. Or a dead end. If the vent led nowhere, they'd be doomed. But the air intake must connect to the exterior. If each room had an independent system to avoid cross contamination, as Opio had stated, then they'd only encounter one set of filter braces in the double box system. But what if the assemblies were too narrow to traverse? Or what if they couldn't remove the filters? The list of potentially insurmountable problems grew.

But the die was cast. They'd either escape or die. Worrying wouldn't increase their chances of survival.

"Got it off," Opio said.

Nathan slipped his phone out of his pocket and illuminated its light. He peeked under his arm at her. She eased a wire-coated blue filament out of its metal frame.

He smiled. "It wasn't locked—"

"Sh." Opio pointed at a trapdoor in the duct, which maintenance must use to replace the filter.

"Keep going."

She moved the filter aside and crawled forward.

Nathan shuffled back and banged his knee on the frame. He grunted and bit his lip to keep from crying out. He wanted to loose a string of expletives. The danger and ridiculousness of their situation made him angrier by the second.

More noise from below. Had Yemeni's men heard them? Did they suspect they'd entered the ventilation system? Speculating wouldn't help.

"There's an intersection," she said.

"What?"

"A cross shaft," she said. "Left or right?"

Nathan envisioned the building's layout. The corridor for Level 4 had started east and then turned north. Then followed the vent back east. Which would mean turning right here—her right, not his—would send them back to the south and the front of the building. He hoped for an exit out the back, but anything beat charbroiling in the rapidly heating system.

"Turn left."

It was a hunch, but there would be more armed radicals out front. At least he'd eliminated three terrorists out back. Yemeni had planned a rapid in-and-out strike to seize Ebola or Marburg, but he hadn't counted on two FBI agents waiting for them, or a stubborn counterterrorism officer who didn't object to dying if he could take out a few with him. Yemeni couldn't have anticipated the resistance.

Opio shuffled around a corner. He reached the intersection and used it to turn around. She moved ten yards ahead. Her scrawny body was all bone and muscle, like a jungle cat. Nathan bumbled through the filter cowling after her. He moved faster facing forward.

Things were looking up. The most serious diseases had been incinerated, and they were still alive, though it must be over one hundred degrees in the vent. His shoulders brushed against the sides as he moved, and the tight confines darkened the edges of his vision. The shaft could've been miles underground, with no sunlight, no way out—except forward. He dismissed the thought and swallowed his growing fear. He willed his pulse to slow. They must be close.

Ahead, Opio stopped and glanced back. She gestured with her chin at another shaft on her left. The ducts were a maze of twisting metal.

"Keep going straight."

"You sure?" she asked.

"No."

She frowned and continued.

He clicked off his flashlight. What if his battery died, and they were stuck in the dark? Terror fluttered through his chest like water rippling over rocks. He forced himself to go slow and stay silent. He turned the corner.

Opio waited beside a filter system.

She tugged a wire-framed filter out of its metal frame. She pushed it to the side. Beyond her, razor-thin lines of gold streaked through metal slats.

Sunlight.

Light sliced through the minuscule cracks between closed louvers. She looked back and smiled. Their way out.

But what waited for them outside?

63

Opio rolled onto her side and dug at the exterior vent cover's louvers with her fingertips. She looked back with frustration plastered on her face. "It won't open."

"Let me try."

She backed up and wedged herself against the shaft. He squeezed past and clambered over the metal filter track that cut into his skin. He grimaced as he inspected the frame. He pried back the rubber seal from the edge and exposed its bolts, held in by eight hexagonal nuts. The screws had been inserted from outside. He grabbed a nut and twisted. Too tight.

He grabbed his knife, but kept it folded. He pressed its spine against a nut and bore down, a difficult maneuver from his awkward position. The nut turned. He repeated the process, and it loosened, which meant the screw didn't turn. The high humidity and rainfall had probably rusted it. He spun the nut, and brown flakes of oxidized iron fell off. He set the nut on the vent.

One down.

He worked the next screw. This would take time. The vent warmed with every passing minute, and the lack of airflow didn't help. He jolted. Would the terrorists notice the lack of sound coming from the vents, or would the humming laboratory equipment create enough background noise?

Perspiration soaked through his scrubs as he attacked the next nut. The longer they remained trapped, the greater the chance of discovery. He couldn't slow or they'd die. He lost himself in the unscrewing, oblivious to his surroundings, something he'd only do in the bowels of a ventilation system. Nathan's fingers ached from unscrewing nuts, and rusted screws rubbed his skin raw. He freed the last nut and spun it off. He caught it to avoid it clanking on the vent. Any sound could cause their demise.

He shook his hand to return blood flow and regain feeling, then he lowered his head to ease his stiff neck. He peered over his shoulder. Opio's phone illuminated her face as she regarded him. What had they done before cell phones? Technology was both a blessing and a curse.

"Almost done," he whispered. "I need to pop out the screws."

"How long?" Her voice sounded raspy, on the verge of panic. Being confined in a dark tunnel had worn her edges raw too.

"Two minutes."

He focused on the grate. He needed to push the screws out. If any of Yemeni's men were standing nearby, they might hear them land. It wouldn't take a genius to understand what the pile of screws below an air duct meant. Nathan was unarmed, and he'd be exposed dangling out of the vent. Once he hit the ground, he could fight. Best case, he'd drop unnoticed and escape with the girls, but realistic planning didn't involve best-case scenarios.

He must protect Opio too. He was the sheepdog, and she needed him. She'd kept him safe in the lab, where he'd been as lost as a toddler, but fighting Islamists was in his wheelhouse, and despite being outnumbered, his experience and skill would give them a chance. He'd choose terrorists over Marburg every time.

The thought of the deadly virus cooled him to his core. What if he'd been exposed? What if he hadn't cleaned his suit enough or decontaminated the bag and all its nooks and crannies, or there'd been a rip in the suit itself or . . . the possibilities were endless. When dealing with deadly viruses, the room for error was close to zero.

Could've been a lawyer.

Nathan turned a rusted screw with his fingers, and the metal cut into him. He pulled up his shirt and gnawed a tiny hole in the fabric. He ripped off a piece of cotton and wrapped the sweaty material around the metal.

He poked the screw, and it fell out through the hole. He listened but heard nothing. He pushed open a louver, and light streamed in. A flash of terror passed through him like an animal exposed in the wild, but unless somebody watched the vent, they wouldn't notice the movement.

Nathan pressed his face against the louver and flinched. It had heated from the sun and would leave a mark on his cheek. He peeked out. The sanctuary gate remained open, and the men he'd killed lay nearby, but no roving groups of terrorists looking for blood.

No sense waiting. Their situation could only deteriorate. This was their chance. He pushed another screw out, and more light streamed in. No one shot at them.

Keep going.

He continued to the next screw and then the next. He removed them all, then reached under the louvers and eased off the vent cover. It moved, then stopped with a clunk. He didn't breathe.

No response.

He pushed harder, but something held the cover in place. Why hadn't he realized they'd lock it to prevent anyone with a wrench from accessing it.

What to do?

To break it open, he'd need leverage. "Come closer."

She crawled behind him until he smelled her perspiration. "What's happening?"

"Brace yourself. I'm gonna push off you."

"It's nice to know twenty years of advanced education make me useful."

Something banged behind and below them. Terrorists searched inside for them. If they heard Opio and Nathan inside the duct, they'd fire—unless they understood the danger of shooting inside a lab filled with deadly pathogens. Filling the air with lead wouldn't end well for anyone.

Nathan bent his knees and placed his soles on her shoulder and hip, the most stable parts of her body. She held the sides of the duct.

"Get ready."

He pushed off and lunged at the vent. He swung his elbow into the corner of the cover, which should house the locking mechanism. A sharp snap echoed, and the cover bent outward. The shaft filled with sunlight. The time for stealth had ended.

Nathan shoved the cover out of the way, and it dangled by a strand of ripped metal. He crawled forward and poked his head through the opening. The sun's glare pierced his eyes, and he squinted. He scanned the field. No terrorists other than those he'd killed.

The Islamists may have heard him as the sound traveled through the ventilation system. The insurgents could fill the shaft with bullets or race outside at any moment.

Nathan crawled halfway out of the shaft—vulnerable. He should be facing backward, but he hadn't anticipated this. Luckily, the ground was only fifteen feet below. He clung to the lip of the shaft and wriggled forward. He had no option but to drop to the ground. If the fall didn't injure him, he'd help Opio out.

He teetered on the edge, steadying himself. He pushed off and his upper body launched out. His legs cleared the duct, and he shifted his weight midair. He squeezed the cowling but couldn't hold on. He fell.

This will hurt.

The ground came at him fast. Nathan contracted his muscles and shifted his legs beneath him—but there wasn't time.

He landed hard.

His knee impacted, then his hip. He threw his weight forward and rolled. His elbow dug into the dirt, and pain shot through his injured shoulder. He pinwheeled twice and stopped.

Red haze filled his vision, and he ground his teeth against the sting. The impact took his breath away. Everything hurt. He waited for the pangs to subside and any injury to show itself. His knee and elbow throbbed, and the shoulder, where he'd taken the bullet years ago, burned as if someone had plunged in a scalpel. He blinked and shook his head. He scanned the yard. No crazy jihadis charged him.

His luck had been awful, and he needed a break.

"Are you hurt?" Opio called from above.

He looked up. She gripped the shaft and peeked out over her knuckles. She seemed concerned.

"Nothing's broken."

"Help me down."

"I need a tactical pause," Nathan said. His body throbbed. Even his ribs ached where he'd twisted. He didn't recover like he had a few years before, and injuries lasted longer.

He surveyed the doors and windows. No sign of his adversaries. He looked past the corpses of the men he killed. More could come running at any second, but right now he was clear.

Get up.

He lumbered up, and bolts of lightning fired through him. This one would take time to shake off. He looked up. "Hang on to the side and swing your legs out. Try to hold on."

"What if I fall?"

"I'll catch you."

"Can you?"

Good question. "I'll break your fall. That much I can promise. Hurry, we won't be alone for long."

She climbed out, and when her feet broke free, she held on. Her arms quivered.

"Drop. I got you."

She let go. He caught her thighs and back, taking on her dead weight. She knocked him backward, and waves of torment crashed over his body. He stumbled but didn't fall. He set her down.

Gratitude flashed in her eyes. Then something else. Something uncertain. "Thank you."

"We've got to locate the girls and get out of here."

64

Nathan shuffled down the steps to the facility's basement with Opio behind him. The tight stairwell kept him in the threshold. He tapped his knuckles against the metal.

If Bridget had fled with the students, he could be announcing himself to terrorists, and that wouldn't go well. But Bridget wouldn't leave him . . . unless the girls had been in danger.

The door handle rattled. Nathan tensed. It cracked open. Nathan stared into the dark sliver leading into the basement. The door swung open and Bridget smiled at him.

"Took long enough," she said.

Nathan and Opio followed her inside. Behind Bridget, Lubega held his AK-47 up, ready to react. Good thing Nathan had knocked.

Opio brushed past Nathan and scanned the girls huddled against the walls. Most looked terrified, but a few had blank expressions—either resigned to their fate or in shock.

"Where's my daughter?" Opio asked.

Bridget scanned the fifteen girls. "She brought in those two, then left." Bridget gestured at the girls Nathan had found with Laker.

"Where is she?" Opio's vocal cords tightened.

"She's looking for you," the first girl said.

Opio grabbed her shoulders. "Where?"

"As soon as we arrived, she left to find you. Out the service door."

Tears filled Opio's eyes. "I must find her."

"Wait," Bridget said. "We've gotta gather everyone and bounce."

"But my daughter—"

"Yemeni's men are here for the viruses."

Opio hardened. "You don't know these men. If they find a pretty girl . . ." She closed her eyes. "They won't just kill her."

Bridget addressed Nathan. "We gotta book into the jungle and hole up until the QRF arrives."

"No," Lubega shouted. Fear had crept into his voice. "The animals stay close, for the carcasses."

"Why would you dump carcasses near your lab?"

"Feeding the predators means we don't go far to trap them."

"Wonderful," Nathan said. "Islamists are searching the building, and they'll be down here any minute."

"I'm not leaving without Laker," Opio said.

Nathan sighed. He couldn't abandon her either.

"You've got that look again," Bridget said.

"I'm going back in," he said.

Bridget gawked. "That's insane. Let's take the girls and skedaddle. I'll take my chances with those animals. Last I checked, lions don't carry AK-47s."

"We're missing Laker," Nathan said. "The virus broke containment in the lab, and crazed Islamists are looking for revenge. I can't leave her inside."

"If we don't extract these girls, they're all gonna die."

"Take them down to the lake and hide," Nathan said. "I'll find her."

"They'll kill you."

"Maybe, but I won't run away and leave her. I can't."

Nobility resided inside the impossible, and terrorists were an enemy Nathan could fight.

The ranger handed him his revolver. Nathan opened the cylinder. Six

.38-caliber rounds. A handgun against carbines wasn't a good matchup. He needed to rely on stealth.

He headed for the service door.

65

Nathan slunk into a dusky hallway with a charcoal-colored concrete floor and scuffed walls. Returning inside bordered on suicidal, but he couldn't leave an innocent girl to suffer the predations of radical Islamic terrorists, especially men raging after he'd denied them their prize. God knew what they'd do to her. At least six terrorists remained. He'd check the basement and then sneak upstairs and search. If he couldn't get through, well, that would be it, but maybe he'd get lucky. He had little chance of finding Laker and getting her out—but he had to try.

Doors lined the hall, and he cracked open the first. Boxes of supplies filled shelves. He proceeded to another room. Maintenance equipment and discarded scientific devices had been haphazardly strewn around the space. A junk room. He checked two more rooms, then stopped at a stairwell beside the elevator. Searching the lab while terrorists hunted them was crazy, and taking a noisy elevator would serve himself up on a platter.

He placed his boot on the first step and ascended, staying in contact with the wall. The stairwell turned forty-five degrees at a landing, and he surveyed the next flight. It emptied into a hallway in the back of the facility, away from where the terrorists had entered.

But they could be anywhere.

He crept up and stopped at the top to listen. Muffled voices in the distance. A door slammed. Yemeni's men searched offices. They must know a counterterrorist response was imminent. Or did they? Cell service didn't work, and they'd cut the telephone lines. Maybe they assumed they had time.

What would Yemeni be thinking? He'd planned this mission to be a quick hit, and their distance from Kampala meant local police probably didn't have many assets. Yemeni had expected to grab the samples and flee, which was why they just murdered the guards. Had Mugisha been on their payroll, or was he a believer? With the chief of security in their pocket, they'd known every inch of this facility. The wild cards had been Nathan, Bridget, and Odongo. Yemeni couldn't have predicted that. They'd tracked him from Europe, but Yemeni couldn't have expected the rapid success from Odongo's enhanced interrogation techniques. If Yemeni's man hadn't broken so quickly, it would've taken days or weeks to discover Yemeni's plan. If ever.

Nathan leaned into the hallway and quick-peeked left and then right. Empty. Administrative offices lined the corridor—a good hiding place while the jihadists focused on the labs—but Yemeni would want to exact revenge on everyone who resisted.

Nathan tiptoed to the first office and looked through its narrow window into the dark. He snuck into a classroom with rows of lecture chairs. A closet door was ajar in the back. Could he be lucky enough to find her in the first place he checked?

He whisked between chairs, careful not to bang into them, because any sound would bring a lethal response. He reached the closet and yanked it open. If anyone hid inside, it would be a frightened thirteen-year-old girl.

The closet was stacked with boxes and books. No Laker.

"Dammit."

The danger and futility of his search sank into his belly. Was it ego or overconfidence that drove him to take risks, or something else? He risked his life, but he did it for a child, and that meant something.

He exited the closet and stopped.

Opio stood in the doorway. She wore an odd expression.

"What are you doing here?" Nathan asked. "It's not safe for you to be—"

Opio pointed at Nathan. "That's him."

She stepped aside, and two men with ISIS headbands stepped into the room. They aimed AK-47s at him.

Nathan froze. His revolver was in his waistband, but they'd slaughter him before he could draw it.

She'd betrayed him. Had they captured everyone in the basement, or had she been working with them all along?

"What's happening?" he asked.

"I'm sorry," Opio said.

A wave of vertigo washed over him. "You're one of them."

"I did what I had to do."

One man shouted something in Swahili, and both approached with their guns pointed at his chest.

Nathan glanced at the single window across the room where sun filtered through a mesh screen. Maybe he could jump through . . . No, he'd never make it.

He had nowhere to run.

66

Opio left the classroom while ISIS members bound Nathan to a chair. One terrorist guarded the door while another tightened the ropes that bound Nathan's wrists. Nathan arched against the backrest in pain. An older man entered the room and approached. He wore black fatigues and an ISIS headband like the others, but he had graying hair, hollowed cheeks, and his tunic hung on him like a tent.

He stopped before Nathan and unslung his carbine. He laid it on the desk with the muzzle pointing at Nathan. The man's movements were precise, as if he gave great thought to everything before he did it, which meant he intended the carbine's position to intimidate Nathan.

He slipped the leather satchel off his other shoulder and set it beside his AK-47. It clinked on the hard surface, signaling it contained something metal. He unclipped its leather straps and flopped open the trifold bag.

Shiny steel instruments filled the satchel. Not good.

At least they hadn't shot him yet. He still breathed air, an unexpected outcome, but what happened next wouldn't be pleasant.

"What do you want?" Nathan asked.

The old man smiled a toothy grin and continued unwrapping the satchel. He removed metal pliers and set them on the table's surface. He withdrew a rusty blade and placed it beside the pliers. He added a dental pick and scalpel to his collection.

Shit.

Nathan glanced at the window. If he could break free from the rope and take out the nearest terrorist, then he could throw a chair through the glass and dive out.

He sighed.

Impossible. The guards would mow him down the second he resisted. These men would torture him, and he couldn't physically resist.

But his mind still functioned—his most powerful weapon.

"I need to talk to Yemeni," he said.

The closest guard's eyes widened, and he took a half step back. He might not speak English, but he'd understood Yemeni's name.

"Tell Yemeni I'm here," Nathan said with more confidence.

They exchanged looks. These men were killers, savages following an ideology that sought death, but Yemeni's name struck fear in them.

"If you kill me, Yemeni will make you pay for it. I have information he needs."

They stared at him. Did they understand his words?

"Yemeni," Nathan said. He enunciated to eliminate confusion. "I want to talk to Ye-men-i." He repeated the name like a hostage negotiator building rapport. "Yemeni wants me alive. He—"

"I want no such thing," Yemeni said from the doorway.

Nathan's world crashed down around him. Yemeni was there, and Nathan's ruse collapsed.

Yemeni strode into the room. "Agent Burke, how nice to meet you face-to-face."

"We'll see each other again. In court."

"Ah, that eternal American optimism. You don't find that in Africa. You've been a thorn in my side for too long."

"It's over," Nathan said. "You didn't acquire the viruses, which means your plans are finished."

"What have you done with my specimens?"

That jolted Nathan. Yemeni didn't know he'd incinerated the deadly viruses. If he thought Nathan had hidden them, he'd need Nathan alive to find them.

Yemeni stormed across the room, his façade of civility gone. "Where is the Marburg?"

Nathan needed to stall. If he admitted he'd destroyed the viruses, they'd have no reason to keep him alive. And worse, he'd give Yemeni more motivation to make Nathan suffer before his death.

"The samples are safe."

"We can play this little game as long as you'd like," Yemeni said. "But in the end, you will tell me everything you know. In fact, you will beg me to allow you to speak. You'll do anything to make your agony stop."

Nathan's stomach hardened into dry clay. He wanted to vomit, but he couldn't show weakness. Yemeni didn't know Odongo had planned an ambush to arrest him, and when Odongo went radio silent, his men would come to investigate. Yemeni would assume he had time, but the QRF could arrive at any moment—if they were coming at all.

Nathan had to stall. Every second they spoke was time Yemeni's men wouldn't inflict pain, and each passing minute increased the chance of rescue. Unfortunately, if the counterterrorism SWAT team stormed the building, the first thing Yemeni would do would be to put a bullet in Nathan's head—but that was preferable to being dissected like a lab rat.

Nathan had learned one thing from all the tight spots he'd been in. Never give up.

"I asked you a question," Yemeni said. "Where did you hide my jinn?"

"Your what?"

"My invisible demons."

"Tell me why you want Marburg."

"You know why."

"How does murdering innocent civilians help you? You're destroying countless lives."

"You're not in a position to question my motivation."

"You've been thorough, from your brilliant escape to this assault. I thought you'd be proud of what you've accomplished."

A thin smile cracked Yemeni's face. "I do Allah's bidding."

"Your God wants you to slaughter thousands of men, women, and children? People who have done nothing to harm you?" Nathan pushed his torturer, not a great idea, but he needed to keep him talking.

Yemeni snorted, and his face hardened. "Nothing to harm me? Your people have oppressed Muslims across the world. You protect Jews and blaspheme Allah with your words and deeds."

Alarm bells went off in Nathan's head. Yemeni's anger focused on Americans, which suggested he didn't plan to spread deadly diseases in Africa. Nathan needed more information if he planned to stop the attack—assuming he lived longer than ten minutes.

"You're targeting Americans?" Nathan asked. "How do you plan to get Ebola and Marburg into the United States?"

Yemeni's eyes narrowed. Could he tell Nathan hadn't asked out of morbid curiosity but because he'd intended to ruin Yemeni's plans? That implied Nathan's belief he could escape, which would make Yemeni question what gave Nathan hope. Nathan could see Yemeni's wheels turning. Was he examining his plan to see what he'd missed? The man was smart. And lethal. A worthy adversary.

"Enough talk," Yemeni said. "It's time for you to give me my prize."

"But you haven't explained—"

"Stop." He looked at the old man standing over his implements. "Cause him torment."

67

Yemeni's eyes glistened with expectation as he stared at the old Islamist standing before him. The man grabbed the desk by its edges and dragged it closer. Its metal legs screeched against the tile like fingernails down a chalkboard. He stopped just out of Nathan's reach—not that Nathan could resist with his hands tied behind him.

The old man hefted a metal implement with a curved blade and serrated edge that looked like a raptor tooth. Were these devices used to dissect animals in the lab, or was this man a professional interrogator who'd brought them from home?

Nathan's pulse quickened, and his breathing grew shallow and rapid. He stared at the surgical blades. This was bad.

The man turned the blade, letting the light reflect off it. He flashed a toothy grin. Nathan fixated on a grain of rice stuck in a space where the man's canine had been pulled.

Fear grew inside Nathan, as if his internal organs wanted to jump up and run out of his body. He forced a deep breath to calm himself.

The man came around the desk. His breath smelled of garlic.

Nathan swallowed hard.

His interrogator twirled the implement between his fingers, then held the blade close to Nathan's face. This old bastard wasn't just seeking information—he enjoyed hurting people. He'd have been a serial killer if this radical Islamic group hadn't put his talents to good use. How many sociopaths were drawn to radical Islam? Al-Qaeda, ISIS, and the Phantoms had become boy's clubs for the criminally insane.

"What did you do with my toxins?" Yemeni asked.

Yemeni's voice surprised Nathan. He'd been so fixated on the blade, he'd almost forgotten Yemeni was there.

Nathan couldn't admit that he'd destroyed the specimens, or Yemeni would have no use for him. "We concealed them where they can't be found."

"Nothing hides forever. You also have a finite amount of time on earth."

Yemeni said that to frighten him—an old interrogator's trick. Fear would dump adrenaline into Nathan's system and make his emotions override his reason—a condition known as going into the black. Yemeni and the interrogator sought to terrify Nathan and activate his primitive lizard brain. Inflict enough pain, and Nathan's primal defenses would do anything to stop it. Evolution had made survival the ultimate goal—yet some things were worth dying for.

"Fuck you," Nathan said.

Yemeni smiled. His interrogator did too. They weren't buying Nathan's false bravado. He was scared, and they knew it. Any human would be petrified at the thought of dismemberment.

"Show Special Agent Burke I'm serious."

The old man stepped between Nathan's legs. Nathan jerked reflexively to block him, but ropes fastened his legs to the chair.

The man grinned wider at Nathan's futile effort. He spread his feet and pressed his knees into Nathan's thighs to keep his legs wide. Things deteriorated fast.

The old man twirled the long handle of the curved scalpel between his fingers, facing the blade down.

"Hurting me won't—"

The old man punched down in a lightning-fast motion without warning or preamble. The blade pierced Nathan's thigh.

Nathan cried out, unable to contain it, then he gritted his teeth and bore down until he muffled his agony into a low groan. He'd take the pain, but he wouldn't give them the satisfaction of hearing it.

The blade punctured all three levels of skin but didn't go deep, and it lacerated the front of his leg, which wasn't the worst place, because his femoral artery ran close to the surface on the interior where even a nick could bleed him out and bring rapid death. Maybe he should hope for that.

No, he'd never stop fighting.

The old man leaned in and sniffed, as if craving the alkaline scent of fear. He scraped the tip of the scalpel down Nathan's thigh toward his knee. The steel burned hot as it severed nerve bundles, and the skin snapped apart. He opened a four-inch gash. Warm blood gushed out and trickled down Nathan's leg.

It hurt. God, it hurt.

And things would only get worse. Nathan grimaced.

"The location of the contagion," Yemeni said. His calm tone, as if getting sliced open in a jungle lab was normal, amplified Nathan's terror.

"If I tell you, you'll kill thousands of Americans."

"I'll make this simple," Yemeni said. "Tell me the location, and when I recover them, I'll free you."

He was talking, which was better than torture. *Tap, tap, tap.* Blood seeped out of Nathan's wound and dripped on the floor.

"What about the children and employees?" Nathan asked. "What will happen to them?"

"Nothing, if they don't interfere."

Yemeni lied. He wouldn't let anyone survive. What had Nathan been thinking? He'd destroyed the samples. Yemeni would kill him and then hunt down everyone there. He'd torture children in front of their chaperones, including Laker. Everyone would die in Yemeni's vain attempt to find his biological stew.

"Things are about to become uncomfortable for you," Yemeni said. "You should be more concerned about yourself."

"I'll take you to the Marburg," Nathan said. A glimmer of hope fluttered in his chest. If he could walk around with Yemeni, he might stall long enough for the police to arrive. Waiting for rescue—the hope of the damned.

"I will not play your games. Give me the location, and when my men recover it, I'll release you."

"It's in the jungle. I can't describe it, but I can show you." Maybe Bridget and Lubega could save him.

Yemeni shook his head. "This conversation is going nowhere. You don't understand who holds the scalpel. Let's see how you enjoy what comes next."

Nathan led a convoluted and complicated existence, but this pain—inflicted for a simple and singular reason—brought him back to the essence of life. This was what it meant to be human, fighting for survival, experiencing the breadth of emotion. Predictable and agonizing. Nathan walked the line between life and death, and one wrong move would send him into oblivion.

The interrogator reached down and unbuckled Nathan's pants with his grubby fingers. Days of grime had accumulated under his fingernails like little black strips. Strange how tiny details stood out in moments of great stress. He yanked Nathan's pants down and brought the blade close.

What a nightmare.

A gunshot shattered the silence.

68

Nathan, Yemeni, and his henchmen looked at the classroom door. Gunfire had come from outside. A single shot near the facility's entrance, then another. Had the QRF arrived to rescue them—or were Yemeni's men hunting children?

Yemeni shouted an order in Arabic. The guard grabbed Nathan's shoulder.

Was this the end? Would they kill him now? Yemeni still thought Nathan knew where the Marburg was hidden, and without him, they'd never find it. But if a counterterrorism team assaulted the building, Yemeni would try to escape, not search for viruses, and that would make Nathan's life worthless.

Yemeni glared at him. Was he thinking the same thing? He'd sacrificed much for this plan. Could he abandon it so close to the end?

"If you attempt escape," Yemeni said, "Ahmed will put a bullet in your brain."

Nathan didn't respond. What could he say?

Yemeni spun on his heels and raced out the door with the other two men in tow. Ahmed remained. He stepped back and pointed his AK-47 at Nathan. His intentions were clear.

A volley of gunfire came from outside, and someone held their trigger down and unleashed a barrage. That had to be the QRF. Local cops wouldn't last long, but if Odongo's men had arrived, Yemeni would be in for a world of hurt. Police training in Uganda was subpar compared to the West, but elite teams received the most, and in Central Africa, they had real-world experience. Counterterrorism agents would be out for blood.

Ahmed adjusted his AK-47. His eyes moved from the door to Nathan. The superior air he'd carried when Yemeni and his militants were there had dissipated. Ahmed looked uncertain. Not good. A nervous terrorist was an unpredictable one.

Nathan tried to appear disinterested, slackening his body as he clawed at the rope behind him. They shouldn't have used rope, because natural fibers stretched, and he only needed an inch to free his hand. He strained against the hemp, trying not to move his torso. If Ahmed caught him, he'd smack Nathan in the face with the butt of his carbine.

Or shoot him.

Nathan jammed his thumb between the rope's coils and squeezed the fiber. A little more space and he'd shimmy his hand back and forth until it broke free. Of course, his legs remained bound, and Ahmed pointed an AK-47 at his chest. But other than that, escape would be easy.

More firearms discharged outside, this time, from both the front and side of the facility. The din of combat echoed off the building and jungle, making it impossible to discern what was happening.

If Yemeni returned, would he take Nathan hostage or kill him? Neither scenario would end well.

Ahmed looked out the back window. He'd conclude the same thing—a police assault. Would he wait for Yemeni, or would he flee while he had the chance? Jihadist's ideology trumped self-interest, and Ahmed appeared to fear a powerful and deadly leader like Yemeni. Ahmed would stay and battle the police to the bitter end—but he'd kill Nathan before they finished him.

Nathan must escape or die.

Ahmed crossed the room and peeked into the hall. He vibrated with tension. The guy was spinning out fast. He turned and faced Nathan. He narrowed his eyes. He contemplated killing Nathan now.

Shit.

Ahmed charged across the room with his muzzle raised.

Nathan gazed down the muzzle. "Don't do it. If you shoot, they'll know you're in here."

Ahmed stopped. He flexed his hand on the carbine's grip. Did he understand English?

"Yemeni needs me alive," Nathan said. "I have the Marburg. Kill me, and your operation's finished. He'll murder you."

Ahmed glanced at the exit. If Nathan could only get free of these ropes, maybe he could grab the muzzle. If he wrestled the AK from Ahmed's grip, he could shoot him and then free himself.

Ahmed ground his teeth, and his eyes darkened as if demons controlled his soul. He pointed the carbine at Nathan's face. The muzzle was within reach, but the rope restrained Nathan's hands.

Nathan struggled, desperate. His heart pounded in his temples. He wriggled his hands. The ropes loosened, but not enough. He needed more time. He wouldn't make it.

"The police will hear the gunshot," Nathan said.

Ahmed glanced back at the door. Then he set his AK-47 on the table beside the instruments. He lifted the curved blade, and the steel glinted in the light. An evil sneer cracked his face.

He grabbed Nathan's hair and pulled his head back, exposing Nathan's neck. Nathan struggled but couldn't break free. Ahmed turned the blade and positioned it over Nathan's carotid artery.

"Don't."

Ahmed jerked and straightened. He looked quizzically at Nathan, then his eyes dropped to his leg.

A dart with a cylindrical chamber protruded from his skin. Its feathers jiggled as fluid emptied into him. He touched the cylinder but couldn't grasp it. He wobbled on his feet.

Ahmed collapsed. His forehead smacked against the tile.

Nathan looked back at the doorway. Laker stood there holding a tranquilizer gun. Her eyes fixated on the man on the floor.

Relief washed over Nathan. "Untie me."

69

In Leila's dream, a faceless man hovered over her, glaring with hatred and murderous intent. Khalil stood behind him with tape binding his hands and covering his mouth. He stared helplessly, trying to communicate with his eyes. The man stepped closer and hovered over her, inches away.

She looked to Khalil for help, but he turned and banged his head against the wall.

Bang, bang, bang.

Blood appeared on his forehead. She tried to run, but her legs wouldn't move.

Bang, bang, bang.

The images disappeared in an instant, and she opened her eyes in bed. Her heart pounded with terror. What was that dream? What did it mean if Khalil—

Bang, bang, bang.

She bolted upright. That sound was real, not a figment from her nightmare. Across the room, Shirin's snoring stopped and then restarted.

Leila cocked her head, listening for the slightest sound, confirmation she'd rejoined the world and wasn't caught in a nether region between sleep and consciousness.

Bang, bang, bang.

That was real. Somebody knocked on their apartment door. She tapped her phone on her bedside to activate the screen. 3:05 a.m. Who would come this late? Her hands trembled.

She swung her legs out of bed and stood still for a moment, gaining her balance. She grabbed her nightgown off the bureau and slipped it over her underwear. She opened the bedroom door and crept into the hallway.

Why didn't she own a gun? Two women and a boy needed protection in a high-crime neighborhood. Maybe she'd marry again someday, but right now, she needed a weapon more than a husband.

She paused by the kitchen, then slipped across the tile floor on her tiptoes and snatched a butcher knife out of its wooden block. She raised it, and moonlight streaming through the window glistened off its blade.

What would you do with a knife?

She padded to the front door and looked through the peephole.

Two NYPD uniformed police officers stood in the hall. A sudden lightness swept through her. She took her first deep breath since waking, but the adrenaline that coursed through her veins kept her on edge.

An officer rapped his knuckles hard against the door.

She jerked back. Why had they come? Was this an immigration problem, or had someone else been killed?

"Who is it?"

"NYPD," an officer with a Spanish accent responded.

New York City had always been a melting pot, and NYPD represented the people they protected. Once NYPD had been almost entirely white, but now people of all ethnicities, religions, and colors filled its ranks.

"May I help you?"

"Yes, ma'am. Open the door, please. Police business."

Leila glanced down the hallway at the cubby where her son slept. Her mother's snoring emanated from the bedroom. She had to let them in. People didn't resist the police, especially immigrants hoping to be granted citizenship. Any arrest could foul her chances and get her family deported back to Iran.

Leila hurried down the hall and hid the knife under a magazine. No sense getting shot over a misunderstanding. She returned to the door and slid the chain out of its bracket. It dangled, and she clicked open the bolt.

She raked her fingers through her hair like a comb and checked to ensure her nightgown covered her.

Leila opened the door.

The first officer looked to be in his forties, with flecks of gray hair poking out beneath his cap. His name tag read Ramirez. The second officer, Blackwood, was younger with high cheekbones and dark circles under his eyes. Movement caught her eye. Two additional officers watched her. What would require four police officers to show up at her door unannounced?

"May we come in?" Ramirez asked with a gravelly voice.

Leila turned to let them in—Middle Eastern hospitality had been ingrained in her—but she hesitated. With her husband gone, only she protected her family from the outside world.

"What's this about, officer?"

"We have a report of a crime," Ramirez said with a tinge of annoyance.

"Everything's fine," Leila said. "We've been asleep for hours."

"Let's talk inside," Blackwood said.

"I don't see what—"

"We have a complaint about a kidnapping," Ramirez said, "and we're required to check the premises, whether or not you agree."

Leila couldn't help but smile as her tension floated away. They'd come to free a kidnap victim—a bogus report. She'd done nothing wrong, and she'd be back in bed laughing about this in ten minutes.

"I work for the court," she said, "and I assure you no one has been kidnapped. Come in and check, but please be quiet. My family's asleep."

She stepped back and let them in. The officers entered and surrounded her. One looked down the hallway and the other peeked into the kitchen. Ramirez focused on her. The young officer shut the door. Then his eyes moved down her body.

Leila grasped the open edges of her gown and pulled it tight.

"What's going on?" Leila asked with more confidence. She hadn't violated the law, yet they'd awakened her and invaded her privacy.

"You're Leila Kabiri?" Ramirez asked.

"I am."

"Who else is here?"

"My son's asleep in the alcove, and my mother's in bed. Please keep your voice down so you don't wake them."

Blackwood continued to ogle her body.

Ramirez smirked. "Turn around and put your hands behind your back." He ripped open a Velcro case and removed handcuffs.

Her fear returned. "I haven't done anything."

"This is for our safety."

"But I didn't do—"

Ramirez gripped her arm and spun her around.

"Please."

He pushed her against the wall and twisted her arm into the small of her back. He slapped on one handcuff, and cold steel dug into her skin.

"Hey."

He twisted her other arm behind her and snapped on the second cuff. The metal ratchets croaked like frogs as he tightened them.

"This is absurd," she said. "I'm an officer of the court. I work as an interpreter at the Southern District of—"

He grabbed a handful of hair and jerked her head back. He slapped thick packing tape over her mouth, like in her nightmare.

Alarm bells rang in her head. This wasn't NYPD procedure. Terror weakened her legs.

Ramirez slammed her into the wall. He turned to Blackwood. "Get the boy."

70

Muffled gunfire echoed outside as Nathan and Laker raced through the laboratory. He held her hand, not that she needed help. She moved better than him. The pain from his laceration radiated through his leg and thumped in his brain. Blood trickled down his leg, but the flow had lessened. He moved as fast as possible, without worrying about Yemeni's men who engaged the police out front.

This was their chance to escape.

They jogged past supply rooms and stopped outside the door where he'd left Bridget and the girls. He wouldn't burst in while a gunfight raged outside, because that would be an easy way to take friendly fire, and he'd come too far to lose Laker now. He rapped on the door to the tune of "Shave and a Haircut."

Two knocks came in response.

Nathan pushed the door open and led Laker inside. Relief washed over Bridget's face. Lubega peeked out the far door and covered the field out back.

"*Munnange*," Laker's friend yelled. She raced across the room and swept Laker into her arms.

"Where's Dr. Opio?" Bridget asked. "She went looking for Laker and didn't come back."

"She won't."

"Is she—"

Nathan glanced at Laker. "I'll explain later. They're fighting Odongo's QRF out front, and Yemeni will want the girls as hostages."

"Lubega spotted a terrorist out back a few minutes ago," Bridget said.

"We need to take him out."

Lubega faced them. "There is another way."

Nathan waited.

"We have boats. We can paddle into Lake Kwania."

"And go where?" Bridget asked.

"Wait for the police to retake the lab," Nathan said, "or paddle west and hike up to the road. Anywhere's better than here."

Bridget frowned. "But the insurgents—"

"We can escape through the mechanical room," Lubega said. "There's an exit behind the boilers."

"Let's go, girls," Bridget said. "Lubega will lead us outside. Everyone stay in single file and be quiet."

The girls looked up with bulging eyes and quivering lips. Except Laker. She had a firm resolve on her face, the same mixture of fear, shock, and determination that Amelia had shown years before when she'd saved Nathan. They all needed to pull it together if they hoped to live.

"Where's my mother?" Laker asked.

"She got away," Nathan said. He didn't elaborate.

Lubega led them into a room humming with equipment. The temperature had to be 130 degrees, and it stank like burning electrical wires. An HVAC rattled behind them as it pumped air-conditioning into the administrative spaces. Giant water tanks lined the wall. Lubega continued to the exit. He kept the muzzle of his AK-47 raised as he eased open the door. Sunlight streamed in.

He peeked out, then glanced back at Nathan. "We go."

They filed out, and Nathan brought up the rear to protect them. He limped from pain as they moved over open ground to the fence. Lubega led them down a sloping dirt path until Kwania Lake glistened before them.

Three tiny *mvule* fishing boats lay on the muddy bank with ropes tied to tree branches. Nathan led half the girls into one boat while Bridget escorted the rest into the other. The girls' shoes clunked on smooth hulls constructed from mahogany and mvule wood, and the sound echoed across the water.

"I can't swim," Bridget said.

"Neither can I," a young girl said with wide eyes.

"Then stay in the boat," Nathan said.

"But—"

"Hurry."

The girls stacked on the decks as Nathan untied the ropes. He climbed into the boat and snatched an oar off the deck, though it looked more like a stalk of celery than a traditional paddle, but it would have to do.

Bridget boarded the other boat and picked up an oar. Shouts came from the jungle behind them.

"Push off with the oar," Nathan said.

He dug the wooden paddle into the muck and leaned his weight against it. The bow spun around. The girls grasped the gunwale, their tiny knuckles whitening against the wood.

Nathan reached forward and plunged the thin paddle into the lake. He tightened his core, dug hard, and propelled them forward. The bow angled left, and he paddled on the opposite side. He'd canoed as a child, though these wider fishing boats sacrificed speed and dexterity for stability.

Bridget rowed too, but ineffectively. Her bow jerked left and right as she took tentative half strokes. She paddled too shallow and splashed the water.

"Two strokes on each side," Nathan said. "Reach farther forward and pull back until the paddle's behind you."

Her face reddened from exertion and frustration. Maybe embarrassment too. She took a longer stroke, and the boat rocked, causing the girls to hold the gunwale.

"Careful," Nathan shouted too loudly. Alerting pursuers wouldn't end well, but if Bridget capsized the boat, they'd have other problems. Deadly ones. Crocodiles, snakes, and other dangerous creatures populated African waters. Did they have piranha in Uganda? Worse, many of the girls couldn't swim, and mounting a rescue operation while terrorists took target practice wouldn't be easy.

He swallowed his fear and stopped paddling. He had to help Bridget.

"Aim for me," he yelled.

She looked up, sweat streaking her face. She rowed on one side, and then the other. Her boat rocked, and the girls clung on. One glanced back at her, clearly not confident in Bridget's skills as skipper.

"I know boats," the girl sitting in front of Bridget's boat said. They were still twenty yards away, but their voices carried across the glassy surface. The girl turned and stood. The boat wobbled, and she stiffened.

"You'll capsize us," Bridget said.

The girl crouched with her fingertips balancing against the gunwale, ready to grab it. She lowered herself back down.

"Give me the paddle," the girl said.

Bridget checked the lake's bank, then handed it forward. Water lapped against their hull. The girl leaned over and paddled. Three quick strokes, and then she contorted her body and paddled on the other side. The boat sped up. She turned the bow toward Nathan and closed on him. She stopped five yards away and glided toward him.

"Throw me the line," Nathan said.

The tiny girl at the very front looked confused.

Nathan pointed. "The rope attached to the bow."

She scrunched up her forehead and looked scared. The girl behind her pointed to the rope dangling from a cleat. The first girl grasped the rope, then looked at Nathan and raised her eyebrows.

"Toss it to me," Nathan said.

The girl with the paddle angled the bow closer to Nathan. The other girl coiled the slimy fiber in her hand, then hurled it across the water.

He caught it.

Nathan looked around. His cleat was in the bow, so where could he tie it off? Their pursuers would arrive soon, leaving no time to screw around. Nathan rose, dropped the wet rope beneath him, then sat on it.

"Hang on." He paddled hard and towed Bridget's boat behind him. They made progress, but not fast enough.

They took too long. Yemeni's men would figure out they'd headed to the water soon enough, and they couldn't hide on the lake. If—

On cue, the leaves rattled in the jungle, and two of Yemen's men burst through onto the muddy bank. One of them held a handgun, and the other slung an AK-47 over his shoulder. Were they fleeing from government troops or hunting Nathan and the girls?

The men shouted and pointed, and snippets of Arabic reached him. Had Yemeni imported jihadis from the Middle East?

Nathan pulled hard on his paddle. The girls looked past him to the shore, their eyes wide with terror, except the frail girl closest to him. Her eyes caught his attention. They were emotionless, resigned. Dead. This girl had seen bad things and optimism did not live inside her.

Nathan glanced back. The men raced down the slope to the lake. Bridget's boat swiveled back and forth behind him, jerking with epilepsy.

The jihadists climbed into the boat on shore and shoved off. The man in front pointed at him. Nathan looked across the lake. He hadn't even reached the middle.

They'd never make it.

71

Sweat soaked Nathan's shirt as he paddled. Bridget's boat tugged and jerked the rope beneath him, and every time she tacked, she slowed them. The jihadists in the last mvule gained on them. His efforts were futile, but he didn't dare stop and shoot it out. The chance of an innocent girl catching a stray bullet was too high.

He had to keep going.

The girl closest to him stared at the water. Her mouth dropped open, and she pointed. Nathan followed her finger where water bubbled thirty feet off the starboard side of the terrorist's boat. A gray mound broke the surface, and two eyes over a giant snout stared back.

A hippopotamus.

It looked like a bald cow straight from Disney casting, but as with Nathan, looks could be deceiving. Hippopotami were among the deadliest African killers. They swam like crocodiles, charged like elephants, and bit like great white sharks. Their massive jaws looked comical but were deadly.

The first terrorist aimed a handgun at the hippo. He held his handgun with unstable hands as he rocked with the boat's motion.

Crack.

The bullet splashed into the water a foot behind the hippo's head.

Crack, crack.

Two more shots hit the water in front of the hippo—though they might not be misses. Water slowed bullets, but they might find their mark.

The hippo aimed toward the pursuing terrorist and raised its head. Had a bullet pierced its thick skin? The handgun sounded like a 9mm, a round too small to kill a dangerous predator.

It submerged beneath the water.

A wake roiled the surface, as if an invisible boat traversed the lake, but this came from below. It bore down on the terrorist's craft. The ripples grew as the hippopotamus picked up speed.

Nathan paddled with a half stroke, unable to take his eyes off the impending confrontation. Two guns versus perhaps the most lethal creature in nature.

The man in the bow fired at the water, and bullets splashed into the wake. Didn't he realize the beast was closer to them?

The Islamist with the AK looked at Nathan. He was fifty yards away, a makeable shot with a carbine. If he fired, Nathan would shield the girls with his body. If they stayed low, the shooter wouldn't get a good angle on them.

The first shooter scanned the water. The wake had closed to fifteen yards. He'd run out of time but didn't realize it. These men weren't Africans and didn't understand the danger.

The hippopotamus burst through the surface ten feet away, like a breaching great white shark. The massive beast must have weighed five thousand pounds. How could it be so fast and agile? It opened its mouth wide enough to swallow a chair. Or a human. It looked at them before crashing back under the surface with a huge splash.

They hesitated, probably out of shock—a vital mistake. They opened fire after the hippo had disappeared beneath the roiled surface. Had they hit it or—

The hippo lunged out of the water, its eyes wild and mouth open. The hippo's jaw crashed down on the gunwale. Wood splintered with a loud crack that echoed across the water. The hippopotamus snapped its jaws inches from the men. The AK-47 fired with no discernible effect.

The boat flipped under the weight, like a child's toy, and ejected the men over the hippo and into the lake. They screamed and thrashed. The hippo disappeared beneath the overturned boat.

One terrorist swam toward the boat, kicking and splashing with fear and lack of technique. The man who'd fired the AK-47 couldn't swim. He thrashed in a panic, struggling to keep his head above the surface.

The first man clung to the overturned hull. He tried to climb onto it but didn't have the leverage.

Movement rippled the water behind the boat. The wake enlarged as the submerged hippopotamus gained speed. It headed for the boat.

The man clinging to the hull screamed and pointed at the wake.

The hippopotamus breached again, half fish, half animal, and all predator. It opened its eyes a foot away from him. He kicked and splashed at it.

The beast unclenched its jaws and snapped at him. An aquatic pit bull. He punched its nose in a pointless defense.

It lunged and engulfed him in its mouth. The hippo snapped its jaws shut, crushing him. He loosed a bloodcurdling scream. The hippo opened its mouth and bit him again, its long bony teeth piercing his flesh and penetrating organs. Cracking bones echoed over the water.

The hippo shook his head like a dog with a chew toy, then disappeared with the man beneath the surface. The water turned oily red.

The first man kicked and screamed as he tried to swim toward shore. He wouldn't make it.

Queasiness flipped Nathan's stomach and bile burned his throat. He watched the drowning man. The man's head bobbed above and then below the water as his movements grew more tired. He slipped beneath the surface and didn't return.

Nathan checked the girls. They sat still, without a peep as they stared at the capsized boat.

In the distance, the gunfire had reduced to an occasional pop. Odongo's men must have entered the laboratory.

Nathan leaned forward and pierced the water with his paddle. He headed back to shore.

The lake wasn't safe—not for anyone.

72

Nathan scanned the water as he towed Bridget back toward shore. That hippo was down there somewhere. Would it be less dangerous now that it had eaten, or would its taste of blood enhance its aggression? No point guessing. He didn't know shit about animals. They needed to get off the lake.

He paddled with all his strength, and the girl in Bridget's boat did too. Every time his paddle touched the water, dread flashed through him. Movies like *Jaws* had instilled a fear of the unknown in him, but this wasn't fiction. A massive beast swam somewhere below them. Or did hippos walk along the bottom?

His tension increased as they neared the shore. The closer they came to safety, the more he clung to life.

The bow of his mvule thunked against the muddy shore. Nathan grabbed the sides for balance, then stepped over the gunwale onto shore. He held it steady as the girls disembarked. He stepped into the shallows, careful not to submerge his laceration. The bleeding restarted with his motion. He surveyed the water for any sign of the hippo, then he dragged Bridget's boat onto land. The girls didn't need encouragement to jump out.

He watched the water as Lubega led the girls up the bank. Hippos were dangerous on land too. The girls reached the path and ascended toward the lab. Nathan hobbled after them.

A firearm popped inside the building. The QRF would struggle to defeat an entrenched adversary. Stuck between an aggressive hippo and desperate terrorists wasn't a safe place to loiter, but they couldn't enter the lab during a firefight.

Nathan caught up with Bridget and Lubega. "We should stay outside, but not in the open."

"Let's duck into the preserve and hole up," Bridget said.

Lubega grimaced. "Too dangerous."

"Every friggin option sucks," Bridget said.

"Let's conceal ourselves in there," Nathan said, "but stay near the fence."

"Not a good idea," Lubega said.

"Better than getting picked off out here," Nathan said. He inched around the corner. The backyard was clear of terrorists, which—

Bang.

Another gunshot from inside. Louder, closer.

"The fight's moving our way," Nathan said. "If they spot us, we're dead."

"Everyone run for the gate," Bridget said.

Nathan lurched forward, and the girls' muffled footsteps thumped behind him. The lack of a police perimeter indicated either a small QRF or strong resistance out front. If the police cleared the building room by room, the terrorists would focus inside, not out, but if any jihadists had second thoughts about martyrdom, they'd flee out back.

Nathan crept forward, alternating his attention between the facility and the uneven ground. Tripping and face-planting wouldn't help anyone. He closed on the fence, almost there.

Movement flashed just outside the gate.

Something waited in the preserve. Nathan held up a fist, a reflexive gesture to signal a stop. The girl behind him plowed into his back, and he stumbled.

"Wait," Nathan whispered. "Someone's out there."

Nathan bladed himself against the fence and approached the gate. He peered out through the bars. A massive lion paced nearby. Its shoulder muscles rippled. It raised its head and sniffed the air, then disappeared.

That could be the disruptor they needed to cover their escape, but it had a downside—being mauled by a lion.

Nathan crept closer and stared through the bars at an angle. No lion. Had the corpses' odor attracted the beast the way blood in the water drew sharks? Did lions have enhanced olfactory senses like dogs? Nathan snorted. Add that to the list of things he didn't know about Africa.

Nathan scanned the jungle's dense vegetation. They could shoot to scare off the lion, but that would alert the killers inside. They had few good options. Maybe they could crouch just outside the gate and—

The lion stepped out from between the trees and considered him.

"Shut the gate," Lubega asked.

The lion trotted forward and stuck its head through the open gate. Nathan backed up, careful not to run and act like prey.

"We outnumber it," Bridget said. "If it charges, everybody fight."

"Lions hunt in packs," Laker said. "There'll be others."

Bridget gawked. "You know about lions?"

"Mama bought me *The World's Animals* book when I was ten."

Nathan scanned the thick undergrowth beyond the lion, but the tree's canopy blocked the sun, casting papyrus bracts into dark shadow. Nothing moved in the still air. The hair on his neck rose. He pivoted to the thick Musizi trees inside the compound. They rose thirty feet, and their pale-gray branches formed an umbrella like stalks of broccoli. A shadow flickered beneath them.

Nathan froze.

Something was there, inside the compound. He stared, unblinking, his senses on alert. A stand of hippo grass rustled beneath the trees, and something tan and muscled moved through it.

Another lion.

The male lion who'd been staring lumbered toward them. Its padded paws and retracted claws made no sound. It moved into the open without fear. What was he doing? The lion's ears pinned back close to its head. It flicked its tail and bared its teeth.

"Everybody back," Nathan said.

"We've got bad guys behind us," Bridget said.

"Better than a pride of lions," Nathan said. "If they attack—"

The lion roared.

The sound blew a chill through him. The lion bared its teeth and crouched. Its muscles rippled as the beast coiled, ready to pounce.

The beast charged.

73

———

The male lion's mane billowed as it raced toward them. Nathan guided Laker and the girls back across the compound toward the nearest building. Bridget led the way, needing no encouragement to retreat.

The lion's paws pounded the dirt, and the thumping triggered an evolutionary fear inside him. Its snorting grew louder as it gained on them, providing all the encouragement he needed.

Bridget reached the building. She grabbed the door handle and pulled.

It didn't open.

She turned, her face a pale mask of terror. "It's locked."

Shit. Nathan looked over his shoulder. The lion closed fast. "Run."

"We can outrun a lion," Laker yelled.

"Head for the maintenance shed," Nathan said.

Bridget bolted for the corrugated-steel structure. If that was locked too, they'd be screwed.

Nathan grabbed a young girl's hand and dragged her with him, willing her to run faster. Lion's breathing grew louder. He didn't dare look back.

Bridget neared the shed and stopped.

"Keep going," Nathan yelled.

She didn't move. She didn't turn. She stared at the jungle beside the shed.

Nathan followed her gaze. Two female lions emerged from the brush.

A trap.

The male lion had charged, driving them toward his pride, who waited in ambush to pounce.

Nathan glanced around, his pulse thumping in his neck and adrenaline tingling his fingers. His breath came short and fast. They were surrounded.

He glanced around, searching for salvation. They couldn't go back without running into the lion, the lab was locked, and the pride crept toward them from the sides of the maintenance building.

The animal pens.

That was all that remained. Their only hope.

"Inside the cage," Nathan said.

"We keep injured animals there," Lubega said.

"I'll take my chances," Nathan said.

Nathan raced to the enclosure. The hasp appeared rusted, and as he approached, he scanned the mesh that enclosed it. Could they scale it? Did lions climb too? The girls crowded around him.

He stumbled to a stop and jerked up the mechanism. The gate swung open.

"Get inside," Nathan yelled.

He held it open. The male lion closed from one direction and the female lions from the other. This would be close.

Nathan stepped inside the gate with his other fingers wrapped through the chain link. He waited for Bridget. For a girl her size, she could move. Fear did that.

She breezed by him, with the lion on her heels. Nathan slammed the gate and closed the hasp.

The lion crashed into the gate, sending Nathan flying backward. He landed, and the impact knocked the wind out of him. The lion fell outside the fence. It rolled back into its paws and shook its head. It showed its fangs.

The gate held.

Nathan waited for his lungs to refill. He took shallow gasps and fought the panic that comes with shortness of breath.

"Are you hurt?" Laker asked. She stood over him with a wrinkled brow.

He flashed the okay sign, still unable to speak.

Bridget joined them and watched the lion pace along the cage. The pride approached and they inspected the fence, looking for a way inside.

Nathan's breath came easier. He sat up. "We're okay."

"If ISIS comes out," Bridget said, "we'll be in a shooting gallery."

His chest ached. "Maybe we can find another—"

Something growled in the enclosure behind them.

"Aw c'mon," Nathan said. "Give me your carbine."

"You got it."

Bridget handed her weapon to him, and he sneaked around a water hole and under an overhang with stacks of dried grass and large rocks. He squinted into the dark, ready to engage.

The growling came from his left. He spun around.

A tiny jackal with a black stripe running down its side crouched in the corner. It bared its teeth, but its ears were flattened back, and it looked terrified. Nathan surveyed the area. The only danger was that forty-pound wild canine.

He lowered the muzzle. "Get out of here."

The jackal slunk back and crouched beside a rock. It wasn't a threat.

Nathan walked out into the light. Everyone stared at him. "It's not a problem, but don't go in there."

"We've gotta bounce," Bridget said, "before they find us."

Nathan scanned the enclosure. "We're safer in here. Take cover behind the rocks. If they survive the assault, I doubt they're gonna come anywhere near a pride of lions. Stay low in case they shoot."

"That's our plan?"

"Time's on our side. We hunker down and wait them out." Nathan aimed his carbine toward the building, and the tension ebbed out of him.

They would survive.

74

Nathan clutched two steaming cups of coffee as he wormed between counterterrorism officers in the Lira Police Station. The Ugandan counterterrorism police had liberated the laboratory, killing every terrorist—except Yemeni and Nathan's torturer, who'd remained unconscious for hours. Taking Yemeni into custody alive, while his jihadists fought to the death, was the perfect example of Islamist leaders unwilling to sacrifice themselves as martyrs. The same dynamic repeated itself across the Middle East as leaders profited from jihad while radicalized youth sacrificed themselves for a misguided cause.

The counterterrorism police and soldiers had brought the wounded and other victims to Lira, the closest big city. Officers moved about nonchalantly, as if terror attacks happened every day. Violence had become part of Uganda's social fabric.

Bridget slumped in a faded plastic chair with a blanket wrapped around her shoulders. The girls they'd rescued lounged against an opposite wall. Most hadn't spoken for hours after their rescue, but they'd loosened up as they realized the danger had passed. Escaping death did that to people. For Nathan, it often manifested as a desire to embrace life, and his post-incident behavior often resembled that of a college kid on spring break.

Nathan plopped down beside Bridget and handed her a coffee. "Cup a joe will help."

"Thanks. I can't believe he tortured you. You got lucky Laker was there."

He stared into his coffee. "Amelia saved me once too, but here I am on the opposite side of the world with someone else's daughter."

"We're not on vacation." She looked fatigued and something else. Pissed off. "That *fuckah* was gonna unleash poison in the US," Bridget said.

Nathan ground his teeth. "Yeah, but not anymore. Jihadists target the West, but he's been solely focused on us. Wiping out the Phantoms must've made him nuts. He's pious and driven to spread radical Islam, but he's still human."

"He hates us."

"With a passion."

"Think any of his men escaped Uganda?"

"Without a doubt," Nathan said. "His tentacles reach across the globe."

"At least we stopped him from stealing the virus."

Nathan replayed the memory of his last moments in the lab. Opio's betrayal stung, and not just from her willingness to partner with monsters but from his inability to spot it.

"I need to talk to her," Nathan said.

"Dr. Opio?"

"They're holding her in a cell. I've got to ask her why she did it."

Bridget stared with dead eyes. "Money, revenge, power . . . the usual suspects. Who cares why? She did it, and she'll pay."

"Yeah, I know."

Across the room, Laker huddled with her friends. She knew her mother had been arrested but not the circumstances. She deserved to know.

What would happen to her? Nathan's heart ached. She was like Amelia in so many ways. Did Nathan's actions mean Laker would grow up without a mother? Like ripples in a pond, Nathan's presence in a Ugandan jungle lab could affect this girl and countless others for generations to come. Those were the hidden stakes police and criminals bet when they gambled with life and death.

Nathan stood.

"You can't resist, can you?"

"Be right back."

Nathan crossed the room, abandoning his steaming coffee. He exited the room and approached the front desk. He waited for the officer manning it to finish a call.

The officer hung up and raised his eyebrows.

"FBI." Nathan flashed his badge. "I need to speak with Dr. Opio, the researcher you arrested at the lab."

"Not possible."

"It's a matter of your national security," Nathan lied.

"The Directorate of Counterterrorism is in charge." The officer's eyes flickered to a nearby door. "She's their prisoner now."

"I'm working with them. I—"

The phone rang again, and the officer picked it up. He pressed the receiver close against his ear. He turned away from Nathan and lowered his voice as he spoke into the phone.

Screw it.

Nathan made for the door the officer had flagged.

Laker appeared beside him. "Can I see Mother?"

She stared with wide, innocent eyes, on the verge of tears. His chest collapsed, crushing his heart. How could he deny her?

He nodded and swung open the door.

Opio slumped on a wooden bench, shackled by a chain connecting her handcuffs to an iron loop.

"Mama."

Opio looked up, and emotions rippled across her face from recognition, to yearning, to shame.

"How are you, *Mwana wange*?" Opio asked.

Laker didn't respond.

"They'll kick us out any second," Nathan said. "I've got to know why you did this."

Her eyes lingered on Laker before they moved to him. "You can't possibly understand."

"How long did you work with them?"

"A few days."

"Then why didn't you give me up in the lab?"

"I . . . couldn't."

"Why incinerate the viruses?"

"They promised they wouldn't hurt anybody, but when they started shooting . . . my daughter . . ."

"You realized you couldn't trust Islamists fighting jihad?"

She fixated on her handcuffs. "They said they'd use Marburg as a deterrent, not a weapon, but when they killed people, I knew we had to destroy the samples."

Ah. It came together for Nathan. "You could blame me for destroying the viruses and not worry about them taking retribution on you or your daughter."

"Yes."

"Why didn't you alert them to our presence in the supply room after we destroyed everything?"

"I planned to wait for them until you climbed into the ventilation system."

"You could've made noise and alerted them."

"They'd might have shot us."

Nathan shook his head. "How can you side with these monsters?"

"To survive in Uganda, one must choose teams. The leadership are all monsters."

"But Laker almost died," Nathan said.

"There wasn't supposed to be any violence."

"Terrorists lie." Darkness clouded Nathan's mind, intensifying his pain. Her naivete was more offensive than her betrayal.

Laker stepped forward but stayed out of reach, as if Opio might bite. "You helped these bad men."

"My *Mukwano*," Opio said. "What I did, I did for you."

"You fed him to those creatures," Laker said.

"This is how the world works."

"He tried to help us, and you betrayed him."

"I had no choice," Opio said.

"He had choices too. He returned for me."

"You don't understand," Opio said. "These are powerful men. They would've taken what they wanted without my help."

Laker stared at the ground. "Now they are dead."

"The strong rule Uganda, and the weak die."

Laker looked from her to Nathan. "They are gone, and this FBI agent is here. Who is the strong one now?"

"You are too young to understand."

The door opened behind them, and the officer from the front desk stormed inside. "Get out. This is very bad. You forbidden."

"Okay, okay," Nathan said. He looked at Opio. "I got what I needed. Let's go, Laker. You can see your mother later."

Laker hesitated. She looked at her mother, then pinched her mouth and walked out.

Laker returned to the room with the other students, and Nathan headed for Bridget, who stood in the hall talking to Agent Hart. The woman had to feel lucky she hadn't gone with them to the lab, but they'd still dumped a pile of shit on her doorstep. She'd be stuck in Uganda cleaning things up.

"It's gonna take them a long time to decontaminate that lab site and unravel what happened there," Hart said.

"The QRF killed most of the insurgents," Bridget said. "That'll make prosecutions easier."

"We need to take Yemeni back to New York," Nathan said.

"We should coordinate with the interagency," Bridget said.

Hart raised her hand. "That's Pretoria's job."

"We should be present when you brief the ambo," Bridget said. "And it wouldn't hurt for us to chat up the station chief."

"We've got it covered," Hart said, annoyed.

"Then it makes no sense for us to stick around," Nathan said.

"Head back to the States?" Bridget asked.

Nathan nodded. "The big question is, did his people escape with pathogens?" Nathan asked. "And based on what the Phantoms did with the fentanyl attacks, Yemeni doesn't think small. Did he acquire pathogens anywhere else? We can't be certain other prongs of his attack aren't prepared."

"You destroyed the Ebola and Marburg," Bridget said.

"Hopefully."

"If any of his people escaped, they'll run for their lives. And once word gets out, anyone he emplaced in the US will be hiding."

"That's what I'd do," Nathan said, "but that's not how Islamists think. Preservation of life isn't a priority. Jihad is about spreading death."

"We caught him. It's over."

"Maybe, but—"

Two hazmat suits entered the police station. Hart walked over to them. She gestured at the room, then her shoulders slumped. A feeling of dread spread through Nathan. Standing unprotected with men in Level A hazmat suits chilled him.

Hart shook her head as she walked over to him. "Want the good news or the bad news?"

"Quarantine?" Nathan asked.

"Yup. For everyone you've contacted until we can confirm no one was exposed. The government doesn't take this lightly."

"How long?"

"Maybe forty-eight hours," Hart said. "They'll start testing immediately."

"What about Yemeni?" Nathan asked.

"Quarantine for everyone," she said, "but that'll give us time to arrange a charter plane back to the US."

"Will Uganda fight it?" Bridget asked.

"I think they want him gone."

"Do me a favor," Nathan said. "When you arrange his travel, don't use the same airline as last time."

75

Terror surged through Leila's veins, pumping her full of adrenaline. She screamed behind the packing tape that covered her mouth, and the sound came out as a gurgle, echoing in her head and throat.

Blackwood, the young cop who'd been ogling her, led two officers toward where Ri and Shirin slept.

No, no, no.

Had these officers been paid to hurt her family? Had Yemeni sent them? Were they even real police?

She must save her family.

The older officer, Ramirez, seemed in charge. He kept his hand between her shoulder blades and pressed her against the plaster wall. Leila bent her knees and spun. He shoved her, but his hand slid off as she rotated.

She sprinted down the hall after the officers. She lumbered with her hands tied behind her, and her bare feet slapped the cool wood.

The last officer turned and raised his hands as she charged.

Allah, help me.

She could crash into him and knock him backward, or kick his knees, but there were three of them and—

Ramirez tackled her from behind. She crashed to the floor, and her head banged against the wood. Everything blurred, and a high-pitched tone whined in her ears. Nausea flipped her stomach.

Ramirez manhandled her onto her stomach and knelt on her back. His boney knee fired electricity through her spine. He bore down with all his weight, making it hard to take a full breath.

She blinked, trying to focus. What just happened? Jumbled thoughts and incoherent images coalesced.

Ri and Shirin.

They were in danger. The reality of the moment flooded back, and horror enveloped her.

She'd fallen facing the wall and couldn't see down the hallway. She turned her head, and her vision twisted, as if the apartment flipped upside down. She fought the urge to vomit or she could choke to death.

She blinked, and the room righted, but everything remained fuzzy, and the light stung her corneas. She had a concussion.

"Who are you?" Ri screamed, his voice shrill and panicky.

Leila shook her head to reorient herself. Her son was in danger, and she had to save him.

"*Mmmph*," she shrieked behind the tape.

Blackwood brushed back the curtain into Ri's alcove and stepped out with his arm around Ri's neck. Ri's feet dangled off the ground.

My God, he's choking him.

Leila pushed against the floor. She could barely move and everything hurt, but she had to reach her son. She slipped her knee beneath her and used a surge of adrenaline to push.

Ramirez toppled off her, surprised by her burst of strength. She twisted and got a foot on the ground. She rose.

Ramirez slammed into her. She pancaked against the floor, and her head thumped off it again. Stars filled her vision. The world spun in unending loops.

"Maman, Maman!"

Ri's voice cut through the static in her brain. Tears filled her eyes. Where was she? What was wrong with her son?

Her stomach turned, and she vomited. Her mouth filled, but the chunky liquid had nowhere to go. Panic rose inside her. She struggled and jerked, trying to spew it through the packing tape. The convulsion subsided, and she swallowed it. She inhaled through her nose, and her sinuses filled with a horrible scent.

Leila threw up again. She would drown in her own puke.

Ramirez yanked the packing tape off.

She convulsed and hurled the contents of her stomach on the floor. She heaved once, twice, three times. Her body clenched, but nothing else came up. She gasped for air and gagged. She coughed and spit.

Ramirez covered her mouth with a tape again.

"No," she screamed.

Voices moved around her. "Help her," Shirin said.

Leila tried to stand, but her body wouldn't cooperate. She gagged, but nothing came out.

Ramirez stayed on top of her. He wouldn't be taken by surprise again.

The nausea subsided, but her head pounded like a drum from the inside out. She looked down the hall through a haze of stars. No one was there. She turned to the living room, and her cheek sloshed through vomit.

Blackwood had Ri by the door. He handcuffed him behind his back and tugged a cloth hood over his head. Ri struggled, but Blackwood held him with little effort. At least her son was alive. They'd handcuffed her mother and taped her mouth shut. The other two officers dragged her into the living room and out of view.

Leila struggled, flopping like a fish out of water on the floor. Would they kill her family? Her life meant nothing, but her son. *Oh Allah, her son.* He was her world, and she'd failed him in every way imaginable.

She strained to look at Ramirez, but he kept his knee in her back. She couldn't move. She could barely breathe. She snorted through her nose and gurgled. The vomit had gone into her sinuses, and the space behind her eyes burned with agony.

The two officers exited the living room. What had they done with her mother?

"Get ready," Ramirez said. "Keep a grip on him."

"Got him."

What would they do? The other officers stacked on the door.

"Moving in thirty seconds," Ramirez said.

He tugged her hair and pulled her face inches from his. His breath reeked of whiskey and meat.

"You know why we're here," he said. "You're planning to talk to the judge. We can't have that. Here's what's gonna happen. You're going back to work tomorrow and you won't report this. When we ask for information, you give it to us. If you tell anyone else, they'll end up like Mr. Mansoor."

They invaded her home to threaten her. Fear turned to hope. They'd let them live. But they'd killed Khalil, as she'd suspected. Tears blurred her vision, and the pounding in her head didn't stop.

"Grunt if you understand."

"Uh-huh." Her throat burned.

"That's good. Because one mistake, and you, your mother, and your son are dead. Understand?"

She groaned.

"If anyone asks what happened to your face, tell them you fell. We're leaving now, and you won't get another warning."

Her heart pounded, but she had to remain calm. She'd give them whatever they wanted to keep Shirin and Ri safe. Her bruises would heal, and her family would survive—if she provided information.

"Oh, and one more thing," he said. "To make sure you cooperate, we're taking your son."

76

The scratchy hemp sack covering Darius's head smelled like chocolate and sugar, like a Bamiyeh. He stumbled blindly up a staircase, bracketed by policeman holding his arms. Their fingers dug into him, and he stifled a cry. Police did this in Iran—midnight kidnappings—for anyone who opposed the regime. Had Maman said something bad about the president? She'd promised they'd be free in America.

He bit down on the rag they'd stuffed in his mouth. The knot dug into his neck. He snorted, trying to breathe, but snot filled his nose. His eyes burned from crying, but the tears had stopped, and his mouth had dried. He had no liquid left.

"Next floor," Ramirez said behind him.

Darius looked back, but his head moved inside the bag. The plastic handcuffs cut into his wrists, and the gag prevented him from speaking. He wailed behind it. Didn't they care he couldn't breathe?

"Shut up," Blackwood said.

Darius counted their steps as they moved. Six, seven, eight. The rhythm of the numbers calmed him. He raised his foot to climb the next step and stumbled on even floor. A landing. They moved to their right, and a door creaked open. His ear popped from changing pressure. They turned him sideways and shuffled him through, and then his feet squished on carpet. Maybe a hallway?

He'd never been up this late. Everything felt unreal, like a nightmare. He'd gone to sleep, and then been awakened by these policemen standing over him. Maybe he was still dreaming.

"In here," Ramirez said.

A key rattled in a lock, then another door squeaked, and they went inside. Everything was dark behind the sack. Were they in jail? Why had they arrested him? If his mother had done something bad, why take him? Had they kidnapped Maman and Bibi too?

Fear weakened his knees. Had they hurt Maman? His eyes watered again, as his body squeezed out the last drops of moisture. He inhaled, and the snot plugged his nose. He panicked. He closed his mouth and blew hard through his nose, clearing the passageway. He breathed rapidly. Didn't they care if he died?

"Should I put him in the bedroom?" Blackwood asked.

"Keep him here and watch him."

Ramirez released him, and Blackwood turned Darius around and then pushed him down. "Sit."

Darius bent his knees, but without the use of his hands, he lost his balance and fell hard on his butt. His back slammed into the wall and his head collided with it. Stars filled his vision. In the total blackness, he floated through space. The pain came, and he moaned.

"Shut the fuck up, or I'll shut you up," Blackwood said.

Blackwood was mean. Darius had seen that behavior before. Cruelty had lived in his house. He loosed a muffled snort. He shouldn't speak. Father had taught him that lesson.

Blackwood ripped off the sack, and the textured fabric scratched Darius's nose. He blinked in the room's dim light. The bag had been over his head for at least half an hour, though he'd lost track of time after they'd dragged him out of his apartment and thrown him into a van. They'd driven for about twenty minutes, and he'd rattled around on the vehicle's metal floor. But which way had they gone? Even if he knew, how would he call Maman? Was she looking for him, or had they arrested her too?

He surveyed the living room's musty furniture and cheap paintings of the Italian countryside. He could paint better than that. Whoever had done them hadn't worried about proportion. He prickled with annoyance and looked away.

The apartment had an open kitchen and a hallway that led out of view. Why was he in someone's residence? Did one of the policeman live there? This wasn't a jail, but he'd never been arrested before, so maybe this was normal in America.

Four policemen had taken him from his home, but only Ramirez and Blackwood were here. Across the room, Ramirez spoke on the phone, and Darius strained to hear his muffled words.

"Yes . . . no problem." He nodded. "The boy's with us. No, he's fine . . . maybe the woman because she—" His face crinkled, and his eyes darted to the other officer.

"Nothing serious. She'll be able to go back to work . . . It's not my fault. You don't know what happens. Things don't always go as planned." He listened for a few more seconds, and then he hung up.

"Problem?" Blackwood asked.

"Usual bullshit."

"What now?"

Ramirez looked at Darius. "We wait. They'll call if we need to bring him down and show him."

Blackwood walked to the window and pulled back aluminum blinds. They crinkled beneath his touch. He peeked outside. "I can see it from here."

"Keep that shut."

"Whatever."

Blackwood returned to Darius and hovered over him, seeming more interested in dealing with him than Ramirez. Both officers were heartless.

Darius's panic returned, and his breathing increased. He snorted, and his nose clogged again.

Blackwood knelt and leaned close. His face tightened like a Persian tombak drum, and his eyes became black holes—like Father's.

"I'm gonna remove your gag, 'cause I can't have you dying on me. Not yet." He chortled and sneered.

An image of Father standing over Maman as she bled on the carpet flashed behind his eyes. He had to get out of there.

"One word, and I'll smack you so hard you'll never wake up. Understand?"

Never wake up. The phrase repeated over and over in Darius's mind. His belly turned colder than Mount Damavand in winter. He nodded. He'd do anything to remove the gag and breathe again.

Blackwood stepped behind him and tugged the rag. "Fuck." He grumbled and loosed a string of profanity as he struggled with the knot. Darius's head jerked back and forth.

The knot loosened, and Blackwood yanked out the rag. The fabric hooked Darius's front teeth, and they moved in his gums. Flame burned through his skull. He gasped.

Blackwood towered over him with clenched fists. "Don't speak."

Darius nodded and stayed silent.

Maman, where are you?

77

Nathan and Bridget exited the FBI's New York Division at 26 Federal Plaza and walked down Worth Street toward the Thurgood Marshall United States Courthouse where they'd arraign Yemeni. A witch's brew of agitation and anticipation bubbled in Nathan's stomach. They turned the corner and approached hundreds of reporters, television crews, and onlookers who spilled off the sidewalks onto the street. Police manned barricades and scanned the crowd for protesters and terrorists. The large public gathering had drawn international media attention and would be a perfect target.

Uganda didn't have an extradition agreement with the United States, and they'd been uncooperative for years, but they'd quickly agreed to a judicial removal to get Yemeni out of their country. That had surprised Nathan at first, but terrorism trials were complicated. And dangerous. The Ugandan president probably hadn't relished drawing radical Islamists like a magnet. To sweeten the pot, the US administration had offered incentives, but the details remained murky. Whatever had happened, FBI agents and US marshals had taken Yemeni into custody and flown him from Kampala back to the US within seventy-two hours. This time, the marshals used their own jet.

Nathan and Bridget had cleared quarantine, and both the Uganda Ministry of Health and US State Department had given them clean bills of health. None of the students or scientists had been exposed to the Marburg that contaminated the lab, yet two dead terrorists had contracted it. Bullet holes in their hazmat suits hadn't helped.

"We better bury this fucker," Bridget said.

"I've argued for civilian judicial prosecutions for terrorists," Nathan said. "I like transparency where everyone can witness a fair trial, but with foreign terrorists, I'm rethinking my philosophy."

"Now, you sound more like a Boston cop."

"Defendants need trials, but treating them the same as citizens doesn't work. We catch most high-value targets overseas in austere environments, where it's difficult to gather evidence. It's unfair to force agents operating in a hostile country to gather forensic evidence while they're taking fire. Holding us to the same legal standard isn't possible."

"I've been saying that for years," Bridget said. "If they think—"

A uniformed cop blocked their path and held up his hands.

"FBI," Nathan said.

They badged their way around the barricades and entered the courthouse. They stopped at security, secured their firearms, then proceeded to courtroom 318, which was used for most significant arraignments. Yemeni had landed at Westchester County Airport for the second time in two weeks, and US Marshals and FBI agents had transported him to the Metropolitan Detention Center in Brooklyn. Early in the morning, they'd used an armored vehicle to deliver him to Southern Manhattan, and he'd been held in solitary lockup awaiting his arraignment.

Spectators packed the courtroom, and Bridget and Nathan wormed through the boisterous crowd. The judge could have closed it to the public, but the emotional wounds from the murdered passengers remained raw, and Americans wanted revenge.

They showed their credentials to two marshals and a court security officer who guarded the courtroom well, and then they walked to the prosecution table.

White, and another AUSA Nathan had seen but didn't know, combed through documents. White looked up and let out a long breath. "About time."

"You don't need us for this," Nathan said.

"I do if the judge has questions, or the defense surprises me with a curveball, or—"

"Okay, okay. We're here. What can we do?"

"White looked down at the open folders on the table and scraped a hand through his hair. He looked nervous, which was unusual, but so was the size of the crowd watching him. And the stakes. Screwing up this case would end his career.

"You got this," Nathan said.

White glanced at him. "I know." He looked vulnerable.

The door to lockup opened, and four court security officers entered and scanned the audience. One of them leaned back through the threshold and gestured. Two marshals escorted Yemeni out. He wore slacks and a button-down shirt, clothes the Ugandans had given him after they'd burned his contaminated clothing. His hands and ankles remained shackled.

The court room fell as quiet as a tomb, as they lead Yemeni past the bench, to the defense table. The defendant had inflicted historic death and destruction, and everyone wanted to see him. His eventual trial would be closed, because they'd use classified information for his prosecution, but for this—an arraignment—no such protected information was required.

"I'll be over here," Bridget said. She exited through the wooden gate into the spectator area.

Nathan pulled out a chair and sat beside White, but he didn't take his eyes off Yemeni. The killer appeared older and frail, so different from how he'd been in Uganda. Yemeni sat at the defense table and spoke with his attorney through the interpreter, Leila.

Yemeni looked up and caught Nathan staring. A glimmer flashed behind Yemeni's eyes. Or had Nathan imagined that?

"All rise," the bailiff announced in a booming voice that resonated off the cavernous ceiling. "The honorable Judge Byron Jefferson presiding."

A portion of paneling opened in the wall behind the platform, and Magistrate Judge Jefferson entered. He climbed onto the dais and sat behind his bench. All eyes were on him. The air crackled with anticipation.

"Be seated," Jefferson said with a wave of his hand. "Are we ready, counsel?"

"Yes, Your Honor. Liza Dawson representing Mr. Yemeni."

"Sam White for the government. We're ready to proceed."

"The defendant will rise," the judge said. "You are Omar Yemeni?"

Leila interpreted through her headset, but Yemeni just stared at the judge with black orbs full of hate.

"Does Mr. Yemeni understand the interpretation?" Jefferson asked.

Indignation flared Nathan's nostrils. Defendants, even the worst people on earth, received every deference and accommodation in American courts. That was a positive attribute of Western jurisprudence, but that fucking guy spoke English clear enough when he threatened to cut off Nathan's balls.

"We had no problem communicating with Mr. Yemeni before the hearing," Dawson said. "At least language wasn't the issue." Defense attorneys never publicly expressed feelings about their clients. She must really dislike him. Shocker.

Dawson leaned over and whispered in Yemeni's ear. Yemeni looked at her as if she were something he'd scraped off his shoe, then he faced the judge. "That is my name."

A murmur spread through the crowd. Everyone knew they had the right guy, but hearing a voice from a fugitive who'd dominated the news for years was like having the bogeyman speak to them.

"Ms. Dawson has been appointed as your legal counsel," Jefferson said. "Have you had the opportunity to discuss your case with her?"

"I do not recognize this court as a—"

"A simple yes or no. Has your attorney explained the purpose of this arraignment?"

"Do what you will."

"Ms. Dawson, have you conferred with your client, and does he understand why he's here?"

"Yes, Judge."

"Mr. Yemeni, have you read the complaint?"

"Lies."

The judge lowered his chin to his chest, and his jowls flapped out like balloons. "We'll let the jury decide the veracity of the charges."

White summarized the indictment, and the judge made sure Yemeni knew his rights. The proceeding moved to bail. White summarized the violence, severity of the charges, and Yemeni's flight from justice.

"Mr. Yemeni also has significant connections to foreign terrorist organizations," White said, "which amplifies the danger if he's released."

"Counselor?" Jefferson asked.

"Mr. Yemeni hasn't been convicted of any crime, and other than his presence on the airliner, there's nothing tying him to the incident in Westchester. We'd request bail to allow Mr. Yemeni to confer with witnesses in his case and—"

"Counselor, please. I understand your position, but are you seriously advocating for the release of a defendant who has been a fugitive for years and charged with hundreds of murders?"

"Yes, Judge. We request a reasonable bail so that Mr. Yemeni can take part in his defense."

"Denied."

A snicker passed through the audience. The judge set the schedule for motions and a tentative trial date, though everyone knew that would get delayed.

Nathan watched Yemeni while the court dealt with administrative matters. He showed no emotion. Then the judge wrapped up the arraignment and prepared for the next case.

Two court security officers helped Yemeni out of his seat. Dawson raised her hand and said something to them. They stepped back. She leaned in and whispered to Yemeni as Leila interpreted. Yemeni glared at her with disdain. Having a female defense attorney hold his fate in her hands couldn't sit well with a radical Islamist.

The officers took Yemeni's arms and escorted him to the door that led to the temporary lockup area. Two marshals waited beside the entrance.

Nathan scanned the crowd. If somebody planned to make a move, this would be the time. The officers led Yemeni inside, and the marshals followed. The door clunked shut.

Nathan expelled an audible sigh of relief.

Dawson came over and whispered something to White. He nodded, and she headed back to her table to collect her papers.

"What's up?" Nathan asked.

"He wants a proffer," White said.

78

Nathan and Bridget huddled with White and Mark Young, the unit chief of SDNY's National Security and International Narcotics Unit. FBI ASAC Debbie Giacomo listened over Nathan's shoulder.

"We need to do this fast," White said. "He claims he has time-sensitive information."

"Keep it clean," Young said. "Say nothing they can misinterpret as an agreement to cooperate."

"Not my first proffer," White said.

"There's no way the AG signs off on his cooperation," Young said.

"Unless he has something significant," White said.

"I can't imagine what that would be," Young said.

Nathan leaned in. "How about a Marburg release in Manhattan?"

Both men stared at him.

"You think he has knowledge of a WMD?" Young asked.

"No idea," Nathan said. "But it wouldn't surprise me if he floated something."

Young scowled. "Then let's get this done. Keep a low profile, and no leaks that we're talking to him."

Giacomo stood and forced her way into the circle. "I'll make sure nothing leaks."

Why did bosses always feel the need to interject? Did they need to justify their role? Young and White ignored her.

White looked at Nathan. "Meet me at the office as soon as you get him."

"Will do."

Young pulled White off to the side, and they chatted privately.

"That's huge," Giacomo said. "Really big."

She'd dug deep into the thesaurus for that. Nathan had dealt with ASACs like her for his entire career. They hid in their offices and contributed little to cases, other than applying agency protocols and regulations that gummed up every case. In fairness, following policy was their job, but when lives were on the line, mission came first, and the rules be damned.

"If we can stop a domestic attack," Giacomo said, "we'll be heroes."

Why did people who'd never been in harm's way always throw that term around? If Yemeni gave them critical information, and they stopped an attack, that didn't make them heroes. It made them federal agents doing their job.

"How are we doing this?" Bridget asked.

"Let's rally the guys," Nathan said. "We'll have the marshals bring him down to the loading dock and meet our cars. We'll go with Yemeni and bring a marshal with us to facilitate entry in the US Attorney's Office. Maybe we can use their armored vehicle. We'll get a cover team and—"

"No, no, no," Giacomo said. "We've got our number one fugitive in hand, and he wants to flip and join team America. We're not screwing around with logistics while terrorists prepare to unleash Ebola in Times Square."

White walked up to them. "His attorney said it was extremely time sensitive."

Nathan shot him a look. White was a brilliant prosecutor who showed balls in the courtroom, but this was an internal conversation between FBI agents who carried guns for a living. Nathan knew how to keep a defendant alive. And himself. He didn't need White double-teaming him with an ASAC who'd been riding a desk for fifteen years.

"Yemeni has an army of jihadists at his beck and call," Nathan said.

"Everyone with a television knows Yemeni is in court this morning. The security risk couldn't be higher."

"There must be a hundred cops around Foley Square," Giacomo said. "And we've got SWAT on standby. It'd be suicide for Yemeni to attempt an escape."

"I heard somewhere that suicide is in the Islamist's tool kit," Nathan said.

The exuberance melted off Giacomo's face. She glared at him. "Don't get cute with me. Not now. Washington's watching this play out in real time, not to mention the entire front office. We're gonna do this, and we're gonna do it fast."

"Agreed," Nathan said. "But it won't take long to do this right."

"How long?"

Nathan cracked his neck. Five minutes to liaise with the local marshals, then another ten for them to get approvals, maybe more, especially if they requested the armored vehicle. They'd call ahead to get access to the US Attorney's controlled garage space. Then they needed time to get Yemeni through control points, strapped into a vehicle, brief the cover team, then navigate horrific traffic. Even with lights and sirens, they'd have to get around the roadblocks to the office, then take him upstairs to the interrogation room. What a colossal pain in the ass.

"We'll have him up there within the hour."

"Too long," Giacomo said. "Let's do it in the courthouse."

"Not possible," White said. "I attended the marshal's briefing this morning, and they created a security corridor for this. We need to keep him locked down."

Giacomo snapped her gum. "You're overthinking this. Go in the back and grab him. Take him down the marshals' elevator and walk him out the side door. No one's expecting that."

"Too risky," Nathan said.

"You've got a gun and badge," Giacomo said, "and a hundred agents at 26 Fed. If there's a problem, handle it."

Rage heated Nathan's face, and his stomach gurgled, but he didn't lash out. She could accuse him of many failings, but cowardice wasn't one of them. "We're supposed to be smarter than the bad guys and avoid dangerous situations."

Bridget stepped between them and stared at Giacomo. "Nathan's normally not a rule follower, so if he's telling you to get an armored vehicle, do that."

Giacomo crossed her arms. "When you promote to ASAC, you can decide, but until then, follow orders." She looked at Nathan. "Gather a few squad members and walk that asshole over to the SDNY."

"But—"

"This isn't a discussion."

Bridget narrowed her eyes, exuding disdain. Giacomo seemed oblivious that Bridget was about to explode.

"It's your call," Nathan said.

"Yes, it is," Giacomo said. She wagged her finger at Nathan. "And by the way, I know you've done this before. Last year you walked a defendant over for a late-night proffer with one other agent. I was in court that day, and I remember."

Nathan remembered too. She'd been there when Nathan and Three-Balls had escorted a prisoner down the alley after hours. Nathan hadn't liked it then either, and that defendant hadn't been a terrorist mastermind. But complaining wouldn't help. She'd made up her mind, and she was the boss. He would've felt better about following her orders if she earned her position.

He looked at Bridget. "Tell the marshals the plan, before they bring him down."

She grimaced. "What are you doing?"

"I want a brief word with his defense attorney."

"Hey now," White said. "We shouldn't discuss the case without—"

"Just come with me," Nathan said. "I'd like a little more information before we walk this guy over."

79

Leila remained at the defense table in the arraignment court after Yemeni had been led back into lockup. Excitement sizzled through the courtroom, like flashes of heat lightning on the horizon. Hushed conversations droned around her as the judge called the next case.

Dawson said something and then scowled. "Miss Kabiri?"

Leila looked up. "Sorry, what?"

Dawson leaned close and whispered, "You're coming, right? I've asked for a meeting between my client and the prosecutors. I need your assistance."

Leila could fake illness, or refuse because Yemeni spoke enough English to understand, but her tormentors wouldn't accept anything but her complete cooperation. She'd become their conspirator. A pawn in whatever game they played.

"When?" Leila asked.

"Right now."

"Where?"

"Next door. The agents are taking him to the AUSA's office. It could be an interesting proffer, if my client knows anything explosive."

"I'll be there."

Her throat dried from fear and regret. And hopelessness.

"Walk with me," Dawson said.

"I need to file my paperwork. I'll meet you there."

"This can't wait. Mr. Yemeni just sprang this on me, and frankly, I'm surprised the prosecution agreed. If this doesn't happen now, it may never work."

The men who'd taken her son had called and given her explicit instructions to interpret at both the arraignment and the proffer. How had they known about Yemeni's offer to cooperate before his attorney, and how had they ensured she'd be assigned to the arraignment? Had they added another victim to the body count? She didn't dwell on that.

"I need the restroom," Leila said.

"I'll come with you, and then we'll head over."

Dawson didn't trust that Leila would join her, but she couldn't know Leila had no choice. One of Ri's kidnappers had ordered her to divulge where Yemeni's proffer would be held and then attend it.

A court security officer led another defendant wearing an orange jumpsuit and chains to the defense table for his arraignment. The court would churn through a parade of losers and sociopaths, reading charges and making bail decisions. Most in attendance beelined for the exits. They'd come to see Yemeni.

"I'll pop into the restroom, and then we can go," Leila said, trying to sound normal.

Normal. Nothing in her life would ever be the same, not until she got her son back. If he returned. He'd be traumatized and carry emotional scars forever. He could be so fragile.

My boy. My poor boy.

Another defense attorney hovered over the table, waiting for a chair. Dawson gathered her papers and waited for Leila. Leila collected her folder and stood. Her legs wobbled under her. Her body had numbed.

She should devise a brilliant plan to trick her captors into believing she'd cooperate, while feeding them false information and luring them into a trap where police could arrest them and rescue her son.

But that was fantasy. Pure delusion.

One false move and they'd butcher her and her family. Those people displayed zero compassion. They had Ri, and there was nothing she could do to save him. She had to give them what they wanted, or she'd never see her son again.

Leila trailed behind Dawson through the throng of cops, attorneys, and reporters in the hallway. Dawson kept looking back to make sure Leila followed. Did she sense Leila's trepidation and worry she'd skip out of the interview? That wouldn't make sense. A bolt of fear pierced Leila's chest. Had Dawson been corrupted too? Did they hold one of her family members, or had she taken a bribe?

Leila stared hard at Dawson. If she concentrated hard enough, maybe she could see inside the woman's heart and learn her true intentions. But Dawson was a mystery. Leila glanced around. Anyone in the crowd could be working for Ri's kidnappers. They'd gone to great lengths to co-opt her, and they'd be watching. Had they anticipated Yemeni's recapture? Did they want information about other defendants too? Turning her into their mole could bring many benefits to a criminal organization, but now that Yemeni was back in handcuffs and facing the death penalty, her cooperation would be even more important.

She must follow their demands.

"Let's make this quick," Dawson said.

Leila followed her into the restroom. Dawson entered a stall and locked it. Leila waited a beat, then tiptoed back past the sinks and slipped out. A throng of people in business attire, many carrying legal binders, strode through the corridor. Everyone moved with urgency, their faces tight with stress.

They'd told her they would contact her, but what if they'd seen her with Dawson and couldn't approach? What if—

"Where is the meeting?"

Leila jolted and spun around. A thickset man no more than five-four, wearing a cheap suit and faded leather shoes, stood beside her. Stubble covered his chin.

Leila tried to speak, but words wouldn't come. Divulging information was a crime, maybe a felony. But worse, if she gave them the information and they hurt some innocent person, she'd be responsible.

She couldn't live with that.

But she couldn't cause Ri's death either. And if saving him meant she'd spend the rest of her life in jail, then so be it. Her duty was to her son. Her life meant nothing.

"They're meeting him at the US Attorney's Office," Leila said.

"Where, which floor?"

Leila panicked. She hadn't thought to ask. Would Yemeni meet in the Criminal Division's terrorism unit? If she guessed wrong, they'd think she was lying. And lying meant death.

"I don't know. We're headed over now."

The man leaned close, and his body odor assaulted her olfactory senses. "We instructed you to get the location."

"That's all they told me. I'll know when I get there." Dread grew inside her. She'd agreed to violate her oath and help them, but she hadn't even done that well. She was a mess. A bubble of emotion rose inside her, and her eyes teared.

The man reached into his pocket. Was he getting a weapon to kill her for failing?

He removed a cell phone and gave it to her. She accepted it and held it with both hands, as if it were a bird that might fly away.

"Call me the second you know where you're going. My number's pre-programmed. Hit send."

She breathed a sigh of relief. They had a backup plan and would let her cooperate. Ri had a chance. "I'll call you."

He glowered. "You'd better. Or we'll return your son to you in buckets."

80

Nathan and White looked for Dawson, but she'd already left the courtroom. ASAC Giacomo stormed off, saying she had to make a call, and Bridget went to tell the marshals they needed to take Yemeni on a field trip, leaving Nathan and White alone.

"She's probably conferring with the PD's office," White said.

"What could Yemeni possibly get out of this?" Nathan asked. "The US Attorney will never agree to a plea bargain, and I know the FBI won't sign off. This guy killed thousands of Americans, and the AG will request the death penalty."

"If he has the virus in New York, he may cooperate if we take execution off the table."

"He craves martyrdom," Nathan said.

"He didn't when he fought it out with police in Uganda."

Nathan pinched his lips. It didn't make sense.

"What's the problem with listening?" White asked. "Either he has something of value to trade, or he doesn't."

"There's no way we're making a deal with this asshole," Nathan said. "This may be a ploy for him to create a loophole to escape the death penalty."

White's face hardened. He looked down and rolled his tongue inside his lip. "It's not without precedent, but we're fine if we keep it short. We'll ask him what he has, and if he dances around it at all, we'll end the interview."

"And if he gives up a terror cell?" Nathan asked.

"You guys take them out."

"Which creates substantial cooperation."

"He planned a hemorrhagic fever pandemic," White said. "If he has biological, chemical, or nuclear weapons, we've no choice. Unleashing Marburg here could kill thousands."

"Let's say Yemeni gives up a cell, and we take them out. How much leniency would a judge give him?"

White shrugged. "That's the question. If he provides substantial assistance, the judge could sentence him to anything."

"But Yemeni's facing the death penalty."

White sighed. "We're down a rabbit hole. This is all speculation. The judge could give him life, or less, but it's his discretion."

Cognitive dissonance tickled the base of Nathan's skull. "That's what's bothering me. I could see Yemeni offering something of value, and then the judge gives him twenty years. With time off for good behavior and a friendly parole board, he could go free. Fifteen years from now, people will forget what could have happened. I've seen it before."

White looked at his watch. "We have no choice, and we've got to do this now."

Nathan nodded. "I know, but I had to vent."

"Bring him up to thirty-seven. I'll grab a conference room. We'll know soon if he has anything."

White headed for the exit as Bridget returned.

"Put the order in with the marshals?" Nathan asked.

"We can take him outta lockup once they do the paperwork."

Years ago, the marshals transported defendants through a tunnel to the Metropolitan Correctional Center and then took them through a connecting bridge to the US Attorneys' Office. But MCC had closed. Not an ideal situation.

Bridget and Nathan were escorted back into the court's detention area. Yemeni was chained to a bench in his own cell. He'd changed into a brown jumpsuit, the uniform of prisoners and defendants held without bail. He'd need to get used to it. Even if he received the death penalty, which the feds hadn't done in years, his legal team could mount decades of appeals. His judicial removal from Uganda added a layer of legal vulnerability for the prosecution. Between discovery and tracking down witnesses, it could be a year before Yemeni's trial.

The trial itself would last a month. The Phantoms case for which Yemeni had originally been arrested involved thousands of victims who needed justice. Conviction was likely but uncertain. Yemeni had passed orders and facilitated the Phantoms' deadly opioid attacks, but he hadn't participated in them. That was the challenge in prosecuting high-level cases. When cutting the head off the snake—the only thing that made a difference—they needed to prove Yemeni directed the criminality, and cooperators were hard to find. Radical ideologues willing to die for their cause were difficult to flip.

The terrorism case against Yemeni for his actions in Uganda would be easier to win, because Nathan had witnessed those crimes, as had Bridget, Laker, and the other students. Nathan would only need a few believable witnesses to send Yemeni away forever. But the case was fraught with jurisdictional issues, and nothing was guaranteed in a legal system that afforded every defense to monsters who killed without remorse.

But they'd win. He was certain of it.

Yemeni glared at them.

"We're taking you to meet the assistant US Attorney," Nathan said.

Yemeni didn't react.

"I don't understand what game you're playing," Nathan said, "but we'll listen."

"I have information that—"

"Not yet. You have the right to remain silent, and I suggest you exercise it until your lawyer's with you."

Yemeni smirked.

An urge to drive his elbow into Yemeni's nose ballooned inside Nathan. That monster had gleefully killed thousands. In another time or another place—hell, in almost any country outside of the West—Yemeni would be dangling from a rope. Everyone knew what Yemeni had done, and their evidence was strong. The justice system had gone far to ensure innocent people weren't prosecuted, though it still happened, but perhaps they'd gone too far.

A bullet in his skull would be too kind. Yemeni deserved to suffer, like his victims. Thousands of murder victims left tens of thousands of grieving people. And for what? The need to kill anyone who didn't believe in radical Islam? If any good came out of Yemeni's actions, it would be in his exposing his ideology. Westerners had spent too much time putting themselves in other people's shoes. Fundamentalists only wanted one thing—to murder infidels. It was time for people to understand that.

But Nathan wouldn't hurt him. The rule of law meant something, and once it was gone, it was hard to get back.

A marshal approached. "Get him up. We're ready."

81

Darius tucked his knees against his chest and rocked on the floor. He remained handcuffed behind his back, and their rigid plastic cut into his wrists. Nothing was as it should be. They'd missed breakfast time, judging from light streaming between the metal blinds, and neither policeman prepared his oatmeal. Didn't they know the schedule? Six ounces of oatmeal with a tablespoon of milk. Whole milk, not skim, and ladled into the center. What if they didn't feed him breakfast? Panic bubbled inside him. What kind of jail was this?

Blackwood had drifted to sleep about an hour ago. He slumped in a chair with a drop of spittle stuck in the corner of his mouth. His chest rose the way Bibi's did when she stayed up late watching television. Ramirez sat at a tiny breakfast table and stared at his phone. He'd monitored that phone all night, as if it would ring at any second. He was in charge, which was obvious. Was he the other policeman's uncle? Things work so differently in America.

At least they've taken off Darius's hood so he could breathe.

Darius had to pee. He'd been uncomfortable for hours, but Blackwood had ordered him not to speak. He was the meaner one, just like Father. Back in Tehran, Father had beaten him several times, though he hadn't suffered the vicious abuse Maman received. Bibi hadn't protested then, and she hadn't spoken a word when the police arrested him either. Didn't she care?

A twinge of pain contracted his abdomen. He might wet his pants. He'd done that when he was younger. Luckily, Maman had cleaned the sheets before Father had seen. If he wet himself now, would the policemen hurt him?

One, he speaks and gets beaten. Two, he pees and gets beaten. One, two, one, two, one, two . . . The pain came again. Even his numbers couldn't soothe him. He had to pee.

"Excuse me," he said.

Ramirez looked up. Dark bags hung beneath his eyes. "You're supposed to stay quiet."

"I have to go."

"You're not going anywhere, you little shit."

"I mean, I need to make water."

Ramirez fixated on his partner. "Wake the fuck up."

Blackwood jerked awake and grasped his armrest. "What happened?" Drool ran down his chin, and he wiped it off with the back of his hand.

"Some fucking lookout. Take the kid to the bathroom."

Blackwood stood, and his shirt hung outside his pants. He snarled at Darius. Maybe now Darius would get his beating. Blackwood staggered like Bibi in the morning. He grabbed Darius by the collar and yanked him to his feet. Darius's shirt tore. He braced for a pummeling.

It didn't come.

Blackwood hauled him across the room. Darius tried to keep his feet under him, but his legs had fallen asleep. He stumbled.

"Come on," Blackwood said. "I'm not your nanny."

They hated him, but they were still better than the mullahs' policemen. The officer hauled him into a tiny bathroom. Darius stared from the toilet to Blackwood.

"What you waiting for?"

Fear froze him. "I can't make water without my hands."

"Shit."

Between the naughty words and stubble on the man's chin, he didn't seem as much like a policeman as he had the previous night.

Blackwood drew a knife and flipped open a curved blade.

Darius backed away and bumped into the wall.

"Turn around. I've got to cut off your zip ties."

Darius obeyed and Blackwood came close. The hair on the back of Darius's neck rose. Would the policeman gut him like a fish? He yanked up Darius's hands, sending fire through Darius's shoulders. But he didn't cry out. The man hacked away at the plastic, and it snapped open.

"Make it fast," Blackwood said. He stepped out the door.

Darius rubbed his sore wrists. His shoulder ached, and his legs were still asleep.

He wanted to go home.

82

Nathan grasped Yemeni's elbow, controlling the man's arm. Even a handcuffed and shackled prisoner could pose a threat, and he wouldn't give Yemeni an opportunity. Minding the details saved lives. They walked down a back corridor and entered an elevator. Bridget, a court security officer, and two marshals crowded in. They descended to the first floor and exited into the secondary lobby. The corridors had been blocked off in advance, and two armed marshals stood near the exit to the street.

"We need our firearms," Nathan said.

The officer unsnapped his radio and called ahead. Nathan and Bridget hurried back to the primary access point and retrieved their firearms, which they'd secured when they entered the courthouse. Law enforcement officers weren't permitted to carry a gun inside the courthouse, except CSOs and marshals, but this was an exigent circumstance, and a supervisor escorted them back through the interior hallway.

They reached the back where Yemeni waited with the marshals. Nathan exhaled with relief. When dealing with high-value targets who controlled assets worldwide, the unpredictable became the predictable.

Nathan took control of Yemeni, and the group moved to the rear security checkpoint. The access point had been closed all morning. Red ropes attached to brass stands blocked off the double doors. Nathan squinted through the glass past metal detectors to the exterior doors leading to the steps. Two marshals waited for them, and four NYPD officers huddled nearby. People transversed the sidewalk, but no one looked at the closed entrance.

"This is a bad idea," Nathan said.

"Wicked retarded," Bridget said.

Yemeni maintained a placid expression, as if he watched this happen to someone else. Was he in shock from his return to the United States and the horror of a potential death sentence, or had he resigned himself to his fate?

Nathan scanned the street as they descended the steps. Yemeni's leg shackles restricted them to a laggard pace, but Nathan kept them on, because if Yemeni could run, he had a chance. A man and a woman wearing suits stopped and gawked. Nathan watched their hands. Both carried cell phones and appeared to be lawyers attending to federal business.

The arraignment had received enough publicity that everyone in North America must've seen a photo of Yemeni, the man who'd masterminded thousands of opioid deaths. The victims in Westchester had brought him back onto the front pages, and his recapture would dominate the news for weeks. Life or death, freedom or incarceration—human drama too powerful to resist.

Nathan kept a firm grip on Yemeni's arm as they reached the sidewalk. For a man who'd caused so much death and destruction, he felt scrawny and frail, but the darkness lurking inside him remained powerful. Evil existed. Nathan scoffed at most supernatural phenomenon, but he'd seen enough to know wickedness thrived in men, whether a devil, demon, or other metaphysical force. And that malevolent entity lived deep within Yemeni. Nathan felt it.

They crossed the street and turned onto Cardinal Hayes Place adjacent to the now-closed Metropolitan Correctional Center, a gray, depressing concrete anachronism. People who ended up in prison occupied the bottom rung of human experience. It took serious criminality to be charged federally, get convicted, and sentenced to years in jail. Those who'd been housed in MCC exhibited humanity's depravity—ignorant and immoral— the predators who lived among their prey.

The police had barricades on this side of the narrow street, but not at the far end where it emptied onto Saint Andrew's Plaza. They'd barricaded the plaza to vehicular traffic after 9/11. Those attacks had changed the landscape of the city.

Nathan and Bridget moved up the street between MCC and Saint Andrew church toward the US Attorney's Office. The church was constructed from red brick and white stone with massive oval windows, a stark design contrast to the brutalist architecture of the government buildings. Had NYPD checked it before the arraignment? No one had expected this stroll with a terrorist.

Except Yemeni.

They approached the wooden doors, and Nathan's eyes lingered on them. Marshals surrounded them like a presidential security detail. Nathan kept a brisk pace, pushing Yemeni hard. Bridget brushed her jacket back and kept her hand on her Glock. That wasn't protocol, but neither was the movement. Where was the ASAC Giacomo? As always, supervisors made decisions, and line agents paid the price.

They exited into Saint Andrew's Plaza and steered toward a flight of concrete steps that led up to the raised walkway and the entrance to the US Attorney's Office. Nathan mounted the steps and climbed sideways to scan the plaza.

They reached a landing. Through the trees and across Park Row lay NYPD Headquarters at One Police Plaza. Even in proximity to New York's law enforcement hub, they weren't safe. Terrorism sought soft targets, making it almost impossible to stop without some loss of life—especially in a free society with few restrictions on movement.

They continued up the last flight of steps and across the elevated walkway. The office was at 1 Saint Andrew's Plaza in the Silvio J. Mollo Federal Building, a forty-one-floor tower that looked like a Jenga stack. Gigantic pillars gave the building the appearance of an alien ship from *War of the Worlds*.

They paused outside and let the marshals enter first. A moment later, one came back and gave the thumbs-up. All clear.

"I thought we were gonna get whacked out there," Bridget said.

"Me too."

They followed the marshal past the front desk, and a security officer buzzed them into the back. The marshals held Yemeni while Nathan and Bridget locked their firearms in security boxes. The security officer handed them the keys, which Nathan pocketed, and they took hold of Yemeni. Bridget and Nathan escorted Yemeni into an old elevator car with two armed marshals and a building security officer.

The marshals and the security officers contracted by the Federal Protective Service could carry weapons inside the court and US Attorney's Office, but federal agents weren't allowed. Controls and authorizations seemed reasonable, but FBI agents could carry on airplanes, yet they weren't trusted to bring them into the office. Absolute nonsense.

They'd arrived, and nothing had happened. Nathan had been wrong— not about following proper protocols—but his gut had told him Yemeni's people would make a play to free him. Nathan's instincts were usually accurate, but he was happy they'd failed him. He'd seen enough bloodshed to last a lifetime.

The elevator dinged, and they got off on the thirty-seventh floor. White stood in the unit's lobby and peered through bulletproof glass. He unlocked the door for them. The security officer and marshals returned to the elevator while Nathan and Bridget took Yemeni into the SDNY's National Security and International Narcotics Unit.

Time to see if Yemeni had information or was just jerking them around.

83

Nathan and Bridget guided Yemeni into a dingy interview room inside the SDNY's Terrorism and Narcotics Unit and sat him at the table, bracketed by his court-appointed defense attorney, Lisa Dawson, and the court interpreter, Leila Kabiri, who had her cell phone to her ear.

"Hello, Ruhi," Leila said. Unlike court, cell phones were allowed in the US Attorney's Office. "I'll be late. I'm interpreting for a proffer on thirty-seven. I'll call you when I'm done."

Leila hung up and slipped her phone into her purse, as Bridget, White, and Nathan took their seats.

"I'm Samuel White, assistant United States attorney prosecuting your case, and you've already met Special Agents Quinn and Burke. Before we begin, I need you to read and sign a proffer agreement. This is a temporary arrangement where you agree to waive your right to remain silent so you can explore potential cooperation with the government." Sam paused to let Leila catch up, but she'd been interpreting simultaneously and finished.

"We don't make promises," Sam continued, "but we won't use anything you say against you if we go to trial, unless you take the stand and contradict statements made here."

Sam pushed a paper across the table, and Dawson scanned it. She turned to Yemeni. "This is identical to the boilerplate I explained to you.

The only difference is they've added your name and the date. Are you ready to begin, or would you prefer Ms. Kabiri translate it for you?"

Yemeni stared at her with disdain, then he smirked at Nathan. "Translation."

Dawson rolled her eyes. Clearly, she'd become exasperated with him in the short time they'd been together. Nathan had interviewed dozens of jihadists from the Middle East, and their inability to answer questions directly made him nuts too. Her conversation with him before the arraignment must've been an exercise in futility.

Sam stood. "Very well. We'll give you a moment to translate the document and answer Mr. Yemeni's questions."

Bridget sighed. This was all performative, but as the prosecution team, they had to ensure the defendant understood his rights and knew the limitations of a proffer. Any miscommunication could later invalidate cooperation or create the groundwork for an appeal. Yemeni would bullshit them, but they still had to do everything by the book.

Sam was already up and had the door open. Bridget followed him, and Nathan shuffled to the door but didn't shut it behind him. He looked at Yemeni, who stared back like the cat who'd eaten a mouse. Had this whole thing been leading to this moment? Nathan had patted him down. Yemeni wore jail-issued coveralls and the marshals had searched him, but he could still have a shank on him.

Nathan's eyes moved to Yemeni's restraints. He remained shackled and handcuffed, but unlike standard lockups, this interview room didn't have a place to handcuff Yemeni in place.

"I'll give you privacy," Nathan said, "but I can leave this cracked open in case there's a problem."

Dawson looked at him with a contemptuous expression he'd received from Ivy League graduates who considered agents to be blue-collar workers with inferior intellects. Many thought gun-toting agents were knuckle draggers who enjoyed inflicting violence.

"Shut it," she said.

Nathan glanced at Leila. The interpreter looked a little frightened, but she was new and unaccustomed to the company of terrorists, especially a mass murderer like Yemeni.

Nathan closed the door. White and Bridget moved away, discussing the case, but Nathan stayed beside the threshold. He cocked his head and leaned close. Muffled murmuring came from inside. He shouldn't eavesdrop on a confidential conversation, but if Dawson or Leila yelled, he'd hear them.

White looked back at him, and Nathan pretended to examine his phone, but he focused on the voices inside the room. If anything banged or a chair leg screeched against the floor, Nathan would barge in, and attorney-client privilege be damned. He wouldn't let either woman get hurt. Not on his watch.

The hushed conversation continued inside for a few minutes, and then Dawson opened the door. Her eyes narrowed at him, but she said nothing. Down deep, her primitive desire to survive had to make her cautious when meeting with a killer. Her dedication to protecting her clients must heighten her suspicion of law enforcement, but the threat to her safety was obvious.

Nathan waved at White and Bridget and followed her inside. They all returned to their seats.

"I've explained the proffer agreement to my client," Dawson said.

"All right, Mr. Yemeni," White said. "Do you understand that you're required to tell the truth, but we're under no obligation to sign you as a cooperator, and this meeting is unlikely to result in any reduced sentence recommendation from this office?"

Nathan shifted in his seat. White's formality was understandable, but calling this savage *mister* irked him. Yemeni had destroyed so many lives.

Yemeni bowed his head in acknowledgment.

"We need a verbal response," White said.

"I understand you won't help me," Yemeni said. "I understand you're my enemy. I understand you're very existence is an offense to Allah."

White looked at Dawson. "I don't know where we go from there."

Dawson scowled. "Mr. Yemeni, you requested this meeting to—"

Leila stood. Dawson cocked her head, and White raised his eyebrows in concern. Leila stared at Nathan. Fear warped her face, and her chin quivered.

Nathan glanced at Yemeni. Had he touched her? The hair on Nathan's neck rose. Something was wrong. Really wrong.

"Is there a problem, Ms. Kabiri?" White asked.

"I need to speak with Agent Burke," Leila said.

"Hold on," Dawson said. "Anything you've interpreted in here is privileged information, and you're not legally allowed—"

"It's not that," Leila said. "It's something else, and it's urgent."

Dawson's forehead furrowed, and she blinked rapidly. "What do you—"

Nathan stood. "Step outside with me."

"This is highly inappropriate," Dawson objected.

Nathan ignored her and led Leila into the hall, shutting the door behind them. "What's so urgent?"

Leila's eyes filled. "We're in danger. We—"

Boom. A thunderous noise from below shook the floor. An explosion.

84

A red haze tinged the edges of Darius's vision as he rocked back and forth on his butt and held his knees. Nothing had happened according to schedule.

Eight, eight, eight. That's when he should have eaten, but the time for breakfast had come and gone, and Maman hadn't told him to get dressed. Now, it must be lunchtime and the policemen didn't feed him. His routine, his existence, had collapsed. This wouldn't do. It wasn't right.

"*Ey vai*," he said. It slipped out. He wasn't supposed to talk, but he couldn't contain his desperation. His entire being protested. His life revolved around the normal, the expected—but everything here was new. The apartment smelled like musk. Where was his mother? Why hadn't she come for him yet? This couldn't stand.

Ramirez gazed up through sleepy eyes, but said nothing. He'd stuck to that same chair since they'd arrived. Blackwood paced around the apartment mumbling to himself as if he battled unseen jinn.

"No," Darius said.

Blackwood raged into the room. "What the fuck did you say?"

Darius rocked. The policeman was furious, but he didn't care. He couldn't live like this. His world spiraled out of control, and he couldn't correct it. These men controlled everything, and they didn't care about him. Why weren't they taking him to the judge?

"No, no, no."

Blackwood came closer. "Shut up."

"You didn't make my oatmeal."

"What the hell are you talking about, you little freak?"

"Little freak, little freak, little freak."

"You making fun of me? You a wiseass? You're not gonna be laughing when I knock out your teeth."

"Take it easy," Ramirez said.

Darius's nose tingled, the way it did before he cried. "You missed breakfast. Missed it, missed it, missed it. Everything supposed to happen at the right time."

Blackwood snorted. "Fuck is wrong with this kid?"

"I need clean clothes, and it's time for lunch. We can't miss lunch, lunch, lunch."

"He's fucking crazy. I'm gonna gag him again."

"Leave him be," Ramirez said. "I'm too tired for this shit."

"Too tired, too tired, too tired."

Blackwood flushed. "I can't take this shit. I'm not gonna listen to this nutcase all day. They're not paying me enough."

"They're paying you more than you're worth," Ramirez said.

Blackwood glared in silence.

Darius rocked. "It's time for lunch. It's time, it's time, it's time."

Blackwood whirled around. "How about I feed you your ears?"

Darius's breath caught in his throat. Blackwood meant it. He'd cut off Darius's ears and make him eat them. How could he hear without ears? He wouldn't hear Maman calling for him.

"You don't like him complaining," Ramirez said, "then feed him. And make me something too."

"I'm not your fucking servant."

Ramirez shoved his chair back and raised to his full height. He didn't seem old anymore. His face sharpened, and he glared at Blackwood. "Go ahead, say that again."

Blackwood swallowed hard. "I'm hungry too. I'll go downstairs and get something from that café on the corner."

Ramirez nodded. "That's what I thought. Egg sandwich and black coffee. And don't take too long. They can call any time."

Blackwood started for the door, then stopped. "Should I go out in the uniform?"

"Gotta be ready. When they call, we grab the kid and head down. And we ain't getting anywhere close to that place without the uniforms."

Blackwood nodded but didn't look friendly. He glanced at Darius. "Happy now, you little shit? I'll get you lunch, but I better not hear another word out of you, capeesh?"

"Another word, another word, another word."

Blackwood scowled. He grumbled as he went out into the hall.

Ramirez glowered. "Don't mistake kindness for weakness. I'll feed you, but if you make noise, I'll stuff you in that closet with a bag over your head. Get it?"

"Uh-huh." A tear rolled down Darius's cheek.

When would Maman come get him?

85

Nathan yanked open the proffer room's door and pointed at Yemeni. "Don't let that fucker out of his seat."

Bridget stood beside her chair. "What was that?"

"Bomb." Nathan slammed the door and raced down the hallway.

A female attorney in a brown pantsuit leaned out of her office. "What's happening out—"

"Stay inside and shut the door," Nathan said.

She jerked back, offended. "Excuse me?"

"Hide under your desk until you get the all clear."

She recoiled with understanding and disappeared inside. Nathan dashed to the lobby and surveyed the elevator bank through the thick glass.

Vacant.

The elevator doors remained closed. Everything appeared normal. Had a bomb gone off at the courthouse or in their building? Something had exploded somewhere, and—

Thud, thud, thud.

Rhythmic thumping came from below, and there was no mistaking the sound of automatic weapons fire.

They were under attack. Yemeni's people were coming for him. That's why he'd requested the emergency proffer. That snake had set them up to give his men a chance to bust him out.

And it could work.

Nathan had little time to plan. What were their options? They could take Yemeni and flee downstairs, but assaulters would have those emergency exits covered, and they couldn't leave innocent people behind. Yemeni had proven he'd kill anyone to effectuate his escape when he'd slaughtered those airline passengers. Innocents weren't just expendable for him to achieve his aim—their deaths were the point. The more civilian lives lost, the more Yemeni would spread terror. A population in fear would pressure lawmakers to appease terrorists, but slaughtering infidels was also the goal. Fundamental Islam forced people to submit or die.

Nathan couldn't flee with their prisoner, nor could he let Yemeni escape. He had to stand his ground, and he only had seconds to prepare.

Jihadists could come up either the elevators or stairwells. Terrorists wouldn't walk up thirty-seven flights, which left the elevator bank. Nathan dialed Bridget, as he watched the elevators.

"Whatcha got?" Bridget asked.

"Take Yemeni and get away from the lobby. Bang on doors and bring everyone with you. Hole up in the last office."

"What's the scoop?"

"They're coming for him," Nathan said. "I'll slow them down."

"You're unarmed."

"If we survive, you'll never catch me without my gun again. Hurry."

"They'll search all the offices. They'll find us."

"We're a hundred yards from One Police Plaza. NYPD will respond. We need to stall."

"Copy."

It would take Bridget time to corral attorneys, and she wouldn't get everyone, but in law enforcement, as in life, doing something was better than nothing. He had to slow the terrorists down, but how? He'd locked his weapon downstairs, and the gunfire had lessened to an occasional muffled pop, so the terrorists had taken the first floor. It wouldn't have been difficult. The armed officers only carried handguns, and even if they had shotguns, they wouldn't offer any real resistance to motivated jihadists.

Behind him, a cup filled with pens and a pair of scissors sat on the vacant receptionist desk. *Scissors.* Nathan snickered. If trained security officers with Glocks couldn't stop them, what chance did he have with a dull blade? Still, it was better than nothing.

Nathan snatched the scissors and stuck them in his pocket. He looked around as panic grew inside him. Maybe he should hide with everyone else. But that would be suicide.

His active-shooter training had shown the futility of hiding while armed assailants went room to room murdering everyone. They had to resist to survive, and if he only had scissors, then dammit, he'd use them. Better to die fighting than cowering like a victim.

He scanned all four hallways, then returned to the lobby. A fire extinguisher hung on the wall. Maybe he could use it to create a cloud to conceal his retreat.

Nathan had taken a counterterrorism course in the great dismal swamp of North Carolina years before, and he'd been a team leader on the red team, acting as a terror leader in practical exercises. He'd employed classic hit-and-run techniques against a superior force and had whittled them down as they chased him. That's what he'd do here. Of course, his red team had been armed with Simunitions.

No sense bemoaning his circumstances. He unclipped the fire extinguisher and took it off the wall.

The elevator bell dinged.

86

Nathan sprinted across the lobby and flattened against the wall beside the bulletproof window. He peeked around the corner. Two men dressed in black clothes and carrying AR-15s exited the freight elevator. One turned toward the opposite wing, and the other came toward him.

Nathan slipped out of sight. The elevator bank was in the center of the building, separating two sets of offices. If only two jihadists came, he could deal with one at a time. He might have a chance if—

Another elevator dinged. More footsteps.

Crap.

A shadow crossed the floor as men moved toward the lobby. He fought the urge to flee. He could race down the long corridor to help Bridget collect attorneys and administrative personnel, but what then? Nathan would need to resist eventually, and if he did that here, he'd give Bridget time to hide everyone.

He couldn't hold out for long, but they only needed to hold out until the feds or NYPD arrived. Would police wait for HRT or SWAT, or would officers come in knowing dozens of staff were in danger? Police gave a little extra effort when their own were involved.

The handle on the lobby door jiggled. Nathan removed the scissors from his pocket and grasped them like a dagger. He dangled the fire extinguisher in his other hand.

Someone kicked the door with a loud bang, and the window rattled. He kicked again. The door held. At least the lowest bidder who'd built this place had done their job. Another kick, then silence.

An AR-15 unleashed a burst, and wood splintered. A cloud of fragments and dust blew into the lobby. Nathan turned his head to protect his eyes and coiled his body.

The door flung open.

Nathan didn't hesitate. He lunged past the window and swung the fire extinguisher.

The first jihadist stepped through the threshold as the extinguisher's cylinder reached the apex of its arc. The metal smashed into his face with a wet smack, as if Nathan had struck him with a water balloon.

A mist of blood and teeth flew into the air. The man crashed against the wall, and his AR-15 clattered to the ground.

Nathan dropped the extinguisher and snatched the weapon.

Another jihadist sprayed rounds. Bullets smacked the safety glass, cracked over Nathan's head, and pierced the far wall.

Nathan ducked out of the doorway and stayed low. The first man's body splayed across the threshold, which would slow them down, but not for long.

Nathan dashed down the hallway. He'd never make it.

He dove into the first office with an open door. He landed on the floor of a tiny office with a single desk and two file cabinets. Nathan scrambled to his feet and faced the doorway. The shooting stopped up front, which meant one thing.

The men were coming.

Nathan mounted his AR-15 against his shoulder. The safety was off and the metal warm, which meant it had been fired, but he had no time to inspect it. Nathan braced his foot against the wall aimed at the hallway. He leaned out, muzzle first.

A jihadist kicked the unconscious body into the lobby, then two men entered with weapons raised. Nathan lowered his front post onto the first man's chest and dropped his finger onto the trigger. He squeezed, and a round exploded out of the carbine's muzzle with a bright flash.

Single action.

The first suspect jerked and tumbled back against the wall. The second man fired, and overpressure from the supersonic round rippled the air beside Nathan's face.

Nathan adjusted his sights and squeezed off three shots in quick succession.

The man's head exploded in a fog of bone and blood. His body crumbled to the floor. Nathan focused on the lobby door.

No one entered.

The unconscious man didn't move. Nathan fired a round into his chest to make sure he stayed that way. Combat could be ugly.

Nathan had a moment, maybe seconds. He lifted his finger off the trigger and rested it on the frame. He adjusted the stock off his sore shoulder and seated it in the hollow between his deltoid and pectoral muscles. He adjusted his grip so the web between his thumb and forefinger pressed flush against the backstrap. He moved his support hand farther out to better control the muzzle. Years of tactical training paid off.

A man poked his face through the entrance. Nathan raised his barrel and fired. The man ducked back. Missed.

The elevator dinged again. How many operators came to rescue Yemeni? They could have hundreds of sleeper-cell agents who'd entered the country illegally. If Nathan had planned the attack, he'd have used a small team carrying AR-15s in duffel bags to take the lobby to allow the larger force to enter unopposed.

They'd expected armed resistance, but not like this. They'd be trying to figure out a way in. Did the hallways connect to the other half of the thirty-seventh floor? A chill of terror breezed through him. If they moved quietly, he might not hear them. If they were smart, they'd take the stairs down one floor and then come up another stairwell behind him. But all that took time, and they had to know NYPD would respond soon.

These guys were blunt instruments, Islamists willing to sacrifice their lives to free their leader. They wouldn't use finesse. They'd attack through—

A jihadist with an AK-47 burst into the lobby and fired a sustained burst at Nathan.

Nathan feathered the trigger and loosed two rounds as he plunged backward into the office. A bullet ricocheted off the metal doorframe and punctured the plaster. The shooting stopped.

Nathan repositioned himself and squatted, to reappear from a different spot. He leaned into the hallway and fired off three quick rounds.

The terrorist grabbed his leg where one of Nathan's rounds had found its mark. Two other terrorists scampered across the lobby and returned fire. They disappeared around the far corner. They were inside.

Nathan's section of the building was shaped like an H with two parallel hallways. Now they could come from either direction, and worse, they could search for the office where Bridget hid Yemeni and the other attorneys.

Nathan should have fled in the opposite direction to draw them away. *Stupid.* Of course, innocent attorneys hid on that side too. The serpent had entered the house.

Time to go.

87

Nathan kept his eyes on the lobby. He clicked the magazine release and removed it. He didn't have time to count the double-stacked bullets, but he hefted the magazine. Too light. He ran low on ammo. He reseated the magazine, and it clicked it into place.

Three terrorists had infiltrated the office, and more on the opposite half of the floor, plus they'd leave people downstairs to repel rescuers. The bodies of the men he'd slain lay with their limbs akimbo in that awkward positioning of the dead. He needed their weapons, or he couldn't protect everyone else.

Nathan fired a round at the lobby to let them know he was still a threat. Hopefully, that would deter them.

He slipped into the hallway, scanning over his front sight. He moved heal to toe, trying to be as quiet as possible—but fast. Dawdling in the hallway's fatal funnel would end with his death.

He reached the first body. The man's eyes were open, and he'd soiled himself. Not a threat. Nathan reached down and tugged the AR-15's sling over the dead man's head and slung the weapon over his shoulder. He proceeded to the second body.

A shadow flashed on the wall. At least one terrorist remained close. They hadn't all tried to circle him. At least not yet.

Nathan glanced back. No one snuck up behind him. He shuffled backward, moving quickly and sacrificing sound for stealth. He needed to get behind cover.

A terrorist peeked around the lobby corner.

Nathan fired, but the man ducked behind cover, and plaster puffed off the wall. Nathan had missed by two feet. That may keep the shooter at bay, but he'd spotted Nathan in the hall and knew he was vulnerable.

Nathan reached the office and stepped inside as the terrorist extended his AR-15 and fired a burst. The bullets were unaimed and scattered, and they slammed into the ceiling and ricocheted off the floor.

Nathan stayed hunkered down. He checked the magazine in the second carbine. The thirty-round magazine probably held twenty rounds. The risk had been worth it.

Nathan eased the charging handle back and confirmed a round sat in the chamber, then he swapped the magazine with the one in his carbine. He could've just switched weapons, but the one he held worked, not a guarantee when using an enemy's firearm. Nathan slung the second AR-15 onto his back.

He'd wasted enough time.

Nathan peeked out, then bolted down the hall. He sprinted and didn't bother looking back. If they heard him and shot, then he'd take his chances. He had to get to the office where Bridget holed up with the attorneys and Yemeni.

Nathan reached the end of the hallway and swung around the corner. No terrorists yet. He hurried to the last office, which the unit's deputy chief used. He flung open the door.

Bridget stepped into the threshold ready to throw a punch.

"It's me."

"Get in."

He entered and shut the door behind him. Yemeni lay on his stomach beside the door, and eight attorneys, including White, huddled against the far wall.

"How bad?" Bridget asked.

"Three are headed our way."

"Wicked beat."

Nathan unslung his second AR-15 and handed it to her. "There's one in the pipe."

She slung the carbine. "Should I ask how you got these?"

"I took out a few."

She nodded. "At least we can fight back."

"It won't be enough. These walls won't stop .223 rounds."

"Everyone behind the cabinets," Bridget said.

Attorneys shuffled behind the metal file cabinets, but they didn't fit, and they resembled clowns climbing into a car. Yemeni rolled onto his side.

"Not you, dirtbag," Bridget said.

"What are we doing?" White asked from the corner.

"I've hunted criminals my entire career," Nathan said, "but since we started this damn case, I've been the prey. I've had enough."

"We don't have a choice here," she said.

"Yeah, we do. I can get aggressive and take the fight to them."

"If we stay down and wait it out, they'll come for us, eventually."

"We wait much longer, and this'll be a recovery, not a rescue."

Bridget nodded but didn't look confident.

Voices emanated from the hall.

White raised his hand like a kid in school. "I don't think we should go anywhere. Let the police handle this."

Nathan started to respond, then turned to Bridget. "Here's the plan. You and me will take Yemeni down the stairs. If the rescue team can't come to us, then we'll go to them."

"We'll never make it to the stairwell."

"They're not expecting aggression. I'm gonna break out and charge them. I'll rout the closest shooters and give you a window to get Yemeni to the stairwell. If you make it, head down and keep going."

"Wait," White said. "You can't leave us here without protection."

"They came for Yemeni. If we survive, we lead them away from here."

"They'll have people in the lobby," Bridget said.

"Stop one floor up and wait. Contact NYPD by phone and vector SWAT to you."

"This is freaking crazy," Bridget said.

"If we wait, they'll pin us down," Nathan said. "They'll shoot through the walls and pepper us with bullets. They'll use suppressing fire to swarm in here and murder whoever's still breathing."

"Then let's get our asses in gear."

Nathan looked at White. "Keep everyone in here and stay low. When Bridget drags Yemeni out, barricade the door with the desk. We'll draw their fire away from you."

White's eyes widened with terror. He was a beast inside a court room in a battle of wits, but he was out of his element confronting flying bullets. Composure came from experience, and battle had become Nathan's world.

White grabbed one end of the desk and Nathan took the other. A round smacked through the wall above them. They dropped the desk beside the door.

Nathan mounted his carbine's stock against his shoulder. He looked back at Bridget. "In thirty seconds, I'll either be dead or I'll have driven them back. Get ready."

Bridget didn't look happy. She jerked Yemeni to his feet. She held his elbow and wrapped her other arm around his neck. She was gonna drag him out whether or not he agreed. Yemeni looked uncertain, as if none of this had gone the way he'd expected.

Fuck him.

Nathan readied himself.

God, help me be strong.

He wrenched the door open and stepped out.

A siren yelped on the street, and Darius flinched. He hadn't moved for hours, and his legs cramped. Blackwood spent most of his time peering through the blinds at whatever was happening outside. The wailing sirens sounded close.

Blackwood let the slats flap shut, then he lumbered across the room to where Ramirez watched out the peephole. They'd heard a murmured conversation and footsteps in the hallway, and Darius had been tempted to shout out, but that would have invited a beating for sure.

"What happens if we gotta show him?" Blackwood asked.

"Then that's what we'll do."

"The Financial District sounds like a fucking war zone. We're supposed to waltz up there with the kid?"

"They'll tell us what to do."

Blackwood shook his head and frowned. "I'm not getting arrested for this shit."

Getting arrested? How would a policeman get arrested?

"You'll do whatever the fuck you're told," Ramirez said. "If they call, we'll take him out and let her see him. That's why we're here."

Blackwood glanced at Darius, then whispered, but loud enough to hear. "What happens to the girl and the kid after that?"

Ramirez's eyes shifted to Darius, and he spoke softly. "He . . . that's up to . . . finish them."

"We gotta kill him?"

"You'll do what you're told, or they'll take care of us too."

Darius's breath came fast, and he tried to control it. He couldn't let them know he'd overheard. He breathed in through his nose and rocked but couldn't erase those words from his memory.

They would murder him.

Adrenaline masked Nathan's fear as he sprang into the hallway. Two jihadists aimed AK-47s, and two more loitered in the open, as if they perceived no threat from their victims. Big mistake.

Nathan fired three quick rounds at the first man without using his sights, then spun and shot at the man on the opposite end of the hall. A bullet flashed past Nathan's face. He crouched and fired at the last two men as they brought their guns around.

Nathan's rounds smacked into their flesh, spinning them. The guy at the corner fired again, and the round slapped the wall beside Nathan.

Nathan aimed at him, and the man slipped behind cover. Nathan edged his sights to the side and shot into the wall. His bullets must've pierced it, because the terrorist dropped his weapon and fell to the floor.

Nathan approached the men he'd shot and fired into their writhing bodies without slowing. He spun around the corner and squeezed off rounds before his mind processed the scene. Two terrorists ran toward him.

Nathan moved as he shot, making himself a challenging target. But the men weren't prepared for his attack. Both turned and fled. Nathan stopped and knelt. He overlaid his front post on the last man. He fired.

The man's back arched, and his arms extended. He grabbed his spine, then stumbled forward and fell. The second man disappeared into the lobby. Nathan retreated. The office door was ajar, and Bridget looked out at him.

"Go now," Nathan said.

Bridget flung open the door and dragged Yemeni out by his throat.

Nathan fired at the far corner. No response.

Nathan, Bridget, and Yemeni headed for the stairwell. Nathan looked back as a muzzle poked around the corner. Nathan fired, and his rounds tore a hunk of plaster off the wall. The barrel withdrew. Nathan shifted his aim six inches to penetrate the wall. He pulled the trigger.

Click.

The most dreaded sound in a gun battle. Out of ammunition.

Nathan turned and raced after Bridget and Yemeni. He caught them as they reached the stairwell. Bridget dragged open the heavy fire door and pushed Yemeni inside.

"*Inkahak,*" Yemeni shouted.

Nathan threw a hard right jab into Yemeni's face. His knuckles collided with Yemeni's teeth, and his lip exploded.

Yemeni's head jerked back, and he banged against the wall. Bridget pinned Yemeni against the landing wall, but he didn't fight. Nathan closed the door behind them.

"Down," Nathan said.

He descended two steps, then wrapped his fingers around Yemeni's cuffs to control him. Bridget held Yemeni's other arm. They reached the next landing.

"I'm out," Nathan said. "What can you spare?"

Bridget ejected her magazine and thumbed out eight .223 rounds. He took them and fumbled with the bullets as he loaded. *Slow is fast.* He took a breath and finished loading.

"Ready?" he asked.

"Move."

"Keep your eyes on our six," Nathan said. "I've got him."

"This douchebag isn't going anywhere." Bridget hooked her elbow around Yemeni's arm and turn sideways. She aimed her carbine up the stairs.

The stairwell enclosure used a closed design, with solid walls on both sides. Nathan pressed his back against the wall and kept his AR-15 away from Yemeni as they climbed down. He sliced the pie, hoping to glimpse a piece of clothing or weapon before they spotted him. Even savvy adversaries flagged themselves with sloppy positioning.

Nathan descended, one foot at a time. Yemeni bumbled behind him, and his weight jostled Nathan, making their maneuver less than acrobatic.

He stayed on the stairwell's interior wall to better address threats, and he kept a grasp on Yemeni. They made too much noise, but their pursuers must've heard them enter the stairwell. Nathan's bold aggression should have diverted the terrorist attention from the innocents in the office, and making noise would continue to draw the terrorists' focus on them. The sudden death of the terrorists' colleagues bought him a minute or two, but it would heighten their sense of danger and fill them with a lust for revenge. Losing comrades did that, but they'd reorganize and mount an assault.

Bridget and Nathan were thirty-six floors above the lobby, and terrorists could have positioned on intervening levels, but that was unlikely. Diffusing their force throughout the building wouldn't make sense. If terrorists waited below, they'd be screwed, but what else could they do?

He stopped. "Call the PD."

Bridget took out her phone and dialed. "No service. Frigging stairwell."

"Or they jammed comms. Let's keep moving."

Nathan continued downstairs with his weapon angled down. The stairwell came into view over his front sight. He leaned out and pointed the barrel. His AR-15 weighed seven pounds plus ammo, and extending the weight with one hand strained his muscles. His shoulder injury burned. The scar tissue and damaged nerves from his old bullet wound had inhibited healing.

Nathan moved around the corner. The lower stairwell was clear. He dragged Yemeni behind him. They stumbled forward, a drunk threesome on the dance floor.

He hurried down the next flight and glanced back. Yemeni looked annoyed. Things hadn't gone as anticipated. Nathan slowed and edged around the next landing. The steps below were clear.

Nathan continued down, picking up speed.

The metal door above them clanged open, and footsteps pounded down the steps—at least five or six jihadists in a murderous thunder. Bloodlust had swept away their caution.

Bridget aimed at the landing above. They should pick up their pace and not get bogged down in a firefight, but they couldn't ignore the threat. Nathan couldn't shoot past Yemeni and Bridget in the confined space, so he relied on her. How many rounds did she have left?

Nathan focused below as they descended. He moved deliberately to allow Bridget a better chance to defend them.

She fired. A man cried out. Nathan jerked around. Blood splattered the wall as a terrorist crumpled onto the steps. A second jihadist poked out and fired.

Bridget screamed.

Bridget lowered her AR-15 and collapsed against the wall. Nathan shoved Yemeni aside and raised his AR-15. He fired. The man who'd shot her flinched and ducked back around the corner. Nathan fired into the plaster, but these were solid walls and his rounds wouldn't penetrate. His round ricocheted with a whine. His ears rang from the clatter, compounding the chaos. Gunpowder tickled his nostrils. The stairwell had become the Seventh Circle of Hell.

They needed to keep moving, but Bridget wasn't going anywhere. She held her thigh, and blood trickled through her fingers.

Two rounds clanked into a fire door below them. More terrorists. They used suppressing fire to clear the landing, which meant they'd enter soon. They must have taken the elevators down to trap them.

Nathan aimed at the door as it swung open and a jihadist stepped onto the landing. Nathan fired two rounds into the man's chest. He fell back through the doorway. The fire door slammed shut behind him.

This was it. They had to fight it out. If the terrorists had a grenade, it would be over already.

Bridget shot from behind him, and a man tumbled down the stairs. More shouts came from above. If Bridget stayed in the fight, they'd have a chance.

Yemeni shrugged out of Nathan's grasp and stepped toward the fire door and freedom, but his shackled legs restricted his movement. Nathan grabbed a handful of Yemeni's jumpsuit and slammed him into the wall.

Yemeni grinned through bloody teeth. The bastard thrived in chaos. There were no sleeper cells in New York preparing to unleash biological hell on Americans. Yemeni only wanted to escape.

Nathan hooked his arm around Yemeni's neck and pulled him off-balance. He dragged him to Bridget. She lay on the ground and used her hand to apply pressure to her wound. Her pant leg had soaked through with blood, but she kept her carbine pointed up the stairs.

Bridget could be dying, but she wouldn't go without a fight. Male or female didn't matter. She had the heart of every paladin who confronted evil.

She was a warrior.

"*Yamut, kafiran!*" a man screamed as he spun around the corner with his carbine up and hate in his eyes.

Nathan pulled Yemeni in front of Bridget as fire spit out of the man's weapon. Yemeni's head snapped back, and he crashed against Nathan.

Nathan fired back with one hand. His muzzle jerked as he sent a stream of bullets upward. The man twitched as the rounds impacted him in the chest and face. He hovered for a second, then fell face-first onto the steps. He spasmed, then stopped moving.

Nathan swept the landing with his barrel, but no one followed the crazed jihadi.

Yemeni leaned against the wall in front of Bridget. Blood splattered his jumpsuit, and he didn't move.

"Cover up," he told Bridget.

"Got it," she said through clenched teeth. Her face scrunched into a mask of pain, but she kept her AR-15 pointed forward. Blood pooled on the floor beneath her. She'd lost a lot, but hopefully not too much. Nathan's instinct urged him to bandage her wound, but tactics dictated he confront the deadly threat before rendering aid.

Nathan pivoted and scanned the stairs below with his finger on the trigger—ready to fire. The door remained closed. The smell of blood and gunpowder hung in the air. He wriggled his nose to ward off his sneeze, because involuntarily closing his eyes wasn't ideal in a gunfight.

A siren yelped thirty-seven floors below, then another until a cacophony rushed up toward him. Boots thumped on the ground.

Bridget and Nathan were both dangerously close to running out of ammunition. They couldn't resist for much longer.

Muffled shots came from the opposite side of the door below them, but no rounds impacted the door. What were they shooting at now? More shouts and firing, this time with the distinctive pop of small arms. Were they using handguns, or was that someone else?

No sound came from above. Had they retreated or were they preparing to charge?

The door creaked open below him and Nathan aimed. The barrel of a handgun and the brim of a cap poked into the hallway.

A cop.

"Blue, blue, blue," Nathan shouted. "FBI, don't shoot."

The muzzle lowered, and the man peeked around the corner. A uniformed cop—the most glorious sight Nathan had ever seen. Help had arrived.

God bless the NYPD.

"We've got suspects on the floor above us," Nathan said, "and an injured agent."

"We engaged upstairs," the officer said. He reached for his radio as more shouting came from above, only this time it was police ordering people not to move. No more shots sounded upstairs.

"Officer down," the officer broadcast.

Three uniform cops wearing heavy tactical vests brushed past him and ascended the stairs. They passed Bridget and glanced at Yemeni as they moved up the stairwell and around the corner.

Nathan hurried to Bridget. "How bad is it?"

"Hurts like a motherfucker."

Nathan replaced Bridget's hand with his own and applied pressure over the wound. "You're gonna be okay."

She looked back at Yemeni. "What about him?"

Blood oozed from a jagged hole in Yemeni's forehead, where a .223

round had smashed into his skull and splintered the bone. A disfigured bump protruded, a sign of the trauma the bullet had done as it scrambled his brain, ricocheting around inside and dislodging bone. Yemeni's eyes and mouth had frozen open, and he stared up with an expression of horror.

"He's gone," Nathan said.

"That *fuckah*."

Nathan had done that. Not directly, but by using him to shield Bridget, he'd put Yemeni in harm's way—a clear violation of FBI protocol. Prisoners in custody were his responsibility to protect, not to put in danger.

But he didn't care. Not a bit.

Yemeni was dead, killed by a bullet fired from one of the Islamists he'd radicalized. Nathan savored the sweet irony like honey. Justice had been done.

Nathan filled with elation from being alive, relief that Yemeni hadn't escaped, and triumph that the terrorist had paid for his sins. At least on this earth. If hell existed, Yemeni would burn for eternity.

His glimmer of optimism flickered along the edges of his mind, then evaporated. Capturing Yemeni had been their goal, and the man was a high-value target—the top of the heap of festering garbage—but his death wouldn't defeat radical Islam. The imam was a product of the system, another cog in the machine.

Islamists who sought a global caliphate didn't just tolerate violence as a tool—they enjoyed it. Killing Jews and other infidels brought them joy. The destruction of non-believers was their goal. Worship Mohammad or be slaughtered. That was their doctrine and their message, yet many in the West didn't believe it. The Sunni and Shiite terrorists who promulgated a supremacist, theo-political ideology intended to conquer the world, and they'd only be stopped when people understood that.

91

Darius sat on the floor of the tiny apartment and banged his head on the wall. One, two, three. He took a breath. *Bang, bang, bang.* He hit his head. Three, four, five. *Bang, bang, bang.*

"Stop that," Blackwood said.

These horrible policemen had kept him hostage for hours, and they showed no sign of releasing him. Everything was wrong. They'd fed him, but with the wrong food at the wrong time.

"This isn't my room. I should be in my room. And my shirt is dirty, and I'm supposed to change my underwear whenever I—"

"Shut the fuck up."

"I need my things," Darius said. "I need my pen and paper so I can draw. I can't think if I can't make my circles and—"

"How about I cut off your fingers?" Blackwood asked. "Would you like that? You'll never be able to draw again?"

That threat hit Darius like an open-handed slap. Was Blackwood serious or trying to scare him?

Ramirez looked up with annoyance. "Stop terrorizing the kid. He's obviously got problems. Give him a pencil and paper so he can fucking draw."

"You want me to give the kid a sharp pencil?"

"You outweigh him by a hundred and fifty pounds, and you've got a gun. Stop being a *coño*."

"I don't need a gun to snap his little neck, but I ain't his babysitter."

"Either give him what he needs, or we gotta listen to this banging and crying all day."

Blackwood snarled at Darius. "Or I can gag and zip-tie him and stuff him in the closet."

"Our job is to keep him alive until they call us. You kill him now, and they'll bury our bodies with him."

"Now who sounds like a pussy?" Blackwood said.

The old policeman glared in silence, and somehow, he seemed more dangerous without speaking. Darius looked from man to man. Would they fight?

Ramirez stood. "Keep him breathing until we know if they need him. After that, I don't care what you do."

"Whatever."

"I'm going out to check on the situation downstairs."

"What's the point. There ain't nothing you can do until—"

"If they call us, we won't have much time, and I want to know what we're facing. You got this?"

"I can handle the little shit." He faced Darius. "If he fucks with me, he's dead."

Darius's chest tightened and he held back his tears. He'd been crying off and on since they'd taken him.

Ramirez gazed out the peephole, then looked back at his partner. "I'll be back in ten minutes."

"Grab me a black coffee."

"Go fuck yourself." He slammed the door behind him.

Blackwood looked at Darius. "I ain't gonna coddle you. Keep banging your head and making noise, and I'll bang it for you until you stop moving. Capeesh?"

"Capeesh, capeesh, capeesh," Darius repeated. What did that mean?

The man sighed. "Fuck it. You want a pen and paper."

Darius nodded, too scared to talk.

"I give you this, and you'll be a good kitten? No more noise."

"No noise, no noise, no noise."

Blackwood snorted. He grabbed a blue pen and notepad off the table and dropped them in front of Darius. "One more fucking word, and I'm taking your teeth."

The words bounced inside Darius's head as he took them.

He drew a large, perfect circle.

92

The US Attorney's Office was a chaotic nightmare. Police swarmed the building, searching offices, but they'd yet to clear most of the structure. Officers from numerous city, state, and federal agencies had responded to the call for assistance. Initial radio calls indicated threats had been neutralized, but tactical teams methodically searched every space. It would take time.

Nathan walked behind the EMTs as they rolled Bridget to the elevator. She writhed in pain from the tourniquet they'd applied to her thigh. A paramedic had run an IV, and her color looked good, considering.

"I'll come to the hospital," Nathan said. "But I want to take a quick look upstairs to assess the damage."

"I'll freaking stay here if you don't mind."

"Meet you at the hospital."

"Come see me after surgery."

"Count on it."

Nathan watched her until the elevator doors closed, then he took another stairwell up to avoid tracking through the crime scene where Yemeni had bled out. Taking a man's life was the gravest action he could take, but in this case, he felt nothing but relief.

The thirty-seventh floor was in disarray. Bodies lay everywhere. Nathan skirted corpses in the lobby and drew a glare from a crime tech. Passive collection of evidence wouldn't be that important since most of the terrorists had been killed, but forensics could lead them to co-conspirators.

Nathan stopped at the conference room. Sam knelt beside Dawson, who slumped in a seat wearing a thousand-yard gaze.

"She hurt?" Nathan asked.

"Traumatized."

"Did they breach the office after I left?"

"A defendant looked inside, but then you fired. They chased after you."

Defendant. Funny how attorneys who inhabited the courtroom characterized those who wanted to murder them. At least Nathan's plan had worked.

A door clicked behind Nathan, and he spun around.

Leila exited an office and gawked at his AR-15.

Nathan depressed his barrel, and his adrenaline dissipated. "It's over."

A tear rolled down her cheek.

"Are you injured?" he asked.

"No . . . it's not that."

"What's wrong?"

She looked down.

The hair stood on Nathan's neck. He inspected the office behind her. Empty. Their discussion before the attack came back to him. She'd tried to warn him, but how did she know?

"Step inside," he said with less empathy.

She entered, and he closed the door but left it cracked open, as he always did when interviewing the opposite sex.

"Tell me."

"I don't know what to say."

"You knew they were coming."

"Yes."

Anger fired inside him. "How?"

She wiped her eyes and her shoulders slumped. "They have my son."

93

Darius stayed still and tried not to bring attention to himself as Blackwood pulled back the blinds and surveyed whatever created the noise outside. The policeman had become agitated—behavior Darius had seen from his father—and he didn't want to invite a beating.

The popping and bangs that had come from the street were not fireworks. He'd wondered why people were celebrating, but the sirens from police cars, fire engines, and ambulances meant people had shot guns. He'd heard gunfire in Washington Heights too, but not like this. Maman had made him lie in the bathtub whenever shooting came from outside, but it had always ended before the sirens came close.

This was different.

People had been shooting for at least fifteen minutes before it stopped. What was going on? Was this a revolution? Maman had told Father they needed one in Iran, but she'd always whispered those words quietly, and whenever she said things like that, he'd slapped her. One time, she'd told him not to be a coward, and that had invited a savage abuse. He hadn't understood that. Maman knew Father liked to hurt them, and she must have known that calling him a coward would end with him hitting her, so why had she done it?

The blinds snapped back, and Blackwood turned and stared at him.

Hate filled his eyes. That was familiar too. A damp fear cooled Darius. This man would hurt and maybe kill him. He wouldn't do it because he had to, but because it would bring him pleasure. He craved violence just as Father had.

Where was Maman?

Blackwood crossed the room and looked through the peephole. He unlocked the door and peeked into the hall, then bolted it again. He dialed his cell.

"Where are you?" He listened. "Why can't you get back? You're in a uniform, for fuck's sake. Just walk through the lines." His cheeks reddened. "They won't ask for ID. They're fighting for their lives, not worrying about an officer carrying coffee."

He bared his teeth. "I asked you for coffee. I've been up all fucking night listening to—" He grimaced. "I only slept for a minute. You expect me to watch this little fucker alone while you're screwing around. What if they call now? How am I gonna bring the kid downstairs alone?" He listened for a moment, then glanced at Darius.

Darius felt the urge to pee. These guys planned to kill him, and Maman wasn't coming.

"Asshole." The policeman jammed the phone into his pocket and glared at him.

Darius focused on the floor. Stay silent, stay still, and project no emotion. Be the chair, be the chair, be the chair. That was an old trick he'd learned the hard way.

Blackwood's dark shadow hovered in Darius's peripheral vision. He hadn't moved. He stared at him, thinking, planning, fantasizing. A single wrong word would draw the man's wrath.

One, two, three. One, two, three. One, two, three. It wasn't working. He needed to draw his circles, or lose himself in a math problem. The paper where he'd been sketching concentric circles lay beside him, but he didn't dare look at it. He closed his eyes and pictured the circles drawn inside each other, all the exact same distance apart. If he focused hard enough, they spiraled and moved. Measurements flashed in his head 1/32 of an inch, 1/64 of an inch, 1/128 of an inch. Tension ebbed, and his shoulders relaxed. He didn't show his comfort, because that used to set Father off too. A giggle or a laugh would draw an angry curse, at best. Then Maman would inter-vene and receive the beating. His punishment. That had been horrible. Better to suffer the sting of Father's blows than the guilt and shame of knowing Mother had been hurt protecting him.

But now, Darius was the man of his house.

The realization came to him in a flash, as if his brain had been illumi-nated from the outside. He shouldn't be waiting for Maman to save him. If he wanted to live, he'd have to save himself, and then help her. His fear didn't matter. His size didn't matter. He must protect Maman.

But how?

Blackwood moved into the kitchen, grumbling to himself. He was mad at Ramirez, and Darius, and probably a million other things. Violent people always found something to upset them. It made them happy. Pummeling Darius would give him the same feeling Darius had when he recited his numbers.

Blackwood glanced across the counter at him, and Darius dropped his eyes to the ground. Blackwood opened the refrigerator, though they both knew it was empty. But it was time to eat, and Blackwood understood Darius would get upset and make noise.

That was it.

Darius had become predictable. He had to be regimented to survive, but if he could overcome his special needs, he could use them against these policemen.

Darius's mind whirled with excitement and intellectual calmness—the same stillness that came over him when he calculated math proofs. One front door to the apartment, two windows in the living room, a tiny window in the bathroom, and at least one window he'd seen through the partially open bedroom door. Those were his only options to escape.

Despite only one policeman guarding him, he still had no chance of overpowering Blackwood, even if he could find a weapon. Darius was small and weak—but his brain wasn't. Maman always told him his intellect made him different from other people, and that meant he was exceptional. He'd never embraced that argument, because always being the other, the strange kid alone on the playground, had made him feel unwanted and awful.

But he was smarter than other kids.

Darius saw patterns and variables. He saw reality as a streaming series of numbers, each value representing the world around him. He may not understand the need for emotion or the expression of it, but he knew logic and reason. He always had. Everything was a problem, a puzzle, begging for him to solve. And he could. Each year he tackled harder physics problems.

And this puzzle of escape would be trivial, if he reduced the factors and confounding variables to numbers. He'd translate his situation into an equation, adding in each potential option for escape, and then settling on the one with the highest probability of success. Statistics 101. He'd mastered that four years ago. Now, he needed to do math to save his life. He glowed inside. Maybe Maman had been telling the truth after all.

He did possess a superpower.

The doorknob jiggled, and Blackwood's head darted up and his hand went to his gun. He stepped out of the kitchen and drew. Was Maman coming to rescue him?

The apartment door opened. Darius held his breath.

Ramirez stepped inside carrying a coffee cup. Darius deflated. This wasn't a rescue.

Ramirez noticed Blackwood's gun and raised his hand in surrender. "Whoa, easy there. I told you I was coming."

Blackwood holstered his gun. "That coffee for me?"

Ramirez sneered as he raised the cup and sipped. He smacked his lips. "Nope. I ain't working for you, and I don't appreciate your shitty attitude."

Blackwood balled his fists. The muscles bulged in his jaw.

"You think you're better than me?"

"I don't think it, I know it. You're an inexperienced little shit with a chip on your shoulder."

"How about I show you how experienced I am?"

They didn't act like policemen. They behaved like street thugs around his school in Tehran, and the guys who hung out at the bodega across from their new apartment had the same look in their eyes. Police in America scared him.

But this was the moment he needed. The extra variable. A distraction for what he had to do.

"Excuse me, please," he said.

"What?" Ramirez asked.

"I've need to make water."

"Then go," Blackwood said without turning around. He continued to glare at his partner.

Both men had become accustomed to Darius's routine, and he'd shown them any deviance would cause a meltdown. Ironically, they too found comfort in his schedule, only for different reasons.

Darius rushed to the bathroom, then paused at the door and glanced back. Blackwood's back was to him, and Ramirez was out of sight.

"You're a tough guy?" Blackwood asked. "Just because they put you in charge doesn't mean you're the better man in this room."

"I'm the best in every room, if you're in it."

"Fuck you."

"Bring *it*."

These guys were morons, like the badge-wearing criminals in Tehran. But this was Darius's moment. He must escape. Fear tickled his belly.

Now or never.

94

Darius tiptoed across the hallway and bladed himself to slip past the partially open bedroom door. A bare mattress lay on the floor opposite a closed closet door. The corner room had single windows on both walls, each with closed aluminum blinds like those in the living room.

The wall across from him faced the front, so he crept to the other wall. That's where the fire escape would be, like his apartment at home.

I want to go home.

He didn't dare pull the cord to raise the blinds because of the noise they'd make, so he twirled their clear-plastic wand between his fingertips. The slats rotated open. Sunlight streamed in. The window was shut and locked with a tiny plastic latch.

No fire escape.

Perhaps it was off to the side. He hovered his face close to the window and peered at an angle. Nothing to the right. He looked out from the other side and leaned closer. His cheek touched the slats and metal crinkled.

Darius froze.

Blackwood's and Ramirez's muted voices came from the living room as they continued their argument. Darius only had a minute before they wondered why he hadn't returned and came looking for him.

Darius snuck to the front-facing window and rotated the blinds open.

This one was locked too. Darius pressed his face against the pane and scanned left and right. No fire escape there either.

That was bad. He'd imagined climbing down an iron fire escape to the street and escaping. They were on the third floor, or maybe the fourth. Outside, tall buildings made of white granite surrounded them. Government buildings. Emergency lights from police cars two blocks away reflected off the street. That's probably where they'd been shooting. He could open the window and scream for help, but would anyone hear him over the traffic and sirens?

What to do?

The window high on the bathroom wall was too tiny to squeeze through, and he'd have to cross the hall again. The policemen's voices intensified, but their restrained volume betrayed their fear of drawing attention. That need to stay quiet had kept their argument from breaking into a fist fight, but that wouldn't last.

The building had a façade of white stone with uneven, protruding surfaces, not unlike the bark along the trunk of the Zagros field elm in his garden in Tehran. That was the answer.

I can do this.

He grasped the cord and slowly pulled down, inching up the blinds. The slats collapsed into each other, and their combined weight made them sway.

Tink, tink, tink. The slats tapped the glass.

Darius stopped and glanced at the door. Blackwood's voice rose in anger.

Darius raised the blinds almost to the top, then tugged the cord to the side to lock them in place. He eased the pulley back, making sure they didn't drop.

He unlatched the plastic lock and pushed the bottom sile up. The wood had swelled and jammed against the frame. He shoved with all his strength, and it slid up its tracks.

It squeaked.

He froze. The argument continued. Darius never took more than a few minutes in the restroom, and they'd come for him soon.

He had to go.

The window was open enough, but a screen blocked his way. Darius depressed the latches that held it in place. He slid it up. The metal shrieked as it scraped the rail.

The policeman stopped talking.

Darius didn't breathe. If they came now, they'd catch him and kill him for sure.

A footfall creaked in the hallway.

Darius peeked out and looked down. Fifteen meters to the street. A fall would kill him. No one was on the sidewalk below, but across the street, people watched the police spectacle, and vehicles slowed as drivers' heads craned. He could yell, but no one would hear.

Behind him, someone rapped on the bathroom door. "Hurry up," Blackwood said. He sounded pissed.

The base of Darius's skull tingled. If Blackwood caught him, he'd beat Darius to death. Anger equals pain. A equals B. He'd seen that before.

Darius reached out and found a handhold. He lay on the track, and the metal scratched his belly. He shimmied across it the way he'd crawled under his bed in Tehran to hide from Father.

The breeze blew across his face. It felt like freedom. He had to escape, even if he fell.

He squeezed the textured stone until his fingers ached. He pulled his knee through and braced one foot on the stone.

The bathroom door creaked.

"The little fucker's gone," Blackwood yelled.

Out of time.

Darius withdrew his other leg, and the metal sheared skin off his shin. He felt little pain. Fear overwhelmed everything.

He extended his leg and jammed his toes against a stone. He pushed against it and pulled with his hands to create tension—just like he'd done climbing his tree in Tehran.

He pressed his toes into a few centimeters of protruding stone and grasped the pointy edge. He balanced and stepped out with his other leg. He found an edge.

"There he is." Footsteps pounded across the bedroom floor.

Darius clung to the stone beside the window, his body free of the apartment, but still within reach of the window. He looked up. No balconies, no fire escape, no gutters—nothing to cling onto for safety. He'd have to climb down. He—

Blackwood's head poked out. "Get back in here, you little fuck."

Darius moved without thinking. He stretched and grasped a stone, then pulled his upper body away from the window. The policeman reached for him, but his fingers only brushed Darius's shirt.

Darius stepped away, praying to find a foot fall. His shoe slid off a rounded flake, and his weight transferred onto his fingers. His hands screamed in defiance. But letting go meant death, and Darius wasn't ready to die. His mother needed him.

His fingertips gripped a crimp in the surface, and he pulled himself up. He'd done the same move when he'd slipped off a branch in Iran and held on with one hand. His legs dangled beneath him.

His toes found a horn in the stone, and he stood.

"I'm gonna fucking kill you," Blackwood said.

Darius reached up and slid his fingers across the façade until he located another crimp. He pulled himself up and away from the window. He located another foothold and shuffled to the corner.

"So help me, you little fuck, I'll murder you. I'll rip your fucking arms off. I'll—"

Darius blindly reached around the corner, and his fingers touched a jug that protruded off the side. He couldn't look without losing his balance, so he grasped it and swung onto the other wall. He held on to a tiny gargoyle with the face of a laughing child.

The statue's jovial expression and the perfect spacing between gargoyles calmed him. He moved across the building as if he swung from branch to branch.

Darius looked down at a window ledge. He could lower himself one floor at a time, but he must hurry. The policeman had stopped yelling, which meant they'd headed for the stairs. If Darius didn't beat them down —they'd kill him.

Darius grasped the pointy edge of a stone at chin level. He descended and his fingers found a tiny pocket. He inserted his finger and searched for a foothold. His toes touched an edge, and he transferred his weight onto it.

This was easier than climbing smooth bark, and fear motivated him. Not from terror of falling but of the policeman. Blackwood had said he'd rip off Darius's arms. Darius believed him.

Darius stepped onto a window ledge. He breathed deeply to relax, then lowered himself over it. He found another edge and continued down. But would he make it in time?

95

Nathan stood in the office and focused on Leila. Tears streamed down her face, and she transformed from a powerful woman into a young girl before his eyes. His anger bubbled up and energized him. This woman had betrayed them and worked with those animals from the inside.

"They'll hurt Darius," she said. "Please, help me."

"Start over," he said. "How are you connected to these terrorists?"

"I didn't know this would happen."

"Not what I asked."

"They said they wanted information."

Nathan suppressed his rage and transformed into an analytical investigator. He threw an internal switch and shut off his emotions. He became a law enforcement machine—void of human frailty.

"How did they contact you?" Nathan asked.

"It happened slowly. People asked me about my case. They questioned my loyalty to Iran. They—"

"Who?"

"My boss, Mr. Massimi, then a man named Lucas Robert tried to bribe me in the cafeteria, and a man threatened me in the stairwell at home."

Her eyes widened as she spoke, and she seemed to gain energy as her words poured out. She found relief in confessing. She appeared truthful.

"Who threatened you?"

"He called himself Gharagöz. He threatened my family. An NYPD detective did too."

Nathan jolted. "A detective threatened you?"

"Well, not explicitly, but he grabbed my arm and—"

"Who was he?"

She shook her head. "I never saw him before, and he didn't give me his name. He stopped me in the courthouse."

Nathan would need to chase down that lead and identify the detective, if the man even worked for NYPD. He'd investigate all of it.

"You didn't report it?"

"At first, I wasn't sure anything was technically illegal. I wondered if it was all in my mind. Then Gharagöz made it clear my family would die if I told anyone. When they demanded more information, I told my friend. He warned me they were dangerous, but then a hit-and-run driver killed him."

"That interpreter?"

"Khalil Mansour. I got scared."

Nathan had so many questions, but Leila's child was in the hands of murderous bastards who wouldn't think twice about killing him.

"When did they take your son?" Nathan asked.

"In the middle of the night. They knew I would assist Ms. Dawson and Mr. Yemeni. They—"

"Where is your son now?"

"I don't know." Her voice came out thin, almost inaudible. "They killed people. I shouldn't have . . . I could have fought them."

Empathy softened his anger. She'd been in a tough place, an impossible situation. His protective instincts kicked in. "They would've killed you."

"I don't care. My life is meaningless without Darius. Help me save him. I'll do anything."

Nathan should advise her to retain a criminal attorney because of her legal vulnerability, but he only cared about rescuing her son. He couldn't take the loss of another innocent, especially a child.

"Think about exactly what they told you. How and where would they return him to you?"

"They said Darius would come home after I gave them the proffer location. They said they'd bring him here, so he must be close."

Dread seeped into Nathan's bones. These guys were killers, and anything they'd said had probably been lies. They may have already killed her son. Why leave another witness, unless they needed him for leverage? If she'd had second thoughts, they may have planned to use her child to pressure her. If she demanded proof he was unharmed, they'd need the son. Darius could still be alive.

"You called them from the proffer?" Nathan asked.

Her eyes drifted to her shoes. "Yes."

"Show me the number."

Leila unlocked her phone and scrolled to her recent calls. She displayed the number.

Nathan cracked open the door. "Sam, I need you in here."

White glanced up with alarm and hurried across the hall. Dawson hugged herself and stared at the wall.

"Yemen's men took her son," Nathan said. "They extorted her to give up our location."

White jerked in surprise. "She's involved?"

"I'll explain later. Right now, we need an emergency trace on this number, and a team to find her son. We won't have much time. Once they know Yemeni's dead, they'll kill him."

96

Leila walked beside Agent Burke as he escorted her out of the US Attorney's Office and down the walkway into Saint Andrew's Plaza. She wore an FBI windbreaker and cap with the brim pulled low over her eyes. Burke also wore a cap low to conceal himself.

Red emergency lights flickered everywhere as a hundred police officers from different agencies rushed around. Burke held her elbow and guided her down the steps. Burke had called his office and activated a team to respond to Ri's kidnapping. They were headed to the FBI office at 26 Federal Plaza so agents could debrief her.

"Keep your head down," he said. "If they're watching, they can't know you're cooperating."

"Why didn't we stay inside?"

"The building will take hours to clear, and I want to be mobile in case we get a lead."

"Do you think . . ." Her throat closed and her eyes filled. "What are the chances . . ." She couldn't finish her thought.

"We'll do whatever we can. I promise."

She believed him. Her capitulation to terrorists filled her with shame, and her worry over Ri made it difficult to function. She walked with stilted movements and had to think about each step.

What if they killed him? Her life would be over.

They moved around the police barricades and pushed through the crowd of onlookers. He stepped onto Center Street.

"The office is a couple blocks away."

"Is your partner meeting us there? The girl, I mean. I can't remember her name."

His face hardened. "She's on her way to the hospital. Yemeni's men shot her."

"I . . . I didn't know. I'm sorry."

He nodded and led her across the street.

How could she have cooperated with those animals? They had Ri, but giving them what they wanted didn't make him any safer, and now that Yemeni had been killed, his men had no reason to extort her. Maybe they'd want to keep their mole on the inside to tell them—

"Maman?" Darius said.

She froze. His voice. Had they killed him and his spirit sought her out?

Burke stopped and looked at her. "What's wrong."

"I heard him. I—"

Darius stepped beside her and touched her arm.

She looked at him, frozen. "Do you see him?"

"Maman, what's wrong? Why are you wearing that?"

"Ri! What are you . . . how did . . ." Leila wrapped her arms around him and pulled him into a bear hug. She lifted the boy's feet off the ground and squeezed him. She kissed his head and ruffled his hair.

"Maman, stop."

"My boy, my boy, my beautiful boy." Her voice broke with emotion as she filled with endorphins. He was alive. Somehow, he'd escaped those monsters.

"You're embarrassing me." He rocked in her arms and brought her back to the moment. He always balked at displays of emotion, especially in public. This would throw him into a fit. She pulled back in and released him from the hug but gripped his arms with her hands, unwilling to let him go.

Burke scanned the crowd. "Where are the men who took you?"

Darius pointed down the street. "They're in an apartment over there, but they probably left."

"Why did they let you go?" she asked.

He smiled and his eyes beamed. He looked proud like when he wanted to show off for her.

"I escaped."

She gasped. "Tell the truth. How could you flee armed men?"

Nathan dialed his phone and continued to survey the area.

Darius stared into the distance the way he did when he worked on math proofs and disappeared inside his head into a world of brilliance and logic she couldn't understand and never would.

She waited and watched him. Her son, her glorious son.

He blinked and refocused on the world before him—the real world. "They wouldn't let me eat or go to the bathroom on time. I have my . . ." He looked down bashfully. "You know, my routines."

"That must've made you crazy."

"It did. I cried—" He stopped, embarrassed. "It upset me. They untied me to help me calm down. They let me draw to keep me quiet."

"Then how did you—"

"They learned I needed my schedule, like always, but then I remembered something you said."

What did he mean? "When I said what?"

"You told me neurodivergence was a superpower. You said people thought my rituals were strange, but I was just different—better in some ways, like how I get top grades and understand physics better than my teachers."

"That's true, my baby." She wanted to snatch him back into her arms, but he needed to boast about how he'd escaped—and she needed to know.

"I showed them I had to follow my schedule, and they understood. They anticipated I'd do everything they said at the correct times, or I'd break down. They expected me to follow the schedule, but I used the part of my ability that helps me understand things. I applied logic and solved it like a chess problem. I did what you said and used my superpower."

"Like a chess—"

"I waited until they were comfortable and anticipated my schedule . . . then I broke my routine."

She jolted. Ri had followed his routine for his entire life, and the few times he'd been forced to break it, he'd exploded in fits and it had taken hours to recover. What she'd initially diagnosed as uncontrolled rage and mental illness, had merely been the loss of his coping mechanisms he used to understand the world. And now, he'd used reason and willpower to trump his phobias and break the cycle. He'd willed them into a sense of complacency, then summoned the courage and strength from a well she didn't know he possessed and escaped.

"Tell me how."

"I pretended I had to pee, and I climbed out the window."

"The fire escape?"

"Nope."

Fear weakened her legs. He could've been killed.

"Did they see you?"

"Yeah, but I beat them to the street."

"How did you find us?" Nathan asked.

"I saw the courthouse, and I knew Maman was there."

Leila looked at Burke. "It's impossible."

"A miracle," Nathan said.

Miracle. The world swirled in her mind. "What does that mean?"

"Your boy did something you thought was impossible and saved himself. I'm not overly religious, but something gave him that strength, and God is as good an answer as anything else."

"Allah saved Ri?"

"Your god and mine aren't the same," Nathan said. "But call our creator whatever you want. I believe someone had a hand in saving this boy, and no amount of rationalization will get me off that."

She wanted to object and tell them they believed different things, but something about what he said resonated deep inside her. Maybe he was right. And here was Ri. Her son. Her world. Everything she cared about. Somehow, he found the courage to overcome his limitations and use it as a weapon against his captors.

Whether or not there'd been a miracle, he'd survived. Her eyes burned, and tears flowed down her cheeks.

Ri was alive.

97

Butterflies fluttered inside Leila as she signed into the visitor's log at the US Attorney's Office. She'd surrendered her interpreter credentials after the incident, but she'd come at the behest of AUSA White. He'd asked her if she had an attorney, and when she'd said no, he'd told her she was free to bring one, but it was her decision.

She'd come alone.

The interior door opened, and a young woman stepped into the lobby and looked at her. Leila had seen her before. She wasn't an attorney but some kind of intern. Was that condemnation in her eyes?

"Ms. Kabiri?"

"Yes." Leila's voice came out hoarse and weak. She cleared her throat. "I'm Leila Kabiri."

Leila's stomach hardened as they rode up in the elevator and exited on the thirty-second floor. Terrorists had decimated the terrorism and narcotics unit with bullet holes in doors and walls, shattered windows, and bloodstained carpets. It would take time to make the space habitable for attorneys, and even then, the horror from that day would make it hard for many to return. Would she ever go back? Would she have a job? Or her freedom?

She'd become complicit the moment she'd given the proffer location to

Ri's kidnappers. The terror attack had claimed thirteen lives. And she could be looking at anything from a couple of years in jail up to life, depending on how they charged her.

The intern badged into the section and led her through the lobby. The office was a mirror image of the terrorism unit upstairs. Leila followed her down a long hallway and stopped outside a conference room. Leila looked in.

Agent Burke and AUSA Samuel White sat at the long table. They didn't have any folders or papers on the desk—just them.

"Come in," White said.

She stepped into the room, and her stomach tightened like it did before her husband came home.

"Sit." White motioned to a chair.

She slipped into the seat across from them and wrung her hands. Maybe she should have brought an attorney with her. White and Burke represented the government, and adversarial party. They possessed the power to lock her up forever, but she'd been through hell with them, and that experience had bonded them together in a way only survivors of trauma shared.

Somehow, she trusted them.

White forced a smile. "From the look on your face, I can tell your stressed, so I'll get right to the point."

"Okay." She spoke so softly they probably hadn't heard.

"I've consulted with the US Attorney and DOJ on this. We could've charged you as a co-conspirator, and for a dozen felonies, including terrorism and murder. That would've exposed you to decades in jail, at a minimum, and potentially life."

The room shifted beneath her, and she touched the edge of the table with her fingertips for support.

"Could have?" she asked.

"Agent Burke stood up for you," White said. "He's been your biggest advocate."

"Yemeni's men kidnapped your son," Burke said. "I have a daughter about your son's age, and I understand how that can warp your thinking. It's hard to imagine your desperation to save him."

"I didn't know what to do, but the moment I called them, I knew I'd made a terrible mistake. I had to warn you."

"Even as distraught as you were, and with your child's life hanging in the balance," Nathan said, "you still trusted me and spoke up."

"And that warning you gave Agent Burke," White said, "is a reason I've agreed to not seek an indictment against you."

Leila's breath caught in her throat. The room brightened. Had she heard him correctly?

"You're not arresting me?"

Burke shook his head. "I won't put you in jail for the rest of your life and orphan your son because you had a moment of weakness. You were out of your mind with worry, and you panicked."

She'd been certain she'd receive a lengthy prison sentence, and best case, a shorter one. She'd been ready to accept her punishment. Not being charged hadn't seemed a possibility.

Tears filled her eyes. "Thank you."

"No need for thanks," White said. "Duress is a legitimate defense, and quite frankly, with the exigent circumstances, I'm not sure I could get a jury to convict."

Leila's heart pounded. her shoulders dropped as her stress lifted. She had the urge to race home and shower Ri with love and kisses. They'd be together, thanks to her little boy's cunning, and thanks to Burke for saving her. She owed him everything.

Burke shifted and frowned. "It's not all good news. You won't get your job back. The court won't risk exposing you to sensitive information after this incident. If something happened again, they'd be liable."

"I understand. Of course. I wouldn't expect . . . I didn't think I'd walk out of here a free person."

"What will you do now?" Burke asked.

She gnawed on her lip. She'd steeled herself for a long stay in a federal detention facility, and she'd lacked the hope and imagination to envision a future. But that's what she had now—possibilities.

"I'll go home and be with my son."

"No, I mean for work?"

"Darius is my job, my only priority. I'll be a mother to him. He's my world, and you gave him back to me. And you too, Mr. White. You gave me my life back."

"Will you be okay?" Burke asked.

"I'll find another way to earn money for us. The private sector may need a Persian interpreter."

Nathan grinned. "Would you be interested in working for the FBI?"

"They'd never hire me after this."

"Perhaps not, but I would. Iran is a perennial problem, and I'll need a Persian and Arabic translator. I'll sign you up as a source, or maybe I can call in a favor and get you hired by a sub-contractor. We'll figure it out."

"I don't deserve that."

"You deserve it more than you know," Burke said. "Terrorism claims many innocent victims. It shatters lives, including yours. You faced an impossible situation and yet you tried to do the right thing."

Guilt tickled the edges of her conscience, but she wouldn't let it spoil the moment. She'd survived. Ri had survived. And not only wasn't she being carted off to jail, but she'd be able to work with this amazing agent and defend her new country.

"Want the job?" Burke asked.

Leila smiled. Her future lay before her, ready for the taking.

98

Nathan parked his personal car in the FBI's Washington Division's garage and left Amelia in the passenger seat while he ran upstairs. He spent every moment with her since returning from New York, and she'd been clingy. Who could blame her? She'd seen the news coverage during the attack and thought he'd been killed. Bridget getting shot hadn't helped, despite her good prognosis.

He avoided the other agents in his office as he made his way to Rahimya's office. He needed to have a life-altering discussion with her, and the seriousness of the situation subdued him.

Yemeni, the criminal mastermind who'd eluded him, was dead. In the past few years, Nathan had uncovered the secrets behind Havana Syndrome, stopped the opioid attacks, and exposed China's unrestricted warfare. He'd almost died many times while investigating criminals and terrorists—a risk he accepted because the United States needed defending. The country was safer, but his family had paid the price for his vigilance. Reagan was married to another man, and Amelia had almost been killed. What if he'd died in Uganda and left her fatherless?

He reached his floor and rubbed his aching shoulder. Scar tissue sent tingles down his nerves. He'd never healed properly after getting shot, and maybe he never would. Most things didn't improve with age, except wine and scotch. Experience made him wiser, but it had also worn down his spirit. How much injury and death could he witness before the scar tissue formed on his soul?

He stopped outside Rahimya's door and inhaled a calming breath. He blew it out and opened her door.

She looked up from behind her desk. "You sounded serious on the phone. What's this you've got to tell me?"

"I'm done," Nathan said.

Rahimya cocked her head. "What are you saying?"

"I've done enough damage to my family. I lost my wife because I put my career first, and now I'm hurting Amelia. I'm gone way too much, and that's got to change."

Her face softened. "Listen, the past four years have been a whirlwind. Our country has teetered on the edge, and you're the reason we've avoided catastrophe."

Nathan looked down at his hands. He'd never learned to take compliments without filling with embarrassment. Acknowledging his contribution was kind of her to say, but many people had given everything to protect the country, and some had paid the ultimate price.

"I appreciate your support, but I had no choice. Our way of life was it stake, and I had the investigative skills, so I had the obligation, no, the *duty* to fight."

"Then how can you hang it up?"

"I have a duty to Amelia too."

Rahimya's face pinched. "You're resigning?"

"The thought has crossed my mind. The idea of taking Amelia and holing up in a small house in the woods has become a waking fantasy."

"You'd go insane."

"Yeah, I know."

"Then what's the plan, and don't take my asking as any kind of approval. You belong right where you are."

His insides hollowed out again. He'd invested so much in his career and fought so hard to put himself into a position to fight terrorism. How could he walk away? It felt self-destructive. But his job as a father was to give his daughter the best childhood possible.

His job had almost killed her, and her psychological scars remained. The least he could do was give her a normal childhood, or at least something resembling it. She needed safety, security, and the chance to sleep through the night without waking up and wondering if her father would ever come home. Leaving counterterrorism would hurt his career, but the smile on Amelia's face when he broke the news to her would mean everything.

"I want a nine-to-five job," he said.

"Take the GS-14 test. If you promote, you'll be tied to a desk most of the time."

He nodded. "Thought about that, but I can't handle being a bureaucrat."

"No offense. Then what?"

"I was hoping you could pull a few strings to land me a GS-13 position at headquarters. Maybe a staff coordinator or liaison job with limited travel so I can have weekends at home."

"That doesn't sound like you."

"This isn't about me."

"And you'll be happy?" Rahimya asked.

"I had to travel around the world to find my way back home. By confronting evil, I understood virtue. If all I do is raise Amelia, I'll be a success."

She nodded with that skeptical look childless people had when talking to parents. "If I make these calls, and you transfer, you won't be able to return for a long time."

Nathan's stomach knotted. She was right. This decision would dictate how he spent fifty hours a week for a few years. But Amelia had sacrificed for him, and now, it was his turn. He could live with that. This was the honorable decision. He wouldn't pay lip service talking about putting family first, he'd do it.

His queasiness dissipated. "Make the call."

Rahimya scratched her chin. "How about I give you twenty-four hours to let it sink in?"

"It's sunk in, deeper than the *Titanic*. I made my decision."

Rahimya sighed. "I owe you, and if this is really what you want, I'll help."

"Thanks." Butterflies fluttered with excitement inside him. Or fear.

Rahimya leaned back in her chair and gave him a funny look. "What does Meili think about your decision?"

"We haven't discussed it."

"Oh?"

"We decided to take a break."

"I see." Rahimya broke eye contact. They rarely discussed their personal lives, which was one reason he enjoyed working for her.

"Is that part of this?"

He sighed. "Amelia's waiting for me downstairs."

"Call me if you have a change of heart."

"Thanks, boss."

He headed downstairs, and doubt gnawed at him. Why had Rahimya brought up Meili? Meili had been as absorbed in her career as him, but maybe he'd used work as an excuse for their failing relationship. Had he immersed himself in his case to ignore Meili's reluctance to commit? Maybe her rejection meant he had a flawed personality, or worse, an imperfect character. Would leaving his fast-paced job lay bare his flaws while taking away the one thing he'd been good at?

He relinquished his career for the noble cause of tending to his family, but would he be miserable? He turned his back on his calling, which felt heaven sent. And he was good at his job. Didn't his having talent attach a concomitant duty to exercise it? If his skills made the world a better place, wasn't he obligated to keep doing it?

Shit.

At least he wasn't leaving the FBI. He could seek justice in another position that kept him off the pointy edge of the spear. Being the number one man through the door was where he belonged, and if he didn't do it, someone else would. What if the agent who replaced him failed his next mission, or worse, died?

He entered the garage, and Amelia's face brightened when she spotted him. He got in and fired up the engine.

"What's wrong?" Amelia asked.

"Why do you think something's wrong?"

"Your face."

She was her father's daughter. He'd made a big decision to bench himself and care for her, but it was the right one. She was worth it, and he'd be fine. Maybe.

"I'm leaving the group and getting a job at headquarters."

"Why?"

"To spend more time with you, and less time getting shot at."

"But you're a hero."

"I'm not, and I don't know what that means."

"You risk your life."

"If being a hero means doing something dangerous, every cop and soldier is a hero."

Her eyes moistened. "You almost died."

"You're talking about the airport?"

"You got shot at the zoo. You've done so many cray-cray things."

"Lots of agents worked those cases, and everyone took risks. I'm a cog in a big machine. Those who've given their lives for our country are the heroes."

"But they gave you an award."

"Awards can be arbitrary, and a hunk of crystal and gold doesn't make me a hero."

"You are to me."

Nathan sighed. How'd he get so lucky to have an incredible girl like her? She was intelligent and strong, with his best qualities, and so far, none of his worst. She'd even saved his life. Like Laker.

"There's something else I have to ask you," Nathan said.

Amelia tensed and made little fists. "The last time you told me that, you divorced mom."

"It's nothing like that."

"I know you and Meili broke up."

"It's for the better. I thought marrying her and having a baby would bring me happiness, but she didn't want a commitment. I need to make myself whole to find contentment, and that means being a good father."

"Sorry."

"Sometimes people aren't meant to be together. I'll find someone else. Love will come." An image of Leila floated behind his eyes.

"Enough drama. What did you want to tell me?"

"Remember that scientist's daughter who saved my life in Uganda?"

She laughed. "Little girls save you a lot."

"I'll take salvation any way I can get it."

"Okay, but what's your point? Spit it out, Dad."

"Laker's mother will rot in jail, and Laker has nowhere to go. I thought—"

Amelia's eyes widened. "You're bringing her here?"

Smart girl. "She's a witness in the case, and her life is in danger in Uganda, so we're getting her a visa, anyway. Eventually, her relatives will step up, but until then, she needs a home."

"For how long?"

"As long as necessary. You okay with her staying with us?"

Amelia smiled. "Yaas. Slay. I've always wanted a sister."

Nathan pulled her into a tight hug.

"You're squishing me," she said. "Let me go."

"Never."

Line of Fire
Ian Hale Series #1

Betrayed. Hunted. Driven by duty.

Born into a legacy of heroes, Ian Hale ascended from the 75th Ranger Regiment to Delta Force, dedicating his life to the cause of freedom. But when a Black Hawk crash ends his military career, he is left searching for purpose—until Sentinel offers him a fresh start. A private military firm known for its high-stakes operations, Sentinel promises danger and noble causes, the perfect match for his skillset. Or so it seems.

Hale's latest mission is simple: rescue a kidnapped business executive from South Sudan. But when his team is ambushed and slaughtered, leaving Hale as the sole survivor, he's forced to confront the truth—he's been set up. Someone wants his team dead, and they'll stop at nothing to finish the job.

Now, Hale is a man on the run, hunted by enemies who underestimate his resolve. With only his loyal handler, Laney Shaw, to trust, he launches a one-man war for the truth, uncovering a conspiracy that traces back to the very heart of the nation he so loves.

But Ian Hale was born for this fight, and surrender isn't an option. It never was.

Logan Ryles, author of the acclaimed Prosecution Force series, returns with a gripping new thriller, *Line of Fire*—the explosive first installment in the *Ian Hale* series. Packed with relentless action, high-stakes intrigue, and a hero you won't forget, this debut is perfect for fans of Brad Thor, Jack Carr, and Jack Slater.

**Get your copy today at
severnriverbooks.com**

30% Off your next paperback.

Thank you for reading. For exclusive offers on your next paperback:

- **Visit SevernRiverBooks.com** and enter code **PRINTBOOKS30** at checkout.
- Or scan the QR code.

Offer valid for future paperback purchases only. The discount applies solely to the book price (excluding shipping, taxes, and fees) and is limited to one use per customer. Offer available to US customers only. Additional terms and conditions apply.

ACKNOWLEDGMENTS

I've been fortunate to receive incredible encouragement and support from my colleagues, family, and friends. Thanks to my wife, Cynthia, Farahat Higgins, my parents, James and Nadya Higgins, and my mother-in-law, Sanaa Nessem.

Thanks to Andrew Watts, Amber Haddock, and the entire Severn River Publishing team. Special thanks to Julia Hastings for shepherding my book through the process and to Lisa Gilliam for editing my manuscript.

My writing group, The Royal Writers Secret Society has been with me from the beginning. International Thriller Writers, the Chessie Chapter of Sisters in Crime, and the Northern Virginia Writers Club have encouraged me along the way.

I greatly appreciate Tom Young for sharing his aviation expertise with me. Any errors are mine alone.

Last, but not least, thanks to my readers. If you enjoy this thriller, I'd appreciate a rating or review on Amazon. I love seeing readers' comments, and you're welcome to email me at Jeffrey@JeffreyJamesHiggins.com. Thanks for your support!

ABOUT THE AUTHOR

Jeffrey James Higgins, author of the Nathan Burke Thrillers, is a retired supervisory special agent who writes thrillers, short stories, scripts, creative nonfiction, and essays. He has wrestled a suicide bomber, fought the Taliban in combat, and chased terrorists across five continents. He received the Attorney General's Award for Exceptional Heroism and the DEA Award of Valor. Jeffrey has been interviewed by CNN, National Geographic, and The New York Times. He's a #1 Amazon bestselling author and has won numerous literary awards, including the Claymore Award, PenCraft's Best Fiction Book of 2022, and a Reader's Favorite Gold Medal. Jeffrey is an active member of the Authors Guild, The Virginia Writers Club, International Thriller Writers, Sisters in Crime, and the Royal Writers Secret Society. His first three thrillers are *Furious, Unseen,* and *The Forever Game.*

Sign up for the reader list at
severnriverbooks.com